LOVE-GRE

Nile's lips mov
felt the first jol
core, then slowly spread through her body
like a slow flame, as he claimed her.

She welcomed this sensuous invasion, allowing
his fingers to move down the front of her
shirt and deftly undo one button after another.

The moment Nile's warm, rough hand closed
around her, Maddie felt him retreat from
the kiss. She groaned in wordless protest and
sought to pull him back.

"Love-greedy woman," he whispered,
amusement in his voice. "I just want to be
able to see your face while I do this. . . ."

SEEK THE WILD SHORE

by

Leslie O'Grady

AN ONYX BOOK

NEW AMERICAN LIBRARY

A DIVISION OF PENGUIN BOOKS USA INC.

PUBLISHER'S NOTE

This book is a work of fiction. Names, characters, places, and incidents either are the product of the author's imagination or are used fictitiously, and any resemblance to actual persons, living or dead, events, or locales is entirely coincidental.

Copyright © 1989 by Leslie O'Grady

SIGNET, SIGNET CLASSIC, MENTOR, ONYX, PLUME, MERIDIAN
and NAL BOOKS are published by New American Library,
a division of Penguin Books USA Inc.,
1633 Broadway, New York, New York 10019

First Printing, October, 1989

1 2 3 4 5 6 7 8 9

PRINTED IN THE UNITED STATES OF AMERICA

Author's Note

Of all the sources consulted about the Amazon, two were invaluable: *Lizzie: A Victorian Lady's Amazon Adventure,* compilied by Tony Morrison, Ann Brown, and Anne Rose; and *The River That God Forgot,* by Richard Collier.

Special thanks also to orchid enthusiast Hank Kelly for his inspirational tales of Victorian orchid hunters, and to my grandmother for Zosia's story.

Last but not least, to Michael, for always being there.

1

"Miss! Women are not allowed in the Explorers Club!"

Maddie stared at the man in the green uniform and raised her brows in mock astonishment. "Now, that is surprising, since members of my own sex have explored China, the Amazon, Arabia ... I myself have traveled through dangerous and uncivilized parts of Africa under the most appalling conditions anyone has had to endure." She widened her devastating blue eyes further. "And you mean to stand there and tell me my presence is not welcome here?"

Red-faced and bristling with indignation, the majordomo said, "I don't make the rules, miss, I only enforce them. And one of those rules is that only men are allowed in the Explorers Club. I must ask you to leave quietly, or I shall be forced to remove you myself."

Even as the majordomo spoke, he hunched his broad shoulders and leaned toward Maddie as if trying to conceal her offensive presence from several male members who had just entered the club's foyer. He failed. A distinguished-looking man with snow-white hair and mustache noticed Maddie at once and glowered at her.

He shook his head and said to his companion, "Next they'll be wearing our trousers and demanding the vote."

Chuckling at such a preposterous notion, the two men disappeared through a pair of formidable mahogany doors guarded by a fierce wooden figure of a Zulu warrior, his shield and short spear poised as if to repel those who would dare assault such a sacred all-male bastion.

Maddie saw all closed doors as a challenge. She had the urge to fling them open and foist her unwelcome presence on those very people who would seek to exclude her. But today she resisted the impulse. She had more important matters to contend with.

She gave the majordomo her most persuasive smile. "I am not here to force myself where I am not wanted, Mr. . . . ?"

"Biddle."

"Mr. Biddle. I am here to call upon a Mr. Nile Marcus." She paused. "He is a member of this club, is he not? And he is staying here?"

Biddle nodded. "Mr. Marcus is indeed here, but I'm afraid you cannot see him. Unlike some clubs in London, the Explorers Club does not have a receiving room for ladies, you see."

Maddie understood only too well.

She reached into her handbag, took out her card, and handed it to Biddle. "It is imperative that I see Mr. Marcus immediately. Perhaps you would be so kind as to give him my card and tell him I am here waiting to speak to him."

As Biddle took the card and read the name printed there, a perceptible change came over him. His eyes widened in disbelief, and his cold, hostile demeanor melted like ice in summer sunlight.

"You're Maddie Dare?" he said. "Of the *Morning Clarion?*"

She was accustomed to having her name recognized, and smiled graciously in acknowledgment. "Yes, I am."

Biddle grasped her hand in a crushing grip and began pumping it. "Miss Dare, you don't know what a pleasure it is for me to meet you! You are the best reporter the *Clarion* has ever had—the best reporter any newspaper has ever had, I'll be bound—and I wouldn't miss one of your articles even if my house was on fire and burning down around me."

"Why, thank you, Mr. Biddle." Maddie blushed with pleasure, for she never tired of hearing her work praised by an enthusiastic and responsive public. "Which articles were your favorites?"

"The ones you wrote from Africa. When I read your account of being surrounded by hostile savages, I broke out in the shivers and my hair stood on end." He smiled sheepishly. "I should have known who you were the minute you said you had been there. Not many women have."

Now that Maddie had the majordomo sufficiently awed, she pressed home her advantage. "If you would fetch Mr. Marcus for me . . ."

Biddle glanced around to see if anyone were watching, but the foyer was empty now. "I'll do better than that, Miss Dare. You can meet in our manager's office as privately as you like."

"Oh, I wouldn't want you to get into trouble on my account, Mr. Biddle."

"Don't worry about that, Miss Dare. Our manager is gone for the day, and I'm sure he wouldn't mind, you being so famous and all. Now, if you'll just follow me . . ."

Looking around one last time to make sure no one was observing them, Biddle ushered Maddie through the foyer as if she were the queen herself.

She followed him down a narrow corridor, and he showed her to a small quiet office devoid of such trappings of conquest as Zulu warriors and tigerskins strewn on the floor. He indicated one of two chairs before the desk and left her to go in search of Nile Marcus.

Maddie remained standing, suddenly assailed by fresh doubts and misgivings. What if Nile Marcus didn't agree to her proposition? Then what would she do?

I will simply find someone else, she thought to herself.

But there was no one else qualified to undertake such a long, dangerous mission. Only two other men in all of Great Britain had the specialized knowledge and experience she required; one of them was away on a two-year expedition to Tibet and the other had out-and-out refused her just today, lecturing her indignantly on the sheer lunacy of a woman managing such an undertaking. That left only Nile Marcus.

Maddie was as adept and tenacious as a bloodhound when it came to tracking people down and ferreting out information about them. She had learned that Nile Marcus was the only child of the late Rose Marcus, a celebrated and indefatigable lady traveler whose globe-trotting exploits rivaled those of Isabella Bird Bishop and Mary Kingsley. Her husband, Jason, now also deceased, was something of a mystery, content to remain in England with their son while his wife was abroad. Nile—named in honor of the Egyptian river—apparently had inherited his mother's restlessness, for most of his adult life he had been earning his living by traveling throughout the tropics, hunting rare orchid specimens for private collectors, nurseries, and botanical gardens—whoever had the finances to pay for such an arduous and dangerous expedition. Lately, though, his customary success had eluded him.

Maddie smiled to herself. He wouldn't refuse. A

man down on his luck couldn't afford to, and that gave her a distinct advantage.

Alerted by the sound of footsteps coming down the corridor, Maddie composed herself and waited.

Suddenly the door swung open and Biddle entered the office, his massive, broad-shouldered form hiding the man behind him.

"Miss Dare," Biddle began in his most formal tone, "I would like to introduce you to Mr. Nile Marcus. Mr. Marcus, this is Miss Maddie Dare of the *Morning Clarion*."

Then he stepped aside to reveal Nile Marcus himself.

In his conservative dark suit, the man resembled a banker, not the daring adventurer of Maddie's fertile imagination, and she felt irrationally disappointed. But upon closer inspection, she was relieved to find that even such staid clothing couldn't conceal the vitality and raw masculinity that radiated from him as palpably as heat from a fireplace on a cold winter's day.

The moment Maddie's gaze flew up to Nile Marcus' face, she felt a shiver race up her arms. She had never seen such a handsome man, and she couldn't have torn her eyes away from his bold-featured visage even if she had wanted to. Only a relentless tropical sun could have lightened his unruly brown hair with streaks of gold, and bronzed his strong, clean-shaven face so that it made his pale brown eyes appear tawny by contrast.

And what eyes! They seemed to glitter with some strange inner fire as they flicked over her, casually taking her measure. He must have liked what he saw, for one corner of his wide, sensuous mouth rose in an appreciative smile.

Oh, my, Maddie thought as she tried not to let this compelling man fluster her.

As he came toward her, Marcus moved silently

and gracefully, like a man accustomed to easing himself through dense jungle undergrowth, and there was an air of wariness about him, of always watching and listening for the unexpected.

I feel as though I'm sharing a cage with a jaguar, Maddie thought in wonder as she watched his restless eyes inspect every corner of the room, then settle back on her with disconcerting and unabashed masculine curiosity. Some primitive feminine instinct warned her that he was not a man to be trifled with.

Maddie recovered herself, stepped forward, and extended her hand. "It's a pleasure to meet you at long last, Mr. Marcus."

She was a tall woman, accustomed to looking lesser men straight in the eye, but this time she was forced to look up at him.

A hand with strong brown fingers and callused palm closed around hers in a firm grip. Maddie was startled to feel the scorching heat of his touch all the way up her arm, and she almost pulled her hand away as though she had grasped a white-hot poker.

He must have noticed how much he had jarred her, for a shadow of an amused smile touched his mouth as he said, "Miss Dare, a pleasure," in a deep, rough voice.

Introductions made, the discreet Biddle slipped away, closing the door behind him and leaving Maddie alone with Nile Marcus.

"Thank you for agreeing to see me, Mr. Marcus," Maddie said.

"I was curious as to why a newspaper reporter would want to see me." Those tawny eyes darkened suspiciously, turning the color of sherry. "I don't give interviews, you know."

"I know. But then, I am not here for an interview."

"Then why are you here, Miss Dare?"

Maddie took a deep breath and said, "I want to hire you. That is, the newspaper I work for, the *Morning Clarion*, wants to hire you."

He raised his brows at that. "Hire me? To do what?"

"My fiancé is lost somewhere in the Amazon jungle, and I want you to help me find him."

Marcus started, and then stared at Maddie as though she had addressed him in some foreign language. Without warning, he gave a sharp bark of laughter. "Miss Dare, surely you can't be serious?"

"Oh, but I am, Mr. Marcus. Quite serious."

He smiled, then shook his head, turned, and started for the door. "This has been a most interesting conversation, Miss Dare, but a complete waste of my time and yours."

Despite the long skirts of her redingote, Maddie moved swiftly and managed to block the door before her quarry had a chance to escape.

"Please, Mr. Marcus," she began, facing him. "All I ask is fifteen minutes of your time. Hear what I have to say. Then, if you don't wish to help me, I promise I shall walk through this door and you'll never see me again."

Annoyance flickered in the depths of his eyes. "Miss Dare, I—"

"Please. Just hear what I have to say. I promise it will be well worth your while."

He stepped back a pace, a glimmer of grudging admiration in his eyes. "You are devilishly persistent."

She smiled disarmingly but remained blocking the door. "One has to be, if one is to succeed as a newspaper reporter. You will hear me out?"

He hesitated, then said, "All right. But I doubt if I'll change my mind."

Oh, you shall, Mr. Marcus, Maddie said to herself. I'm going to give the performance of my life.

The man stepped back into the room with the litheness and grace of a cat, and offered Maddie a chair. After she seated herself, he did likewise, drawing up his left leg until his ankle rested on his right knee. The deliberately casual gesture called attention to his long legs and strong thighs.

With great effort, Maddie kept her eyes on his face and leaned toward him to impress him with her sincerity. "My fiancé is a photographer with the *Morning Clarion*. Part of his job is to travel abroad, taking photographs of the landscape and people of foreign lands to serve as models for illustrations. Well, a little over a year ago he was sent to the Amazon to do a series of photographs about the rubber boom."

Maddie blinked, forcing tears to fill her eyes. "Mr. Marcus, no one has heard from him in over six months. Not one word." Her last sentence ended on a watery sniff.

The tears worked. Judging from Marcus' panic-stricken expression, he was utterly at a loss. He might have been brave enough to face down a hundred perils of the jungle, but when it came to a woman's tears, he was as helpless as a baby.

Finally he reached into his breast pocket, pulled out a handkerchief, and pressed it into Maddie's hand.

"There, there, don't cry," he said gently. "Six months isn't so long when you consider the great distance the mail must travel. Besides, the mails are slow there."

She dabbed at her eyes. "But I had been receiving a letter from him every week, and the newspaper received photographs almost weekly as well, whenever he reached some outpost of civilization and could mail them. Then suddenly they just stopped coming."

"And you think he's disappeared?"

Maddie swallowed hard and nodded. "What else could have happened to him?"

"Many things, but to jump to the conclusion that he's lost . . ."

"Ben Thomas and I are very much in love and were to have been married last week. I don't think he would have missed his own wedding for any reason, do you?"

Those eyes raked her up and down and he grinned mischievously. "No, not with such a beautiful fiancée to come home to."

"Thank you." Maddie felt her cheeks grow warm. Damn the man! He obviously enjoyed flustering her.

Nile Marcus sighed and ran his hand over his jaw. "I don't mean to upset you, Miss Dare, but you do realize that your fiancé could be dead."

Maddie bolted to her feet and turned away from him. "I realize that," she replied in a trembling voice. "I know that the Amazon is a lawless place with untold dangers awaiting the unwary." She turned to him so he could see the tears filling her eyes again. "But I refuse to believe that Ben is dead unless I do everything that is humanly possible to learn what happened to him."

Marcus rose and cleared his throat. "I'm sorry, but I can't lie to you. It's unlikely that he has survived."

"And I cannot spend the rest of my life living with that uncertainty! To face day after day, month after month, not knowing whether he's dead or alive, wondering if I had done everything humanly possible to find him . . ." Maddie looked at him helplessly.

Marcus' heavy brows came together in a scowl. "Something puzzles me. Why must you go along on such an expedition? Why don't you just hire someone to search for him and report back to you?"

"Because I refuse to remain behind and twiddle my thumbs. I am not that kind of woman."

Nile gave her a gentle smile. "The Amazon is no place for a lady."

"But I am not a lady, Mr. Marcus, I am a newspaper reporter. And I'll have you know that I am no stranger to adversity, having braved all the hardships of Africa to deliver supplies to a group of stranded missionaries in the midst of an intertribal war. Ask our mutual friend Mr. Biddle. He can tell you all about my exploits."

Marcus rolled his eyes toward the ceiling. "Damnation and hellfire! Don't tell me you are one of those women who traipse around the world poking your noses where you are not wanted."

"Your attitude does surprise me, especially since your own mother was just such a woman, to judge from her books."

Even beneath his tanned skin, Marcus paled slightly. "My mother was killed in a fall while trying to cross the Rocky Mountains," he said coldly. "Her tragic, senseless fate should serve as a lesson to all the rest of you."

Maddie sensed at once that he disapproved of independent women. She would have to tread carefully.

"Be that as it may, Mr. Marcus, if you were to agree to this expedition, you would have to agree to my accompanying you as well."

Marcus scowled. "Do you have any knowledge of the Amazon?"

"Of course. I know the heat is appalling and that there are untold dangers there."

He gave a snort of derision. "Spoken like a bright little schoolgirl who has memorized her lessons to impress the teacher."

He grinned, baring strong white teeth, as he strode toward her. Maddie resisted the impulse to take a step back, and held her ground as he came to a halt only inches away, those unusual eyes alight with determination.

"You are an uncommonly beautiful woman, Miss Dare," he said, his voice low and silky, "but you wouldn't be, once the Amazon was through with you."

He reached out and grazed her cheek boldly with the backs of his fingers.

Maddie jumped at his touch, surprisingly light and as gentle as being brushed by a butterfly's wing. Again, a delicious frisson of pleasure enveloped her, even as she fought the spell this man was trying to weave around her.

The deep, hypnotic voice went on relentlessly. "That appalling sun would soon burn your milky white skin to a crisp. And the jungle undergrowth would catch and snarl your golden hair so much that even a comb would do no good."

"Then I'll wear a hat."

Her quelling response must not have been what he expected, for he stepped back a pace and stared at her in surprise. He recovered himself at once and tried a different tack. "Are you afraid of snakes, Miss Dare?"

"Not particularly."

He shook his head. "I suspected you would say that. But I don't mean the harmless variety found slithering in the English garden. I'm speaking of poisonous ones that drop from the trees without warning, and the giant anaconda that dwells near rivers and streams. They grow to twenty feet, you know, and are capable of suffocating a man. Or a woman."

Maddie suppressed a shudder and managed to shrug diffidently. "I've encountered snakes in Africa, and I've lived to tell the tale."

"Well, if they don't scare you, there are ants that

can paralyze a man—or a woman—with their painful sting. And of course, I mustn't forget flesh-eating fish capable of reducing a man—or a woman—to a mere skeleton in minutes."

"They're called piranha, I believe," Maddie said coolly, growing weary of his attempts to dissuade her. "But I trust you would come to my rescue if I ever had the misfortune to fall into a river."

A flicker of a smile passed across his mouth. "I would do my best, but there would be no guarantees."

Maddie pounced, her eyes widening eagerly. "So you will agree to accompany me on this expedition?"

"Damnation and hellfire!" he bellowed. "Hasn't anything I've said penetrated that thick skull of yours? Of course I'm not agreeing to it! I am merely trying to convince you to give up such an insane idea!"

Then he shook his head contemptuously. "A woman going to the Amazon . . . Why, your trunks and bags alone would be enough to scuttle an expedition before it even started!"

"I'll have you know I travel with a minimum of such feminine encumbrances."

"And what about your maid?"

"Maid?" Maddie echoed, suppressing the urge to laugh. "Mr. Marcus, I work for a living, just as you do. I can't afford a maid. I travel alone."

"Women in Brazil never go out without a chaperon."

"Then I'm afraid you'll just have to do."

Backed against the wall, he took refuge in anger. "Are you deaf as well as stubborn? I've told you the Amazon is no place for a woman!"

"Oh, come now, Mr. Marcus!" Maddie snapped, her patience worn out at last. "There are European women living there. I've heard Manaus is quite the cosmopolitan city, rivaling even London and Paris in every luxury and amenity. Why, they've even built an opera house there. An *opera house*, Mr. Marcus, in the middle of the jungle!"

He folded his arms across his broad chest and grinned lasciviously. "Of course there are women in Manaus, but not the kind I suspect you associate with."

His smile died and he studied her again. "There are other dangers for a beautiful woman such as yourself. Under its veneer of cultivation, Manaus is a wicked, wicked place, the most decadent city on earth. There are men there who would sell you, and men who would just as eagerly buy you. You could disappear, never to be seen again."

"Once again, I would trust you to see that such a fate didn't befall me, sir."

"How can you be sure you can trust me?" Marcus' arms fell to his sides and he moved closer with negligent grace. He deliberately let his gaze fall to Maddie's lips.

She held her breath, half-dreading, half-anticipating what this unpredictable man would do next.

"Did you know I have an unsavory reputation when it comes to women?" he purred, those tawny eyes darkening. "Once we were alone in the jungle, who knows what might happen? I could try to force my attentions on you."

He reached up and caressed the line of her jaw with his fingertips. "So tempting . . ."

Maddie ignored the slamming of her heart against her rib cage and refused to flinch from his touch and its sweet threat. "You don't frighten me."

"Then you're a fool."

Without warning, he took her face between his hands and his mouth swooped down on hers for a hard, punishing kiss.

Maddie barely had time to draw another breath before a jolt of pure delight rocked her back on her heels. When she opened her dazed eyes, she found herself staring at her indignant face reflected in the depths of Nile Marcus' triumphant golden eyes. She didn't shriek in terror, swoon, or slap him. She calmly grasped both his wrists and dislodged the hands that still cradled her face.

"You've proved your point, Mr. Marcus," she said, fighting to keep her voice steady, "but I also know that you're an honorable, highly principled man. If you contracted to protect and guide me, that is what you would do."

He looked chagrined that she had called his bluff, and stepped back. "Still, an unmarried woman going off with an unmarried man . . . Think of the scandal, your own reputation . . ."

"I think my fiancé's life is more important than any scandal or even my own reputation."

Marcus threw up his hands in disgust and whirled away from her. "There's just no reasoning with you! Well, my answer is still no. Find some other fool to accompany you."

"There is no one else!" Maddie wailed. "Sir Calvin Stone is in Tibet at the moment, and Colonel Beswick wouldn't hear of taking a woman on such an expedition."

"Sir Calvin is a lucky man and Beswick has more sense than I've ever given him credit for." He bowed. "Good day to you, Miss Dare. It's been . . . an interesting fifteen minutes."

He started for the door.

Once again, Maddie was there ahead of him, barring his way. "Wait, Mr. Marcus! Before you go, please listen to one more thing I have to say."

"Miss Dare, I—"

"Please! If you won't be moved by my desire to be reunited with the man I love, then perhaps you'll be compelled to act in your own self-interest."

He stopped in his tracks and regarded her suspiciously. "What do you mean by that? Come, Miss Dare, quickly! My time is valuable."

"The *Morning Clarion* will be financing the expedition, and I can assure you that you will be generously compensated." Maddie hesitated, then plunged ahead recklessly. "I have also learned you are in straitened financial circumstances, Mr. Marcus."

The blood drained right out of the man's face, leaving his tan skin drawn and muddy, and he grew very still. "Where did you hear such a vicious lie?"

"Is it? I beg to differ. I am a newspaper reporter, Mr. Marcus. It is my business to learn all I can about my subject."

He looked as though he could cheerfully throttle her with his bare hands. "Damnation and hellfire! You're wrong!"

Maddie stepped away from him, and to her relief, Nile Marcus didn't bolt out the door in disgust. At least she had his attention.

"I know that you make your living by obtaining orchids for wealthy collectors," she began. "I also know that these flowers are very fragile and delicate—that is why collectors pay such high prices for them. And because they are so delicate, transporting them across the Atlantic can be quite perilous. Many of them die before reaching England's shores." She hesitated. "Am I right so far?"

"You're always right about everything, aren't you?" he demanded.

"Not always. But I do know your last two orchid-hunting ventures were abysmal failures. After months of backbreaking work on your part, none of the plants survived the ocean crossing."

Marcus raised his head even as he seethed in frank resentment. "A mere temporary setback, nothing more. Many hunters experience a disappointing expedition or two. It's a hazard of the profession."

"But now your regular customers are reluctant to hire you. Once burned, twice shy, as the saying goes. Why should they finance one of your expeditions if they're not going to recoup their considerable expenses?"

"Because in spite of a temporary run of bad luck, I'm the best and they all know it. True, some of them may not want to hire me now, but they'll come around. They always do."

"You're sure of that."

"As sure as I'm standing here."

"But it could be months—even a year—before someone in England hires you, Mr. Marcus. I'm offering you a position now that could be profitable to you immediately."

"And that is . . . ?"

"Not only will the *Morning Clarion* finance this expedition and pay you handsomely, they will also agree to let you hunt orchids while we are there. And pay all shipping charges, of course."

Marcus dismissed her offer with a wave of his hand. "That's no inducement, Miss Dare. The most accessible parts of the Amazon have been picked clean by unscrupulous hunters with no regard for the plants themselves. Rare orchid specimens there are now scarce."

"I didn't know. But even if you couldn't hunt orchids, you would still be well-paid for the expedition. I might add that you will not be held responsible should any . . . mishap befall me, and you will be paid even if we cannot locate my fiancé. Think of it as an interim position until something better comes along." Maddie smiled at him. "You can't lose, Mr. Marcus. If anything, you can only profit."

"So you think you have me right where you want me with your little blackmail attempt?"

I believe I do, Mr. Marcus, Maddie said to herself. But she merely shrugged. "It's not a question of blackmail. I can't force you to accept my offer. You are free to refuse."

"Well, contrary to what you may have been led to believe," he said, smiling in triumph, "one of my former employers may have another assignment for me. And if that is the case, you shall be journeying to South America without me."

Maddie sighed. "If he does, I wish you all the best. But if he doesn't, my offer is still open. You may find me at the *Morning Clarion* if you should change your mind. I believe Mr. Biddle gave you my card."

After wishing Nile Marcus good day, she turned and left the office, conscious of a pair of tawny eyes boring into her back.

Once she left the Explorers Club, Maddie went to the curb to hail a hansom cab and return to the *Clarion*'s offices.

Just as she was about to raise her hand, a masculine voice at her side said, "Allow me, miss." Maddie turned to see none other than the white-haired gentleman who had resented her presence so vocally in the Explorers Club.

But now that Maddie was out of that exclusive male bastion and looking as unthreatening and helpless as a normal female, the gentleman deigned to overlook his former indignation and graciously summon a hansom for her.

When a cab pulled up to the curb and the gentleman handed Maddie inside, she leaned forward with an encouraging smile that brought an expectant twinkle to his eye.

"I just want you to know," she murmured demurely, "that someday we *will* wear your trousers, and we *will* have the vote, and we *will* be admitted to your Explorers Club."

Then she signaled the cabbie and left the astonished white-haired gentleman sputtering in her wake.

"Damn that woman!" Nile muttered to himself as he stood at the window in his upstairs room and stared down at the hansom cab just pulling away from the curb.

Judging from the outraged expression on old Parker's face, the bold Miss Dare had said something outrageous to annoy him as well.

Nile suspected the brazen Maddie Dare enjoyed annoying people, especially men.

Feeling suddenly confined, he stripped off his jacket and waistcoat, then yanked off his cravat. There. He felt more comfortable and unrestricted. Lying down on his bed, he laced his fingers behind his head and stared at the ceiling, his thoughts filled with the audacious Maddie Dare and her outrageous proposition.

He hadn't known what to expect when Biddle came to him in the coffee room and told him a lady newspaper reporter wanted to see him. Half-expecting a wrinkled old spinster with graying hair caught up in a bun, he had been startled to come face-to-face with a lovely young woman who couldn't have been more than twenty-five years old.

Only a blind man could have been impervious to such fresh, radiant beauty. But Nile suspected that Maddie Dare was one of those women who used their looks ruthlessly to get what they wanted. By carrying herself at her full height of nearly six feet, she could intimidate her victim physically by towering over him. That perfect oval face with its flawless ivory complexion, straight nose, and full rosy mouth could beguile with its beauty, and one promising glance from her smoldering blue eyes could turn the most rational of men into a blithering fool.

However, Nile was not a blithering fool. He rarely let a pretty face cloud his good judgment.

Nile scowled. She was just too bold and too ambitious for his taste. He was old-fashioned enough to still believe that women were meant to stay home where they belonged, cherished and protected, not allowed to roam around the world willy-nilly. If the whole idea of taking a woman up the Amazon weren't so ludicrous, he might be tempted to accept Miss Maddie Dare's offer just for the challenge of putting her in her proper place.

Unfortunately, he had no time to tarry. He needed another expedition and he needed it fast.

He rose, jammed his hands into his pockets, and paced around his room like a caged animal, stopping at the window to gaze out across the steep rooftops of London. March in England in the year 1897 was so damned depressing. The atmosphere was so cheerless and gray, from the flat leaden sky pressing down on the city like a tombstone, to the stone buildings beyond. Nile shivered, still unused to the cold after the shimmering steam heat of Brazil, and a wave of homesickness washed over him.

He longed for vivid colors to startle his eyes—bright blue sky, deep green jungles, vibrant tropical orchids, and parrots in various shades of yellow and crimson. Instead of clopping hooves and the relentless din of so-called progress, Nile yearned to hear the scream of the wild jaguar in the night and awake to the raucous roaring of the howler monkey at dawn. He would rather sweat than freeze any day.

"I've got to go back," he muttered between clenched teeth. "I need another expedition."

He smiled to himself as he reached for his cravat and began retying it.

"Well, Miss Maddie Dare," he muttered to his reflection in the mirror, "I have a few trump cards of my own to play. Nile Marcus isn't quite down and out just yet."

Spirits soaring, he grabbed his coat and left the Explorers Club.

Maddie strode through the busy editorial room of the *Morning Clarion*, barely taking time to acknowledge the greetings of her fellow reporters as she headed straight for Sam's office.

"I wouldn't go in there if I were you," one of the men seated at a desk warned her. "Our leader is in a foul mood."

"We'll see," Maddie replied as she knocked on the door.

When a masculine voice bellowed, "What do you want?" she gave her coworkers a theatrical shudder, opened the door, and went inside.

"They were right," Maddie said, closing the door behind her. "You are in a foul mood."

The man behind the large oak desk leaned back in his swivel chair and smiled. "Not anymore."

Maddie smiled at him fondly. She owed her career to Sam Vincent. Seven years ago, when she was just eighteen and pounding on the doors of every newspaper in London begging for work, only Sam was willing to see beyond her beauty and inexperience and hire her for her writing ability alone. During those early years, he had taught her how to ferret out the news and how to refine her copy so that it sang; then he gave her every chance to prove herself. Maggie had repaid his faith in her a hundredfold, and she had come to think of him as a benevolent uncle.

Maddie took off her redingote and pulled the

hatpin from her straw boater, setting the hat down on the desk before seating herself.

Sam Vincent regarded her quizzically. "So, did he believe your cock-and-bull story?"

"Of course. Do you doubt my persuasive powers?"

Sam just grunted and shook his head. "Then he agreed to accompany you to Brazil to search for your long-lost fiancé?"

Maddie's gaze fell away as she smoothed the skirt of her black shirtwaist. "Not exactly."

"What? Do you mean to tell me Maddie Dare has failed? I can't believe my ears."

Her head shot up. "I never fail ... well, almost never, and well you know it, Sam Vincent. This is only a momentary setback. True, Mr. Marcus didn't agree to accompany me. The poor deluded man still believes one of his former employers will hire him for another expedition. But I left him my card and told him to contact me if he should change his mind." She crossed her fingers and smiled. "And he will."

Sam shook his head. "You're always so sure of yourself."

"Faint heart never won fair maid, as they say." Then she added, "Of course I'm confident. One has to be if one is to succeed as a journalist. You taught me that."

He held up his hands as if in surrender. "I know, I know. But you can be too confident, Maddie, and someday it's going to be your undoing."

"Never."

Seeing that this particular conversation was going nowhere, Sam changed the subject. "What's this Nile Marcus like? Young, handsome, and dashing, I suppose."

"Of course. The epitome of a legendary tropical explorer. Bronzed skin, sun-kissed hair, eyes a woman could drown in ..."

And as for his kiss ... she thought, as her face grew warm from the memory.

Sam guffawed and shook his head. "I was afraid of that. Fallen in love with him already, have you?"

Maddie looked appalled. "Sam Vincent, how can you accuse me of such a thing? I'm an engaged woman!"

"Sorry, I forgot. But answer my question, Maddie," Sam admonished her. "What is this Marcus fellow really like?"

Maddie hesitated as she recalled Nile Marcus' entrance into the Explorers Club office, the way he took possession of a room and dominated it by sheer commanding presence without even saying a word.

She grew serious and chose her words carefully. "I've heard Marcus described as tough and dependable, but also hot-tempered, and one who prefers working alone. I can testify to his being hot-tempered," she added ruefully. "He's also sure of himself to the point of arrogance."

"What do you mean?"

"Even though I'd stake my life on the fact that he's on the brink of financial disaster, he acted as though he were going to find another expedition tomorrow."

Sam shook his head. "He's either deluding himself or—"

"Or he knows how good he really is."

Sam fell silent as he leaned back in his swivel chair. Then he said, "And you would feel comfortable traveling alone with such a man? Would you really trust him?"

Maddie said nothing as she recalled Nile Marcus asking her that very same question. "You can put your mind at rest, Sam. I don't think Mr. Marcus approved of me or my profession very much, so you needn't fear he would try to force his attentions on me, if that's what you're afraid of."

"That's exactly what I'm afraid of."

Maddie had her own misgivings on that score, but she kept them to herself and just smiled. "How sweet of you to worry."

"I do worry," he said gruffly, looking away. "I know the weaknesses of my own sex all too well, and I'm sure this Marcus fellow isn't exactly a green boy when it comes to women."

Maddie could testify to that, but all she said was, "This is all needless speculation, since he hasn't agreed to accompany me yet."

"Why not?"

Bitter resentment flashed in the depths of her eyes. "Oh, for the usual stupid, senseless reasons, of course. I am a weak, helpless woman who would swoon at the sight of a snake. And Mr. Marcus feels that the Amazon is 'no place for a lady,' as he so eloquently phrased it. Honestly, Sam, when he said that, I felt like kicking him in the shins."

Sam's face clouded and he rose from his desk to walk over to the windows overlooking Fleet Street. "I'm not so sure he isn't right."

Maddie twisted in her chair. "Sam!" she wailed in consternation. "Don't tell me that you, of all people, are going to back out on me now, not when everything has been arranged with Ben?"

"I'm not so sure I like the idea of you putting yourself in such danger again, Maddie. I worried myself sick every day you were in Africa, wondering when I'd receive a telegram telling me you'd drowned in some river or been eaten alive by cannibals. From what I've heard, the Amazon is even more dangerous. Man-eating fish, natives with blowguns shooting poisoned darts . . ."

She rose and went to him. "But I won't be in any danger. I'll only go as far as Manaus, I promise, and let the big brave man go the rest of the way by himself. I'll be as safe there as I am in London.

We've worked it all out with Ben. Once he is rescued and we are reunited, my long-lost fiancé and I will return to England to wild acclaim and adulation."

Sam sighed. "I have a better idea. Why don't we just call Ben back and forget all about this harebrained enterprise?"

"We've been all through this before, Sam," she began gently, to reassure him. "It's for the good of the *Clarion*, and what's good for the paper is good for us. You know what a story like this will do for circulation, not to mention our reputations. Think of the headlines: 'INTREPID REPORTER SEARCHES JUNGLE FOR LOST LOVE.' "

Sam looked at her long and hard, then broke out into a grin of surrender. "We're a well-matched pair of rogues, aren't we?"

Maddie returned his smile. "That we are, Sam Vincent, that we are."

"Now, I believe you have a story due . . ."

"I always have a story due."

Giving Sam a quick smile, she left his office for her own desk.

But as she sat down to write, she found herself unable to concentrate on the story at hand and she wound up staring at a blank sheet of paper. Her thoughts kept flying back to her interview with Nile Marcus.

He was a difficult man to forget.

She could still see him as he came striding into the room like a jungle cat on the prowl, every sense alert for danger. The man was so feline, he could probably see in the dark. There was also something feral about him, an unmistakable wildness from having been a stranger to civilization for so long. Maddie had seen that same quality in some of the traders and big-game hunters in Africa, but never as strongly as in Nile Marcus.

Her thoughts turned to what Sam had said in his office: " . . . you would feel comfortable traveling alone with this man?" Alone with Nile Marcus, a formidable man who disdained strong-minded women . . . She would be dependent on his wits and strength for her very survival. How would Maddie, so used to being in control of a situation, deal with stepping aside, even for her own good? The mere thought made her shiver, and not in fear.

"You're worrying for nothing, Maddie Dare," she muttered to herself as she scratched out an offensive line of copy. "He hasn't agreed to this yet."

Yet when she thought of his wicked golden eyes, she found herself hoping that he would.

2

"Damnation and hellfire!"

Luckily for Nile, he was the only occupant in the first-class compartment of a train clattering its way across the Kent countryside back to London, so he could feel free to swear to his heart's content.

When he ran out of curses, he sat back in his seat and tried to let the clickety-clack of the rails soothe him. He focused his attention on the familiar rural landscape that had once been home to him. Today the dark storm clouds scudding low in the sky made the rolling green hills, fruit orchards, and oasthouses look as bleak and gray as he felt inside.

He had just come from visiting a prominent orchid collector he had often dealt with in the past, shamelessly prevailing upon an old friendship to get him the expedition he needed so badly.

The man had refused him kindly and so regretfully, claiming that he had just sent another collector off to Burma and couldn't possibly afford the expense of two simultaneous expeditions. Come back in a year's time, he said.

A year might as well be an eternity.

Nile sat back with a low groan of disappointment. He had exhausted all of his options. There was nowhere else for him to turn.

Then he remembered the card in his pocket.

He sat back in his seat, took out the card, and studied the name printed there in bold black lettering. Immediately a tantalizing vision with spun-gold hair and bewitching blue eyes danced in his mind's eye.

Nile ran his hand through his hair and groaned. Did he really dare accept her offer? To be in such close proximity to a beautiful woman—even one belonging to another man—for months on end . . . It was more of a temptation than any red-blooded man should be expected to endure.

Maddie Dare was trouble; he could feel it in his bones. But now he had no choice.

Nile paused in the doorway and scanned the bustling, cavernous room for any sign of her, but all he saw were men. Men hunched over desks, scribbling. Men looking harried as they scurried back and forth like caged mice. Men standing in groups of two or three looking down at papers in their hands and talking in low, urgent voices that seemed to ebb and flow.

Nile could sense the tension and expectancy hanging in the air as thick as cigar smoke. Even the din was punctuated by the faint staccato tap-tap-tap of typewriting machines and the occasional startling ring of a telephone in the background. Whatever happened in London, or the world for that matter, these people learned of it first, and Nile supposed some would find such knowledge exhilarating.

But he had come here to find Maddie Dare, and find her he would.

"Excuse me," he said to a man seated at one of the desks. "Is Maddie Dare here?"

Without looking up from his writing, the man grunted and jerked his head in the direction of a group of people standing at the far end of the room.

Nile thanked him and started walking in the direction indicated. Just as he approached, the men suddenly became aware of him. Each stopped what he was doing and just stared at Nile as if some rare mythical beast had just entered their midst. He ignored their curious gaping, focusing his attention on the woman he sought.

Even though Maddie Dare was dressed unobtrusively in a black skirt and a crisp white shirtwaist with leg-o'-mutton sleeves, she still stood out because of her sex and her pale golden hair. Unlike her coworkers, she was unaware of Nile's presence. She plucked out a pencil she had stuck in her chignon and began writing something down on the pad she held. She started walking, so absorbed in what she was doing that she was oblivious of her surroundings.

It wasn't until she nearly bumped into Nile that her concentration was broken. She started and her head flew back. "Oh, excuse me!" Those enormous blue eyes widened even further in surprise. "Why, Mr. Marcus!"

"Miss Dare."

She clutched her papers to her bosom. "I must confess I am surprised to see you here. Have you decided to accept my proposition, then?"

He nodded solemnly. "Against my better judgment and with grave reservations."

If she was curious as to what had made him change his mind, she had the good sense not to ask. But she couldn't suppress a radiant smile of childlike excitement. "Excellent. I'd like you to meet my editor, Sam Vincent, and we can iron out the details."

Nile followed her to a closed door at the other end of the room and stood silently while Maddie Dare knocked.

"What do you want?" a voice bellowed from within.

Undaunted, the woman glanced back at Nile.

"Don't pay any attention to our tame bear. Sam's bark is much worse than his bite."

Then she opened the door and went sailing in.

As Nile stepped into the office and quickly looked around, Maddie closed the door behind them, saying, "Mr. Marcus, I'd like you to meet Sam Vincent, the managing editor of the *Clarion*. Sam, this is Nile Marcus, who has just agreed to accompany me to Brazil to search for Ben."

With his pale complexion and stooped shoulders, Sam Vincent looked like the type of man who had been born behind a desk and would probably die there. But Nile knew better than to be fooled by the outward softness, the balding head, and the paunch pushing Vincent away from the edge of his desk. The man's gaze was direct and challenging, indicating the tough, shrewd mind necessary to rise to such a position of power and authority. Right away Nile realized he mustn't underestimate this man.

Vincent rose slowly from his swivel chair, and Nile could see he was as tall as Maddie.

"Mr. Marcus, a pleasure to meet you."

Nile felt that calculating gaze rake him up and down, but the expression in those sharp eyes remained veiled, keeping Vincent's assessment of him a secret.

"Vincent," Nile said.

"Well, why don't the two of you sit down and we can discuss the expedition." Once they were all seated, Vincent leaned back in his chair. "I'm sure Maddie has already apprised you of the situation."

Nile nodded. "She has. She wants someone to guide her up the Amazon to search for her lost fiancé."

"Yes. The *Clarion* will finance the cost of the expedition and pay whatever expenses you incur while in Brazil. We shall also pay you a salary of 1,000 pounds for your services. Agreed?"

The amount was more than he had hoped for, but Nile kept calm so as not to betray his own eagerness. "Fair enough. But I have a few conditions of my own as well."

He sensed Maddie stir in the chair beside him and glance at him sharply. "And what conditions are those, Mr. Marcus?"

"When we reach Brazil, I give the orders," he said, looking directly at her, "and you will do whatever I say without question."

Rebellion clouded her clear gaze. "Until death do us part?"

He grinned. "Precisely."

"I'll agree to that," she said, but Nile could tell she wasn't at all pleased.

"Also," he added, "you're doing this at your own risk. If something happens to you, I'm not responsible."

"Agreed," she said.

Now he turned his attention to Vincent. "And, if at any time Miss Dare calls the whole thing off and returns to England, I still get my money."

The other man hesitated, and for one instant Nile thought he was going to refuse the outrageous stipulation. But Sam Vincent nodded in assent.

"Good," Nile said. "We all understand each other, then."

Vincent added, "We can put this all in writing, if you prefer, Mr. Marcus."

"Not necessary," Nile said, rising. "I'm a man of my word, and I trust you are too. I'll buy the supplies we need and book us passage on the next ship bound for Lisbon."

"Why will we be leaving from Lisbon and not Liverpool?" Maddie asked.

"Traveling on a Portuguese ship will let us mingle with the natives," he replied. "I'll also give you the name of a bank in Manaus where you can wire additional funds. Manaus is an expensive city, and we'll need the extra money once we arrive."

He nodded first at Maddie, then at Vincent. "Good day to you both. You'll be hearing from me."

Before Nile could turn, Vincent said, "Oh, and, Marcus, there's one other matter we neglected to mention."

"What's that?"

"The *Clarion* will be carrying a series of articles about the expedition—'LADY REPORTER SEARCHES FOR LOST LOVE'—that sort of thing. Naturally, we'll want to introduce you to our readers as the man who will be embarking on this quest with Maddie."

Nile felt his temper soar, but kept it in check. He turned to Maddie and said, "I thought I told you I never gave interviews."

"So you did, but I think such articles could be of great benefit to you in the future."

That piqued his interest. "How?"

"It would show all the doubters and disbelievers that someone had enough faith in Nile Marcus to hire him for another expedition. Perhaps it would also bring you to the attention of prospective employers as well."

She was a clever one, all right, knowing just the right convincing argument to use to win her case.

"I doubt it. Orchid collectors are a rather small and select group. They all know each other and tend to hire the same men to hunt for their plants."

Vincent intervened. "The articles are part of the package, Marcus. If you won't agree to an interview . . ." He shrugged eloquently.

Nile stood there in silence for a moment as he considered their demand. "All right. I'll agree to the interview."

Then he wished them good day again and left.

*   *   *

When the door closed behind Nile Marcus and his footsteps died away, Maddie turned to Sam. "What do you think of him?"

Sam made a grimace of distaste. "He's a shrewd one, all right, but I don't like him."

Maddie's brows rose in surprise. "I've never known you to make such a harsh judgment of someone, based on a first impression, Sam. Why don't you like him?"

"Just a bad feeling I have. He reminds me of Caroline Lamb's description of Lord Byron."

" 'Mad, bad, and dangerous to know'?"

Dangerous. Oh, yes.

"That's the one. And he's too cocky by half."

"Oh, don't let his arrogance fool you." She stuck her pencil back in her chignon and grew reflective. "Despite that air of confidence, I suspect his last chance to find a backer must have fallen through—that's why he came to the *Clarion*. We were his last resort."

"Maddie, you're a damn fine reporter—one of the best—but you're no judge of men."

She raised her head indignantly. "I beg your pardon! I think I'm an excellent judge of men. I came to work for you, didn't I?"

"That's different. I'm a capital fellow, honest and trustworthy. But this Marcus . . . I don't know, Maddie."

"Sam, you're clucking like a mother hen again."

"I can't help it. You're like a daughter to me, and I don't know if I like the idea of your going off to South America with that man."

Maddie leaned forward, her face shining with intensity. "Sam, whatever your personal feelings about Nile Marcus, he's the best man for the job. I know. I've investigated him thoroughly. He knows the Amazon as well as you know these offices, and he's accustomed to extricating himself from dangerous situations. I'd trust him with my life."

"Need I remind you that's exactly what you will be doing? Are you sure you want to risk it? He seems awfully eager to absolve himself of any responsibility for your welfare. I have visions of him abandoning you in some jungle somewhere if the going gets tough."

Maddie shook her head. "Everyone who knows him says he's a man of honor and integrity. I don't think he'd do that to me, Sam."

"If you're sure . . ."

"I am. I do trust him. Besides, I wouldn't want to miss this adventure for the world."

Sam shrugged in surrender. "Then it's all settled. But I still wish you weren't going."

Maddie rose, rounded the desk, placed her hands on Sam's shoulders, and leaned over to kiss the beginnings of a bald spot on the top of his head. "Thank you for not calling it off."

He swung around to face her, causing her to step back. "I would never keep you from doing something you really wanted to do, Maddie. I would never hold you back. You're too good a reporter."

"I know you wouldn't, Sam. And I appreciate it."

A faint smile touched his mouth. "Enough of that sentimental stuff, Dare. Get back to work."

"Yes, sir, Mr. Vincent. Right away, Mr. Vincent." She saluted him smartly just before flying out the door.

A cloak of bone-chilling drizzle had begun to drape itself around the city late that afternoon, and by the time the hansom cab pulled up in front of Maddie's red brick terrace house in Dover Street, she was cold, tired, and shivering uncontrollably.

She paid the driver, disembarked, and hurried up the slick front steps. Once inside, she breathed a sigh of relief and performed her evening ritual of lighting the gaslights, putting the teakettle on, and exchanging her shirtwaist and corset for the unrestrictive comfort of a velvet Liberty dress.

Later, curled up before a cozy fire in the drawing room and sipping her milky tea, Maddie regarded her surroundings with a feeling of pride. True, she didn't own the terrace house, but she paid its rent faithfully with money earned by her own endeavors, and it was the first real home she could call her own.

It was her refuge from the world, a haven of solitude only a privileged few people had ever entered, and one which was not shared by so much as a cat or a bird. Not only had Maddie decorated the five small rooms exactly to her taste in an outdated but comfortable aesthetic style, she was her own maid and cleaned them herself, for dusting, mopping, and scrubbing increased her feeling of being inexorably bound to the place, of its truly being hers.

Maddie set down her empty teacup and crossed the drawing room to the windows overlooking Dover Street, and closed the curtains to shut out the world. She returned to her seat by the fire, feeling oddly melancholy tonight. She would miss her home with its comforting domestic routine. But she was buoyed by the thought that it would be waiting for her, as always, when she returned.

She poured herself another cup of tea and thought of Nile Marcus, wondering how they were ever going to endure each other's company for the next eight months or more. She was going to a strange, exotic land with a virtual stranger. There was no telling what could happen.

Maddie recalled his penetrating hawklike gaze and she shivered. When Nile Marcus looked at her, she felt as if he were looking right through her, down into her very soul, searching for all her secrets. In all her years as a reporter, she had never met a man like him, so compelling, so commanding. And proud.

She remembered the expression on his face when she mentioned his straitened financial circumstances, the look of bleak despair that vanished so quickly she thought she had imagined it. That look was like a dagger twisting in her conscience, and for one instant Maddie felt ashamed of herself for humiliating him.

She rose and set down her teacup. "I'll make it up to him somehow," she said aloud.

Meanwhile, she had plans of her own to make for the expedition. Nile would be buying supplies and booking their passage, but Maddie still had to decide what personal items to take. She had assured him she traveled without the usual feminine encumbrances, and to accomplish that feat required careful planning.

Whirling on her heel, Maddie went to make her supper and then get down to work.

The moment Nile stepped out of the carriage after Maddie and Sam, he regarded the scene before him with ill-disguised disgust.

Half of England must have turned out to see them off, judging by the sea of people crowding the Southampton dock below the *Northstar*, the steamship that would take him and Maddie on the first leg of their journey. The atmosphere was as joyful and as raucous as a circus sideshow. The moment Maddie appeared, the crowd cheered so loudly they drowned out the band playing a rousing rendition of "Rule, Britannia," and hundreds of Union Jacks beat the air wildly in a flurry of color. A banner proclaiming "Good Luck, Maddie," stretched high above the crowd.

"Is all this your doing?" Nile asked Maddie, who was smiling and waving to the crowd and obviously relishing all the attention.

"Of course," she replied under her breath, still smiling and waving. "That's why I wrote all those articles, to call attention to the expedition."

"And you succeeded," Sam Vincent said, "as always."

Nile recalled the first of the articles that had appeared two days after he agreed to the expedition. The headline had read, "LADY REPORTER TO SEEK LOST LOVE," and chronicled the account of how *Clarion* reporter Maddie Dare was determined to go to Brazil to search for her missing fiancé. In the articles that followed, the *Clarion*'s readers were treated to hair-raising descriptions of the dangers their brave Maddie would face, as well as an illustration of the practical split-skirt explorer's costume she had designed for herself.

And there had been that article about Nile.

A wry smile twisted his mouth. He had to admit that part of him had been flattered by it, for the article depicted him as a courageous adventurer capable of fighting off bloodthirsty savages with one hand while wrestling an anaconda with the other. But another part had been appalled by the dishonesty of it. He made his feelings known in no uncertain terms to Sam Vincent and Maddie, but they assured him there could be no harm in embellishing the truth a little.

"I think it's time for you two to go aboard," Vincent said. He extended his hand to Nile. "Good luck, Marcus. And be sure to bring our Maddie home safely, or you'll answer to me."

Nile shook his hand. "Thanks for the vote of confidence, Vincent. I'll do my best."

"Don't worry, Sam," Maddie said, reaching out to give her employer a farewell hug. "We'll all be back before you know it. And I'll send you articles whenever I can."

"See that you do," Vincent said, his eyes unnaturally bright. He cleared his throat as he stepped back. "You'd better board the ship before it leaves without you."

"Good-bye, Sam," Maddie said, then turned to wave to the crowd one last time.

Suddenly the crowd surged forward, pressing against the ropes that restrained them, and their good wishes filled the air.

"Good luck to ya, Maddie."

"Hope ya find your Ben and come home safe and sound."

"We'll miss you, Maddie!"

Just as Nile began following Maddie up the gangplank, he heard a shrill female voice in the crowd squeal, "Ooh, that Nile Marcus is ever so handsome, don't you think?" followed by, "Imagine going into the jungle alone with the likes of him!"

Maddie must have heard it too, for she turned and grinned at him. "Well, clearly you have your admirers, Mr. Marcus."

He gave her a dry look, then pasted a smile on his face and waved. He was totally unprepared for the collective "Aaah!" of feminine adulation that rose and filled the air.

Shaking his head at the absurdity of it, he followed Maddie the rest of the way up the gangplank, gladly leaving the shouting, screaming throng below for the solitude of the open sea.

Maddie stood at the rail, waving and smiling until the people on the docks could no longer see her. Then she glanced at the man standing at her side. Now that they were finally alone together, she wondered if they would get along. In all the preparations for the expedition during these last two weeks, there had been no time to sit down and really talk, except for the one time Maddie had interviewed him. And even then, Nile Marcus revealed precious little.

The man seemed a million miles away, his perfect profile etched against the gray English horizon.

"Well," Maddie said, "that was quite a rousing sendoff, I must say."

"You enjoy all the adulation, don't you?"

She gazed at him steadily. "Yes, yes, I do. I enjoy moving people with my writing, and being recognized for it."

"Well, no one will know who you are when we reach Brazil."

"No one knew who I was when I went to Africa, either, but it didn't make any difference to me."

Nile just gave her an inscrutable look.

Maddie gripped the railing hard. "Mr. Marcus, we are going to spend a great deal of time in each other's company, and I would suggest we at least make the effort to be civil to each other."

"I was hired to find your fiancé. Our agreement didn't say anything about my having to be civil to you."

Maddie felt her cheeks grow warm. "My, we certainly are blunt."

"That's the way I am. Get used to it or start swimming for shore."

She gave him a sidelong glance. "You don't like me, do you?"

"Not especially."

"Why?" she asked, stung. "You don't even know me."

"Well, I don't like what I've seen so far." He turned to face her, those golden eyes glittering with animosity. "You did try to blackmail me."

The accusation in his intense gaze made Maddie feel guilty for what she had done. "I'm sorry. Truly

I am, but I was just doing my job." She looked up and extended her hand. "Will you accept my apology?"

"I'm a private man," he said, rudely ignoring her outstretched hand as he leaned against the railing and stared at the vanishing English coastline. "I resent people prying into my personal life."

Maddie's hand fell back to her side and she colored with embarrassment. "I never expected you to be the type of man who bore a grudge, Mr. Marcus."

"I'm not."

Before Maddie could blink, he had turned away from the rail with his customary feline grace, grasped her hand, and brought it to his lips. "Apology accepted. And I'll try to be civil to you from now on. No guarantees, though."

Then he released her, grinned, and strode away, his abrupt turnabout leaving a stunned and bemused Maddie staring after him.

3

Maddie stood at the rail of the *Esperança* and sighed in relief.

Last night's storm was over. Black, roiling waters that had crested in frightening twenty-foot-high waves were now green and calm again, and the damp deck rocked as gently as a cradle beneath Maddie's feet instead of pitching her from one end of her cabin to the other in the high, howling wind. The sky was an endless stretch of tranquil blue, as if to compensate for the storm's ominous black thunderclouds and jagged forks of lightning.

Maddie swallowed hard and shuddered.

The *Esperança* had been out to sea for five days, and Maddie prayed for fair weather for the next five days it would take the steamer to reach the Brazilian port city of Pará.

She adjusted the tilt of her parasol to shade her from the morning sun, growing fiercer and hotter the nearer they came to the tropics, and she regarded Nile Marcus' closed cabin door in annoyance, wondering when he was going to come out.

Suddenly the cabin door swung open, and the man himself emerged, bowing his head so he could pass through without conking himself against the doorjamb. This morning, his state of semidress was hardly suitable for the presence of a lady. His white lawn shirt was left unbuttoned carelessly at the throat, the deep V revealing a strong neck and a sprinkling of dark hairs on his powerful chest. The snug black trousers accentuated his flat stomach, slender hips, and strong thighs. Unlike the dark suit he had worn in England, these clothes suited Nile Marcus perfectly.

Oh, *my*, was Maddie's only rational thought.

She couldn't take her eyes off him as he shrugged his broad shoulders like a lion awakening from a long sleep and straightened to his full height. Then he took a deep breath of clean salt air, expanding his brawny chest so that it strained his shirt buttons.

Maddie swallowed hard as Nile exhaled. She felt so warm in spite of the cool sea breeze brushing her flushed cheeks. Then she thought of Ben's light-hearted laughter and felt like herself again.

Nile turned and noticed her standing there, watching him, and walked toward her.

Maddie glided forward with a welcoming smile. "Why, good morning, Mr. Marcus."

He nodded civilly and even managed a smile. "Miss Dare."

"What a beautiful morning," Maddie said. When Nile made no reply, she added, "Judging by this sunshine, it's difficult to believe we ever had that horrible storm last night."

"Were you frightened?"

"I was terrified out of my wits, especially when I was flung out of my bunk. I thought we were all headed straight for Davy Jones's locker."

Her blunt admission seemed to startle him, for he looked over at her. "The intrepid Maddie Dare frightened by a little storm at sea? My, my. Whatever would your loyal readers say if they knew?"

"If I do my job properly, they will shudder and fear right along with me."

"Hmph."

Maddie looked at him. "Do I detect a note of disapproval in your tone?"

He grinned insolently, a flash of strong white teeth. "I think a woman can make better use of her time and her, er, attributes ..." He let his gaze drop to the vicinity of her breasts and linger there a shade too long. "... than cavorting around the world, subjecting herself to danger while terrorizing the local populace."

"Such as ... ? Come, do enlighten me."

Nile Marcus leaned against the rail and crossed his arms, a spark of mischief lighting the golden depths of his eyes. "A woman should marry, tend her husband's house, and bear his children—which I'm assuming you will do if we find this fiancé of yours."

"Not 'if,' " Maddie said, " 'when' we find this fiancé of mine. I have every confidence in you, Mr. Marcus." She adjusted the tilt of her parsol. "Even though I shall be married to Ben Thomas, I shan't give up my post at the *Clarion*."

Nile raised his thick brows. "And what if your husband insists that you do?"

Maddie smiled slowly. "He wouldn't. That is the difference between you."

Something like anger hardened the man's features to stone. "And if you should be blessed with a child? What would you do then, Miss Dare? Farm the poor mite out to some unfeeling relative?"

"Is that what your mother did to you?" Maddie regretted the impetuous words the moment they passed her lips.

Nile sucked in his breath with an ominous hiss. All color fled from his lean cheeks, and for an instant his self-assured facade was stripped away, revealing an expression of such pain that Maddie wanted to cradle him in her arms like a lost child.

Fortunately for her, she resisted the impulse.

Nile balled his hands into fists and ground his

teeth. "That, Miss Dare, is none of your business." He turned on his heel.

"Mr. Marcus, wait!"

He whirled around and glowered down at her, his hands on his hips. "Yes?"

"I'm sorry," she said without preamble. "It was very thoughtless of me to say what I did. I didn't mean to pry into your personal life."

"I believe I've warned you about that before," he growled, obviously still furious. "Now, if you'll excuse me . . ."

Maddie stepped aside and he disappeared into his lair, slamming the door behind him with a resounding crash.

She stared at the closed door for a moment, then turned and walked back to her own cabin.

Once inside, she picked up pen and paper and started to write her article about last night's storm at sea, but after writing a few sentences she flung down her pen in disgust.

She couldn't stop thinking of Nile Marcus.

The look on his face when she made that careless remark about his mother was burned in Maddie's mind like a hot brand. Had he felt abandoned as a child because his mother left him and his father while she went traveling the world? Was that why he was so hostile to her and adamantly opposed to a woman accompanying him to the Amazon?

Maddie rose and began pacing her narrow cabin, her journalist's instincts whetted by the tantalizing puzzle that was Nile Marcus.

She went to one of her bags and took out a worn photograph of Ben. Maddie felt her stomach lurch just looking at him, for he was a handsome man—too handsome for his own good, Sam had always said. Ben's pale blue eyes sparkled with invitation, while his lopsided grin was wicked and worldly.

But compared with Nile, Ben was blessedly uncomplicated.

Perhaps I should just confront him, she thought. No, that wouldn't do at all. He'd just snarl at me and tell me to mind my own affairs. And if I really angered him, he's just hotheaded enough to call this whole expedition off and send me packing on the next ship back to England. All our plans would be shot to hell, and Sam would be none too pleased.

Maddie tapped her foot impatiently as she slipped the photo of Ben back into her bag. Then she smiled.

Be forewarned, Mr. Marcus, she thought. Before this is all over, I'm going to know all your secrets, or my name isn't Maddie Dare.

She picked up her pen again and began to write.

Two hours later, luncheon was announced, so Maddie put away paper and pen and strolled alone over to the dining room. Much to her surprise, Nile was already there and rose when she entered.

Maddie hesitated for a moment as she studied those tawny eyes for any hint of animosity, but now they were as bland as a baby's. She assumed he had forgotten—or at least forgiven her—for that careless remark.

After greeting the Portuguese captain in fluent French, Maddie noticed that the other passengers weren't here yet.

She turned to Nile. "Aren't the others joining us?"

Just as Nile shrugged, the door opened and the other passengers began filing in.

When Nile saw who was first, he smiled slowly and said, *"Bonjour, Mademoiselle D'Arqueville."* Then he rounded the table and held out her chair for her.

The statuesque brunette Frenchwoman smiled beautifully, murmured, *"Merci beaucoup, Monsieur Marcus,"* then seated herself with a coquettish glance up at Nile, who was trying valiantly not to stare down at her magnificent bosom.

She was followed by the twins, two blond, buxom Polish girls barely out of their teens, who spoke neither French nor English and had long surnames that Maddie couldn't even pronounce, let alone remember. They looked up at Nile shyly as he assisted them to their chairs, then nodded at Maddie and the captain.

They were followed by another Polish woman named Zosia, who did speak a little French and served as their interpreter.

Last came Senhor Calistro.

Maddie suppressed a shudder the moment the thin, swarthy man glided into the room as noiselessly as a snake. She couldn't help it. There was just something about him that made her flesh crawl. With his short, pointed beard and cold dark eyes, all he needed was a white starched ruff around his neck and he could have posed for a painting by Velázquez. But there was an air of ruthlessness about him that reminded Maddie more of Torquemada and the Spanish Inquisition. If the eyes mirrored the soul, then Senhor Calistro had none, for those pitch-black orbs were as expressionless as obsidian.

I wonder what they are all doing here together? she thought, her gaze encompassing all the women, so beautiful and elegantly attired in expensive gowns. *I know they all came aboard together in Lisbon, and Senhor Calistro appears to be their chaperon. Chaperon . . . he acts more like their jailer, always herding them together like cattle, never letting them out of his sight for so much as a solitary stroll around the deck.*

Suddenly Maddie felt those cold black eyes on her and she shivered in spite of herself. She forced herself to meet his gaze and even managed to nod civilly at him.

Once everyone was seated and the captain said grace, an appetizing luncheon of freshly caught fish was served.

At first, everyone except Senhor Calistro made polite, inconsequential chatter in four languages about last night's storm and today's beautiful weather. But as the meal wore on, Maddie became more determined to learn something about her fellow passengers. She sensed a story here, and damned if she wasn't going to find out what it was.

She caught Zosia's eye.

"Forgive my curiosity, *mademoiselle*," she began, "but South America is so far away from your homeland. Why would you leave there to journey so far?"

"We have accepted positions as governesses," Zosia replied.

Maddie, who couldn't imagine the ingenuous twins being anyone's governesses, forced herself to smile.

Senhor Calistro spoke for the first time, his voice soft and as slick as a film of oil on water. "There are many wealthy families in Manaus, *mademoiselle*, who wish to engage European governesses for their children. And they do pay so much more handsomely than anyone in Europe."

Maddie forced herself to meet his unblinking stare. "I am assuming, *senhor*, that you represent such families in their quest?"

He nodded, but the ensuing silence told Maddie he wasn't about to elaborate.

"And you, Mademoiselle D'Arqueville?" Maddie persisted. "Why are you traveling to Brazil?"

"I am visiting relatives in Manaus," she replied. "Senhor Calistro has graciously offered to escort me." She glanced at Nile. "A woman traveling alone is prey to so many dangers, don't you agree, Monsieur Marcus?"

Maddie was on the verge of disputing the Frenchwoman's assertion by citing herself as a prime example; then she thought better of it. Somehow she thought such a lecture would be lost on Mademoiselle D'Arqueville.

As Maddie expected, Nile said, *"Oui, mademoiselle."*

Senhor Calistro blinked once and said to Maddie, "And what of you, Mademoiselle Dare? Why are you traveling to Brazil?"

When she told him she was a newspaper reporter determined to find her missing fiancé, Senhor Calistro just stared at her. Then he smiled, a quick baring of sharp, lupine teeth.

"You are very brave, *mademoiselle*," he said, "to make such a hazardous journey alone. Women in my country would not be allowed to do this."

"But she's not alone," Nile said in his deep, lazy voice. "I am her guide . . . and her protector."

Under any other circumstances, Maddie would have bristled at Nile's choice of the word "protector" to describe his relationship as her employee. But she sensed something unspoken pass between the two men, of territory being staked and a claim made, and she held her tongue.

When Calistro's gaze fell away and he resumed eating, Maddie knew that Nile had won the wordless masculine battle. She let out an imperceptible sigh of relief and turned her attention back to her food.

Nile continued to converse with Mademoiselle D'Arqueville and the captain, but his thoughts were on Maddie, now eating so demurely.

Damn her prying, he thought. Hasn't she realized by now what kind of man Calistro is, and why these women are with him? I hope she isn't foolish enough to try to interfere.

If she did, he would just have to stop her before she placed both their lives in jeopardy.

* * *

After luncheon, Maddie retired to her cabin and Nile didn't see her for the rest of the day.

But hours later, when he emerged from his own cabin, he saw her standing by herself on the ship's deck and staring at the sunset.

She was hatless, and the warm rays of the setting sun turned her pale hair into the molten gold that the Incas had once picturesquely termed "sweat of the sun." A cool breeze pulled out several soft locks, forming tendrils to frame her face and caress her cheeks. With Maddie's head held high and proud, showing her perfect profile silhouetted against the sun like a halo, Nile thought she looked almost angelic.

Maddie glanced at him as he joined her; then she leaned against the rail.

"It's beautiful, isn't it?" she said, squinting out across the ocean. "I've never seen a sunset quite like this before."

Nile followed her gaze at the setting sun, now a dull orange globe poised over the horizon for its evening easement into the sea. The clouds around it caught its lambent fire and turned various shades of red and purple in the oncoming twilight.

The tranquil scene soothed him, and for a moment he even forgot why he was annoyed with Maddie.

He said, "Wait until we're on the Amazon. By day, all you see is an impenetrable wall of jungle, but when the sun sets . . ." Suddenly at a loss for words, he shrugged.

Maddie reached up to tuck a stray lock into place. "Go on. Tell me what it's like."

At first he thought she was goading him into making a fool of himself, but when he glanced down, her expression held no hint of mockery, just sincere interest.

"The dying rays of the sun shine directly into the jungle. It lights up the tree trunks so you can tell exactly what kinds of trees they are—rosewood, mahogany, figs, chocolate trees. And the foliage . . . I've never seen so many shades of green in my life."

"Why, Nile Marcus," Maddie murmured, a teasing glint back in her eye, "I believe beneath that adventurer's facade lurks the soul of a poet."

He shrugged. "I was never one for poetry, or books for that matter. I just know what I see, and you asked me to describe it, that's all."

"Well, you did a splendid job. Have you ever thought of putting it down on paper and becoming a newspaper reporter yourself?"

"I wouldn't want that. Prying into other people's lives all the time, elbowing your way in where you're not wanted . . . Doesn't sound like work a man—or a woman—could be proud of."

Maddie's head jerked around, and her eyes smoldered with such anger that Nile almost stepped back out of striking range. But all she did was smile and purr, "And I suppose picking flowers is work a man could be proud of? Sounds like something a . . . dandy would do."

Nile felt his cheeks grow hot, and his fingers itched to throttle that slender white neck. "Damnation and hellfire! A dandy, am I?" He stepped forward until he was almost nose-to-nose with her. "Well, your life may depend on this *dandy*, Miss Dare, and you'd do well to hold your tongue."

To his consternation, she merely laughed. "My, my, how prickly we've become." She shook her head. "And as for holding my tongue . . . You should know by now, Mr. Marcus, that I never do that."

But she had, at luncheon with Senhor Calistro. Nile felt his anger drain away as he wondered why.

Maddie shivered. "Well, it's been wonderful sparring with you, but the evening has turned cool and I think I shall return to my cabin. Good night."

As she started to walk away, Nile stayed her with a hand on her arm. She stopped and turned, surprise in her eyes.

"Yes?"

"At luncheon today, when I told Calistro I was your protector, you didn't deny it."

"Why, whatever do you mean?"

"Come, come, don't play the innocent with me. An outspoken, independent woman such as yourself would never sit still for a mere male calling himself her protector. Yet you did. I'd like to know why."

To his surprise, she didn't try to evade his question with some glib comment. Her demeanor was grave as she said, "I am not a fool, Mr. Marcus. There is something about Senhor Calistro that makes my flesh crawl. I know it is in my own best interests to let him believe you are my protector. That is why I did not refute your claim."

"Most prudent of you."

A faint smile touched her lips. "*I* thought so."

Then she wished him good evening again, turned, and started walking toward her cabin.

Nile watched as she glided across the deck, her hips swaying just as gently as the deck, her long skirts showing a faint outline of her long, shapely legs with every stride. When she reached her cabin, she looked over her shoulder at him and nodded, then disappeared inside.

He turned and leaned against the rail. The sun was already nearly submerged in the sea, and the lack of light was rapidly turning to twilight.

Without warning, the sea swallowed up the last of the sun and settled down for the night. The only sounds were the creaking of the ship, like an old man cracking his bones before sleep, and the soporific lapping of the waves against the ship's hull. Then came the faint voices of the Portuguese sailors below deck as they sang some mournful love song.

Nile listened until he could no longer endure it. Then he strode back to his cabin.

The following morning, Maddie was standing on deck, watching Senhor Calistro and his women at the other end.

The way the man kept such close watch on them reminded Maddie not so much of a shepherd guarding his flock, for that was too gentle and benevolent an image, as of some African tribesmen she had once seen escorting cattle to be slaughtered.

Maddie twirled her parasol in annoyance as indecision gripped her. Should she go to the captain and tell him what she suspected, or should she just hold her tongue and let the women go to their fate?

Before she could decide what to do, Nile's cabin door opened and he emerged. He came to join her.

"Good morning," he said. "I trust you slept well last night?"

"Good morning. I slept very well, thank you."

He looked around. "I see that our fellow passengers are taking their morning constitutional."

"Yes. I tried to converse with Mademoiselle D'Arqueville alone, but Senhor Calistro said it would be rude of us to exclude the other women." She turned to Nile. "I thought it most odd."

Nile shrugged. "Calistro is just overprotective of his charges."

"I don't think that's it at all."

"Oh? And what do you think, as I'm sure you're about to tell me?"

Maddie looked him squarely in the eye. "I think they're prostitutes."

Nile didn't flinch. "Very astute of you."

Maddie sighed. "Oh, dear. I was afraid of that."

Nile placed his hands on the rail and stared out to sea. "Well, what did you expect?" His voice was low and edged with anger. "When you first approached me about accompanying you to the Amazon, I warned you about Manaus and the kind of place it is."

" 'Wicked,' I believe you said. 'The most decadent city on the face of the earth.' "

"Yes. So you had better get used to seeing many things that affront your feminine sensibilities." He glared at her. "And keep your nose out of other people's affairs, or you'll place both our lives in danger."

"You needn't worry," she said coldly. "I am here to find Ben, not liberate the brothels of Brazil."

"See that you don't, or wherever we are, so help me God, I'll put you on the next ship back to England and the expedition is off."

Maddie said nothing for a moment and watched Senhor Calistro usher his women back to their cabins. When Nile's anger finally receded, she said, "I am curious about something."

Nile gave her a dismayed glance. "What now?"

"Is Calistro some sort of procurer?"

He nodded slowly in assent. "The lowest of the low. He makes special trips to Europe regularly to find extraordinary women for men rich enough to pay for the best."

"Fascinating."

Nile's golden eyes glittered with mischief. "Take Mademoiselle D'Arqueville. She's not only beautiful, I'll wager she knows just how to set a man on fire."

Maddie knew he was deliberately trying to embarrass her with such frank conversation, but she refused to give him the satisfaction of seeing her discomfited. She raised her brows and replied coolly, "I'll wager she does."

He tried again. "Some rubber baron will make her his mistress and install her in a grand *palácio* in Manaus."

"I'm sure he will, at least until he tires of her and seeks someone more beautiful and more ... accomplished. And what of the twins and Zosia?"

Nile shrugged. "Polish mistresses are the most highly prized of all. Dark Latin men prefer their blond hair and fair skin. As for the twins, I suspect they'll go to a man of certain tastes."

His sordid implication was too much for Maddie. Provoked at last, she whirled on him, blue eyes blazing. "How can you be so cold and unfeeling? They're barely older than children! Don't you care what happens to them?"

"Of course I care what happens to them!" Nile retorted. "What kind of monster do you think I am?"

Maddie felt her cheeks grow warm. "I . . . I didn't say you were a monster."

"Give me some credit. I'd like nothing better than to break Calistro's neck with my bare hands and feed him to the sharks. But all that would do is get me arrested and thrown in some Brazilian jail to rot. Those women are with Calistro because they want to be. Kindly remember that before you go storming off to rescue them."

Maddie took several deep breaths to calm herself, then demurred. "You're right, of course."

"If there's one thing I've learned out here, it's to mind one's own business. And I'd suggest you do the same. Understand?"

"Perfectly," Maddie replied, even as she seethed inside.

"Good. We understand each other, then." Nile

extended his arm to her. "Come, I'll escort you to breakfast."

Later that morning, when Maddie was back in her cabin, her thoughts were haunted by the other women.

As a journalist, she had been exposed to another side of life that most people preferred to think didn't exist, a nebulous underworld where every unspeakable vice was practiced with relish in private by those very same people who decried it in public. While not the crusading sort, Maddie never failed to be appalled by the blacker side of human nature and man's hypocrisy.

She tried to start a new article for Sam about Calistro and the women, but the words just wouldn't come. She set down her pen in frustration and began pacing the tiny cabin.

What can I do about it? she wondered. Talk to the women and try to convince them to return to Europe? Chances are, they won't even listen to me. They've chosen their path.

"Nile's right," she muttered. "I should just mind my own affairs and concentrate on finding Ben."

Then she put her paper away and tried to forget, but several evenings later, an incident occurred that would ensure that the women remained in her memory for a long, long time.

As Maddie sat in the stifling cabin, she could feel the perspiration rising on her skin. No sooner did she dab at her forehead and neck with her handkerchief than they were damp again from the oppressive heat.

"What I wouldn't give for a cool English rain," she muttered to herself as she wiped the moisture from her brow for the hundredth time. "But don't let Nile hear me say that."

Maddie was just about to leave her cabin for a

stroll in what she hoped would be cool night air, when the sound of raised voices coming from the adjacent cabin caused her to pause.

She listened. First there was a low, indistinct voice. This was followed by a loud, hysterical female voice speaking rapid, breathless French.

"No! That's not true! You said we were to be governesses."

Maddie stood stock-still, not daring to breathe. The low voice spoke again, followed by the heart-rending sound of sobbing.

Squaring her shoulders, Maddie rushed out of her cabin and knocked on the adjoining cabin's door.

"Zosia, are you all right?" she called.

The door opened. Maddie stepped back, surprised to see none other than Calistro standing there, staring at her out of cold unblinking eyes.

"I heard sobbing," Maddie said, trying to peer around the man into the cabin.

Calistro stepped forward smoothly and closed the door behind him. "A mere misunderstanding, Mademoiselle Dare. I suggest you return to your cabin."

"The woman is upset. I would like to attend to her."

"That will not be necessary."

Anger burned Maddie's cheeks. "Senhor Calistro, if you don't open that door this instant, I'll—"

"Cease your meddling at once, *mademoiselle*. If you do not, not even your brave protector will be able to save you."

Calistro spoke softly, without raising his voice, but there was such menace in his tone that Maddie felt the fine hairs on her arms rise. She didn't doubt for an instant that this evil little man had the power to carry out such a threat.

Without another word, Maddie whirled on her heel and returned to her cabin, where she stood shaking with relief. She had been threatened many a time in her career, and she had always faced those threats undaunted. But this time even she was afraid.

She noticed the sobbing had stopped.

An hour later, Maddie decided to stroll around the deck before retiring for the night.

As she left her cabin, she glanced around and was relieved to find Calistro was nowhere to be found. She was alone.

Maddie breathed deeply of strong briny air, letting the blessed coolness of it wash over her moist skin and calm her. The ocean was tranquil tonight and a round full moon hung high in the sky, its edges hazy and smudged.

Then Maddie heard the sound of a door opening, followed by light, hurried footsteps crossing the deck. She turned in time to see Zosia place her hands on the rail, then hesitate for a second, as if contemplating some course of action.

Just as Maddie was about to call out a greeting, the woman hoisted herself onto the rail, her intention plain.

For one endless second Maddie could only stare at her in horror. Then she found her voice. "Zosia!" she cried, running forward to stop her.

But the woman would not be deterred. With another push, Zosia hauled her legs over the rail and disappeared over the side, shattering the stillness with her scream and leaving a stunned Maddie to claw helplessly at thin air.

She leaned over the rail and watched in horror as Zosia plummeted headfirst, her arms outstretched as if protesting the fate she had chosen for herself. Then she hit the water with a resounding splash, and the greedy waves rose up to accept the sacrifice, swallowing her whole.

Maddie didn't wait to see if Zosia would bob to the surface. "Man overboard!" she bellowed, pounding on cabin doors as she raced to the bridge for help.

A door opened and a dark figure loomed before her. Maddie found her headlong flight stopped by a chest as hard and broad as a stone wall and a pair of strong hands grasping her arms. She found herself staring up into Nile Marcus' sleepy, scowling face.

"What's wrong?" he snapped.

"Zosia just jumped overboard. She . . . she killed herself."

Nile just stared at her, his eyes bulging with shock. Then he muttered, "Damn!"

Maddie tried to pull away, but he held her fast. "Alert the captain. We've got to help her."

Someone had already alerted him, however, for an alarm bell began clanging and suddenly the deck was filled with light, hurried footsteps, and sailors shouting in Portuguese as they rushed to lower a lifeboat to search for Zosia. Maddie ran aft, followed by Nile, and when she got to the rail, she frantically searched the moonlit sea for any sign of the woman.

Nothing broke the calm surface.

Maddie clutched at the railing, despair welling up inside of her. She was barely aware of Nile standing at her side, conversing with the captain in an urgent, authoritative voice. All she could see in her mind's eye was the hapless woman plummeting into the dark, implacable sea, her thin shrill scream of realization echoing through Maddie's consciousness.

She didn't realize someone had been addressing her until she felt insistent hands on her shoulders, gently turning her away from the sea. She came face-to-face with Nile again, but this time his expression was kind and sympathetic. For the first time, she realized he was shirtless, the well-defined muscles of his shoulders and arms rippling beneath smooth skin with the slightest movement. But she was still reeling from events that were more shocking than the sight of a half-naked man.

"They're going to look for her," he said quietly, his hands lingering on her shoulders, his touch firm and soothing as he held her steady, "but her chances of survival . . ." He shook his head.

Maddie swallowed hard, fighting back helpless tears. "I saw her. She jumped. She just hauled herself over the rail and deliberately *jumped*."

She shuddered as she finally succumbed to shock, her knees wobbling.

"Easy," Nile warned, pulling her against him as she started to fall.

Maddie stiffened, intending to draw away, but by that time his left arm had encircled her waist, imprisoning her, while his right hand drew her head down to his shoulder, then slid down to rest lightly in the middle of her back.

"Don't fight me, Maddie," he whispered, his cheek against her hair. "Not this time."

She closed her eyes, and with a soft sigh of surrender gave herself up to the comfort he was offering. Her arms slid around his narrow waist and she pressed closer, clinging to him as a child would cling to a cherished toy after a nightmare. With her cheek nestled against his bare shoulder, she took deep, shuddering breaths to calm her quaking insides, letting the warm, spicy scent of Nile's skin fill her nostrils. Gradually, when her strength returned and the light-headedness faded, she stirred.

"Feel better?" Nile murmured against her hair.

Maddie nodded, but made no attempt to leave the comforting circle of his arms, for she knew she would feel bereft without his strength buoying her.

Nile's arm fell from her waist and he dislodged her gently.

And a bit reluctantly, Maddie thought in wonder as they parted.

For a moment she thought he was going to kiss her as he had that day in the Explorers Club, but he made no move to do so.

"Will you be all right now?" he asked, an unfathomable expression in his eyes.

She nodded, startled by his boundless kindness. This was a side of Nile Marcus she had never seen, that of a gentle, compassionate man able to console as well as command. "I'll be fine, thank you."

"Why don't you go back to your cabin and try to get some sleep?" Nile said. "I'm sure the captain will tell you when—if—they find her."

Maddie didn't feel like resting. The initial shock had worn off, and now her journalist's mind was clear and bubbling with questions demanding answers.

But she needed time to think, so she acquiesced to Nile's suggestion. She even allowed him to place his hand beneath her elbow and guide her through the somber crowd of onlookers.

On the way, they passed the other women and their keeper. Mademoiselle D'Arqueville's face was impassive, betraying nothing, while the twins stood huddled together, confusion written on their faces. The moment Maddie's gaze met Calistro's blinkless stare, she felt her fury rise.

She was certain he was responsible for Zosia's suicide, and she was going to see him pay.

Nile stopped, presumably to say a few comforting words to the women, but Maddie kept right on walking. When she entered her cabin, she closed the door and waited for word of Zosia.

4

"There's nothing you can do," Nile said to Maddie the following day as they stood together on deck.

He watched Maddie grasp the rail so hard with her free hand that the knuckles turned white. When she looked up at him, even the shadow from her parasol couldn't hide the outrage glittering in her eyes like a hot blue flame.

"The captain made that perfectly clear last night," she replied, biting off the words.

Nile suppressed a yawn, still weary himself from the tense, grueling aftermath of Zosia's suicide. All the passengers had been summoned to the captain's cabin to give their accounts of what had happened before and up to the moment the woman had jumped. They had stayed there until one in the morning, and when all the accounts were given and they were finally allowed to retire, nothing had been resolved.

Maddie smacked the rail with the palm of her hand. "I told the captain that Calistro is responsible. I'd bet a year's pay he never told Zosia the truth until last night."

Nile sighed as he recalled the emotional scene in the captain's cabin. Despite all of Nile's warnings to stay out of it, Maddie had accused the stone-faced Senhor Calistro of luring the women to South America under false pretenses, so they would become whores, not governesses, as promised. When

Zosia had learned the truth, she chose to take her own life rather than endure the unbearable shame.

Now Maddie mimicked the captain's shocked, affronted tone. " 'Oh, no, Senhorita Maddie, you are mistaken. I have known Senhor Calistro for years. He is a fine man, an honorable man. He would never do such a thing, never.' "

She looked over at Nile. "I wonder how much Calistro paid the captain to turn a deaf ear to my accusations?"

"Probably a great deal," Nile replied. "Bribery is a way of life here. You can't fight it, so you'd best get used to it."

Maddie dabbed at her damp brow and flushed cheeks with her handkerchief. Nile had to admire her for not once complaining about the stifling heat, but he noticed she had changed into a dress of thin, light cotton and had removed its high collar for comfort. He himself now wore the uniform of the tropics, a suit of crisp white linen that was rapidly wilting into a mass of creases and wrinkles. A broad-brimmed Chile hat shaded his eyes from the blinding sun.

Maddie grumbled, "Perhaps the authorities in Pará will believe me."

"You intend to report this to the police?"

"Of course I do! A woman died because of Calistro, and I intend to see him brought to justice!"

Nile fought down his rising temper and tried to remain calm. He hoped against hope that she would listen to reason. "And what do you think that will accomplish?"

"Justice," she snapped.

Nile swung his body toward her and rested his elbow negligently against the rail. "Are you proposing to give up the search for Ben Thomas?"

"Of course not."

"I'm just warning you that bringing Calistro to justice could take months."

"Surely not."

"Oh, yes. First of all, what proof do you have that Calistro was responsible for Zosia's death? Did he push her? No. He wasn't even on deck when it happened, so it's your word against his. Besides, Calistro has many powerful friends in high places, former customers, no doubt. And, if pressed, I'm sure Mademoiselle D'Arqueville would swear that all the women knew exactly why they were going to South America before they left Europe."

Maddie's face fell, and she stared out to sea.

"So," Nile continued relentlessly, "the odds are not in your favor. The authorities in Pará would have no reason to detain Calistro, and you would lose precious time."

She was silent for the longest time, and Nile could almost hear her mulling over his words and grappling with the truth. Finally she sighed deeply in surrender.

"You're right, of course."

"When it comes to the Amazon, I am. You hired me for my expertise, and I'm giving it, so the least you can do is take my advice."

"It's just that I hate injustice. When I see it, I feel compelled to try to do something about it."

He looked down into her troubled blue eyes and felt guilty for having been so harsh with her.

"That's an admirable trait," he said gently, "but you're just going to have to curb it while we're here. You'll be in Brazil soon, not England. People won't take kindly to your interference."

"You needn't worry, Mr. Marcus," she said. "I am here to find Ben, and that will always be my first priority."

"Good. We understand each other, then."

"Perfectly."

She turned her attention back to the sea, but from the hesitant glances she kept darting at Nile, he knew there was something else she wanted to say.

He gave an exaggerated sigh. "Out with it, Miss Dare, before you explode."

She looked over at him, a faint wash of pink color staining her high cheekbones. "You were very . . . kind and considerate to me last night when I was so upset," she murmured. "I just wanted you to know how much I appreciated it."

He couldn't tell her that he had drawn her into his arms because something in her eyes had touched him. Perhaps it was her bleak despair or vulnerability, or perhaps he just needed to hold someone himself.

Instead, he brushed aside her thanks with a gruff, "You would have collapsed if I hadn't."

"Thank you anyway."

They fell into an uneasy silence, each alone with his own thoughts.

After a few moments Maddie turned to him and said, "If you don't mind my asking, how long have you been living in the Amazon?"

Nile almost reminded her that his personal life was his own business, but then, he was feeling mellow and decided the question was innocent enough. "Fourteen years," he replied. "Ever since I was sixteen."

"And what made you decide to settle here? The world is so large, and there are so many other places where a man can make his fortune. Australia . . . China . . . Africa."

Nile shrugged. How could he answer her when he didn't know the answer himself? But he tried. "I suppose because it seemed so exotic to me, as unlike England as a country could be."

"And what did you do to earn a living, once you arrived?"

"Anything and everything. I worked on a *fazenda*—"

"A *fazenda*? What's that?"

"A cattle ranch. I worked there for a while, and when I grew bored with herding cattle, I went to work for a shipping company."

Maddie was regarding him with blatant curiosity. "You obviously didn't learn about the jungle or collecting orchids in a shipping company."

"No, I owe that to a man named Providence Brown."

"Providence. That has a distinct Puritan flavor to it. Is that his real name?"

Nile smiled and shook his head. "He's an American who came from someplace called Providence, Rhode Island. Someone started calling him that, and it stuck. Come to think of it, he's never even told me what his real name is. He lives on the river with his common-law wife, and he taught me everything I know about survival in the Amazon."

"You speak of him with great affection. You must hold him in high esteem."

"I do," Nile said. "He was more of a father to me than my own father ever was."

He regretted revealing so much of himself the moment the words slipped out of his mouth, especially when he saw a spark of interest light Maddie's eyes. The snoop picked up on every nuance of speech, every innuendo.

He said, "I'm counting on Provvy to help us find Thomas. If the man is still alive, Provvy will know it."

"He sounds like an interesting character," Maddie said. "I'll be looking forward to meeting him. Perhaps I'll even write an article about him."

Nile turned to go. He had told Maddie Dare enough for one morning. "We should be reaching the mouth of the Amazon in another hour." He yawned. "I got precious little sleep last night, thanks to you, so if you'll excuse me . . ."

He tipped his hat, turned, and strode off.

Maddie watched his cabin door close behind him; then she turned her attention back to the sea. As she listened to the water sloshing and lapping against the ship's hull, she couldn't stop thinking of last night. She could still see the dark shape silhouetted against the moon as Zosia hoisted herself over the railing with such resolve, still hear the woman scream as she plummeted into oblivion. Maddie shuddered at the memory of greedy waves closing over Zosia's head for the last time.

Out of the corner of her eye Maddie saw something move, and when she turned her head, she saw Calistro saunter across the deck as if he owned the *Esperança*. He didn't even look in her direction.

White-hot rage coursed through Maddie and she had to grip the rail to keep her emotions under control. Calistro was as responsible for Zosia's suicide as if he had pushed her himself. But he was going to get away with it, and there was nothing Maddie could do about it.

She clenched her jaw in frustration. Nile was right. She had no proof, and without proof, the Paranese authorities would not detain Calistro.

Just forget it, Maddie, she admonished herself. Pretend Zosia's death never happened. Once Calistro and his women leave the ship, you'll never see them again. Nile warned you that the Amazon was unlike any other place on earth, but you wanted to come anyway, so you'll have to play by their rules.

He had surprised her. Maddie hadn't expected him to reveal any part of his past to her, for he resented her personal questions so fiercely. Yet for once he had let down his guard and spoken freely of his early years in Brazil and his friendship with the man called Providence Brown. What had Nile called him? "The father I never had." Another tantalizing piece of the puzzle that was Nile Marcus presented itself.

Feeling smothered by the oppressive heat, Maddie returned to her cabin to nap.

An hour later, Nile awakened her to tell her the ship was approaching the mouth of the Amazon.

As Maddie stood on deck with Nile and stared out over the horizon, she felt disappointed. All she saw was a thin strip of land in the distance silhouetted against the hot blue cloudless sky. Then she noticed the water. It was changing from the vivid, almost transparent blue of the tropical Atlantic to a muddy opaque bronze.

Maddie stood transfixed. Never had she seen such a sight in her life as the might of the freshwater river clashing in mortal combat with the saltwater sea. For a moment she felt as though a huge bronze hand were trying to ward her off, to push her back to where she came from. But as quickly as the feeling of foreboding came over her, it passed, to be replaced by the excitement Maddie always felt when on the verge of a great adventure.

Then Nile informed her they would be leaving the *Esperança* once they docked in Pará, some eighty miles upriver. They would remain there for several days while Nile acquired supplies; then they would take a Brazilian steamer on to Manaus.

They would never see Senhor Calistro again, and that suited Maddie just fine.

Two days later, Maddie was standing on the wharf in Pará, shading her eyes against the blazing sun as she stared at the steamer docked there.

"The *Rio Madeira*," Nile said beside her. "Now you'll travel the Amazon as the Brazilians do. Think of how authentic your articles for the *Clarion* will be."

Maddie ignored the tinge of mockery in his voice and proceeded to study the *Rio Madeira*. The steamer was larger than Maddie had expected and consisted of three levels—a lower deck, upper deck, and topmost bridge—each surrounded by a railing and open-work sides that made the ship resemble a bird cage.

"It looks rather open," she said. "I don't see many cabins."

"That's because there aren't many," he replied. "Most passengers sleep in hammocks strung across the decks. It's a lot cooler that way."

"I'm sure it will be a novel experience," Maddie said blithely.

"Oh, you won't have to worry. Since we're traveling first class, thanks to the generosity of the *Clarion*, on the upper deck, we'll have cabins. They're quite luxurious, I might add, with bunks and shower baths and even a water closet." He grinned wickedly. "You'll think you're traveling on an ocean liner."

Maddie raised her brows. "Somehow, I doubt that."

"If the accommodations aren't to your liking, it's not too late to take a return ship back to England."

"Sorry to disappoint you, Mr. Marcus. You're not getting rid of me that easily. You're going to have to work for your fee."

"We'll see," he said ominously. "Our journey hasn't even begun yet." Then Nile looked around and added, "We'd better board before the second-class passengers do."

"I presume those are the locals," Maddie said as they walked toward the gangplank.

Nile shook his head. "They're immigrants from Spain who have come to work the rubber *estradas*.

Poor bastards. They don't know what fate awaits them."

"Aren't there enough Brazilians to do the work?"

"There are never enough," he replied, "and I can't say that I blame them." His golden eyes held Maddie's. "It's a hard life. Would you like to work in the middle of the jungle, miles from anywhere, eking out a meager livelihood tapping rubber trees, and owing your soul to your *patrão*? I think not."

Before Maddie could comment, she and Nile were being greeted by the captain, and they were ushered forward to choose their cabins. As Nile had promised, the cabins were rather large and luxurious.

Once they were back on deck, Maddie eyed the many hammocks strung across it with misgivings.

"They don't look very comfortable," she said.

"They're very comfortable, once you get used to them."

While Nile turned to speak to another passenger, Maddie went over to the nearest hammock and sat gingerly on the edge as it shuddered and wobbled. When the contraption stopped moving, she gamely swung her legs into it. Without warning, the hammock bucked away as if it were alive, and with a shriek of surprise Maddie went tumbling to the floor, where she landed with a resounding thump.

Nile was towering over her in an instant, peering down anxiously as he extended his hand. "Did you hurt yourself?"

"Only my pride," she muttered, struggling to her feet.

"Haven't you ever been in a hammock before?" he said. "I thought all English ladies whiled away their summer afternoons in hammocks."

"Not this particular Englishwoman," Maddie retorted, glaring at the hammock in distaste.

"You'll never survive on the Amazon if you can't master the hammock," he said, going over to demonstrate. "The trick is to sit right in the center, then swing your legs into it."

He did so, and unlike Maddie, did not fall out.

Maddie applauded. "Well done, Mr. Marcus."

Nile grinned and went to get settled in his own cabin.

Later, Maddie stood at the rail as the *Rio Madeira* pulled away from the wharf and started on their journey. She recalled a photograph Ben had sent her of the Pará wharf, the stately colonial buildings a bland sepia tone, the boats and people frozen in a moment of time. She wondered if he felt frustrated that he couldn't convey the exotic, pulsating life of the place, the blazing white buildings roofed with contrasting red tiles, the bobbing boats and native canoes, the variety of the people—black descendants of African slaves, Europeans, Indians, and mixtures of all three. Or was he content just to record the image for posterity?

She smiled to herself. She would have to ask him when they found him.

Maddie turned and went to get acquainted with her fellow passengers.

Several days later, as Nile sat down to dine on the fine meal served to the first-class passengers, he decided there was cause for celebration.

After successfully navigating between and around the thousands of forested floating islands in the channel above Pará known as the Narrows, the *Rio Madeira* had entered the main Amazon River without going aground or experiencing any other mishap. Here, the muddy brown river was truly impressive; at some points it was so wide, the shore could not be seen from either side. The only signs that land was near were huge clumps of floating grasses and weeds and mauve-colored water hyacinths.

Sipping his glass of Cordon Rouge champagne while listening to Maddie conversing with their dinner companions as if she had known them all her life, Nile savored the peaceful evening on the river, for they were rare. The ship had endured the daily afternoon thunderstorm, with the high wind whipping up the river before the deluge. But that had ended long ago. Now the setting sun was turning bronze water into a winding road of fiery red, a path leading to the unknown.

Sitting silently while Maddie talked, Nile had to admire her pluck. She approached this venture with the curiosity and enthusiasm of a child, asking so many questions Nile had to resist the urge to throttle her into silence. She retired to her cabin for only a few hours to write her articles, then would be at his side again.

If the Amazon isn't the death of me, Nile thought wryly, then Maddie Dare's questions will surely finish me off.

As darkness encroached and the champagne and conversation flowed more freely, Nile realized that something was very wrong with Maddie. She had grown uncharacteristically quiet, and whenever anyone spoke to her, all she would do was grin a silly little smile and nod her head. But when she rudely propped her elbow on the table like a tavern wench and cradled her cheek in her hand, Nile knew it was time for Maddie to retire for the night.

He rose. "Miss Dare, may I escort you to your cabin?"

She gave him an owlish stare. "But it's not time to go to shleep."

"Oh, but I think it is," he replied with a grim smile. He walked around the table to where Maddie was seated. "Gentlemen, if you'll excuse us . . ."

"Don't want to go to shleep," Maddie said.

"Yes, you do." Nile pulled her to her feet and prayed she wouldn't collapse.

She sighed. "If you in . . . inshist."

"I do." Slipping his arm around her waist to guide and support her, he led her across the deck to her cabin. He hesitated at the door for propriety's sake, wishing that the only other female first-class passenger, a Portuguese merchant's wife named Senhora Ramos, hadn't retired early, so she could have helped Maddie undress.

"Thank you," Maddie said gravely, with all the dignity a tipsy woman could muster.

"You'll be all right?"

"Yesh." She looked steady enough, but looks could be deceiving.

"Good night, then."

No sooner did Nile close the door than he heard a resounding thump. He opened the door to find Maddie lying on the floor, evidently the loser in her attempt to reach her bunk.

Shaking his head, Nile went down on one knee and slipped an arm beneath the unconscious woman's back, bringing her up into a sitting position, where she revived with a small groan.

"Did you hurt yourself when you fell?" he asked.

"Head's shpinning," she murmured, her head lolling against Nile's shoulder as she sagged against him.

For a moment he gazed down at her upturned face, so beautiful in spite of its silly little grin, and the urge to kiss her suddenly swept over him. Her ivory skin looked so soft, and her full rosy lips as tempting and succulent as strawberries. With his arm around her corseted waist, he longed to draw her even closer.

When he heard voices coming from the deck, sanity asserted itself.

"Stand up, Maddie," he said, rising and hauling her up with him.

She muttered a feeble protest, but managed to stand, though her legs were wobbly, for she sagged against him again, her soft full breasts pressing against his chest so tantalizingly.

Nile caught his breath at such unexpected intimate contact and tried to fight his own body's involuntary response with superhuman strength. But he had been without a woman so long that Maddie's feminine closeness was like a match to dry tinder. Nile felt his pulse quicken and his breathing deepen. He swallowed convulsively to ease the dryness in his throat. When he felt the sweet ache starting in his groin, he knew he had to get away from her, fast, before he reached the point of no return and did something he would certainly regret in the morning.

As his hands went to her narrow waist to steady her so he could step back away from her, Maddie's eyes slowly opened and she looked at him. Her stare may have been unfocused, but even by the feeble light of the cabin, there was no mistaking the raw desire there.

Her eyes held his hypnotically as her left hand slid up his chest and behind his neck, her fingers tangling in his hair so seductively. With a small sigh of expectation, she closed her eyes again and held his head steady so she could reach his mouth with her own.

At first Nile was too stunned by her bold advances to resist. Was this wanton the same woman who acted as though she were beyond feeling desire for any man?

He tried to pull away again, but her lips were so soft and warm, and tasted faintly of champagne as she kissed him with surprising ardor, not resisting him the way she had that time in the Explorers

Club. Nile thought fleetingly that it was the kiss of an experienced woman before his own head began to spin, wiping away all rational thought.

When her smooth, moist lips parted beneath his own and she tried to deepen the kiss with her beguiling tongue, Nile thought he would explode and shatter into a million pieces. Part of him wanted to take what she was so freely offering, to teach her not to kiss strange men with the abandon of a street-walker, but the sound of voices brought him quickly back to reality.

He grasped her wrists and parted from her, breathing hard, preparing to give her the verbal set-down of her life, but when she teetered and collapsed in his arms, he realized she was too drunk to know what she was doing.

You were kissing someone, but it wasn't me, he thought as he swung her effortlessly into his arms and set her down in the middle of her bunk.

Then he turned on his heel and left Maddie Dare to sleep it off.

Late the following morning, as Nile finished his breakfast of rolls and *cafèzinhos*, small cups of strong black Brazilian coffee, Maddie emerged from her cabin.

Even he felt a twinge of sympathy as he watched her progress. She took slow, mincing steps as if the steamer were being tossed to and fro by rolling ocean waves rather than gliding along the smooth river, and every once in a while she would wince at some soft noise. And she looked faintly puzzled at her fellow passengers' expressions of solicitude or barely concealed mirth.

Nile rose as she approached the table. "Good morning," he said, holding a chair for her.

"Good morning," she murmured softly, seating herself.

Nile couldn't resist the opportunity to tease her. "Feeling a bit under the weather, are we? You do look green around the gills this morning."

Maddie gave him a baleful stare. "I believe I had too much champagne last night."

"That is an understatement. I wonder what the loyal readers of the *Clarion* would say if they saw their Maddie in such a state?"

"They would take me to their hearts as one of their own," she retorted with a sniff.

Nile just shook his head.

When the waiter brought more rolls and a *cafèzinho* for Maddie, she turned her attention to her breakfast, signaling to Nile that she was in no mood for more conversation.

As he stared out over the rail at the verdant jungle onshore, he wondered if she remembered kissing him so shamelessly last night.

Feeling devilish, he said, "Do you remember anything about last night?"

Maddie looked at him over her coffee cup; then her bleary-eyed gaze slid away and a faint wash of pink stained her pasty cheeks. She muttered something unintelligible.

"I beg your pardon?"

"I said," she replied in an annoyed voice, "that all I remember about last night is collapsing in my cabin. When I next opened my eyes, I was lying in my bunk and it was morning!"

"Nothing else?"

"Nothing else."

Nile felt irrationally disappointed. Most women remembered his kisses for a long time afterward.

Maddie sat there in silence for a moment, gravely studying him. "I made a complete fool of myself, didn't I?"

Nile decided he would make her pay for her affront to his male vanity. "I'm afraid so."

Maddie closed her eyes and groaned. "What did I do? Dance on the table?"

"Much worse, I'm afraid." He hesitated for effect. Then he said, "First you proposed to Herr Schnitzler, then you grabbed Dona Isabella's prayer beads right out of her hands and threw them overboard."

"Senhora Ramos' prayer beads?" Maddie turned crimson with mortification and buried her face in her hands. "I didn't!"

"You most certainly did. You even offered to jump in and retrieve them, but we managed to restrain you. It took five men."

"No!"

"Yes. And a good thing, too, because a hungry caiman swallowed them, so you never would have gotten out alive."

"Was the *senhora* upset?"

"The poor woman was inconsolable, crying and wringing her hands. I've never heard such caterwauling in all my life."

Maddie dropped her hands and sighed. "I shall apologize to her and offer to replace them."

"I don't think you can. They're some precious relic from the Middle Ages and have been in her family for centuries. They're priceless."

Maddie groaned.

Nile was fully prepared to keep fooling her for hours, but when Senhora Ramos herself walked by fingering the beads that had supposedly become caiman food, he couldn't contain himself any longer. Nile burst out laughing.

Realizing she had been the brunt of an elaborate joke all along, Maddie glared at him. "That was not very amusing, Mr. Marcus."

"On the contrary. You should have seen the expression on your face when I said that you offered to dive in after the prayer beads."

Maddie's lips twitched with the effort of repressing a smile. "You are a most convincing liar. I almost believed you."

"Perhaps that will teach you not to overindulge in champagne."

"I have learned my lesson, but be warned. I fully intend to get back at you at the first opportunity, when you least expect it."

He smiled. "In that case, I'll be on my guard."

They sat in silence while Maddie finished her breakfast and regained some of her color; then they rose and went to stand by the rail.

Without warning, a large creature with glossy pink skin leapt out of the water, arched high into the air, and with a flick of its tail dived back into the muddy depths, its body barely disturbing the surface.

Startled, Maddie stepped back a pace. "What was that?"

"A freshwater dolphin, the red *boto*," Nile replied. "The natives believe they are endowed with supernatural powers."

Her face lit up with curiosity. "Such as?"

"Most of the tales are rather ribald and more fit for a dockside tavern than the ears of a gentlewoman."

"Rather risqué, are they? Oh, come, come, Mr. Marcus," she wheedled. "You should know by now that nothing shocks me."

"Very well. They believe the male *boto* can assume human form to come ashore and seduce young ladies of the village."

Much to Nile's surprise, Maddie didn't laugh or express the skepticism of the average Englishwoman, confident of her moral superiority to "inferior" races.

She looked pensive. "I have heard that many countries have similar legends of animals that assume human form to take human lovers. In Scotland, they believe seals can take human form."

"The selkie."

"Tell me, is there any way the young lady can tell her lover is this *boto*, rather than a real man?"

Nile had to look away as he tried to keep a somber face. "Yes." He cleared his throat. "His feet are on backward."

Maddie looked incredulous, and then a small burble of laughter escaped from her. "Thank you for warning me. If a strange man should approach my bunk and try to seduce me, I shall check to make sure his feet are pointing in the right direction."

Nile, who wasn't accustomed to gentlewomen engaging in such flippant and frank conversation, suddenly felt annoyed with her. "And have strange men often approached you, bent on seduction?"

The laughter died in her eyes, replaced by a steely look of indignation at his insult. "As you so often say to me, Mr. Marcus, that is of a personal nature and none of your concern!"

Maddie whirled on her heel and went storming off, head held high and back straight.

Nile watched her glide away, then turned his attention back to the river. Ever since Maddie had kissed him last night, he had seen her in another light, that of an attractive woman capable of responding to a man and inciting passion in return. Had she and her fiancé ever been lovers? he wondered. That possibility both angered and disappointed him, but he didn't know why. After all, she meant nothing to him.

He wiped his brow with the back of his hand. The oppressive humidity was finally getting to him, that was all.

Without warning, another dolphin broke the surface of the water close to the ship and looked straight at Nile with eyes that seemed almost human in their awareness. The creature made a sharp, high-pitched sound similar to mocking laughter, then plunged back into the river.

By lunchtime Maddie's anger toward Nile had cooled, and she managed to have a civil conversation with him during the meal. Both pretended no harsh words had ever been exchanged.

Later, as the *Rio Madeira* passed the mouth of the Tapajós River, Nile summoned her to the rail so she could see the quiet town of Santarém nestled on its banks.

But it soon became apparent to Maddie that Nile was preoccupied. His face was as black as a thundercloud, and he kept clearing his throat as though something he wanted to say kept getting stuck there.

Finally he blurted out, "I'm sorry for what I said to you this morning. It was uncalled-for, and I was out of line."

His contriteness both startled and astounded her because he was such a proud man. The words "I'm sorry" didn't come easily to him.

She turned. "Yes, you were out of line, Mr. Marcus, and I hope it never happens again."

"It won't." He gave her his most disarming smile. "Unless, of course, you provoke me beyond reason."

Maddie chuckled as she returned his smile. "In that case, apology accepted."

Nile Marcus was revealing himself as a man of many surprises.

Once the air cleared between them, they conversed without animosity. But Maddie noticed a subtle change in him. Ever since last night, Nile had been regarding her with a knowing look, as though he had discovered something about her she didn't want anyone to know. She wished she could remember what had happened between the time she fell down in her cabin and the next morning, but the memory was lost in the champagne-induced mist. Somehow she knew it was the key to Nile's strange behavior.

Well, she thought, I have plenty of time to remember what happened.

In two and a half days, they would be arriving in Manaus, and there the real adventure would begin.

5

Manaus.

After seeing the astonishing sight of two rivers, the bronze Amazon and the pitch-black Rio Negro running side by side like two ribbons where their waters met, Maddie thought she had seen everything. But she wasn't quite prepared for her first sight of Manaus.

As Maddie stood at the rail, elbow to elbow with the other passengers for her first look at this Paris of the jungle, she felt a surge of excitement pass through those assembled there. Some murmured excitedly and pointed, while others stood awestruck and mute. Only Senhora Ramos was unmoved as her thin lips pursed in disapproval and moved in silent prayer while her fingers flew over her beads.

Maddie squinted, trying to pierce the shimmering heat haze blanketing this glittering city wrested from thick wild jungle that still bounded it on three sides. At first, all she saw was a fleet of multinational ocean liners and steamboats packed together alongside floating wharves that rose and fell at the river's command. Beyond the wharves were more familiar white buildings topped with red-tile roofs similar to the houses Maddie had seen in Pará, and a sharp cathedral spire somberly pointing the way to heaven. Then her eyes fell on a building with a beautiful blue-and-gold dome rising majestically from its vantage point on a high hill overlooking the city.

Maddie nudged Nile, standing beside her. "What is that building?"

"That's the Teatro Amazona," he replied, "the opera house."

"Oh, my. So that is the opera house I've heard so much about. I'm impressed."

"It's impressive, all right. Technicians and laborers from all over Europe were given free passage just to come here to work on it."

"I'd love to go inside. Perhaps we could attend a performance."

"Only if the *Clarion* pays for it."

"Don't worry," Maddie said. "I'm sure Sam has wired all the funds we'll need."

"I hope so, otherwise this expedition is over before it's begun. Manaus boasts that it's one of the most expensive cities in the world, and that's too rich for my blood."

But Maddie wasn't listening. She kept glancing around like a curious bird. "We don't seem to be moving at all. Why aren't we docking?"

"Ships carrying immigrants upriver to the rubber plantations never dock in Manaus," Nile explained. Then his eyes turned cold. "Poor bastards. By this time, they've seen the jungle. They know what's in store for them. If they were allowed to go ashore, most of them would run away and never come back. So the privileged first-class passengers such as ourselves will be taken ashore by a *lancha*, a launch. The rest will remain here to do what they were hired to do, no matter if they've changed their minds. God help them."

Maddie could think of nothing to say.

Soon the launch drew alongside the *Rio Madeira* and she disembarked with the other first-class passengers. She knew it would be best if she looked straight ahead and didn't think of those bleak faces staring after her with both yearning and resignation. Their destinies awaited them farther upriver.

As the launch passed one of the ocean liners, she noticed it was the *Esperança*, and searing memories of Zosia threatened to overwhelm her.

"Look," she said, placing a hand on Nile's arm. "The *Esperança*."

He seemed to read her mind. "Don't dwell on what happened," he said harshly. "There was nothing you could have done to prevent it."

"So I keep telling myself, but somehow it doesn't help."

Nile said nothing in response, but she could feel his annoyance flaring as brightly as a flame.

Maddie took a deep breath to calm herself, and almost choked on an acrid, unpleasant odor reminiscent of a fire doused with water and left to smolder for days. She wrinkled her nose in distaste. "What is that terrible smell?"

"That is the perfume of Manaus, *senhorita*," one of the other passengers replied. "Rubber."

Maddie fell silent as they approached the teeming wharf. She was a journalist here to record her experiences for the *Clarion*'s readers, so she would have to be very objective and observant.

The moment Nile took her hand to assist her out of the launch, Maddie felt a small shiver of anticipation and excitement run down her spine. When Nile drew her arm through his protectively, Maddie clung to him, grateful for his tall, imposing presence that seemed to intimidate those around him.

Nile guided her along the noisy, teeming wharf, weaving his way among determined-looking tourists carrying battered fiber suitcases, country bumpkins who stopped abruptly to gawk up at the city, and black-clad old women with passive wrinkled faces that bespoke harsh lives of unceasing toil.

They were every color from white to black and reddish brown, but they all shared a common goal: they had come here expecting to make their fortunes.

Maddie found herself wondering what Ben had thought of Manaus as he took his first photographs. Had he felt the frenzied optimism that she sensed among these people, and had he tried to capture it for posterity?

Maddie's voracious gaze took in everything, especially the many women dressed in identical swirling red skirts sprinkled with large green stars, Christmas colors that jarred the eye and looked so out-of-place here in the tropics.

"Who are those women?" Maddie murmured.

Before Nile could reply, one of them sauntered up to him, her shapely hips swaying suggestively as she gave him a wide, inviting smile that promised much. To Maddie's astonishment, the woman's strong white teeth were filed into points and set with what glittered like diamonds in the brilliant light.

After looking her up and down in blatant appreciation, Nile grinned, shook his head, and said something in Portuguese, his tone heavy with regret. The woman gave a disappointed shrug, flicked a curious glance at Maddie, then drifted off to accost another man.

"Never mind," Maddie said just as Nile was about to speak, "I just answered my own question." Then she added, "Why do they file their teeth that way? It makes them look positively rapacious, like sharks. And what are their teeth set with?"

"It's the fashion among women of that sort. Their teeth are filed and set with diamonds."

"Diamonds?" she squeaked in disbelief.

Nile nodded. "It's to show how highly valued they are."

Maddie frowned as she watched the woman moving from man to man, and she was suddenly over-come by a feeling of oppressive sadness.

"Do you suppose we'll find the twins among them, or Mademoiselle D'Arqueville?" she said.

Nile looked at her, his expression indicating that she had tried his patience for the last time. "I thought we had agreed you weren't going to dwell on the unfortunate ladies of the *Esperança.*"

"I can't help it."

He lowered his head so she could hear him mur-mur, "These women are common riverboat whores. Calistro's women will serve only one master and be well cared for."

"Somehow, that doesn't reassure me."

"It wasn't meant to." Nile's golden eyes were as hard as coins. "I don't want to hear you mention those women again, do you understand me?"

Maddie felt her own temper rise at his peremp-tory tone, and she drew away. "How can you be so unfeeling?"

He shrugged. "Call me whatever names you like. I never waste time dwelling on matters I can't change, and I suggest you do the same, or you'll never survive out here."

Chastised, she fell silent as she took his arm again, and said nothing as they made their way to the custom house.

By the time they had gone through customs and arrived at the Grand Hotel Internacional, Maddie's mood had lightened considerably. She knew from Ben's glowing, descriptive letters that the Grand Hotel was as fine and luxurious as any in London or Paris, but he hadn't quite prepared her for the magnificent lobby with its ornate rose-marble pil-lars and a string orchestra filling the air with soft, soothing music.

However, she was most delighted by the fact that her room had a real bed, not a hammock, clean sheets, and running water. When she told Nile she planned to bathe for hours and then take a nap, he told her he was going out for the rest of the afternoon to contact some old friends in the city, well-connected individuals who might know of Ben's whereabouts.

Content, Maddie decided to avail herself of every luxury civilization provided while she still had the chance to enjoy it, because she had a feeling deep in her bones that it wasn't going to last. Though she had promised Sam she would remain in Manaus while Nile went upriver in search of Ben, she had no intention of ever keeping that promise.

As Nile strode through the streets of Manaus, he shook his head in disgust.

This boom will never last, he said to himself. If they think it will, they're deluding themselves. They can build all the European palaces they want. They can send their laundry and their children to Lisbon and Paris. They can install trolleys and railroads to their hearts' content, but the jungle will win in the end.

There was ample evidence everywhere to support his contention. As Nile passed a rubber baron's palace done in the style of a Roman palazzo, he noticed the grandiose effect was marred by several large green lizards clinging to one of the outer walls and swinging their tails idly. Glancing up, Nile also saw four black vultures circling in the hot blue sky, drifting as they waited to swoop down into the streets and dine on garbage thrown there and left to rot in the heat.

In addition, the moist tropical air was pungent with the exotic smells of sweet sugarcane rum; roasting Brazil nuts; spicy cloves, cinnamon, sassafras; and tonka beans, alien odors that destroyed any carefully cultivated illusions that this was really a European city.

After walking for another half-hour, Nile finally arrived at his destination, a modest, unpretentious house set back from the quiet street.

He knocked, and a few seconds later a servant answered the door.

"Senhor Marcus to see Senhor Belgrave," Nile said. "Is Don Winston at home?"

The servant nodded and showed Nile to what, in an English home, would be considered the drawing room. While Nile waited for his friend to receive him, he glanced around the large sunlit chamber, searching for any telltale signs of feminine habitation such as frilly cushions a man was afraid to lean on, or collections of bibelots too fragile for his examining hand. There were none. The room had not changed since his last visit, remaining unabashedly masculine. Nile didn't know whether to be pleased or disappointed.

At the sound of footsteps, Nile turned in time to see his old friend Winston Belgrave appear in the doorway.

"Marcus!" the other man cried with a mixture of astonishment and obvious pleasure.

Then he strode toward Nile and the two men embraced, grinning and laughing as they pounded each other on the back.

When they parted, Winston Belgrave stood back and shook his head. "I couldn't believe my ears when Bento told me who was here. I thought you were in England trying to wheedle another expedition out of one of your greedy, slavering collectors."

"I was, but I'm back on an expedition of a different kind."

Belgrave raised his pale brows. "Oh? Well, before you tell me all about it, have a seat, O King of the Orchid Hunters. What can I get for you? Champagne, to welcome you back? Or will brandy do?"

"Brandy," Nile replied, seating himself and stretching out. "I've had quite enough champagne to last a lifetime, thank you."

Belgrave grinned as he strode to a nearby table and poured two generous brandies from a cut-crystal decanter. "One can never have too much champagne, old friend."

Though five years Nile's senior, Winston Belgrave looked five years younger because of his thatch of straight fair hair, boyish face, and slight build that belied his physical strength. Yet there was nothing effeminate about him, his movements smooth and confident as he crossed the room and handed Nile his glass.

Once Belgrave was seated, he raised his glass in a toast. "To old friends."

"To old friends," Nile echoed, then sipped his brandy.

Belgrave's green eyes sparkled. "So, Nile, tell me about this expedition of yours before I expire of curiosity. Will you be seeking emerald mines? A lost city of gold, perhaps? Heaven knows there are plenty of those to search for."

"Nothing that exciting, I'm afraid," Nile replied. "I'm on a manhunt."

Belgrave raised his brows. "A manhunt? Whom are you hunting? Anyone I know?"

Nile reached into his breast pocket, removed one of several worn and wrinkled photographs of Ben Thomas that Maddie had given him, and handed it to his friend.

"You don't know him, but you may have seen him," Nile said as Belgrave studied the photograph. "He's a photographer for an English newspaper called the *Morning Clarion*. He disappeared while taking photographs, and I have been hired to find him." As Belgrave returned the photograph with a shake of his head, Nile added, "Since you are an exporter and a member of the English community, I thought you might have seen him."

"He doesn't look familiar, but I can certainly ask around. Perhaps someone else has seen him."

"Thank you. Any assistance you can give would be greatly appreciated, especially since the man's fiancée has accompanied me."

Now Belgrave's fine fair brows rose almost to his hairline. "The man's fiancée? You mean to tell me that you came here with a woman? My dear Marcus, you must have been mad to agree to it!"

Nile shrugged and took a draft of brandy. "She was part of the deal, and the money was too good to resist. So I'll try my best to do the job and hope she gets out alive."

Belgrave rose, looking annoyed as he jammed his hands into the pockets of his white Irish linen suit. "Dear Lord, Marcus! How could you? You know the Amazon is no place for a decent, God-fearing Englishwoman!"

Nile didn't take offense because he knew his friend too well, and what private demons drove him. He snorted. "Maddie Dare fears nothing, not even God, and as to her being decent, that is open to debate."

"Her name is Maddie Dare?"

Nile nodded, and while Belgrave seated himself and laced his fingers together in rapt attention, proceeded to tell him all about Maddie Dare and her quest.

When Nile finished, Belgrave just shook his head. "You're mad, you know that?"

"If I am mad, then Miss Dare is a certifiable lunatic."

"Wherever are you going to find this photographer? Where do you even start looking for him?

You know how large the Amazon is and how many tributaries it has. It's going to be like finding the proverbial needle in a haystack."

Nile shrugged. "Perhaps not. The last letter our intrepid Miss Dare received was from Manaus. In it, her beloved stated he was going to travel upriver. As to whether he arrived there, or took a detour, we don't know."

"So you'll go upriver."

"Yes, we'll show his photograph at all the settlements along the way and hope someone has seen him so we can follow his trail." He shrugged. "If we can't find him, Miss Dare will give him up as lost and return to England, where she belongs."

Belgrave scowled thoughtfully as he crossed the room to stand with his back toward Nile. "I'm assuming you'll stop to see Provvy."

Nile hesitated for a moment before saying, "And Amaryllis of course."

Belgrave just stared out the window wordlessly, but Nile noticed the way his back stiffened, the fingers of one hand flicking open and closed restlessly. Then a soft, heartfelt sigh emanated from the man.

"Give her my love, will you?"

"I have a better idea. Why don't you come with us and give it to her yourself?"

Now Belgrave did turn his head, his eyes filled with a look of torment and bittersweet longing. Then it was gone in an instant.

"Oh, no, my friend," he said with a laugh as he pushed his forelock out of his eyes. "I'm the last person Amy would want to see, and you know it."

"How do you know? When's the last time you've seen her?" Nile demanded.

"About six months ago, just after you left for England. She had come to Manaus for supplies and we happened to cross paths through no fault of my own. She told me Fred had died."

Nile's eyes widened in shock, and all he could do was stare at his friend, dumbfounded.

When he regained his voice, he whispered, "Not Fred." Then he took a large swallow of brandy that caused his eyes to water. "What happened?"

"He was bitten by a bushmaster. Need I say more?"

Nile paled as he shook his head, for he knew the bushmaster was one of the most feared and deadly of all poisonous snakes in the jungle. He didn't envy Fred that kind of death.

"How has Amy been bearing up? She and her brother were very close, as I recall."

Winston's fingers flicked. "She looked heartbroken. And lost. And tired. I had all I could do to keep from locking her in this house and never letting her go back."

"Then why didn't you?"

Belgrave's only reply was a snort of derision, because he knew as well as Nile the answer to that question.

When Belgrave fell silent again, Nile prodded him with, "And what else did she say to you?"

"She was still as hostile to me as if I were Satan incarnate."

"I'm sure she still loves you," Nile said lamely.

Belgrave shook his head. "That's just wishful thinking, old friend. I lost Amy's love the moment I chose Mammon over the Lord and proved our ultimate unsuitability."

Nile didn't know what to say to that.

Belgrave sighed deeply. "Enough of this dwelling on the past. I'd like to meet this Miss Dare of yours and tell her that I'll do everything I can to help locate her fiancé. Perhaps we can have dinner together and go to the opera afterward. Since she is a newspaper reporter, perhaps she'll find our fair decadent city inspiring. Shall we go together tonight?"

Nile rose. "Why don't we plan for tomorrow night?" He grinned lasciviously. "I have plans myself for this evening, plans involving the lovely inventive ladies of the Phoenix or Chloe's. It's been a long, rough journey and I'm in dire need of relaxation."

Belgrave muttered, "Someday your excesses will be the death of you, Marcus."

"But what a way to go, eh?" Nile said with a chuckle. He looked at his friend, then said, "Why don't you come with me? You may not realize it, Winston, old friend, but you've been without a woman too long."

When Belgrave raised his hand in protest and shook his head, Nile said, "Unless your taste runs to little boys now."

Belgrave went very still and his face turned crimson with repressed fury. "If anyone else had said that to me—"

"He'd be a dead man," Nile finished for him.

"You sorely try the bonds of friendship, Marcus."

Nile stirred uneasily, knowing he had pushed the other man too far. "I know it's not true," he muttered by way of an apology. "I only said it to get a rise out of you."

"Well, you've succeeded, and it's insulting nonetheless."

Nile scowled at him. "Dammit, Belgrave! You can't be a monk for the rest of your life because Amaryllis won't have you. Celibacy may be natural for priests and monks, but it isn't natural for the rest of us mere mortals."

Belgrave burst out laughing, his good humor returning like the tropical sun after a thunderstorm.

"Perhaps not to you, old friend, but I'm still too much the missionary to consort with whores."

"Then find a wife. I suppose there are still one or two respectable females left in Manaus. You're reasonably attractive, wealthy ... Some well-connected banker's daughter would make you a fine wife and advance your career."

Belgrave smiled slowly. "Perhaps I shall take a fancy to this Miss Dare of yours."

Nile shuddered in mock horror. "You'd live to regret it, Belgrave, believe me. She's a virago if ever there was one." He looked over at the clock on the wall. "Well, I think it's time I left, my friend. I've got to go down to the docks and earn my exorbitant wage looking for this Thomas chap."

"I'll send the carriage for you tomorrow night at six o'clock," Belgrave said, escorting Nile to the door. "Don Antonio Aguirre has invited me to use his box at the opera at any time, so we'll go to a performance afterward."

Nile extended his hand. "I'll be looking forward to it."

"And I'm looking forward to meeting your Miss Dare."

"She is not *my* Miss Dare, and I'll thank you to remember it."

Belgrave gave a throaty chuckle when Nile bade him good day and left.

As Nile walked back to the hotel, he couldn't stop thinking of Winston Belgrave. He was probably the last man left with any semblance of morals in this decadent city, and Nile wondered how he could resist so many forms of temptation after his initial fall from grace. And there were so many to choose from.

Nile was not a man given to facile religious allusion, but when he thought of Winston Belgrave, a fallen angel came to mind. Not Lucifer, but one of the lesser ones. In his case, he had not lost heaven, but Amaryllis. Somehow, Nile suspected that his friend felt they were one and the same.

Drawing nearer to the hotel, Nile heard the familiar cry of, "Lottery tickets! Get rich," so he stopped to buy one with the *Clarion*'s money. If he won, he could always send Maddie Dare back to England and stay in Manaus a wealthy man.

He thought of the beautiful willing women of the Phoenix and decided this was going to be his lucky night in more ways than one. But first he had to report to his employer and escort her to supper.

"So, Mr. Marcus," Maddie said after their waiter seated them across from each other in a secluded corner of the hotel's crowded dining room, "have you been able to learn anything about Ben yet?"

He picked up his menu, written in French, and began studying it. "You could contain your eagerness until after we've ordered. The food is excellent here. You'll find none finer outside of Paris."

"And I suppose I had better eat hearty while I still have the opportunity," she murmured before turning her attention to the menu.

"Exactly, because it'll be roast monkey and fried parrot instead of filet mignon once we're on the river."

Maddie's eyes widened and sparkled with mischief over the top of her menu. "Eat roast monkey and deprive a hurdy-gurdy man of his prime attraction? Never!"

Nile gave her a long stare. "I wouldn't be blasé about it if I were you. Once we leave civilization behind, every seemingly inconsequential decision we make could mean life or death."

Maddie sobered instantly. "I'm well aware of the seriousness of our undertaking." Her smile became cajoling. "But for the time being, we are in this beautiful city, so why not enjoy it?"

Before Nile could say another word, the waiter returned to take their orders. When he left, Maddie said, "Now, what have you learned this afternoon?"

"Patience, Miss Dare. We've been in Manaus for barely eight hours, so don't expect miracles immediately."

"Oh, I don't," she replied as she looked around the room at all the finely dressed diners posing as Parisians. "I merely would like an accounting to make sure Sam is getting his money's worth out of you."

Nile snorted. "If I manage to bring you back alive, he'll be getting his money's worth."

"Come, come. Stop glowering at me like a disapproving uncle. Ah, look. Here comes the waiter with our champagne. Let's drink up and enjoy ourselves."

"As you did on the *Rio Madeira*?" he couldn't resist saying.

Maddie winced at what she remembered of that night, and her pale cheeks suffused with a warm rosy glow. "You would have to remind me. Not very gentlemanly of you, I must say."

Nile just smiled at her chiding as he thought: Your behavior was not very ladylike.

As the waiter set a tall fluted glass of champagne in front of her, she said, "I promise you that I shall limit myself to one this evening."

"Please do. I have no wish to carry an insensible woman back to her room."

Her blue eyes darkened with curiosity. "Is that what you did that night on the *Rio Madeira*?"

It isn't what *I* did, Nile thought to himself, it's what *you* did, throwing yourself at me and kissing me shamelessly.

"I escorted you back to your cabin, yes," he said.

Maddie just chuckled at that. "Poor beleaguered Mr. Marcus."

Beleaguered indeed. If she she only knew . . .

When Nile had his glass, Maddie raised hers in a toast. "To the success of our expedition."

"To coming back alive."

"Tsk, tsk. Always the pessimist."

"A realist."

Maddie just smiled and sipped her champagne in silence as she continued to look around the room.

Nile sat back and studied her. If he didn't know better, he could have sworn that Maddie Dare had spent the afternoon closeted with a lover. Her lips were as moist as if she had been kissed repeatedly, and her eyes both dark with secrets and light with high mirth. Only a lover's whispered words of passion could bring such a glow to a woman's smooth skin. The air around Maddie Dare virtually hummed and crackled with vitality and exuberance, and Nile had to find out why.

"You seem unusually animated this evening," he said conversationally, though as he said it, it came out like an accusation.

Maddie leaned forward, her expression eager and intense. "I have had a most productive afternoon, that's why. I finished several articles for Sam, and in all modesty, I must say they're some of the finest I've ever written."

"Oh," was all Nile said.

Maddie ignored his lack of enthusiasm. "It's incredible. The moment I put pen to paper, the words just flowed. Images kept coming back to me." She sat back and said fervidly, "I can't wait for Sam to read them."

"What did you write about?"

"Oh, Pará, the trip on the *Rio Madeira*, our arrival in Manaus," she replied. "I'll mail the articles tomorrow, then write another series on Manaus before we leave." She hesitated. "But I digress. You were about to tell me about your day in Manaus."

As the waiter set their plates before them, Nile told Maddie that he had gone to the bank and found sufficient funds from the *Clarion* awaiting him, as promised.

"We have an invitation to dinner tomorrow night, by the way," he said, and told her of Winston Belgrave.

"I'll look forward to meeting him," Maddie said. Then she grinned. "I am curious as to just what sort of man calls you friend."

Mellowed by the champagne, Nile smiled good-naturedly. "What type of man do you think that would be?"

Maddie's smile died and her expression grew pensive. "Someone brave and quite obstinate."

Nile snorted. "If that's what you think, then you'll be surprised."

Their conversation veered off into neutral territory, and as the meal progressed, Maddie kept stifling yawns, assisted, no doubt, by her solitary glass of champagne. When they finally finished the expensive, elegant meal, Nile offered to show her more of the city, but she played right into his hands by claiming to be tired.

That left his conscience clear to spend the rest of the evening as he wished.

Later, as Nile left the hotel and hurried toward the docks, his thoughts kept turning unbidden to Maddie. The intense look on her face as she discussed her work had approached the fervor of sexual transport. He found himself wondering if any mere mortal man could cause the sublime ecstasy he had seen on her face tonight. Somehow he doubted it. He had seen the same look on his mother's face whenever she returned from her travels, talking incessantly of the pagodas of China or the jungles of Burma. And he had never failed to notice the look of disappointment on his father's face as he listened, the knowledge that what he offered this woman would never be enough.

Feeling melancholy, Nile crossed Cathedral Square and soon entered a narrow side street illuminated only by bright lights spilling out from the clubs and bars situated there. The tinny strains of piano music filled the air, punctuated by harsh, shrill laughter and the sound of glass breaking. Nile felt for the knife in his belt, reassured by its presence. A prudent man never went unarmed in Manaus.

As he approached the entrance to the Phoenix, he noticed two figures embracing boldly in the light from a window. Nile was relieved to see that one of them was a woman, for in a wicked city like Manaus, one was just as likely to see two men locked in a fervent embrace.

As Nile walked by, he couldn't help staring. He didn't notice the woman's face, just that her blue silk surah gown fitted so tightly it looked as though it had been sewn on the lush body, cupping her rounded derriere in a way that left nothing to the imagination and invited a man's touch. Hot and willing, she was plastered to her escort as tightly as wallpaper, her huge round breasts nearly squeezed out of the low-cut gown, her mouth glued to his as her hips ground against his groin, a titillating promise of what was to come if he could meet her price.

Just as Nile was passing, the couple broke apart, probably from a simple lack of oxygen rather than shame. The man said nothing when he caught Nile staring, just grinned and reached over to squeeze a nearly bare breast. When the woman noticed she was being observed, she gave Nile a shark's sharp, glittering smile before slipping her arm through her escort's possessively and sauntering away with a saucy wiggle of her hips and a backward glance of invitation over her shoulder, leaving a trail of cheap perfume and acrid arousal in her wake.

She would do. Or any one of hundreds like her.

But another image intruded on Nile's memory, of a fresh, lovely face turned toward his, so innocent despite its desire.

He steeled himself against the intrusive vision and reminded himself that sometimes a good dose of wickedness was just what a man needed, so he forced himself to concentrate on rounded derrieres and ample breasts.

Nile resolutely pushed aside the swinging doors of the Phoenix and went inside.

6

Maddie had been out of sorts with Nile Marcus all day.

As she stood before the mirror patting one last stray hair into place before going downstairs to the lobby, where Nile was hopefully waiting to escort her to dinner at his friend's house, Maddie found it difficult to contain her annoyance.

She had wasted an entire day, and it was all Nile's fault.

When she had sent word to him requesting his presence for luncheon before the tour of the city he had promised, she received a curt note saying only that he was indisposed, having come in rather early that very morning. His indisposition had unfortunately lasted well into the afternoon. So Maddie remained in her room, stewing and cursing him roundly, for as intrepid as she was, she had seen enough of Manaus to know it was not some sleepy English village where a woman could walk about unescorted without fear of being molested on the church steps.

"I'll bet he went whoring," she muttered aloud, smoothing her brows with the tip of her little finger.

Finished at last, she stood back for one final appraisal of herself. She smiled at her lovely reflection, satisfied with what she saw, for while she was all too aware of her gilt-and-ivory beauty, she knew it to be a double-edged sword, just as capable of making her life difficult as easy where men were concerned.

Still, she was glad she had thought to pack one evening gown among her more utilitarian garments, and that the flowing light blue silk with the modest neckline had managed to survive both the voyage and the careless, grasping hands of the customs men. For she had heard that the ladies of Manaus dressed in Parisian silks and stiff taffetas in defiance of the appalling tropical humidity, and while Maddie's simple gown could not compete with such extravagant finery, at least it would not brand her as provincial.

Shaking out her skirts one last time, she turned and left her room for the lobby.

As Maddie came sweeping down the main staircase, oblivious of the appreciative stares of several gentlemen in evening attire, she scanned the lobby for any sign of Nile. After a long search, her questing eyes found him just as she reached the bottom of the stairs.

"Good evening, Mr. Marcus!" she murmured as she glided up to take his arm, momentarily forgetting her anger with him.

When he winced at the timbre of her voice and Maddie noticed that those golden eyes were bloodshot as well as deeply shadowed with fatigue, her annoyance returned in full force. But she held it in check. There would be time enough to make her displeasure known to him later, in private.

Nile glanced down at Maddie's gown as they walked through the lobby. "I thought you said you traveled light, without the encumbrances of your sex."

"My one indulgence," she replied, ignoring his accusatory tone. "And," she added, glancing around at the other elegantly attired women eyeing her up and down from behind their black lace fans, "a most prudent one."

"Do you intend to take it upriver with you?"

"Of course. I intend to wear it when you go shooting monkeys for our supper. They will be so astounded by the sight, the poor creatures will fall into the cooking pot in sheer stupefaction."

Nile's lips twitched with the effort of suppressing a smile, but as they left the hotel, all he said was, "There's Belgrave's carriage."

Somehow, Maddie was not astonished to find the carriage as fine as any she had seen in London or Paris, for she was learning swiftly that this city wrested from the jungle considered itself the equal of any on earth in sophistication and went to great lengths to prove it. The horses, she noticed before Nile handed her inside, were glossy, matched chestnuts of some high-stepping Spanish strain, undoubtedly imported from the fine breeding farms of Andalusia.

Once seated on squabs of glove-soft leather, her skirts arranged around her, Maddie waited for Nile to take his seat before confronting him.

"I am most annoyed with you," she said as the coachman cracked his whip and the carriage began moving.

One heavy brow rose in something like amusement. "And what transgression have I committed this time, Miss Dare?"

Maddie took a deep breath to strengthen her resolve. She and Nile Marcus had been getting along tolerably well of late, and she didn't want to strain their tenuous relationship further by reminding him that he was her employee. But at the same time, she could not countenance his behavior.

"You were supposed to escort me around Manaus today," she said, "but I believe you spent the day in bed, which, I'm sure I don't need to remind you, is a waste of the *Clarion*'s money. I had to remain in my room, when I could have been searching for Ben.''

His eyes smoldered with anger, even as his face grew very still. ''Damnation and hellfire, you're not my keeper! Even the lowliest servant is entitled to an evening free now and then.''

''I will not dispute that. Whatever you choose to do with your free time is your own business, but when it affects my work, I will take issue with it.''

He grinned lazily, a mirthless baring of strong white teeth. ''And what will you do if I persist in carousing away my nights and sleeping away my days like the worthless fellow I am? Give me my notice and send me packing?''

Maddie knew the futility of making empty threats, especially to a man like this. She said very calmly, ''Of course not. I am just reminding you that you agreed to do a job for the *Clarion*, and you're not the kind of man who goes back on his word.''

He sighed then, for she had surprised him by discussing her complaint rationally rather than shrieking or nagging. ''You're right, of course,'' Nile admitted, but his voice was still tight with resentment. ''It won't happen again.''

''Thank you.''

Knowing that that was all the apology she would ever get out of him, Maddie turned her attention to the sights of the city to give her anger time to cool.

Later, when she sensed that the atmosphere of hostility had dissipated like a morning mist on the river, she looked at Nile and said gently, ''What is this Winston Belgrave like? If I am to be a guest in the man's home, I would like to know something about him.''

Her conciliatory tone seemed to appease him. ''You'll like him. He's intelligent, amusing, and an excellent host. He also knows everyone in Manaus.

So if anyone can put us on Ben Thomas' trail, it's Belgrave."

"Is he one of the infamous rubber barons I've heard so much about?"

Nile smiled slightly at that. "No, he's a rubber exporter for an American firm. He's not in the rubber barons' league, as he'd be the first to tell you."

"How did you meet him?"

Nile hesitated a moment, as if debating whether to tell her. Finally he shrugged. "I was on an orchid-collecting expedition about seven years ago. My men and I had just finished loading our boats with plants when a boatload of missionaries went aground on a hidden sandbar."

He shook his head. "Poor bastards. Their guide had deserted them and they were just drifting. They were starving in the midst of the jungle's plenty because they couldn't hunt and didn't have the tools for fishing."

"So you saved their lives," Maddie said.

Nile dismissed her praise with a wave of his hand. "Belgrave has repaid the favor more than once."

Now Maddie's eyes widened in comprehension. "Winston Belgrave was one of the missionaries?"

"At the time, yes."

"I find most missionaries to be a sanctimonious lot. All that prayer and pontificating about our immortal souls, you know. The ones I dealt with in Africa did not take kindly to an unescorted lady journalist in their midst."

"Not that I blame them, but Belgrave isn't like that. Besides, I told you, he isn't a missionary any longer."

She sat back against the soft squabs. "A missionary turned rubber exporter . . . how intriguing!

May I ask what made him give up one sort of life for the other?"

Nile's thick brows came together in a grim scowl. "I'll tell you only if you promise not to include it in one of your articles for everyone in England to read. Winston still has relatives there, and I'd not want to cause him embarrassment or heartache."

Maddie was too much Sam's protégée to agree to these terms without weighing the impact of such a rash promise on a potential story. Yet after several minutes of deliberation and against her better judgment she said, "You have my word."

"The riches of the Amazon corrupted him," Nile said simply.

Maddie looked at him. "Then he mustn't have been a man of great religious conviction in the first place if he was corruptible."

"I daresay he had more conviction than most. Yet he was no match for the Amazon. First she broke him, then she rewarded him beyond his wildest dreams."

"And does he regret the choice he made?"

A sad smile touched Nile's mouth. "Not the choice, just the price he had to pay."

"And that was . . . ?"

"He lost the woman he loved."

It was a simple statement of fact, yet spoken with just enough wistfulness to make Maddie sense that Nile Marcus, cold-blooded adventurer that he was, had a sentimental spot for affairs of the heart. This realization so stunned her that she sat there quietly, unable to form a teasing retort.

Finally she said, "How sad. There is no hope for him, then?"

"None. It was the lady's decision to break it off, you see. Winston would have it otherwise." Nile was reflective for a moment, then said, "But in spite of that, Winston is a congenial fellow, and I'm sure you'll enjoy his company. I only told you about his early days because I wanted you to know what drives the man. I trust you'll keep it to yourself."

"I won't go back on my word," Maddie said stiffly.

Nile nodded, apparently satisfied.

Fifteen minutes later, they arrived at Winston Belgrave's home.

As Nile handed Maddie down from the carriage and she looked at the unpretentious house for the first time, she smiled in approval. "I just know I'm going to like your Mr. Belgrave."

Her comment pleased Nile, for his scowl disappeared and he visibly relaxed as he offered her his arm and escorted her to the front door, where he knocked and they were admitted by the Portuguese butler.

No sooner had Nile handed the man his hat than a congenial voice said, "Welcome, my friends."

Maddie looked over in time to see their host come toward her with his hand extended and a wide smile on his face.

As she quickly took Winston Belgrave's measure, Maddie decided that the Amazon must have corrupted him thoroughly, for there was no hint of the self-sacrificing missionary in the man walking toward her with such self-confidence. Slender with boyish good looks, he was nattily dressed in an expensive white linen suit, which, unlike Nile's, hadn't yet wilted from the humidity. Judging from his home and his clothes, Winston Belgrave obviously enjoyed the physical comforts wealth could provide.

The two men were as different as the Amazon from Antarctica. Whereas Nile was a jaguar, wild and untamed, his friend was more the sleek house cat, no less capable of ferocity for all its outward domestication.

"I'm Winston Belgrave," he said in a strong voice

that made Maddie think of a tenor in a church choir, "and you must be Miss Dare."

Maddie inclined her head in acknowledgment. "It's a pleasure to meet you, Mr. Belgrave."

As Winston Belgrave bowed over her hand, a straight forelock of pale gold hair fell forward, and when he staightened, he automatically raised one hand to brush it back with an impatient gesture, causing the emerald ring he wore to flash in the light. Maddie found herself looking into eyes as green as a cat's and just as mysterious.

She waited for those eyes to quickly rake her up and down in the blatant masculine appraisal she was so used to, but Belgrave's gaze merely held her own without so much as flicking up to her hair or down to her exposed shoulders. He was clearly not interested.

So, Maddie thought in wonder, his lost love still has him in her thrall.

"The pleasure is mine," he said. Then he shook Nile's hand and smiled. "So we meet again, O King of the Orchid Hunters."

That caused Nile to grin.

Belgrave gave Maddie a conspiratorial wink. "He's such a modest fellow, you know. Never takes the credit for anything. Did he ever tell you about the time he fought off an entire tribe of headhunters single-handed?"

Captivated by the man's easygoing sense of humor and gentle teasing, Maddie said, "No, he never did. Please enlighten me."

"Winston, hold off!" Nile grumbled. "You'll have her believing you in another minute, and threatening to write an article about it."

Winston just chuckled. "So modest for such a handsome, strapping fellow. All right, I shall hold off for the time being and leave your more thrilling adventures for later. Why don't you both join me in the drawing room for a sherry before dinner?"

While Maddie and Nile were seated and Belgrave began pouring their drinks, he asked her, "What do you think of Manaus?"

"It's unlike any other city I've ever seen," Maddie replied truthfully.

Belgrave nodded, advancing on her with a glass of sherry. "Manaus is a study in contrasts. On one hand, we have such a fine opera house and the latest conveniences such as trolley cars, and on the other, vultures pick garbage off the street."

Nile said, "But at least there is some semblance of civilization here. Once we're out in the jungle, the only law is a Winchester repeating rifle."

Belgrave seated himself across from them. "Here we are on the threshold of the twentieth century, Miss Dare, and most of the Amazon is as lawless and untamed as America's West some fifty years ago. So don't judge the rest of the Amazon by Manaus."

"I wouldn't be so foolish," Maddie said.

Belgrave said gently, "Nile has already told me why you're here, and I just want you to know that I'll help you in any way I can."

"I would be forever in your debt."

Nile added, "If anyone can find out where Thomas went, it's Winston. He knows everyone in this city."

His friend said, "You overestimate my abilites."

"Now who's being modest?" Nile took a swallow of sherry. "Any man would be a fool to underestimate you, Winston."

While they drank, Belgrave asked Maddie to tell him everything she knew about Ben Thomas' route and his habits, and she did so.

Half an hour later, their host looked up as his manservant entered the drawing room. "Ah, here is Bento to tell us dinner is served."

Then he rose and extended his arm to Maddie. "Will you allow me to escort you to dinner, Miss Dare?"

Maddie smiled, took his arm, and the three of them went to dine.

Nile said little during dinner, preferring to sit back and watch Maddie charm Winston.

She was doing an admirable job of it, talking of her wide and varied experiences as a journalist while Winston listened with rapt interest even as he ate or paused to sweep his forelock out of his eyes. Every so often he would direct a question Nile's way like the good host he was, but for the most part Winston seemed content to keep Maddie all to himself.

Nile smiled as he took a sip of his Cordon Rouge. A superficial interest was all any woman would get from Winston, because only Amaryllis claimed his heart.

But, he admitted ruefully, if any woman could sway a man, it was Maddie. Even he wouldn't deny her beauty. Tonight her golden hair, pulled back into a simple heavy chignon resting on the nape of her neck, looked as pale as the moon by the light of the double candelabra gracing the table. Her blue eyes sparkled like sapphires and her complexion had a soft luminescence that came from within. The neckline of her gown bared her white shoulders and only a modest amount of bosom, just enough to intrigue a man without being vulgar.

Nile averted his eyes and took another sip of champagne, thinking of the woman he had seen in the alley last night. Her tight revealing blue silk gown made Maddie's seem fresh and wholesome by comparison.

In a brief flash of insight, Nile realized that for all her contact with the flotsam and jetsam of humanity as a newspaper reporter, for all her frank talk of prostitutes and the boldness of her kiss that night on the *Rio Madeira*, Maddie was still a good, decent woman, an English gentlewoman.

And in several days he would be escorting a good, decent English gentlewoman into hell.

He took too deep a swallow of champagne and choked, riveting attention on himself.

"Are you all right?" Winston asked.

Nile covered his mouth with his napkin and nodded.

"Take a sip of water," Maddie advised.

When Nile's fit of coughing subsided, Winston threw down his napkin and rose, indicating they had lingered over a dessert of fresh mangoes and *cafèzinhos* long enough.

"Come," he said, going to assist Maddie with her chair. "I'd like to show you my greenhouse before we leave for the opera. I think you'll find it most intriguing."

"I'm sure I shall," Maddie replied with a smile, rising and taking Winston's arm.

Nile followed, his thoughts having taken a black turn.

Even in the relative cool of the evening, Winston's greenhouse was as hot and humid as the jungle surrounding Manaus. As they walked in, the pervasive odor of damp earth and exotic vegetation filled their nostrils.

"My orchids," Winston announced.

Maddie looked around. "Did Nile collect these flowers for you?"

"Some of them," Winston replied. "Others I've bred myself."

"What colors!" Maddie exclaimed in wonder, going from one blossom to the next.

To her surprise, she discovered that orchids came in every color of the rainbow, from vivid scarlets, oranges, and yellows to pale lavender, green, and white.

"And the variety is amazing," she added.

Some blossoms were delicately shaped like a lady's slipper, while others were huge and frankly lush. How the orchids grew was just as diverse, with some growing on spikelike stems, and others on logs or in sprays that made them resemble fluttering moths.

The flowers momentarily distracted Nile as his acquisitive instincts rushed to the fore. He walked around the greenhouse, looking for exotic specimens to bring back to England. Once the collectors there saw what he was capable of producing, he was sure to be offered another expedition.

And then he saw it, a *Zygopetalum intermedium* with several blossoms in a brilliant blue he had never seen before.

Maddie had noticed the blue orchids too, and her eyes widened. "Oh, my! I've never seen anything so exquisite!"

Winston joined her and began picking two. "Here," he said, offering them to Maddie. "Every beautiful woman should have flowers for her hair."

Nile winced and groaned inwardly when he saw the orchid plant being defaced so cavalierly.

"Why, thank you," Maddie murmured in delight.

With deft movements she attached the orchids to the base of her chignon, then smiled at the two men.

"Well, gentlemen, what do you think?" A flirtatious sparkle filled her eyes.

Winston brushed his forelock out of the way. "Beautiful," he said.

Nile didn't know what to say. The orchids, with their petals blotched and barred with that rare brilliant blue, enhanced Maddie's eyes and gown and transformed her delicate English fairness into truly exotic beauty.

Knowing two people were expecting him to say something, he finally shrugged. "Looks well enough."

Maddie gave an exaggerated sigh, then said to Winston, "I could be as ravishing as Cleopatra, and he wouldn't even notice."

That's where you're wrong, Maddie Dare, Nile said to himself.

Winston's fingers flicked nervously at his side as though he sensed the sudden rise of tension in Nile. "Shall we be off? We don't want to be late for the opera."

The three of them left the house and filed into the carriage.

When Maddie stepped out of the carriage and saw the Teatro Amazona up close for the first time, all she could say was, "Oh, my," for there were no words to describe such a magnificent edifice.

Standing majestically on the crest of a hill, the opera house stood backed by a fiery red sunset sky that failed to dim its beauty. At its feet stretched a long, wide plaza set in a pattern of mosaic tiles that suggested undulating waves, perhaps of the Amazon River itself.

At Maddie's side, Winston said, "They say it rivals La Scala."

"I've seen La Scala, and it does."

In spite of a row of bushy-topped palm trees growing at the base of the opera house, Maddie could discern a sweeping circular staircase leading to a terrace surrounded by a low balustrade of white stone. Above that terrace rose a balcony supported by twelve tall stone columns, and above that still another balcony supported by another dozen smaller columns. Above that was a semicircular piece set with carvings of classical figures.

As Maddie stared at this monument to man's ambition, she didn't know whether she should applaud or bow her head in awe.

"How much did this cost?" Nile asked, joining them.

"So far, four hundred thousand pounds," Winston replied, "and the costs are expected to go higher. When you consider the building's iron framework was shipped from Glasgow, and the dome's tiles from Alsace-Lorraine ..." He shrugged. "If you can't go to Europe, you bring Europe to Manaus."

Nile just shook his head in disgust. "What opera company in its right mind would come here to perform in the middle of the jungle and risk yellow fever?"

Winston grinned boyishly. "It appears the town fathers are willing to pay quite handsomely for the honor." He looked around. "Why don't we go inside? I guarantee there are even more splendors awaiting you."

As Maddie took Winston's proffered arm and Nile trailed slightly behind to her right, she turned her attention to the other men and women crossing the terrace along with them.

The women astounded her. Even in this oppressive heat, most were wearing gowns of heavy black velvet more appropriate for a cold English winter, the long trains caught up and held out of the way by loops of twisted gold satin cord. Sprays of stiff white egret feathers adorned glossy black hair, and necklaces worth a fortune in diamonds, emeralds, and rubies sparkled in a riot of color around their slender necks.

"Look," they seemed to say, "we may have to live in the middle of the jungle, but we are worthy of London or Paris."

Every so often, one of the haughty beauties would give Maddie a quick appraising glance from beneath heavy lids, then dismiss her as a person of no consequence. Their eyes always lingered, however, on Nile.

But Maddie noticed the unladylike beads of sweat gracing more than one patrician brow and oozing out from beneath heavy diamond necklaces.

After climbing the circular staircase and crossing the terrace, Maddie saw that the balustrade and columns were not of common stone after all, but cool white marble. There was even more marble inside the foyer in the form of a pink marble floor, causing their footsteps to echo hollowly despite the great number of people crowded about, waiting to be summoned to their seats.

Maddie felt appreciative male eyes on her, but she did not intercept their stares, preferring to cling to Winston's arm as he said, "There are several different salons off the foyer."

"And the murals?" she asked, looking around in awe.

"Painted by Domenico de Angelis, Italy's leading painter of sacred murals, I'm told."

He was interrupted by a loud gong. "First call. Let's go to Senhor Aguirre's box."

With a man on either side of her, Maddie moved easily up the wide marble staircase, and in seconds they were at Senhor Aguirre's box. When Winston drew aside the curtain, Maddie could see a man and a woman seated inside.

"Wait here," Winston said.

Maddie turned to Nile. "What do you think of it?"

He snorted. "It's as ostentatious as everything else in Manaus."

"Oh, come now, how can you fault such exquisite taste?

Before he could reply, Winston returned. "Senhor

Aguirre will be delighted to share his box with us. Please come in."

As Maddie entered the box, Antonio Aguirre rose from his seat and turned to greet her. Unlike Nile or Winston, Aguirre was undistinguished. Of average height with a physique that was starting to soften from good living, he was too swarthy for Maddie's taste, with glossy black hair and matching mustache waxed into extravagant points. His eyes were his best feature, huge and so dark they appeared black, and he carried himself with a certain arrogance.

Now those eyes were raking Maddie over, making her feel as though she were clothed only in the orchids entwined in her hair.

"Miss Dare," Aguirre said in perfect English before revealing a gap-toothed smile as he took her hand and bowed over it. "A pleasure."

"Senhor Aguirre, the pleasure is—" Maddie stopped in mid-sentence as his companion turned in her seat and smiled. Maddie was so astounded, she felt her jaw drop. Regaining her composure almost immediately, she exclaimed, "Mademoiselle D'Arqueville!"

"*Bon soir*," the Frenchwoman said. "What a pleasure it is to see you again."

Aguirre looked bewildered. "You ladies have already met?"

"Yes, Antonio. We met on the *Esperança*."

By this time Nile had followed Winston into the box, and was as surprised as Maddie had been to learn the identity of Aguirre's companion. After he greeted Aguirre, they all took their seats, for the opera was about to start.

Maddie barely glanced up at the domed sky-blue ceiling, with its innocent angels and pink cherubs, seeming so incongruous in this tropical land of green jungle and vivid colors, for all she could think about was the beautiful Frenchwoman seated in front of her.

Going to stay with relatives indeed.

So Senhor Calistro had gone to Europe to procure a stylish mistress for Antonio Aguirre, who, judging from the oversize diamond studs winking the length of his shirtfront and the walking cane with its silver jaguar's head, was wealthy enough to afford the best.

Maddie thought of Zosia, and in spite of the heat, she shivered.

She leaned forward and tapped Mademoiselle. D'Arqueville on the shoulder. When the woman turned her head, a question in her eyes, Maddie whispered, "What happened to the twins?"

Mademoiselle. D'Arqueville lifted one shoulder in an eloquent shrug. "I don't know."

Maddie sat back and tried to concentrate on the music, unaware that Nile was watching her.

She is the most beautiful woman here tonight, he thought as he scanned the audience in the orchestra and balconies.

Compared with the rest of the women in their dark dresses and diamonds, Maddie's simplicity and lack of adornment made her stand out all the more. With her pale skin and hair and her blue gown, she looked as cool and as tempting as ice.

Nile shifted in his seat. From this vantage point he could see the tops of her breasts as they rose and fell with her every breath. Ice suddenly turned into fire, and he had to look away before he embarrassed himself.

But not for long.

As he glanced at her, he noticed her eyes had a faraway look and a thin line of concentration appeared between her brows. She was obviously not paying much attention to the music, which he found mediocre at best. When she sighed and looked troubled, Nile knew the reason for her preoccupied air.

Damnation and hellfire! She's thinking of Calistro and those Polish women again.

He knew what she was planning, and he had to stop her somehow.

During the intermission, Winston told Maddie it was customary for everyone to go for refreshments, so they all filed out of Aguirre's box and joined the throng on their way to the foyer.

As Maddie was going down the stairs, she felt a hand grasp her elbow. She looked up at Nile, his face a rigid mask of displeasure, his tawny eyes blazing with anger.

"You look like a bear in search of his supper," she said.

"You asked Miss D'Arqueville about Calistro, didn't you?"

"I merely asked her what had happened to the twins," Maddie retorted, trying to keep her voice low to avoid attracting unwanted attention.

"And what did she say?"

"She didn't know."

"Smart woman," Nile said as they reached the foot of the stairs. "She knows enough not to cross Calistro, and you should do the same."

"But—"

"For the last time, let it rest, Maddie!" he hissed into her ear. "If Calistro hears you've been asking questions about him, you could be in danger."

Then the others were joining them, claiming their attention, and that line of conversation ceased.

Once they reached the promenade, already thronged with people, Aguirre dominated the conversation.

"Winston tells me you are a newspaper reporter, Miss Dare, here to search for your fiancé."

"Yes, Senhor Aguirre," she replied.

He shook his head even as his eyes caressed her. "The wilderness is no place for a beautiful woman."

"As I have told her a hundred times," Nile said. "But she is determined to go."

Aguirre wagged a chubby finger at Maddie, causing his diamond ring to sparkle. "If I were you, I would find a new man, one who would pay homage to your beauty by keeping you at home, out of danger."

Maddie sighed dramatically and clasped her hands to her bosom. "But, senhor, I love him so desperately. I would travel to the ends of the earth just to be by his side."

She thought she heard Nile choke in surprise, but she definitely saw Winston suppress a smile.

"Ah, but affairs of the heart need no explanation," Aguirre said, pointedly reaching for Mademoiselle D'Arqueville's hand and kissing it extravagantly, lest she be out-of-sorts with him for paying too much attention to Maddie.

When he finished, he said to Maddie, "So you will write about Manaus, then, for this newspaper of yours?"

"Yes," Maddie said. "I want to tell everyone in England about your beautiful city."

"That is good. The world must know about Manaus. Too long have we been neglected and denied our rightful place in the world."

"I wish to tell the truth of Manaus," Maddie replied.

Aguirre said, "I am a modest man, Miss Dare, one who does not boast of his great wealth and influence. So I would consider it a great honor to be able to assist you in any way."

"Thank you, Senhor Aguirre," Maddie said.

His gap-toothed smile contained a little too much lechery for Nile's taste, as he said, "Please call me Don Antonio."

Maddie inclined her head graciously.

Winston said, "We are overwhelmed by your generosity, Don Antonio, and would ask that you help us find anyone who has seen this photographer."

"Done," the rubber baron replied.

Nile added, "And a letter of introduction to Mr. Fitch on your plantation would be helpful. We're sure to pass that way upriver."

"You have my word that Mr. Fitch will assist you in any way."

Just then, the gong sounded.

Aguirre said, "You must come to dine at my *palácio* tomorrow night. I would like to show the senhorita what true Brazilian hospitality is."

"We would be honored, *senhor*," Nile said, accepting for them.

"Splendid. I shall be expecting you tomorrow night at eight o'clock."

Then they returned to Aguirre's box for the rest of the evening's entertainment.

When the opera was over, Maddie was surprised when the carriage took Winston home first, then continued on to the hotel. But when Nile said, "Now we can talk in private without being disturbed," she knew he had planned it that way all along.

Maddie pulled the wilted orchids from her hair. "Please spare me another lecture about Calistro."

"Damnation and hellfire! I would gladly do so if I thought it would do any good!"

Maddie glared at him. "All I wanted to do was find out what happened to the twins. What could be the harm?"

Nile rolled his eyes heavenward in exasperation. "Calistro obviously procures for Aguirre, who, in case you hadn't noticed everyone bowing and scraping to him tonight, is a wealthy, powerful man.

Cross him and you'll find yourself in some brothel, and even I won't be able to get you out."

Maddie gave him a teasing smile. "Such heart-warming concern for my welfare."

"I'm merely fulfilling my promise," he replied stiffly.

Her light mood vanished. "So Winston thinks Aguirre will be able to help us find Ben."

Nile nodded. "He may claim to be a modest man, but he's as ruthless as they come. He knows people and how to use them. He also controls the river we need to use, so it's important to keep on his good side."

Maddie's brows rose in astonishment. "He controls an entire river?"

"Oh, yes, an entire river, the Juruá. His rubber kingdom is there, and he's got his own private army of some six hundred men to control it."

Maddie gasped. "Six hundred men?"

"Six hundred men along the length of the river, all armed and all without consciences. Provvy lives nearby, as well as some missionary friends of Winston's, so Aguirre's good graces are important."

"I'm looking forward to dinner with him tomorrow night," Maddie said. "I think an interview with an authentic Amazonian rubber baron would be of great interest to the *Clarion*'s readers."

"Don't you become of great interest to him, or you'll find yourself taking Miss D'Arqueville's place."

She smiled mischievously. "I'm not worried. You'll rescue me."

Nile gave her a withering glance but said nothing all the rest of the way back to their hotel.

Beneath the filmy layer of mosquito netting, Maddie couldn't sleep. The night air was hot and listless, with nary a breeze to cool her skin. She placed her hands beneath her head and stared out into space, trying to quell her tumultuous thoughts.

Nile was right. Her preoccupation with Calistro was going to jeopardize the entire expedition. But she couldn't help it. Every time she thought of the fate that awaited those poor innocent girls . . .

"You can't change the world, Maddie," she muttered to herself. "Forget them, or you'll never find Ben."

Everything was going according to plan. Once Nile began making inquiries and showing Ben's photograph, someone was sure to come forward with news that a man matching Ben's description was heading upriver. She trusted Ben to leave an obvious trail, just as they had planned.

All she had to do was wait.

Closing her eyes, Maddie finally slept.

7

With steam rising from the earth after the usual late-afternoon downpour, Aguirre's *palácio*, built in a decidedly English style complete with steeply pitched gables and mullioned windows, resembled a manor house Maddie had once seen in Devonshire, on the edge of Dartmoor. But she was not surprised. She had already seen one Turkish minaret, a Swiss chalet, and two German baronial palaces side by side on the same street, each edifice trying to outshine the other.

She looked up at Nile. "If it weren't for the palm trees, I'd swear we were back in England."

Nile snorted in disgust. "It's an outrage against nature."

Winston grinned at Maddie as he clapped Nile on the shoulder. "Our King of the Orchid Hunters here is a man of simpler tastes. Just give him a thatched hut with whitewashed walls, wicker furniture, and a hammock, and he's content."

Nile just muttered, "Let's go in, shall we? The sooner we get this over with, the happier I'll be."

"He's never been one for the social graces," Winston explained to Maddie in an aside that was just loud enough for Nile to overhear. "I've been trying to civilize the brute for years now, but he just won't cooperate."

Nile joined in the bantering with, "Yes, just throw me a slab of raw meat for my supper when I growl."

"Ah, but I didn't hire him for his social graces," Maddie replied as they walked down a path paved with mosaic tiles, earning her an oblique look from Nile.

Winston appeared perplexed. "Then why did you hire him, if I might ask?"

Feeling devilish, Maddie said, "For his muscles. As a weak, defenseless female, I needed a strong man to carry my bags and fan me with a palm frond when the heat prostrates me."

Nile stopped in his tracks and whirled around. "Damnation and hellfire! If you think I—" He stopped himself in mid-sentence when he saw that Winston and Maddie were laughing at him.

"I . . . I don't mean to laugh," Maddie said, trying to control her mirth and failing. "But you can't mean to say you believed me?"

A wicked gleam danced in Nile's golden eyes. "Didn't your mother ever teach you not to tease a hungry dog?"

And without another word he turned and strode up to the front door, leaving Maddie and Winston to compose themselves and follow in his wake.

A liveried butler answered the door, led them through a cavernous foyer, and into what the English would have called a drawing room. As the visitors were announced, Senhor Aguirre and Mademoiselle D'Arqueville rose to receive them.

"Welcome to the *palácio* Aguirre, my friends," the senhor said with a gap-toothed smile.

Aguirre and his mistress were both dressed in matching black evening attire glittering with diamonds, although Mademoiselle D'Arqueville's jewelry was more restrained this time.

After greetings were exchanged, Aguirre said, "Champagne for everyone."

When Nile gave Maddie a stern warning look,

she said, "Just sherry for me, Senhor Aguirre, if you please."

Aguirre looked affronted. "But a beautiful woman deserves to drink nothing but the best."

Maddie smiled apologetically. "I'm afraid champagne makes me rather ill."

He bowed. "Far be it from me to contradict the wishes of a lady. Sherry it is, *senhorita*."

Then Aguirre clapped his hands sharply and another servant appeared out of nowhere to pour their drinks into gleaming goblets that Maddie didn't doubt were of pure silver.

Aguirre said, "I see you are admiring the goblets."

"They are very beautiful," Maddie replied, examining the ornately decorated stems more closely.

"The Incas called this precious metal 'tears of the moon,'" their host said, "while gold was 'sweat of the sun.'"

"What picturesque terms!"

Aguirre's dark eyes sparkled flirtatiously. "My countrymen were—are—gifted with a picturesque turn of phrase."

When everyone had a goblet and was seated, their host proposed a toast.

"To rubber."

As Maddie raised her heavy goblet, she thought she detected a look of annoyance on Mademoiselle D'Arqueville's beautiful face at not being the object of her lover's tribute, but it passed almost as quickly as it appeared.

"So, Senhorita Dare," Aguirre said, "what do you think of my *palácio*?"

Maddie let her gaze rove over the lavish oil-painted murals on the walls. "It is certainly one of the most splendid houses I've ever seen, senhor, rivaling many of the stately homes of my country. You are to be commended on your excellent taste."

The obsequious words almost stuck to the roof of

her mouth, but she managed to force them out. Aguirre was a vain man, and if she wanted him to help her, she would have to pander to his vanity.

Aguirre's barrel chest puffed out like a pouter pigeon. "Even though I am a modest man, I must say that I have spared no expense." He waved his hand, indicating the white-marble-topped table before them. "This marble is of the finest imported Carrara, and the base is made of solid gold, more 'sweat of the sun.' It was so heavy, it took six men to carry it inside. I do not seek to boast, you understand, merely to inform you."

"You are a man of exquisite taste, *senhor*," Winston said, raising his goblet.

Nile said nothing, and when Aguirre looked at him expectantly for his tribute, Maddie managed to kick Nile in the ankle.

He winced, but instead of glaring at her, Nile forced a smile. "Exquisite taste and great power."

Aguirre beamed while his mistress looked amused.

"Come," their host said, rising. "You must see the rest of my *palácio*."

They rose and followed obediently.

By the time they finished, Maddie could see the virtue of simple whitewashed walls and wicker furniture. There was so much ostentation as to be vulgar. Upstairs, the walls of the ten bedrooms were all lined with shot silk in muted, exquisite colors of blue and gray, and cluttered with massive suites of furniture that had traveled five thousand miles from London. She found herself wondering how much sweat was given and how many tears were shed to pay for such grandeur.

They went downstairs and dined sumptuously on costly imported delicacies; then they returned to the drawing room and Maddie began interviewing Senhor Aguirre about his rubber empire. Two hours later, they left with what they had come for, a concrete plan to help find Ben Thomas.

For the next several days Maddie spent most of her time alone in her hotel room, writing her articles and a letter to Sam, while Nile was out on the docks showing Ben's photograph to everyone. Every evening, they would dine together in the hotel dining room, but the news was not encouraging. Though Nile spoke to hundreds of people, no one remembered seeing the English photographer.

After dinner, when Maddie bade Nile good night and returned to her room, she would stay awake for hours, pacing the floor, worrying about Ben, wondering why he hadn't left her an easier trail to follow.

But on the fourth day, just when Maddie was ready to admit that something had gone very wrong with this adventure, she received the news she had been waiting for.

When notified that a man was waiting in the lobby to see her, Maddie hurried downstairs to find Winston eagerly pacing the floor.

The moment he saw her, his boyish face lit up and he rushed toward her. "Good news."

"About Ben?" Maddie asked eagerly.

Winston nodded. "Aguirre contacted me this morning. One of his men spoke to the captain of a steamship that just returned from upriver. He recognized your Mr. Thomas from the photograph and said he remembered him because he carried a camera and kept taking pictures with it."

Maddie could have fainted with relief. "So Ben did go upriver. Did the captain say how far?"

"To Tefé," Winston replied. "So, assuming he didn't turn around and return to Manaus, he must be continuing his journey upriver."

"That sounds like something Ben would do,"

Maddie said. "He would want to photograph as much of the land and people as possible."

"At least you have somewhere to start."

Maddie smiled and rested her hand on his arm. "Thank you, Winston, from the bottom of my heart."

His green eyes danced. "Don't thank me, thank the very modest Senhor Aguirre. All of our unctuous flattery the other night bore fruit, despite the high cost to our self-respect."

Maddie laced her fingers together. "I'm so excited! Now Nile and I can get under way."

"Come to dinner tonight," Winston said. "We can celebrate."

"Thank you. I'd like that, and I'm sure Nile would as well."

"Splendid. I'll send my carriage for you at six."

Then Winston set his Chile hat in place, wished Maddie a good day, and left.

Nile was drinking too much of Winston's champagne for his own good, yet he couldn't seem to stop himself.

Late that afternoon, after he had returned to the hotel from yet another numbing, fruitless search for anyone who had seen Ben Thomas, he found Maddie waiting for him in the lobby, her face glowing with excitement. She told him that their search had finally met with success: Ben Thomas had been seen journeying upriver.

At the time, Nile had both shared her exultation and felt a sharp stab of relief. At long last, their expedition would finally get started. He would be able to rent a boat, take on supplies, and do what he was being paid to do. With any luck and a greater part of skill, they would find the tiresome Thomas in some riverside town, innocently taking his photographs, oblivious of his beautiful fianceé's concern for his whereabouts.

But now, as Nile sat across from Maddie at Winston's dining-room table, he felt assailed by fresh doubts and misgivings.

I must have been out of my mind to agree to this in the first place, he said to himself. She'll never survive. Look at her. She belongs in a ballroom, not the jungle.

Tonight Maddie looked as fragile and delicate as one of Winston's orchids. She had worn that damnable blue gown again, with a thin band of grosgrain ribbon around her neck as her only ornamentation. Her hair was swept to the side, where it tumbled seductively over her left shoulder and nearly covered her breast.

Nile thought of that milk-white skin filled with black blisters from the bites of sand flies, and he felt his resolve weaken once again.

I can't do it, he thought. I just can't do it. Let the *Clarion* sue me for going back on my word. I don't care.

The sound of someone calling his name brought him out of his reverie, and Nile found both Maddie and Winston staring at him strangely.

"You looked a thousand miles away just then," Maddie said.

Winston grinned. "A thousand miles upriver, no doubt."

Nile took another swallow of champagne.

Maddie leaned forward, her eyes shining with excitement. "Now that we know Ben headed upriver, what will be our next step? Will we make the journey on another steamer like the *Rio Madeira*?"

Nile shook his head and stared at the tiny streams of bubbles in his glass. What did he care what happened to her? She knew the dangers and the risks. Why should he be responsible for some uppity addle-brained woman who didn't have the good sense to stay home where she belonged?

"They run too infrequently and we'd be at the mercy of the captain's schedule," he said. "I propose to hire a launch with the *Clarion*'s money."

"That way," Winston said, "you'll be able to search for Thomas at your own pace and navigate the shallower waters. It will also be large enough for you take all the supplies you need."

"Sounds splendid."

"Damnation and hellfire, it's not splendid!" Nile set his glass down so forcefully the stem snapped with a sharp tinkling sound.

The silence at the table was deafening as Maddie and Winston froze and stared at him in astonishment for what seemed like an eternity.

Then Winston rose. "Let me take that for you," and he removed the shattered glass gingerly from Nile's hand.

"What's wrong?" Maddie said quietly, her eyes soft with concern.

Nile held her gaze. "Everything. Our deal is off. I'm not taking you with me. The Amazon is no place for a woman."

Maddie's cheeks grew crimson with raw fury, and her nostrils flared like an enraged bull's. With her eyes as dark as sapphires, she brought the flat of her palm down on the tabletop with a sharp smack, causing the cutlery to jump.

"You listen to me, Nile Marcus," she said between clenched teeth, "a deal's a deal. We've been over this a hundred times. You're not backing out on me now, not when I've come this far."

"You can stay here in Manaus with Winston and wait for me to return."

"No."

"I'll bring Thomas back to you, but I'll do it alone."

"I said no!"

"And I say *yes!*" he roared, jumping to his feet

and facing her, his hands on his hips. "It's too dangerous."

Maddie was on her feet in an instant. "You made an agreement with the *Clarion*, and I'm holding you to it."

"We're in South America now. I doubt if such an agreement is valid down here." He smiled slowly. "I can disappear into places where no one could find me, not for a hundred years."

"Fine. Break your word. I never should have trusted you in the first place. You're a blackguard of the vilest sort. You're obviously not an honorable man."

"Name-calling isn't going to work. I've been called worse."

She regarded him in silence, her eyes narrowed in anger. Then Maddie gave a little shrug, and the anger seemed to fade.

"Fine," she said, her voice brittle. "If you won't take me with you, I'll find someone else who will. You're not the only man who knows the Amazon. Perhaps Senhor Aguirre will be kind enough to recommend someone to me."

"Don't threaten me. Trust Aguirre, and you not only won't find Thomas, you'll wind up in a brothel servicing his *seringueiros*."

Maddie turned crimson and gasped.

"Nile . . ." Winston warned him.

Maddie's chin came up a stubborn notch. "I'm going upriver, Nile Marcus. With or without you."

"You stupid little fool!" Without another word, he jammed his hands into his pockets and went storming off for the peace and quiet of the greenhouse.

Among the plants, he stood there for a moment, breathing deeply to cool his anger and to quiet his racing pulse. Then he ran his hand through his hair, and gradually he felt the burning rage leave him.

A minute later, Nile heard footsteps coming toward him. He turned around, fully expecting to see Maddie ready to badger him into submission again, but it was Winston who entered the greenhouse.

Winston didn't speak at first, just regarded Nile curiously for a moment. Then he said, "May I presume on a very old friendship to ask you what that outburst was all about?"

Nile lifted one shoulder in a negligent shrug. "It's obvious, isn't it?"

"No. I thought it was all settled between you. Why the change of heart? It's not like you to go back on your word."

"I must have been insane to agree to take a woman up the Amazon, any woman, even that . . . that . . ." He groped for a word, then gave up.

Winston shook his head. "Forgive me, old friend, but I suspect it's more than that. Amaryllis has been living upriver for years, and you even admire her for her courage and strength. Maddie is just like Amy, one tough lady who appears to know how to take care of herself in the face of adversity."

When Nile made no comment, Winston said gently, "Come now, what's really bothering you? You know you can talk to me and it won't go beyond this room."

Nile sighed. He should have known he couldn't keep anything from Winston. The man was just too damned perceptive. He forced the words out. "Dammit! I care for her."

His friend was silent for a moment, then murmured, "I see."

"No, you don't see, dammit." Nile whirled on him. "I don't care for her the way you care for Amaryllis."

"How, then? Enlighten me."

Nile hesitated while he collected his thoughts in his fuzzy brain. "When Maddie first came to me in

England with this plan of hers, I agreed to it because I was down on my luck and needed the money desperately. If some brazen fool of a woman wanted to risk her neck, who was I to stop her? I would take her where she wanted to go, and if she survived, fine. If not . . ." He shrugged.

"But now that I've come to know her, I feel more responsible somehow." Nile sighed in frustration. "I can't explain it."

Winston nodded sagely. "If something happened to her, you'd feel the same as if Amaryllis or I came to harm. You've come to know her better over the last couple of weeks and now you care for her as a friend."

"That's as good a way of putting it as any."

"Why don't you tell her that? Perhaps she'd change her mind."

Nile snorted. "And risk losing a precious story for her newspaper? Not likely."

Winston walked over to one of his plants, a rare tulip orchid from the Andes. "Then you have no choice but to let her accompany you."

When Nile opened his mouth in protest, Winston raised his hand to silence him. "Hear me out. If you don't take her, she will go to Aguirre or someone equally unsavory for help, and meet a fate worse than anything that could befall her in your company."

Winston took a step forward and placed his hand on his friend's shoulder. "Don't you see? The only way you can keep her from harm is to keep her where you can watch her at all times, and that means taking her upriver with you."

Nile knew defeat when he saw it staring him in the face. "You're right, of course. That is the only way, short of locking that she-devil in your attic and throwing away the key."

His friend grinned. "That is not an option, I'm afraid."

Nile regarded Winston out of narrowed eyes. "You're a shrewd man, Belgrave."

"For a former missionary?"

Nile laughed at that. "For a Borgia."

Winston pushed his forelock out of his eyes. "Come. Let's tell Miss Dare that she'll be going upriver after all."

They found Maddie standing before one of the dining-room windows and looking pensive. The moment she heard them return, she turned and looked directly at Nile. "Well?"

"I never go back on my word," he said.

She let out the breath she had been holding. "I didn't think you would."

"Now that that's all settled," Winston said, "won't you stay for dessert?"

They sat down to finish their meal, and when conversation resumed, it was cordial in tone, as though Nile's outburst had never happened.

Later, in the carriage, Maddie said to Nile, "What made you change your mind?"

Nile replied with a diffident shrug, "I decided if you really were bent on self-destruction, who was I to stop you?"

She opened her mouth to make a stinging retort, then thought better of it. But as Maddie settled back quietly against the squabs, she knew there was another reason for Nile's having a sudden change of heart. As hard as he tried to hide it, the big brave adventurer was concerned for her welfare. Of course, his masculine display of overprotectiveness was unwarranted, but she found it sweet and touching nonetheless, especially in a man used to keeping his softer emotions locked tight inside.

He was thawing toward her, of that Maddie was certain. The change was about as perceptible as a snail's step, but it was there nonetheless. In the

short time she had known him, he had gone from
overt hostility to indifference, and now concern.

She smiled to herself in the darkness. This was
going to be an interesting expedition indeed.

Three days later, Maddie caused heads to turn
and conversation to cease as she strode through the
hotel's lobby.

She doubted if the fashionable citizens of Manaus
had ever seen a woman dressed as she was that
morning, but she was going upriver, not to the
opera, and she had selected her garb to suit the
occasion.

Maddie wore a wide-brimmed hat to protect her
from the fierce sun. Instead of having to fuss with
hairpins, she wore her hair in a simple solitary
braid that hung down to the middle of her back.
She had dispensed with her corset altogether for
comfort's sake, and she relished the unrestricted
feeling beneath her long-sleeved white shirt, though
judging from their shocked and outraged expressions, the good citizens of Manaus did not approve.
Doubtless they did not approve of her custom-made
divided skirt either, for its scandalous hem came
down to the mid-calf of her knee-high leather gaiters rather than the floor.

Nile, however, approved. He looked her up and
down, then muttered, "Sensible. Now, let's get going.
Winston's carriage is waiting to take us to the docks."

"Where is Winston?" Maddie asked, hurrying to
keep up.

"Working. He promised to see us off, though."

"I was hoping he would. I like him."

"And he likes you. Lord knows why."

Maddie caught the teasing undertone and just
laughed.

Once they were seated in the carriage, she said,
"You've bought all the supplies we'll need?"

Nile nodded. "All bought and paid for, thanks to the *Clarion*. They've already been packed on board the launch."

"Good. And my mountain of luggage?"

"That also." Nile was silent for a moment as he looked at her. "You're taking only one bag?"

Maddie smiled. "I told you I traveled with a minimum of feminine fripperies."

His eyes were filled with grudging admiration. "So you did, but I didn't believe you."

"I won't be a hindrance to you, Nile," she said, her smile fading. "I meant it when I said I can take care of myself in a crisis."

He folded his arms over his broad chest. "That remains to be seen."

"All I ask is that you give me the benefit of the doubt and let me prove myself."

"Fair enough."

They fell silent for a while, though between them there was enough restrained excitement to explode the carriage.

When they arrived at the docks and Nile handed Maddie down, he hesitated as he looked up at her. "I know this is a waste of breath, but I'm going to say it anyway. There's still time to change your mind."

"Not for all the tea in China. Or perhaps I should say, all the rubber in the Amazon."

He threw back his head and laughed then, a rich rumble of sound that came from deep within him, turning his eyes light gold with mirth.

Maddie realized that she truly enjoyed hearing Nile laugh with such abandon. It was a pleasant sound that gladdened her and sent her spirits soaring.

Then she took his proffered hand and stepped down in time to see Winston come striding toward them.

After scrutinizing Maddie from hat to gaiters, Winston took her hand and bowed low over it. "You look positively dashing. I guarantee you'll have every lady in Manaus copying your look within the week."

"Somehow I doubt that," Maddie replied, "but it's preferable to mincing about in a dress."

Winston brushed his hair out of his eyes. "Well, I hope you have a safe and successful voyage, Maddie Dare."

Nile rolled his eyes to the skies. "Damnation and hellfire, I was afraid of this. He's going to give you one of his maudlin farewell speeches."

Winston ignored him. "As unpalatable as this sounds, do whatever Nile says. I know he's an insufferable and overbearing oaf, and he does tend to think his way is the right way of doing things, but to give the devil his due, he does know the Amazon."

Nile interrupted him with, "Can you keep this short, Belgrave? We haven't got all day."

Winston ignored him again and continued with, "He'll keep you safe."

"I expect him to," Maddie replied as tears stung the backs of her eyes.

Then Winston leaned forward and kissed her on the cheek. "Good luck and Godspeed. I'll pray for your safe return."

"Don't believe him," Nile muttered. "He hasn't prayed in years."

But after Maddie bade Winston farewell, she noticed that for all of Nile's seeming imperturbability, his eyes were unnaturally bright as well.

Nile excused himself for a moment and drew Winston aside. "Is there anything you want me to tell Amaryllis?"

A shadow passed across Winston's boyish face. "You can tell her that I still love her, for all the good it will do."

"I will. You never know. She may have a change of heart one day."

"Oh, no, my friend. I'm afraid that will never happen. I've become one of the damned in her eyes, a lost soul beyond redemption."

"Then since she is in the business of saving souls, I should think she'd appreciate the challenge of saving yours."

Winston shook his head. "I'm afraid it doesn't work that way, my friend."

Nile didn't know what to say to that, for Winston's resignation was so deep, there was no arguing with it, so he just grasped his friend's shoulder in a comforting grip, turned, and left.

Winston didn't stay to see Nile and Maddie off. He had work to do. Work was all he had, these days.

As he sat alone in his comfortable carriage and thought of Amaryllis, he felt the deep abiding sadness all the way down to his soul. His soul. . . . He wondered if he had one anymore. He must, in order for him to feel such acute pain and longing for another human being.

He could still visualize her even through the years that separated them as surely as the miles, for she always avoided him when she came into Manaus, once or twice a year. Amaryllis Gates, with her soft brown hair and cool mist-gray eyes so quick to warm with laughter and blaze with righteousness. Of average height and slender of figure, she radiated energy and zeal for the cause she thought greater than life itself, spreading the word of the Lord.

He remembered too well how he had once shared that fervor.

And it had almost cost them their lives. That same unshakable faith that had sustained Amaryllis when their party of missionaries became lost on the Amazon had been the undoing of Winston Belgrave. He realized then what a coward he really was, and that he had no desire to be martyred in the service of the Lord. He was destined for another kind of life, an easier life, one that didn't demand such terrible sacrifices. He found his destiny in Manaus, even though it meant losing Amaryllis forever and making the most terrible sacrifice of all.

Winston passed one hand over his eyes, trying to banish the image, but it was no use. Her vision danced before him, as tantalizing as a mirage in the desert.

He thought of the one time he had dared to kiss her, the gentle innocence of it, and how it had ignited in him both a sinful yearning for more and a disdain for it in the arms of other women.

But it was Amaryllis' companionship he craved. Physical unions were not as lasting as spiritual ones. Passion could never take the place of laughter and mental intimacy.

Winston looked out the carriage window and hesitated. There was still time for him to turn around and ask Nile if he could join the expedition. Perhaps if Amaryllis saw him again, she would realize how much she loved him.

He groaned in despair. It was no use. He and Amaryllis were fated always to be apart. God, in his infinite wisdom, had seen to that.

Maddie shook her head as she watched the carriage rumble away.

"I wish I could help him somehow."

Nile said, "When we reach the mission, you could try to talk sense into Amaryllis." He drew Maddie's arm through his and started walking down the wharf. "Not that it would do any good. Amaryllis Gates has always been a single-minded woman."

Maddie grinned mischievously. "I like her already."

"I've never understood missionaries. They're always so sure their God is the only one, and they're going to make sure everyone else in the world thinks so too."

"That's an unpopular opinion, but I quite agree. I think it's time we stopped turning the natives into good little Englishmen just like ourselves and appreciate their cultures for what they are."

He grinned. "What have we here, a traitor to the empire?"

"A woman of uncommon sense," she retorted.

Nile stopped where a small boat was moored. "This is it. Come aboard and meet our captain."

Maddie was impressed with the small steam launch, a sturdy-looking craft that would be their home for many weeks. There was a high smokestack toward the rear, and a large steering wheel up front. Covering the open-air deck was a roof that would provide blessed shade from the incessant sun.

No sooner did Maddie step on deck than a dark-skinned man with a merry face came up from below.

Nile greeted him in Portuguese, and the man smiled a toothy grin.

"This is Jayme, our captain," Nile said to Maddie. "He speaks only Portuguese, so I'm afraid you won't be able to countermand any of my orders."

"Clever of you to hire him." Maddie smiled and extended her hand to Jayme, who whipped off his hat and said something in Portuguese.

"He says you are a beautiful lady, and he is honored to have you as a passenger on his humble *lancha*," Nile translated for her.

"Tell him that I am honored."

After Nile did so, he said, "Now, would you like to see your cabin? I'm afraid it's not as large as the one on the *Rio Madeira*."

The cabin was barely large enough to turn around in, and windowless, but at least it had a bunk and a door that could be closed to give Maddie privacy. Her bag and her medicine box were already there, stuffed into a corner.

"My cabin is right across from yours," Nile said. "Jayme sleeps on the deck."

He disappeared inside, and when he came out, he was holding a Winchester repeating rifle. "A gift for you. I'm assuming you know how to shoot one of these."

He threw it at her.

Expecting him to do something like that, Maddie caught it expertly with one hand, then automatically checked the ammunition chamber to make sure it wasn't loaded, earning her a rare smile of approval from Nile.

"Even though I'm a modest woman, I'll have you know I'm rather a crack shot."

Nile gave an exaggerated sigh. "Somehow, I expected you would say that."

"It's no idle boast, my friend. I even went on a shoot at Sandringham, with the Prince of Wales, and was the only woman shooter present."

His thick brows rose. "I am impressed. But grouse are hardly unfriendly savages with blowguns and poison darts."

"Don't worry," she said, her teasing mood gone. "I'll do what I have to do when the time comes."

Why, I believe you will, Nile said to himself.

When they went back on deck, Nile said something to Jayme, who bustled to do his bidding.

Nile turned to Maddie. "Say farewell to Manaus, and pray you live to see it again."

They were on their way at last.

8

If hell were as hot as the Amazon, Maddie decided she was going to mend her ways.

Even though the launch's roof provided shade from the searing sun, it was still hot, the moisture-laden air as heavy and smothering as cotton batting. No sooner did Maddie dab at her brow and neck than more sweat rose on her skin, turning her camisole and pantaloons into wet rags. Finally she abandoned the futile activity and concentrated on her surroundings, hoping intellectual activity would distract her from the appalling heat.

Jayme was at the wheel, humming some tune so bittersweet that it could only be about unrequited love, while Nile was absorbed in cleaning and oiling the Winchesters to prevent them from rusting.

Maddie watched as his large hands, with their strong, blunt fingers, stroked the gun barrel with a clean cloth. There was a gentleness to his touch that was almost a caress, and she found herself wondering what it would be like to have those fingertips sliding over her skin so deftly.

It's the heat, Maddie, she warned herself. It's giving you strange fancies. You'll never get through this if you let Nile Marcus distract you.

Maddie sighed. A mere five hours away from Manaus, and already she was bored. The river, with its impenetrable green line of jungle on either side, was monotonous at best, but then, she was looking at it from the river, not from the inside. Once, they passed a steamer full of waving passengers coming in the opposite direction, and another time they saw several dugout canoes filled with Indians that turned out to be friendly. Maddie's interest stirred when a cluster of thatched huts on stilts at the river's edge came into view, but the launch didn't stop.

Maddie closed her eyes, letting her head loll back. She thought of England in late October and could almost smell the cold, crisp fall air expectant with winter, and feel the rain on her face.

A hand on her shoulder shook her out of her reverie. Maddie opened her eyes to find Nile crouched beside her chair, his worried face inches from her own.

"Are you ill?"

"No. Just indulging in a pleasant daydream, that's all." She didn't elaborate, knowing if she so much as hinted she was thinking of England, he'd use it as an excuse to send her back.

He swung to his feet with his customary feline grace and looked down at her. "You sure? It's not too late to turn back."

Maddie smiled lazily. "Thank you for your concern, but I'm sure. Sorry to disappoint you."

"Suit yourself." Nile took the guns and disappeared below.

When he came up, he went to Jayme and conversed for a few minutes, then went to stand at the rail. Maddie rose and joined him.

"I'm curious about something. How does Jayme navigate the river? I've noticed that sometimes he steers the launch into the center of the river, and other times he hugs the shore. Yet he doesn't use a map."

"I'll ask him and translate for you," Nile said,

then turned to their captain and asked him Maddie's question.

Jayme smiled, obviously flattered by Maddie's interest, and began speaking in rapid Portuguese.

"The Amazon is like a woman, *senhorita*. Even though you cannot read what she is thinking, you can sense her mood, if you know how to look.

"First you must learn to read the river, and listen to what she tells you. Everything on the river tells you something. Watch the floating leaves, logs, and even the foam, because these things always seek the sea and will tell you where the water runs fast and deep. If you want to know where the sandbars hide, watch the calm water above them, or follow the ripples. And always choose a channel between two steep banks rather than sloping ones, because that's where the water will be deepest."

"Fascinating," Maddie said as she smiled, thanked him, and let him get back to his work.

Nile said, "You'd better remember all that just in case something happens to me or Jayme and you're forced to navigate the launch by yourself."

"Oh, don't worry, I shall." Maddie studied him in silence for a moment, then said, "Now it's your turn to tell me how you go about collecting orchids."

A wry smile touched his mouth. "You mean you don't know? You seem to know everything else about me."

"Except that."

"When I go into an area, I hire natives familiar with the jungle. We go in on foot, or sometimes by mule, depending on the terrain. When I find a bed, the men chop down trees containing the plants."

"Why is it necessary to cut down the entire tree? Why not just take the orchids themselves?"

"Because they're parasites. They depend on their host tree for life. The plants are better apt to survive the journey back to England if they're still attached.

"Once the orchids are collected, they're placed in Wardian cases. These are small boxes that simulate the humidity of the jungle, like little individual greenhouses."

Maddie said, "Then you ship them to the nearest ocean liner returning to England."

"Yes. But," he added, "sometimes they don't survive the ocean crossing, as you so eloquently reminded me when we first met."

She ignored the bitterness in his voice. "What is the most number of orchids you've collected on one of your expeditions?"

"About ten thousand, from four thousand trees."

Maddie stared at him, speechless with amazement.

Nile grinned. "Why so surprised? You don't think I'd risk life and limb for just one or two plants, do you?"

"No, I suppose not. Is this sort of venture profitable?"

"If it's rare enough, one plant can fetch as much as one thousand guineas."

Maddie took a step back, as if staggering physically under the weight of such information. "Oh, my. I think I'm in the wrong line of work."

Nile snorted. "Those are few and far between, especially now, with so many of the accessible orchid beds picked clean, and so much competition to find the rarest specimens."

"You mean there are others like you wandering out here?"

He nodded. "Some nurserymen have as many as twenty collectors hunting for rare specimens all over the world. Some represent Kew Gardens and others the Horticultural Society. And, of course, there are the wealthy private collectors."

"Ah, like the man who refused to finance another expedition for you."

Nile's eyes darkened. "Exactly."

"Oh, don't look so fierce," Maddie teased. "If he had financed your expedition, you and I wouldn't be standing here right now, embarking on the adventure of a lifetime."

"I must remember to thank him," Nile said.

His acerbic comment caused Maddie to chuckle. "You should know by now that I'm immune to your insults."

"You do have a thick hide, I'll say that for you."

They both fell silent, each alone with his thoughts, while Jayme's bittersweet song filled the air and the rhythm of the engine seemed to keep time.

Maddie turned to the man beside her. "What do you get out of it, Nile? Why do you risk your life to satisfy some rich man's whim? Is it the adventure?"

Nile looked at her long and hard. Finally he said, "I do it for the satisfaction of it. My goal is to seek the rarest of the rare. If I find it, and can bring it back safely, then I'm doing what not many men can do.

"It may not seem important, collecting flowers, but I like to think I help bring something rare and beautiful into people's lives."

Moved by his simple eloquence and sincerity, Maddie said, "I feel the same way about my writing. I do something that not everyone can do. But I do it, and do it well."

She regarded Nile's stern profile out of the corner of her eye, half-expecting him to launch into his usual diatribe about a woman's proper place, but for once he kept silent.

Then he excused himself and went to talk to Jayme again.

Maddie returned to her chair and tried to resume her writing, but Nile's words intruded on her thoughts. So that's what drove him, a need to set himself apart in some small way from the millions of other human beings inhabiting the planet. She understood that need all too well.

Jayme broke into song again, this one a sprightly, sparkling tune that freed Maddie of her philosophical musings and made her want to dance a little jig. She resisted the impulse, deciding that Nile's conventional system would never withstand the shock, and instead started writing again, not stopping until suppertime.

They moored the launch for the night just as the sun was going down, bathing the river in red-gold light.

Nile watched as Maddie wrinkled her nose in distaste at their supper of jerked beef and tinned peas.

"In another day I shall be ready for that roast monkey you promised," she said.

He widened his eyes in mock horror. "And deprive a hurdy-gurdy man of his principal attraction? I'm surprised you would even suggest it."

Suddenly a flock of parrots burst from the jungle and flew across the river in a fluttering riot of green, yellow, and vivid red feathers, their raucous screams shattering the stillness and startling Maddie so that she jumped.

"In that case, a succulent parrot would do," she muttered, eyeing the birds balefully.

Nile just smiled and shook his head, while Maddie fell silent to finish her supper.

He leaned back in his chair, feeling oddly contented as he surveyed the river, its placid surface broken by the big fish feeding and a *boto* or two leaping into the air. As reluctant as he was to admit it, he was enjoying Maddie's company. She was stubborn and infuriating, but she was also witty and amusing, teasing him out of his foul tempers with her quick repartee.

She had survived her first day well, never complaining about the oppressive heat, though as Nile well knew, one day did not an expedition make. What would she be like after five days of heat, mosquitoes, and tinned peas?

Nile felt his contentment snatched away as quickly as a fly was snatched by a fish arcing into the air. But then he remembered what Belgrave had said. Better to have this headstrong woman with him where he could keep an eye on her rather than with someone else who might take advantage in more ways than one.

She had insisted on coming along, so she would just have to endure the discomforts as best she could.

Maddie set down her tin and said, "I can't tolerate it any longer." Before Nile could ask her just what it was she couldn't tolerate, she leaned forward in her chair, extended her right leg, and began unfastening her gaiters.

"I feel as though I'm wearing a suit of armor," she said, intent on her task.

Nile felt his cheeks grow hot and he averted his eyes. "Must you undress in public?" he muttered between clenched teeth.

She stopped and stared, her blue eyes wide. "I'm not undressing. I am merely removing my gaiters."

He couldn't tell her that the gesture reminded him of a woman sitting on the edge of a bed, slowly removing her stockings as an arousing prelude to lovemaking.

He fought to keep his voice steady. "Please do so in the privacy of your own cabin."

A fiendish smile played about her mouth, and for a moment Nile expected her to make some comment that would make him want to get up and throttle her. But Maddie always seemed to know just how far she could push him, and this time she wisely held her tongue.

"As you wish," she said, rising, and going below.

Damnation and hellfire, you sounded like such a prig just then, he chastised himself. You'd think you never saw a woman undress before.

But those women had not been respectable, and for all her forward talk, Maddie Dare was still an English gentlewoman when all was said and done.

She emerged, smiling. "There! That feels so much better."

As she took her seat again, Nile couldn't help stealing a glance at her legs. The absence of the heavy leather gaiters revealed Maddie's slender well-turned ankles and part of the gentle curve of her shapely calves before they became hidden in the folds of her skirt.

He dragged his eyes away and swallowed hard, waiting for Maddie to make some infuriating remark.

He was spared, however, with the arrival of the mosquitoes, a nightly ritual on the river.

First Nile heard Jayme slapping at his bare shoulders, then heard a distinctive humming about his ears, followed by a stinging sensation on the back of his neck. He slapped at it.

"Mosquitoes," he said to Maddie. "Don't let them bite you. You could catch yellow fever, and the last thing I need is a sick woman on my hands."

Maddie brushed at her face. "Persistent, aren't they? And as thick as smoke."

Then, as Nile watched, she unrolled the veiling around the crown of her hat and pulled it down, where it formed a screen to protect her face. When she tucked it around her braid and into the neckline of her shirt, the insects couldn't alight and sting her face or neck.

When Nile slapped at his cheek to kill several

that had alighted there, Maddie said, "Perhaps you should let me rig up something for your hat as well."

"No need," he replied. "One gets used to them after a while."

She shrugged. "Well, suffer, then."

Nile glared at her, but said nothing.

They all stayed on deck, the silence punctuated by slaps and oaths, until finally even Maddie had had enough trying to keep the voracious insects off her exposed hands.

"I think I shall retire now," she announced to Nile, even though it wasn't yet seven o'clock.

After wishing him and Jayme good night, she disappeared below once again.

Hours later, as Maddie lay beneath the mosquito netting covering her berth, she couldn't stop thinking of Nile and his reaction to her removing the gaiters.

He had looked so shocked, one would think he had never seen a woman removing an article of clothing before, especially one so innocent. Yet Maddie knew that he had had his share of women and was surely used to seeing them undress.

She smiled to herself in the darkness. For such a worldly man, he could be as straitlaced as a country parson.

Then Maddie's smile died. His respect for her was actually touching, because there had been men in her past who hadn't deemed her worthy of such respect. And any woman unconventional enough to pursue a career as a journalist was always fair game to certain kinds of men always striving to force her back, to put her in her place. Nile might resent her occupation, but at least he had scruples and he wasn't cruel.

Maddie smiled to herself again. She was glad he hadn't called her bluff when she threatened to have someone else take her upriver. The search for Ben Thomas would have been over before it had begun, because Maddie never would have entrusted her safety so completely to another man. Certainly no one Senhor Aguirre recommended.

She turned over on her side, and soon the gentle rocking of the launch lulled her to sleep.

The following morning, Maddie rose early to the lionlike roaring of howler monkeys, only to find Nile already up and about, and Jayme fueling the engines.

Nile seemed preoccupied with his own thoughts, so Maddie left him alone and ate her breakfast of jerked meat in silence. After telling her that they would soon be stopping at a small village to take on more coal, Nile went below deck.

About eleven o'clock, Maddie noticed they were approaching some semblance of civilization at long last. She could see people on the riverbank who stopped to stare at the approaching launch, and as they rounded a bend in the river, a bustling village of docks and thatched huts appeared out of nowhere.

When Nile joined her, Maddie asked, "May I go ashore?"

"Why would you want to? There's not much to see except a few thatched huts. Besides, we won't be staying long, and there will be other villages. We're going to take on coal and be on our way."

Maddie smiled. "Whatever you think is best."

Nile looked at her oddly, but decided not to question his good fortune at having Maddie so complaisant this morning.

Once they docked, Nile and Jayme went off in search of coal, leaving Maddie to sit there and observe the populace going about their daily lives.

As she sat there patiently, she noticed a group of men and women who looked to be natives going down to the riverbank. The men, clad only in loin-cloths, eased themselves into the water and called back to the women, their voices laughing and cajoling as they motioned for them to come in. Maddie averted her eyes for a moment, for she knew that when the women dropped the colorful woven blankets wrapped around their bodies, they would be naked underneath.

She smiled to herself as she wondered what Nile would have to say about naked women bathing so brazenly in the river.

"As long as they aren't Englishwomen," she muttered, "he'd probably stare."

When she looked up again, the bathers were in the water, laughing and splashing.

Watching them bathe, Maddie found herself thinking how wonderful it would be to go for a swim, to immerse herself up to her neck in cool, refreshing water and lather up from head to toe with lavender-scented glycerine soap, one of the few indulgences she had brought along with her. She would ask Nile about it the moment he returned.

As if her thoughts conjured him, Nile came striding down the dock, with Jayme not far behind. Nile noticed the bathers right away, and when one of the women stepped out of the water, her black hair dripping and bronze skin glistening, his eyes unabashedly drank their fill.

The moment he stepped on deck, Maddie said, "I'm assuming the river is safe to bathe in?"

Before Nile could answer, there came an ear-splitting shriek of terror from the bathers that sent both him and Maddie rushing to the rail to see what had happened.

All of the bathers rushed out of the water, some screaming in panic as they struggled to escape some unseen foe. Two of the men were holding a third man by the arms and dragging him along. When they were safe, the man on the ground clutched his left leg, his face twisted in a grimace of pain as he babbled hysterically.

"What happened?" Maddie asked Nile. "Was he attacked by piranha?"

Nile shook his head. "Stingray, most likely. The poor bastard probably stepped on it and got stung for his pains."

"Will he survive?"

"Probably. Oh, he'll be in agony for a day or so, but he'll live." Nile studied her for a moment. "Does that answer your question about the safety of bathing in the river?"

"But surely—"

"Let me tell you about bathing in the Amazon," he said with exaggerated patience, his eyes hardening. "First of all, there are stingrays that hide in the mud of the shallows. There are also piranhas, which you already know about. And there are caimans, Brazilian alligators, though you can discourage them from pulling you under and drowning you by gouging out their eyes. That is, if you have the strength and you don't panic. Last, but not least, there is the candiru."

At the mention of the word "candiru," Jayme suddenly snickered, pointed to his groin, and muttered something in Portuguese that made him laugh even harder.

Nile said nothing.

"And, pray tell, what is that?" Maddie demanded irritably, not sure she wanted to know. "You're obviously not going to enlighten me unless I ask you."

"The candiru is a tiny transparent fish about one inch long. It is tiny, but it can be even more fearsome than the piranha to those foolish enough to bathe in these waters."

When he purposely hesitated to make her ask, Maddie obliged with, "And why is that?"

"It lodges itself in certain bodily orifices and can't be removed."

It took Maddie only two seconds to comprehend what Nile was saying in his delicate, oblique way. When she did, her entire body turned bright crimson with a mixture of fury and embarrassment.

"That's disgusting!"

Nile shrugged. "Oh, I agree. But you did ask."

"You tricked me into it."

"I merely wanted to discourage you from bathing in the river."

That mollified her. "Well, you have," she mumbled. "Most effectively. Thank you for the warning."

"Think nothing of it. I'm just doing what I'm being paid to do."

He left Maddie standing there staring at the man on the riverbank.

They had a second uneventful day on the river, but by the time night fell again, Maddie knew that something was very wrong with Nile.

She had spent the entire afternoon writing and wondering how she could tell the *Clarion*'s readers about the candiru in such a way as not to offend their sensibilities or cause Sam Vincent to have an apoplectic seizure. Every once in a while she would look up from her work and try to engage Nile in conversation, but when he replied in words of one syllable and seemed intent on keeping to himself, she soon gave up and left him alone.

She first suspected something was amiss when they dined on more tinned peas. Maddie noticed that Nile's fork shook slightly as he ate.

"Are you all right?" she asked. "Your hand is trembling."

When he looked over at her, she noticed his eyes were dull, their irrepressible sparkle gone.

He brushed her concern aside with a stalwart wave of his hand. "I'll be fine. I just feel a little queasy, that's all. I suspect it's the peas."

"Have they gone bad? Then you mustn't eat them. You'll get sick if you do. And need I remind you, there's no doctor on board."

Suddenly Nile's strength seemed to seep out of him right before Maddie's eyes. He slumped in his chair, his head lolling forward onto his chest as his left arm fell listlessly to his side, causing the tin to drop from his nerveless fingers and roll across the deck, scattering the bouncing peas in all directions.

"Nile!" Maddie cried, jumping to her feet and reaching for him.

Nile's eyes closed, and before Maddie could catch him to break his fall, he pitched forward, toppling his chair and hitting the deck with a heavy thud that shook the boards beneath Maddie's feet.

"Nile." Maddie sank down on her knees beside his unconcious form and struggled to roll him over onto his back. He was heavy, but she managed to do it.

"Dear God, he's shivering!" she said to Jayme, who had come running and now stood peering down at them while he babbled in Portuguese.

Maddie lifted Nile's head and cradled it in her lap, smoothing back his hair as she thought fast. "Nile! Can you hear me?"

His eyes fluttered open, but he stared up at her without recognition. His teeth were chattering together in audible clicks.

"Nile," Maddie said, stroking his rough cheek, "was it the peas? Please, you've got to tell me so I can do something to help you."

He opened his eyes, struggling to focus, and for a

moment his vision cleared. "Malaria," he murmured, as another spasm shook him.

Maddie felt a surge of relief. "I have quinine in my medicine box. That should help."

Suddenly Nile's shivers became so violent they shook his entire body. "Freezing."

Maddie's heart went out to him when he drew his knees up to his chest and curled himself into a ball in a pathetic attempt to keep himself warm. He looked so helpless and forlorn, a Goliath felled by a mosquito.

Maddie gently set his head down, rose, and hurried below deck to her cabin. She opened her medicine box, took out a small bottle of quinine powder, and went running back upstairs to Nile.

He was convulsed by shudders, and for the first time, Maddie felt truly frightened. What if he should die? What would happen to her then?

He's not going to die, she told herself as she hurriedly mixed the powder with a little water so he could be able to take the medicine.

When Maddie dropped back down beside him, Nile's eyes opened, his gaze silently beseeching her to help him. "So cold," he muttered. "Can't get warm."

She lifted his head. "I have something to help you. It's quinine, but you've got to drink it." When she held the cup to his lips, Nile tried valiantly to drink, but his teeth were still chattering so badly he couldn't manage it. Maddie drew the cup away.

"Try again," she said.

This time Nile choked and sputtered, but he got the liquid down.

That accomplished, Maddie decided it would be best to get him into bed. Motioning to Jayme, who had been hovering around like a spinster aunt, Maddie pantomimed what she wanted him to do. Grinning and nodding, Jayme grabbed one of Nile's arms while Maddie took the other, and between the two of them they managed to haul the semiconscious man to his feet, where he swayed precariously.

Before Nile's knees could buckle, Maddie slipped beneath his arm so she could support his weight with her shoulders while Jayme did the same on the other side. She staggered and almost fell when Nile swooned and threw most of his weight against her, but Maddie was a tall, strong woman herself and she managed to keep them both upright, though she knew she'd pay for it tomorrow with aching muscles.

"Nile, wake up!" she said. "We've got to get you to bed, but you've got to help us. Please!"

The urgency in her voice must have penetrated the sickness, for Nile revived long enough for him to regain his footing while Maddie and Jayme steered him below deck and into his cabin.

Once Nile was stretched out in his bunk, Maddie wiped her forehead with the back of her hand and allowed herself a moment to catch her breath while she decided what to do next. She smiled and thanked Jayme, then shooed him away.

Nile was still shaking with the chills. As Maddie watched him suffer so, her own helplessness infuriated her. There had to be something more she could do for him.

A blanket. She needed a blanket to keep him warm. Perhaps then the fever would break.

But they hadn't brought any blankets with them. Who needed blankets in the stifling heat of the Amazon?

"Cold," Nile muttered. "So cold."

There was only one thing for Maddie to do.

She walked over to the bunk and sat on the edge, taking care to draw the mosquito netting around them. Although the bed was narrow, there would be just enough room for Maddie if she and Nile lay on their sides, as he was doing now, facing the wall, his broad back toward her.

Maddie swung in, straightening her skirt and slipping her arm around his waist so she could draw him tightly against her, letting him share her body's warmth. Even though his body was as hard and strong as iron, he was shuddering helplessly against her, still caught in the grip of the malaria attack.

Nile Marcus is the last man in the world I ever thought to wind up in bed with, she thought to herself, smiling in the darkness.

She held him that way for what must have been hours, listening to his erratic breathing and incoherent mutterings. Then she noticed that he wasn't shivering as violently as before.

"Warm now," he murmured, just before falling asleep.

Soon the fever would come, followed by drenching sweat as it left the body. Hopefully, with the quinine, the fever wouldn't be as bad.

Maddie brushed her lips against his hair, closed her eyes, and slept.

When a groggy Nile opened his eyes, he found himself surrounded by darkness. Where was he? When he gradually became aware of his surroundings, he was alert enough to comprehend that he was in bed with a woman.

Whoever she was, she felt good. Her warm, sweet breath tickled his neck and her soft breasts pressed provocatively against his back. She must have been curled against him, because her lower body was hugging his bottom and her legs were molded to the backs of his. He felt her arm tucked around his waist possessively, as if she would never let him go.

She moaned softly and stirred in her sleep, rubbing against him unself-consciously, like an affectionate cat desiring to be stroked. Nile felt himself grow hard in response to the innocent gesture. He couldn't tell who she was in the darkness, and why they were both still clothed, but what did it matter? She wouldn't have been in bed with him if she didn't want him. And he certainly wanted her. Their clothes could come off in due time.

He closed his eyes and murmured, "Luizhina," the name of the woman he had wound up sleeping with that first night in Manaus.

He grasped her arm, and in one quick twisting motion managed to slip beneath her and slide onto his back while he rolled her on top of him. The woman struggled from the depths of sleep with a gasp of surprise, but before she could protest, Nile pulled her head down so he could kiss her.

Her lips felt as good as the rest of her, soft, pliant, parted slightly in drowsy surprise. Nile took advantage with consummate skill, teasing her lips with quick, darting thrusts of his tongue, and finally plunging it home.

Her entire body went rigid at the intimate assault, and she squealed in denial, fighting to pull away from him even as he held her fast and deepened his kiss. She began thrashing about and pushing at his shoulders, but all her struggles were doing was arousing him even further. He had to take her now.

Nile stopped kissing her long enough to murmur, "Ah, my sweet Luizhina, don't fight me," to the shadowy figure poised above him, fighting him like a wildcat and gasping for air.

"I am not your 'sweet Luizhina,' and if you don't let go of me this instant, I'll make you wish you had never been born."

The familiar voice was like a dash of cold water on sizzling coals. Nile released her at once and felt Maddie leap off him as though he were a leper. As he lay there, panting raggedly and trying to gather his scattered wits, he heard her fumbling about for something while she cursed him roundly under her breath.

When the lamp was lit, she turned to face him. Even by lamplight, Maddie's eyes were as dark as the night sky and glittering with rage as she eyed him fearlessly. Her cheeks were flushed and her nostrils distended like those of a wild creature poised for flight.

"What in the hell did you think you were doing?" she growled.

He swung his legs over the edge of the berth and held his aching head in his hands. When it cleared somewhat, he looked up and glared back at her. "Why should I defend my actions?" he snarled. "Didn't anyone ever tell you what happens to a woman who gets into bed with a strange man? If anyone deserves an explanation, I do!"

"You had an attack of malaria and were freezing. I was only trying to keep you warm."

Nile cradled his head in his hands again as dizziness sent his cabin spinning. So that's why he felt as though a herd of cattle had run over him.

"I didn't expect to be mauled for my pains," Maddie said indignantly.

He looked up at her. "I'm sorry. I didn't know what I was doing, so that makes us even."

She scowled down at him in puzzlement as she buttoned the top button of her shirt. "Even? What are you talking about?"

"The night on the *Rio Madeira*, when you drank too much champagne?"

"I remember."

Nile smiled slowly. "That's precisely my point. You don't remember what happened, do you?"

"Nothing happened. I passed out, that's all."

He shook his head. "You kissed me. You brazenly threw yourself in my arms and kissed me."

Maddie's eyes widened and her color fled, making her face look spectral in the lamplight. "You're lying. You're just saying that to get even with me."

In spite of feeling weak from battling malarial chills, Nile managed to rise and crossed his arms over his chest. "You really astonished me that night. There you were, a woman engaged to one man, and kissing another. Not very ladylike of you. In fact, you were quite the wanton."

"I don't believe you."

"It's true. And if I hadn't resisted, you probably would have thrown me into your hammock and ravished me right then and there, so don't accuse me of trying to maul you."

Maddie stared at him for what seemed like an eternity. Finally she swallowed hard. "I . . . I'm sorry for lashing out at you like that."

"Apology accepted. You had no business coming into my bed for whatever reason and then making me feel like some kind of depraved monster when I reacted as any normal male would."

"I know, and I'm sorry," she said, her head lowered contritely. "I shouldn't have made you feel that way. And if I behaved badly on the *Rio Madeira*, I apologize for that as well."

When Nile felt the dizziness wash over him for the third time, he sank onto his bunk and cradled his forehead in one palm. He felt a hesitant hand on his shoulder, and when he looked up, Maddie was by his side, looking both sheepish and solicitous.

"Are you sure you're feeling better now?" she asked. "Would you like a headache powder or water?"

He managed a wan smile. "I think the King of the Orchid Hunters will live to see another day, but I'm parched. A cup of water would be appreciated."

Maddie went above deck and returned moments later with a tin cup brimming with fresh water that Nile drank gratefully, savoring the coolness as it slid down his throat. He thanked her and handed the cup back.

"You know, Maddie," he said soberly, "I am many things, but I'm not the kind of man who takes what isn't freely offered, especially from a woman."

A shadow appeared in her eyes, a shadow that Nile couldn't fathom. "There are men who do," she said, almost to herself; then the shadow disappeared and she added, "But I know you're not one of them."

"No, I'm not. I would not have gone any further once I knew who you were. You must believe me. You have no cause to fear me, in that regard."

Maddie nodded quietly in acceptance, then wished him good night and headed for the door.

"Maddie?"

She stopped and turned, a question in her eyes.

"Thank you for helping me."

"You're welcome."

Then she was gone.

Once Maddie was back inside her own cabin, she undressed quickly, as her clothes were still damp in the places they had touched Nile's fevered body. Beneath the sharp odor of sweat, she could detect Nile's own masculine scent, faint but unmistakable.

After she crawled into her bunk, her stiff, sore muscles groaning in protest, she lay on her back with one arm flung across her forehead. She closed her eyes and relaxed, but a powerful image of Nile remained in her mind, refusing to be dislodged by something as puny as sleep. She could still feel those steel-muscled arms around her, crushing and imprisoning her, still taste his hard, demanding kiss.

Maddie shifted over to her side, her thoughts in a turmoil. His response had been frightening, a surge of pure masculine desire flowing from him with animalistic urgency. If Nile hadn't come to his senses in time . . .

"But he did," she murmured aloud, "and he told you you have nothing to fear from him."

Still, as sleep began to overtake her, she wondered.

9

The following morning, Nile felt strong enough to go above deck. He found Maddie already seated in her chair, writing.

She looked up from her work, her eyes filled with solicitude. "Good morning. How are you feeling today?"

"Much better."

He could tell by the way she abruptly looked away that she was recalling what had happened between them last night. He wondered if she repeatedly recalled the incident the way he did.

Maddie risked another glance. "I'm delighted to hear it."

He came up to her chair and looked down at her.

"Thank you for what you did for me last night," he said. The words didn't come easily, especially in the light of day, for he was a proud man unaccustomed to apologizing. "I don't know of many other women who would have risked climbing into bed with a strange man, no matter what the circumstances."

Maddie flashed him a confident smile. "But I've already told you, I'm not like other women."

Once her boast would have infuriated him. Now he only chuckled at her audacity. "I'm beginning to believe you."

Her smile died. "I only did what I had to do."

"Nonetheless, you took a great risk."

"No, I didn't. As you said last night, matters would have gone no further once you realized who it was."

Her trust shook him. "You're so sure," he said as he stared out over the water at the jungle beyond.

"I am. We have an agreement, remember?"

He smiled wryly. "Our verbal contract. Of course. How could I forget?"

As if his word of honor could deter him if he really had wanted her.

Maddie was silent for a moment. Then she said, "Why didn't you tell me you had malaria?"

"I didn't think it was of any consequence. I haven't had an attack recently."

"And these attacks just come upon you suddenly?"

He nodded.

"When did you first contract the disease?"

"Two years ago. I had been out here twelve years without catching it, and then my luck ran out." He turned and looked at her. "There was an epidemic, and I survived. Many who were stricken didn't."

"You're very fortunate."

Nile grinned. "When I have an attack like I did yesterday, I wonder."

"But at least you're still alive. That counts for something."

"You're right. It does."

Then he excused himself and went to talk to Jayme about the rough part of the river he knew would be coming up soon. When Nile was through, he noticed that Maddie had written several pages of her latest article.

"May I read it?" he asked.

Her astonished expression was almost comical to behold. "You really want to?"

"Yes, I do."

"You've never wanted to read one before."

"Well, I do now." He frowned at her suspiciously.

"Why are you so reluctant to let me read it? Does it have me doing something farfetched, such as fighting off a tribe of savages with my bare hands?"

"Nothing like that." She extended the papers to him. "It's about your malaria attack. It's so typically tropical that I thought my readers might be interested in it."

He took the papers and gave her a stern look. "So, my sufferings are to provide excitement at the English breakfast table, is that it?"

Maddie tried to keep a straight face and failed. "By the time I'm through with you, you'll be as famous as Buffalo Bill Cody of America's Wild West." She drew her hand through the air as though Nile's name were written on a music-hall marquee. "Marcus of the Amazon . . ."

Nile just shook his head and stalked off to read the article.

As he pored over Maddie's bold, clear handwriting, he was surprised to discover that the account of his malaria attack was straightforward and devoid of the exaggeration she was prone to.

One particular paragraph caught Nile's attention, and it was so startling that he had to reread it:

As Mr. Marcus fell to the floor, I rushed to his aid. When I saw he was unconscious and shuddering with chills, I, dear reader, experienced a fear such as I had never known since embarking on this expedition. What if he died? Not only would I lose a valued friend and companion, I would be alone in the Brazilian wilderness with only the captain of our launch to guide and protect me from the dangers of the river and jungle. I was not confident of this man's abilities. Faced with such a prospect, I was determined to save Mr. Marcus any way I could.

When Nile finished, he felt as though he had just read Maddie's secret diary. So, she thought of him as a valued friend and companion, did she?

He handed the papers back to her. "It's very good."

Maddie looked surprised, as though she had expected him to find fault with her work as a matter of course; then she recovered herself with a smile. "Thank you. I'm glad you approve."

Then she returned to her writing, and Nile went to check the Winchesters and ammunition. They would be coming to a small settlement soon, and he intended to dock and shoot them some fresh meat for supper.

The settlement was nothing more than a collection of several huts and a ramshackle pier on the edge of the riverbank, but the inhabitants welcomed them warmly. Nile left Maddie to practice her nonexistent Portuguese on their hosts, while he went into the jungle.

Half an hour later he returned carrying his kill by its feet.

Maddie greeted him with a woebegone expression. "Poor parrot," she murmured, eyeing the lifeless bird swinging from Nile's hand.

"This is not a parrot, you green girl, it's a *garcia*," Nile replied, "a type of pheasant, and we both know how delectable they are."

"Well, in that case, I shall have no objection to eating it."

Nile grinned as he sat down and began gutting his kill with the knife he wore in a sheath strapped to his right calf. "I didn't think you would. Of course, if you would rather have some tasty anaconda, that can be arranged. I saw one slithering along back there in the jungle. It was at least thirty feet long. Enough meat for a week."

Maddie gave him a feeble smile. "I think I prefer

the *garcia*, thank you." She was silent for a moment, then said, "I don't mean to sound fault-finding, but why did you only kill one? Wouldn't it be prudent to offer our kind hosts something for their hospitality?"

Nile shrugged as he began plucking the bird with practiced ease. "This is your first visit to the Amazon, so I'll overlook your ignorance. A man hunting with a rifle in the jungle only gets one shot because the noise scares the rest of the game away. That's why the Indians hunt with blowguns and darts dipped in *wourali*, a deadly poison. Noiseless and deadly. With the racket I made, I'm lucky I got one *garcia*."

Maddie looked properly chastened. "Oh, I see."

Nile chose three of the largest, prettiest feathers and handed them to her. "A souvenir."

She smiled, thanked him, and promptly stuck them in the brim of her hat. "There. Now I have a chapeau worthy of Ascot."

He laughed at that. "Now, all we need is a fire and we'll soon be dining royally."

Then he rose, and Maddie joined him as he walked toward the huts.

Late that afternoon, after their fresh, sumptuous meal, they were back aboard the launch and on the river again, listening to one of Jayme's haunting love songs as they watched the twilight sky turn a brilliant orange behind the jungle.

Maddie sighed contentedly. "That was so delicious. I feel as stuffed as a Christmas goose."

"After jerked beef, even anaconda would taste delicious," Nile replied.

"Forgive me if I appear skeptical."

"I've eaten it on more than one occasion, and I'll have you know it tastes like chicken."

"When I was in Africa, I was told alligators taste

like chicken. It would appear that every strange creature on the face of the earth tastes like that humble domesticated fowl. Certainly they must be related somehow."

Nile laughed at that, a rich, melodious sound that echoed over the water; then he lapsed into silence, though it was a thoughtful rather than a brooding one.

We appear to be getting along so well, Maddie thought as she watched him close his eyes and lean back in his chair. He doesn't seem as resentful of me as he first was. We've become friends rather than employer and employee.

Maddie decided to take advantage of the mellowness of the moment.

"Nile, I know you've warned me off on several occasions, but would you mind terribly if I asked you some questions about your mother?"

Then she held her breath and waited for the explosion that would roundly put her in her place and end all discussion of Rose Marcus.

His eyes flew open, but they didn't ignite with fury this time. "Is this for one of your articles?"

"No. I wish to satisfy my own curiosity, which, as you know, is prodigious."

He hesitated as if considering something. Then he shrugged. "What do you want to know?"

Maddie fought to contain her excitement, for she had to proceed carefully lest she outrage him. "What was it like growing up with her? From her books, she seems rather . . . daunting."

He put his feet up against the rail, leaned back in his chair, and steepled his fingers. His eyes took on the thoughtful look of one who is peering back in time.

Nile began with the chilling words, "I don't think my mother ever really wanted me. You see, she was the daughter of a successful brewer in Kent, and when her father became ill, she actually ran the business because her only brother was something of a ne'er-do-well, concerned only with the high life of London."

Maddie raised her brows. "I never knew that about Rose Marcus, and I thought I knew all there was to know about the woman."

"It was a well-kept secret. She never told anyone, even when her travel books were published and became so successful. My father always said it was an unpleasant part of her life that she would rather have forgotten."

"But why, if she were so successful at it?"

"Because nine years after she married my father, her own father died. Instead of leaving the business to my mother, who had kept it afloat and deserved it, my grandfather settled a generous inheritance on her, but left the brewery to his son and heir."

Maddie was aghast. "The ne'er-do-well? But why?"

"Simply because my mother was a woman, and my grandfather didn't believe a woman should hold such a position of power and authority."

"Why, of all the stupid, idiotic . . ." Maddie sputtered, her indignation flowing like molten lava. "But she proved herself more than capable of doing the work."

"That didn't matter to Grandfather."

"Your grandfather was an ass."

Nile grinned at that. "I quite agree. I never liked him myself. He was a wrinkled, prune-faced tyrant who was never content. All of us, from the maids to me, stood on our heads to please him, but it was never enough. Not only did he demand my mother's constant attention like an overgrown baby, he didn't even pay her one shilling for running the brewery. At that time, we could have used the money, too."

Maddie just shook her head at the injustice of it.

"Mother was later vindicated when her brother ran the company into the ground and it had to be sold at a loss, though that was of little consolation. She was always bitter about it."

"I don't blame her one bit. I'm sure I would have been as well."

Nile ran his hand through his hair. "But she took her bitterness and frustration out on me. I was only eight years old when she suffered this blow. She was never a demonstrative woman, and afterward she became positively cold and withdrawn, always treating me as an annoyance, an impossible burden. When she came into her inheritance, that's when she began traveling the world."

"Why didn't you and your father go with her?"

"My father was a chemist and had to work, to provide a home for us and put food on the table. While mother's inheritance was substantial, it didn't make her independently wealthy. So she chose to use it to finance her travels."

He sighed. "I felt abandoned. My own mother had deserted me both physically and emotionally, and I couldn't understand why. Many were the nights I cried myself to sleep. And she would be gone for months, sometimes a year or more, at a time. When she did return, she never seemed glad to see me, and she never acted guilty or remorseful for leaving us. She stayed only long enough to write a book—then she was off again."

"Didn't your father object to being separated from his wife for so long a time?"

"Once, after my mother's death, I asked him that very question, only I wasn't as diplomatic about it. I accused him of being weak and spineless, of letting her dominate him. I demanded to know why he didn't insist that she stay with us, where she belonged. And do you know what he told me?"

"No," Maddie said softly, her heart going out to him. "Tell me."

"He said that when you truly loved someone, you wanted what was best for her, even if that meant losing her."

She felt tears sting her eyes. "Your father was a very wise man."

"I didn't think so at the time. That's when I came out here to make my fortune." He smiled. "It was one of the few places on earth my mother hadn't visited."

"You sound so bitter."

Nile swung his legs down, righted his chair, and stood up. "I suppose I am. But it's a devastating blow for an impressionable child, to have your own mother reject you so completely. She might as well have put me in an orphanage for all the times I saw her after that. My father tried to be both mother and father to me, and I had a succession of governesses and tutors, but it wasn't the same."

Maddie wanted to go to him and just put her arms around him, but she restrained herself. She didn't think Nile would appreciate the gesture.

Instead she said, "That all happened when you were a child. You're a man now. Couldn't you put it all behind you?"

"What's that old saying? 'As the twig is bent, so grows the tree.'"

Maddie attempted to lighten his mood. "Well, if that were true, then what am I, a country parson's daughter, doing out here in the wilds of the Amazon? I should be down in Somerset, doing endless charitable works for the church and leading an exemplary life."

Nile chuckled at that. "There are exceptions to every rule, and you do seem to break your share of them."

"I do, don't I?"

Nile's mood changed abruptly and he became serious once again. "So, now that you know the whole sordid story, what do you think of the great Rose Marcus?"

He was asking her to choose sides, and she knew it, but Maddie couldn't compromise her ideals even to ease his pain.

"I'm sorry for what she did to you," she said, "but I can understand what drove her."

Nile smiled wryly. "I knew you would say something like that." But at least he didn't condemn her for saying it.

He slapped his neck. "Mosquitoes. I think I'll retire before they eat me alive."

Just as he was about to disappear below, Maddie said, "Nile?"

He stopped and turned. "Yes?"

"Thank you for telling me about your mother. I know it couldn't have been easy for you."

"It wasn't," he replied, then was gone.

Maddie decided to remain on deck awhile longer, listening to Jayme humming softly as he moored the launch for the night.

As she sat in the rapidly dwindling light, she thought of Nile and what he had just told her. Since he had confided in her, the pieces of the complex puzzle that was Nile Marcus were falling neatly into place.

Now Maddie knew why he had resented her at first: she reminded him of his mother. Like Rose Marcus, Maddie Dare was a strong-willed, independent woman, committed to traveling her own road. And like Rose Marcus, she needed something more out of life than the simple pleasures of home and hearth. But would she desert any child she knew needed her so desperately?

Ghosts from her past materialized without warning, and she shivered once before banishing them to where they belonged.

The last of the light died, and Jayme started to light the lantern. Maddie rose, wished him good night, and went to her cabin.

The sudden bucking of the launch almost threw Maddie from her bunk. She awoke quickly, every sense alert, and she hastily dressed, not even taking time to braid her hair. When she went topside, she could see it was already morning and that she had overslept.

She found a worried-looking Nile conferring with Jayme, who had lost his easygoing air and was jabbering in Portuguese as he gesticulated wildly.

"What's wrong?" Maddie demanded, joining them.

Nile turned, his golden gaze lingering on her unbound hair for a moment. "Rapids," he replied. "We're coming to a particularly dangerous part of the river."

Maddie felt her skin tingle at the prospect of danger. "Will we be able to navigate it?"

"We should. Jayme has traveled this part of the river before. He just has to guide the launch carefully."

"What can I do to help?"

"Just sit tight and stay out of our way."

His peremptory tone caused Maddie to scowl at him in annoyance, but she did as she was told. Now was not the time to challenge Nile's authority.

"Shall I go below?" she asked.

"No. If the launch breaks up, you'd be trapped and drown. You'd better stay on deck with us. Hold on to the poles supporting the roof and stay away from the rail. I'm just warning you that I'm not going in after you if you fall overboard, so don't."

"I won't," Maddie said, grabbing the nearest pole and planting her feet firmly on the deck.

While Nile and Jayme conversed in rapid Portuguese, Maddie remained silent so as not to distract them. Instead, she kept her eyes on the river, trying to read it as Jayme had taught her. Here the Amazon had narrowed, and the water did seem to be moving faster toward them, rushing at them, trying to push the stalwart little launch back. But already the engines were chugging away to propel them forward slowly but surely, foot by foot.

As the launch rocked, Maddie could see white foam churning ahead, and she presumed there were rocks hiding just below the surface to trap the unwary. Ahead of her, she could see Jayme playing the wheel as though it were a fine instrument, sometimes turning it just a little, other times giving it a long, steady turn that sent the launch veering off to the side and almost pitched Maddie onto the deck.

Maddie craned her neck, trying to see over the side, and she held her breath as she saw one ugly black rock after another appear to rear up out of the water as if alive. Just when she expected the launch to crash into one, it veered away.

She lost all track of time. Her fingers were numb with the strain of grasping the pole and her legs felt stiff from constantly bracing herself. Nile never looked over at her once, keeping his worried eye on Jayme and the river.

Suddenly Nile shouted, "Hang on!"

Fear dried Maddie's mouth as she tightened her grasp and braced herself. She felt the jolt through her entire body at the same time as she heard the scraping sound of the hull dragging itself along a hidden rock. Maddie waited in terror for the launch to split apart and fling them at the river's mercy, but nothing happened.

Just as suddenly, it was over.

She realized at once when they were finally free

of the rapids. The river felt different somehow as it released them from its grip. The launch shuddered once, as if sighing in relief, then steadied itself and chugged on. A grinning Jayme turned to them and said something that made Nile laugh.

"What did he say?" Maddie wanted to know.

"He said you brought us luck. The Amazon didn't want to take the life of a fellow member of her sex, so she decided to spare us poor men as well."

"Tell Jayme I thank him for the compliment."

Nile did so, then went below, still chuckling to himself. When he came up a minute later, he told them the rock they had scraped hadn't punctured the hull, so they were safe for the moment

Once the danger was over, Nile felt the tension drain from his body as his muscles loosened like an uncoiled spring. Jayme looked too exhausted to even sing, while Maddie sat down and began combing her hair.

As Nile watched the comb slide effortlessly through that shimmering waterfall of golden light, he felt a familiar rush of desire building deep within his groin. There was nothing like triumphing over danger to trigger his aching need for the blessed physical release only a willing woman could provide, but this time it was quite inopportune.

He took a deep breath and looked away, but he fancied he could still hear the erotic rustle of her hair as she combed it, the exciting crackle of static electricity. He wanted to bury his face in its silken heaviness, then sift it through his fingers.

Nile tried to put her out of his mind by thinking of Provvy's settlement, not far away on the Juruá, and how he was looking forward to seeing his old friend again, but it was no use. Tantalizing visions of Maddie kept intruding persistently.

Nile recalled her smooth, demanding lips against

his that night on the *Rio Madeira*, and the feel of her body against his when he was fighting the malarial chills. So sweet, yet so sensual. Enough to make a man forget promises and damn the consequences.

At his own peril, he risked a glance at her and saw that she had set down her comb and was beginning to braid her hair. He watched in rapt fascination as she proceeded without even looking at what she was doing, as though each fingertip were set with an eye.

It's lust pure and simple, he muttered to himself. I'm a man and she's a woman, and we're stuck together on the same boat, without a brothel in sight. I wouldn't be human if I didn't desire her.

But he couldn't have her. Aside from the fact that he had promised to be responsible for her well-being during this expedition, Nile would not poach on another man's preserve. Maddie was engaged to Ben Thomas, and Nile would respect that and keep his distance. He had some scruples left.

Still, as he watched her tie off the end of the braid, she didn't look or act like a woman who belonged to a man. She didn't have that air of unapproachability, that emotional distance and complete lack of interest in other men caused by devotion to only one man. Nile also thought it odd that Maddie didn't chatter on incessantly about her beloved, as the few engaged women he had known did. In fact, she seldom even mentioned Thomas at all—contradictory behavior for a woman who was traveling thousands of miles to find her lost fiancé.

Nile shook his head. He was grasping at straws, trying to find a way to rationalize what he wanted to do.

"There," Maddie said, her task completed. She

faced Nile. "When will we be arriving at Provvy's settlement?"

"In about another hour we'll reach the mouth of the Juruá River," he replied. "Provvy's settlement is about another hour upriver."

"Good. I'm looking forward to meeting him."

Nile was looking forward to seeing his old friend too. At least Provvy would be able to take his mind off Maddie.

An hour later, the launch entered the mouth of the Juruá River.

Another hour later, they rounded a narrow bend in the river, and the dock to Provvy's settlement came into view.

Nile scowled, not liking what he saw—or rather, didn't see.

Maddie, standing beside him, noticed the look at once. "Is something the matter?"

"There are no boats tied to the dock."

"Perhaps your friend is away."

"Even when Provvy is away, there's always a launch or a canoe docked here. He's a trader. People are always stopping by to see what he has to sell."

Maddie looked around. "Where is Provvy's house?"

"It's in the jungle," Nile replied. "After we dock, we walk down a path, and Provvy's house is set in a clearing."

"Does he live there alone?"

Nile shook his head as Jayme began edging the launch toward the dock. "He's lived with a Norwegian woman named Inge for the last seven years. One day the rubber barons decided there weren't enough women for their workers, so they persuaded the government of Manaus to empty the brothels and send the women upriver. Inge was one of those women. She decided she preferred Provvy to one of the *seringueiros*, and they've been together ever since."

Maddie said, "It must be a difficult life for a woman, after the relative civilization of Manaus."

"Inge didn't seem to mind. From what she told me, her life in Norway was no bed of roses. And I daresay she finds loving one man preferable to loving dozens."

"I daresay."

The launch nudged the dock and Jayme moved to secure his boat. Nile grabbed one of the Winchesters, stepped out onto the dock, then extended his hand to Maddie to help her down.

The dock creaked and groaned, so Maddie hurried across it. "It doesn't seem very stable," she said to Nile, who was glancing all around as if he expected to be ambushed at any moment.

"Something's wrong," he said flatly. "Provvy always maintained his dock."

As Maddie and Nile stepped off the dock, she could see the path he had spoken of, a narrow trail that led into the black depths of the jungle and was promptly swallowed.

Nile, who was holding his rifle as if he expected to use it, stopped and turned to Maddie. "You'd better stay here with Jayme."

"And let you go in there alone? Not on your life."

Anger darkened his eyes to gold. "I thought we agreed I would give the orders on this expedition and you would obey?"

"We did, but if I took the other Winchester, two guns would be better than one."

"All right. If you want to be foolhardy, who am I to stop you? Go get the other gun."

Maddie went back to the launch and returned seconds later with the other rifle.

"Follow me, and keep your eyes open," Nile said, and started down the path.

Maddie felt her heart begin to pound as the jungle wrapped her in its silent green embrace. This was the first time she had actually entered the jungle since arriving in Brazil, and the grandeur of it took her breath away.

She looked up, but the thick-trunked trees were so tall they met overhead like some great cathedral ceiling and blotted out the sky. While the path was clear, enabling her and Nile to move rather quickly, Maddie could see that the vines and undergrowth were already beginning to encroach on it. She looked everywhere, on guard for poisonous snakes or unfriendly Indian faces peering at her through the underbrush, but luckily, she didn't see any. Or perhaps she was just walking too fast to notice.

Finally Maddie could see light up ahead. When she came into the clearing, she felt as though she had stepped out of a tunnel into daylight, and it blinded her momentarily. When Nile stopped suddenly and swore, Maddie knew something was very wrong.

"What is it?" she demanded, trying to look around his broad shoulders.

He stepped aside. "See for yourself."

There, in the center of the clearing, was a house. Maddie didn't need to hear the despair in Nile's voice to know that it was deserted and had been for some time. The veranda running around it had collapsed in several places, and the thatch in the roof had a large, gaping hole in one end.

"What happened?" Maddie said, aghast.

"I wish I knew." Nile's voice was heavy with worry.

"The place looks abandoned, as though no one has lived here for years." She turned to him. "I take it Provvy and his woman were living here the last time you visited."

"Oh, yes," Nile replied.

"I wonder what happened that caused them to leave? And where are they now?"

"That's what I'd like to know," Nile muttered between clenched teeth. "It would have to be serious for Provvy to abandon his home like this."

Maddie took a step forward. "Perhaps we should look around. He may have left a clue as to his whereabouts."

Nile grabbed her arm, stopping her in her tracks. "Stay out of there. The snakes have probably taken it over."

Maddie blanched and took a step backward. "Whatever you say." Then she looked up at Nile. "What do we do now? Where do we go from here?"

"We go to the mission. Perhaps Amaryllis knows what's happened to Provvy and Inge. And if she doesn't, perhaps the rubber men do. Aguirre's *estradas* aren't far from the mission."

They went back the way they had come and returned to the launch.

Once they were back on the river again, Nile found himself wound tighter than a spring. Something terrible had happened to Provvy; he could feel it deep in his bones.

If his friend had simply packed up and moved elsewhere, he would have left word for Nile in Manaus. No, this had been Provvy's home since Nile could remember, and for all the American's bluster about being a drifter without a country, he had put down the deepest, most tenacious roots of anyone.

Soon they would be coming to the mission. Nile prayed that Amaryllis had some answers.

10

The jungle was encroaching on the little cemetery. In another month the simple makeshift gravestones would be overgrown with greedy twisting vines and brush.

Amaryllis stood there in silence, her hands folded and her head bowed humbly to pray for the souls of the departed.

"The Lord is my shepherd, I . . ."

Her lips moved, but the rest of the words wouldn't come, pushed out of the way by stronger thoughts and more forceful images of her beloved Freddie's slow, agonizing death from a snakebite. Now Amaryllis heard her brother's piteous wails of agony echoing loudly in her brain every time she tried to pray. It had been so long since she had last prayed.

Amaryllis sighed, raised her head, and opened her eyes. They had all died, one by one, year after year, since their stalwart little band had first come to Brazil seven years ago to do the Lord's work. Now, with Freddie gone, she was the only one left to carry on. She would have to convert the Indians into renouncing their heathen gods, lead them in Sunday services, and teach their children about true salvation and the Lord. She would also have to deal with the rubber men and their barbaric ways.

She touched the silver cross she wore on a leather thong around her neck and shuddered, feeling as though the burden the Lord had just placed upon her shoulders was too much for her to bear. She tried telling herself that Jesus Christ had borne a far greater burden on the road to Calvary, but for once her faith could not comfort her. She had always seen herself as a stong moral woman, able to face any spiritual or physical test with fortitude and equanimity, but now she was riddled with uncertainty and doubt.

I am losing my faith, Amaryllis said to herself as she turned and walked away from the silent dead. I have lost everyone I ever loved, and now I can't go on. I just can't.

As she slowly walked back to the main house, a vision of Winston Belgrave danced before her eyes. Satan always sent Win to tempt her whenever she was at her lowest ebb, but she managed to resist by turning her thoughts to more spiritually uplifting matters. Now she felt too weak to fight anymore.

She had loved him in the innocence of their youth, when they shared the same ideals and dreams. But then Win had been corrupted by the lure of wealth and she could never forgive him for betraying her like that. She hoped he was happy and content with his money and his harlots. Still, when she pictured the way his boyish face used to light up whenever he saw he . . .

"Why do you torment yourself so?" she muttered savagely, quickening her stride. "Winston Belgrave chose to stray from the path of righteousness. No one forced him."

As soon as the words were out of her mouth, a repentant Amaryllis asked God's forgiveness for her spitefulness.

Just then, a familiar voice called, "Mama! Mama!"

Amaryllis stopped as one of the Indian girls who lived at the mission, a member of the Cammuri tribe, came running down the path toward her.

"Mary, is something wrong?" she demanded, fearing the worst.

"No, Mama," the girl said excitedly. "Visitors."

"Who? Rubber men?"

"No, Mama. A white man and a woman. I see the man before, but can't remember his name. Don't know the woman."

Amaryllis felt her hopes soar. Could it be . . . ? Instead of trying to guess, she gathered her skirts and practically ran back to the mission, with Mary following close on her heels.

The moment she rounded the house and saw the tall man in a white suit standing there, Amaryllis stopped in her tracks. "Nile?" she called uncertainly.

He turned and grinned. "Who else would be crazy enough to come all the way out here?"

When he held out his arms to her, Amaryllis shouted his name with joy and ran to embrace him. As Nile's strong arms wrapped around her in a bone-crushing hug, Amaryllis felt tears of happiness sting her eyes. Nile Marcus had to be a gift from God just when she needed one.

When they parted, laughing, Amaryllis stood back and held him at arm's length. "You don't know how good it is to see you, my dear, dear friend."

Nile's smile died, and his face turned somber. "Winston told me what happened to Fred. I'm so sorry."

She felt tears well up in her eyes. "I know. Thank you. It was God's will, what else can one say?"

Then Amaryllis looked around Nile and noticed the woman Mary had spoken of. "Nile Marcus, where are your manners?" Amaryllis chided him. "Please introduce me to the lady at once."

Nile stepped aside. "Sorry. Amaryllis Gates, may I present Miss Maddie Dare."

The tall young woman, dressed in the most outlandish costume Amaryllis had ever seen, strode forward, her hand extended. "I'm so pleased to meet you, Miss Gates," she said, taking Amaryllis' hand in her firm grip. "Nile has told me so much about you."

As Amaryllis stood there, having her hand gripped hard and shaken, she was bombarded by contrasting impressions. The woman possessed a striking gold-and-ivory beauty that belonged in a Mayfair drawing room, but she radiated a toughness and strength not out-of-place here. And while her warm blue gaze was direct almost to the point of boldness, it was guarded and wary as well. This was a woman whose trust had to be earned.

"I'm pleased to meet you as well, Miss Dare, and—"

"Please call me Maddie."

"Maddie, then, and you must call me Amy. Welcome to our humble mission."

Amaryllis didn't even want to hazard a guess as to why Nile was traveling alone with such a beautiful companion. Fewer things shocked her the older she grew, but the less she knew about Nile's situation, the less she would feel compelled to sit in judgment of her old friend.

Nile, who seemed to read her mind, said, "Maddie and I are traveling upriver, searching for her lost fiancé."

Amaryllis smiled. "Then you both must be tired after your long journey, and in need of refreshment. Come, and once we've eaten, we can talk, for I'm sure you have much to tell me."

"Sounds wonderful," Maddie said.

Amaryllis addressed Mary, who had been hanging back shyly. "Three *cafèzinhos* and some bread, Mary, if you please."

"Yes, Mama." And the girl hurried off to do her bidding.

"Forgive me, but why does she call you her mother when you're obviously not?" Maddie asked, startled.

Nile burst out laughing.

Amaryllis merely smiled. "No, I'm not. They all call me that as a term of respect. I suppose it it because I try to care for them as a mother would her children."

"You must forgive Maddie's blunt tongue," Nile said as they climbed stairs to the veranda that ran all around the house. "She is a newspaper reporter and accustomed to asking people insulting personal questions."

Now it was Amaryllis' turn to be startled. "A newspaper reporter? I thought only men did such work."

"Not anymore," Maddie replied. "And I do apologize if I insulted you."

"No offense taken." Amaryllis offered Maddie one of two battered wicker chairs set at a small table, while Nile chose to lean against the sturdy railing. Once they were seated, she said, "So, you've come to Brazil to search for your missing fiancé."

"Yes." Maddie reached into the pocket of her divided skirt and drew out a photograph. "Perhaps he passed this way. His name is—"

"Ben Thomas," Amaryllis said, recognizing the photograph at once.

Nile straightened. "You've seen him?"

Amaryllis nodded. "He's a photographer for a newspaper, is he not?"

"Yes!" Maddie cried, her face lighting up with excitement. "And you saw him? When? Did he say where he was going?"

Laughing, Amaryllis raised her hands. "Please! One question at a time." When Maddie fell silent, Amaryllis continued with, "He stopped at the mission about six months ago. A most pleasant and charming young man. When he left, he said he was heading upriver for Iquitos, in Peru."

Maddie looked over at Nile. "At least we're on the right track."

"It would appear so."

Just then, Mary appeared carrying a tray laden with three little cups and a plate of sliced bread.

Immediately several insects descended on the food, but Amaryllis just brushed them away nonchalantly and started to serve. "I'm sure you're not used to eating insects with your food, Maddie, but I'm afraid out here they get into everything, so there's nothing one can do but accept it. The natives make this bread from ground dried bananas. It's very tasty."

"There is much I'm getting used to in the Amazon," Maddie said, then shooed the insects away, took a bite of the bread, and pronounced it delicious.

Nile's eyes sparkled with mischief as he sipped his *cafèzinho*. "The insects add a certain flavor, don't you think?"

"And a nutlike crunch," Maddie retorted blithely.

Amaryllis just shook her head. "Nile Marcus, such talk!"

"And he accuses me of having a blunt tongue," Maddie muttered.

Nile's mood changed abruptly, and his faced darkened. "Amy, where are Provvy and Inge? We stopped at their settlement before we came here, and it looked as though it hadn't been lived in for years."

Amaryllis turned white, and set down the piece of bread she was just about to eat.

"What's wrong?" Maddie asked sharply.

"Nile," Amaryllis said, her voice quavering, "I don't know how to tell you this, but . . . Provvy's dead."

Nile stood there still as a statue, his face devoid of all comprehension. "What?"

Amaryllis rose and went to him, taking his coffee

cup from him before he dropped it. "He's dead. And Inge has gone back to Manaus to . . . to resume her old life, I expect."

"Dead?" Nile staggered, then grabbed one of the beams for support.

Maddie just sat there, shocked speechless.

Nile took off his hat and ran a trembling hand through his hair. "When? How did it happen? Snakebite? Fever?"

Amaryllis looked back at Maddie in mute appeal, then spread her hands helplessly. "I don't know of any other way to tell you, Nile." She swallowed hard. "Provvy was murdered."

The three words sounded like stones being dropped in a pond, harsh sounds followed by complete and utter silence.

The expression of shock and pain on Nile's face was too much for Maddie to bear, so she looked down at the table, where a swarm of flies had already taken advantage of the situation to feed on the bread. She made no attempt to brush them off this time. She had no stomach for food now.

Nile choked out the word, "How?"

"He was stabbed."

"Stabbed?" The manner of death surprised him.

Amaryllis nodded. "Inge had been visiting me here, and when she returned to her house, she found Ben Thomas waiting for her, and—"

"Ben?" Maddie's head jerked up. "Ben was there when Provvy died?"

Amaryllis nodded. "He was staying with Provvy at the time, and had just returned from taking photographs, to find Provvy slumped over his desk with a . . . a knife sticking out of his back."

Nile passed a hand over his eyes, and his voice shook. "Who did it? The natives? A *seringueiro*?"

"No one knows. Inge was so hysterical, she even blamed poor Mr. Thomas for it."

"Ben, a murderer?" Maddie scoffed, incensed. "That's preposterous. What reason would he have?"

Amaryllis shrugged helplessly. "Inge claimed that Provvy had acquired some uncut diamonds, and—"

"Diamonds?" Nile interjected. "Where would he get diamonds? There are no diamond mines in this part of Brazil."

"Who knows where Provvy acquired half of the things he had for sale. But Inge claimed Ben Thomas killed Provvy for his diamonds."

"Ben is not a murderer," Maddie insisted. "I refuse to believe he would do such a thing. This woman Inge must have been hysterical to accuse him."

Nile balled his hands into fists at his sides. "And no one sought to find out, I take it?"

Amaryllis fingered the silver cross she wore. "You know our situation here, Nile. There is no law to speak of. Fitch is the only law, but unless he has a personal stake in something, he won't do anything about it."

"Didn't he even try to find out who killed Provvy?"

"He questioned Mr. Thomas, who said he knew nothing about any diamonds or who might have killed Provvy. Then Fitch questioned his men, but of course no one came forward with information. Besides, Provvy wasn't one of his men, just as we here at the mission aren't. If we were massacred tomorrow, Fitch wouldn't care."

After listening to Nile and Amaryllis discussing Fitch in less-than-glowing terms, Maddie wasn't looking forward to meeting Senhor Aguirre's partner.

"And you say Inge went back to Manaus?" Nile asked.

"Yes."

"Why didn't she take up with one of the *seringueiros*?"

Nile's frank question didn't fluster the missionary. "Inge said Provvy was the one love of her life, and she couldn't bear to stay out here any longer, even with another man. I offered her a place with us, but she said a mission was no place for a woman like her, so she went back to Manaus."

Nile smacked the rail with his open hand. "Damn! I wish she had stayed. I want to talk to her."

Maddie said, "Once we find Ben, he could tell us what he knows."

Nile looked at her, his golden eyes glittering dark with interest. "You have a point. Well, now I have my own reasons for wanting to find Ben Thomas just as much as you do. If you'll excuse me, ladies, I want to be alone for a while."

Without another word, Nile strode across the veranda, down the steps, and into the jungle.

Amaryllis sighed. "I hope the dear Lord will give him some comfort. Provvy was like a father to him."

"No death is ever easy to accept," Maddie said, "especially a violent one."

"How well I know that. Out here in the lawless wilderness, one sees so much of it. One tries to feel compassion." Then Amaryllis said, "Enough of this morbid talk. Would you like to see the rest of the mission?"

Maddie would have preferred being alone with her own thoughts in light of this disturbing information about Ben, but she didn't want to be rude to her hostess.

"I'd like that very much," she said, and rose to join Amaryllis on a tour of the mission.

As Maddie followed Amaryllis through the house itself and listened to her hostess extol the virtues of bare wooden floors and curtainless windows in the jungle, she found she could not concentrate. She kept thinking of this day's unforeseen, shocking events.

Poor Nile. Losing Provvy in such a violent manner had affected him deeply. But as much as Maddie wanted to go to him, she realized he needed the time to be alone with his grief.

And what part does Ben play in all this? she wondered. It's not like him to ignore something as heinous as a murder. Surely he could have gotten word to the authorities in Manaus before going upriver to Iquitos, as we planned.

But, as Amaryllis had said, the Amazon was a lawless wilderness, and perhaps Ben had come to realize there was nothing he could do.

"Maddie, is something wrong?"

The sound of Amy's voice broke through Maddie's reverie at once. "I beg your pardon?"

"I was just explaining how the women make flour from the manioc root."

Maddie smiled at the native woman holding a wooden bowl in her lap and grinding the root with what resembled a pestle.

"Do forgive me for woolgathering," she said.

"Don't apologize. I understand," Amy replied.

She continued their tour as though nothing had happened, and Maddie resolved to remain attentive this time.

Later, when Maddie had seen all of the mission and Nile still hadn't returned to the house, she decided now was the time to learn all she could about Amaryllis Gates, to see just what it was about this woman that inspired such undying love in Winston Belgrave and fierce loyalty in Nile Marcus.

It wasn't physical beauty, because Amy possessed only average looks, and the hard life she led beneath the cruel, relentless Amazon sun had taken its toll on what little she did have. Her once-fine English complexion was almost as brown as a field hand's, and scored with deep lines at the corners of her eyes, aging her, as did her rapidly graying light brown hair.

Besides, Nile and Winston were not so shallow as to judge a woman solely on her looks. No, it had to be something else, some elusive inner quality that drew two such different men to her.

When Amy invited Maddie to sit on the veranda to wait for Nile, she decided now was the time to have a little woman-to-woman talk.

"What made you decide to become a missionary?" Maddie asked. "Did you always want to serve God in some way?"

Amy smiled wistfully. "Actually, it began more as a desire to serve my brother, Fred, than to serve God. He was much older, and I kept house for him after our parents died. So when the Lord chose him to spread his word among the heathen of the Amazon, I joined him."

"That must have been a great sacrifice for you, to give up all that was familiar to journey to a dangerous country. Didn't you ever wish to marry and have a family of your own?"

Something flashed in the depths of Amy's pewtergray eyes, then vanished in an instant. "No young gentlemen ever came calling when we lived in England, and faced with the prospect of joining Fred or living alone . . ." She shrugged. "My choice was a simple one, and right for me."

"How long have you been here?"

"Seven years. I first came here when I was twenty-seven. That seems like a lifetime ago."

"Nile told me how you met."

Amy smiled, infusing her face with a warmth that made her look years younger. "Yes. There were eight in our party at the time. He saved our lives."

"So eight of you started this mission."

"Seven of us," Amy corrected, the light dying in her eyes. "One of our party returned to Manaus."

Winston Belgrave.

Maddie waited, hoping the woman would continue talking about Winston, but she fell silent and stared out into the jungle.

Maddie reopened the conversation with, "I'm surprised Protestant missionaries were allowed in this Catholic country."

Amy smiled wryly. "We probably wouldn't be here if it hadn't been for Senhor Aguirre. This is his land. He gave us permission to build the mission. To this day, I don't know why he favors us with his protection."

"To save his soul, perhaps."

"Perhaps. But I think it has more to do with appeasing his English investors."

Then, as Maddie listened, Amy went on to tell her about those backbreaking first years of establishing the mission—wresting the land from the jungle, building houses, establishing trade with the Indians, then slowly and painstakingly converting them to Christianity.

Amy ended her tale with, "So, with Fred gone, I'm the only one left."

"Will your church be sending anyone else to join you?"

She shook her head. "All they have provided us over the years has been modest financial support."

Maddie fell silent. How could this woman expect to carry on here alone, without even one man to protect her?

"Have you ever thought of returning to England?" Maddie asked.

Amy stared at her as if she had gone mad. "There is nothing for me in England. This is my home."

There is nothing here for you either, Maddie thought, except a grave beside your sainted brother's.

Amy frowned and fingered her cross as if seeking

strength from it. "Sometimes I wonder if our work has been worth the sacrifice."

Maddie pounced at once. "What do you mean?"

Flustered, Amy shook her head. "Forgive me for even saying that. Of course the Lord's work is worth any personal sacrifice." But her hands trembled in her lap, and her expression was deeply troubled.

Maddie decided now was not the time to press her, for the woman looked overwrought and on the verge of tears.

Amy composed herself and smiled brightly. "So, how did you ever meet Nile and persuade him to guide you on this expedition?"

Maddie grinned. "I see you know how he feels about taking women"—she deepened her voice in perfect imitation of Nile's—" 'where they don't belong.' "

Amy laughed heartily. "That does sound like Nile. When I first met him, he told me in no uncertain terms that a respectable woman didn't belong in the Amazon and I should go home. I never listened, of course."

"He told me the same thing."

"Nile's a good man and a good friend. He has his weaknesses, but which of us doesn't?"

Now, why, Maddie wondered, is she so quick to forgive Nile his weaknesses and not Winston, who loves her?

While Amy listened, Maddie told her all about her first meeting with Nile and their subsequent journey upriver on Jayme's launch, but she said nothing about Senhor Calistro or Winston Belgrave.

Conversation ceased when they saw Nile come back up the trail.

As they sat together again, with Nile and Amy catching up on old news, Maddie quietly studied the missionary. She could tell something was wrong with her, but it was very subtle and almost undetectable, like a picture slightly askew on a wall. There was a deep, abiding sadness about her, a sense that life was about to overwhelm her. Amy nervously fingered her cross, and her eyes would suddenly turn vacant. She looked tired and worried.

Maddie decided she would talk to Nile about it.

Maddie couldn't sleep. Even though she was used to the eerie night sounds of the jungle by now, every little chirp and strange cry sent her eyes flying open to stare at the ceiling.

When she heard footsteps on the veranda, she pushed the mosquito netting aside, swung out of her hammock, and dressed quickly.

As she had suspected, she found Nile out there, leaning on the railing and staring out into the moonlit jungle. The second he became aware of her presence, he whirled around with arms raised and fists clenched to ward off an attacker.

Maddie raised her hands in surrender. "Only me."

"Don't you know better than to go sneaking up on a man like that?" he growled, keeping his voice low so as not to awaken the sleeping Amaryllis.

"I couldn't sleep, so I thought I'd come out here and let the mosquitoes have a picnic."

"Damnation and hellfire, you won't jest when you get malaria or breakbone fever!"

"Then I'll have only myself to blame, won't I?"

Nile muttered something under his breath about pigheaded women and went back to regarding the jungle out of angry eyes.

As Maddie stood quietly beside him, she could feel the rage and frustration radiating from him in palpable waves, like heat from a roaring fire. His strong, square hands gripped the railing in a chokehold, as though the wood were Provvy's murderer, and a small muscle kept twitching in his jaw as he fought to control himself.

Maddie laid a tentative hand on his shoulder and felt the hard muscles stiffen. "I'm sorry," she said softly. "I know how much Provvy meant to you."

He ignored her touch. "Provvy Brown never had much, but he never cared. What he did have, he always shared, whether it was food or what he knew. He taught me how to fish, how to hunt with a blowgun, how to throw a knife. He knew so much about the Amazon and he taught me to respect it and how to survive."

Maddie's hand fell away. "He sounds like a wonderful man."

"Wonderful? I have no illusions about him. He was unscrupulous when it came to trading. Once he told me the only way for a river trader to make a living was to buy something for a nickel and sell it to someone else for a dollar. And he always did, too."

Maddie smiled at that.

Nile continued with, "I think I'll always remember him the way I first saw him, paddling up the Juruá in his cedarwood dugout piled high with food, clothes, live turtles, guns ... anything and everything he could fit in there to trade."

"That's a nice memory to have," she said softly.

Nile turned and stared over at her. The moonlight bleached all the gold from his eyes, leaving them as black and unfathomable as a tar pit.

"I loved that man, and I'm going to find his murderer if it's the last thing I do," he said.

"But how? It could have been anyone. That will be like searching for a needle in a haystack."

"I think your fiancé is the key."

She inhaled sharply in surprise. "Ben? What could he possibly know about this?"

"He found Provvy's body. Maybe he saw something, someone fleeing into the jungle."

Maddie scowled. "If he saw something, he surely would have come forward and told someone."

"Perhaps."

She stiffened. "Now, look here, Mr. Nile Marcus, I don't like your insinuations that Ben Thomas had something to do with your friend's death."

"Keep your voice down or you'll wake Amy."

"I still resent your insinuations!" Maddie murmured. "I've known Ben Thomas for years, and he is a decent, honorable man. Do you think I'd want to marry him if he weren't?"

He snorted. "Sometimes I wonder."

"Well, thank you very much for your confidence in my judgment!"

Nile whirled on her, a challenge in his eyes. "When was the last time you received a letter from him?"

The conversation's abrupt shift caught Maddie by surprise, and she blurted out, "Six months ago. Why do you ask?"

His eyes narrowed. "Because if he passed this way on his way to Iquitos, he isn't as lost as you thought. And if he isn't lost, why didn't your beloved write to you sooner? His letters could have easily been left at the mission here and Amy would have put them on the next steamer, to be mailed from Manaus."

While Maddie stood there in stunned silence, Nile slapped at his neck and said, "You'd better go inside before you're eaten alive." Then he started walking down the veranda, stopping only to turn long enough to say, "Think about it," before disappearing inside.

Maddie did stay awake thinking when she returned to her hammock, but her thoughts concerned

Nile's suspicions that were coming too close to the truth for comfort.

She knew the real reason why Ben hadn't written to her since Manaus; it was all part of the plan. But Nile didn't know that. All he could assume was that Ben hadn't written to Maddie because he didn't care for her.

Maddie shifted in her hammock. Fiancé ... Ben Thomas was no more her fiancé than Nile Marcus. Of course, Maddie had once hoped that would change when she found Ben and escorted him back to England in triumph. Their proximity on the return voyage would foster closer feelings that would later blossom into love and a future together. Or so she had hoped.

Now she wondered if she had been deluding herself with wishful thinking.

As she rolled over on her side carefully to avoid upsetting the hammock, Maddie forced herself to confront her real feelings for Ben. She thought she loved him, but what did she really know of him beyond his dark good looks and abundant charm? True, they worked together at the *Clarion*, but they had never been really alone together except when on an assignment. Why, Maddie had spent more time alone with Nile these last few weeks than she ever had with Ben.

Then she wondered if she should tell Nile the truth. She had come to trust him, and she was starting to feel guilty about having to deceive him. But if she did that, he would be furious and probably call the expedition off, and she couldn't let that happen. Too much was at stake.

This is no time to change horses in midstream, Maddie girl, she told herself. You'll just have to see this through whether you like it or not. Sam's depending on you. The *Clarion*'s depending on you.

She closed her eyes and finally fell asleep.

* * *

The next morning, Nile awoke to the deafening roar of howler monkeys, dressed quickly, and went out on the veranda, where he found Amy already up and having her breakfast.

"Where's Maddie?" were the first words out of his mouth.

Amy smiled. "And good morning to you, Nile Marcus. Maddie is bathing."

"Is it safe?" he demanded as he seated himself.

"Perfectly. All the women have been using this spot for years, and we haven't lost anyone yet."

Mary materialized out of nowhere with a *cafèzinho*, which Nile accepted gratefully.

Amy said, "With Maddie absent, we'll be able to talk in private."

Nile raised one thick brow. "Uh-oh. When you use that schoolmistressy tone, I know I'm about to get a tongue-lashing. What have I done this time?"

She smiled. "I'm not going to scold or lecture you on the salvation of your immortal soul. We've known each other too long for it to do any good anyway. If you want to escort a beautiful unmarried woman up the Amazon, that is your affair."

"Then why do I get the feeling you're about to box my ears?"

Amy sat back and folded her hands in her lap. "I'm going to do nothing of the sort. It's your own guilty conscience troubling you."

"I have no conscience," Nile said with a chuckle. "You know that."

Amy shook her head. "So unrepentant . . ."

Nile sipped his coffee. "Enough of this banter, Amy, much as I enjoy it. What's on your mind?"

She gave him an odd look. "You're in love with Maddie, aren't you?"

Nile just stared at her out of goggle eyes, then let out an explosive hoot of laughter. "Me? In love with that bossy, demanding shrew? Amaryllis Gates, you've been out here too long. The heat has finally gotten to you."

"Insult me all you like, my dear friend, for you know I'll merely turn the other cheek for more. But I've seen the way you look at her when you think no one else is watching. There is a tenderness in your eyes that I've never seen there before."

"Tenderness in my eyes? I've never heard such drivel in all my life!" Nile rose to his feet and went to sit on the railing, his back toward Amy so she couldn't see him fighting his conflicting feelings.

"Come now. We've known each other too long not to be honest with each other."

Nile twisted at the waist to face her. "I am not in love with Maddie Dare. She hired me to find her missing fiancé, that's all. Once that's accomplished, I'll take my money and never see her again. And good riddance, as far as I'm concerned."

Why did that prospect suddenly make him feel so hollow inside?

"Well," Amy said with a shrug, "if that's the way you really feel . . ."

"I will admit I do feel something for her, but it's simple lust"—Nile grinned as Amy rolled her eyes heavenward to ask her Lord for strength—"my personal favorite of the seven deadly sins."

"So I've heard," Amy retorted dryly.

"I'm just a poor sinner. I never claimed to be a saint."

Amy was silent for a moment, then said, "I like Maddie, even though I've known her for less than a day. She is special. And whether you realize it or not, Nile Marcus, you two suit each other very well."

"Even if what you claim is true—which I doubt—you're forgetting she's promised to another."

An impish sparkle lit up Amy's face. "Engagements can always be broken."

Now Nile was beginning to get irritated. She could sound like a busybody maiden aunt when she set her mind to it. To distract her from extolling Maddie's tiresome virtues, Nile said, "Winston sends his love."

Amy turned as gray as her dress and gripped her cross so hard Nile thought she would jerk it off its leather thong. "I don't wish to hear another word about that man."

"You have no qualms about discussing Maddie with me, so why shouldn't I talk about Win? After all, you loved him once."

Amy rose, her furious eyes the color of hot metal. "That was before he chose Satan over the Lord!" She wrung her hands, took several steps down the veranda, then turned to face Nile when she had control of herself. "I'm sorry for the outburst, my friend. Forgive me for allowing my anger to get the better of me."

"You're only human, Amy. You're entitled to lose your temper like the rest of us."

She closed her eyes and pressed her fingers to her temples. "You only upset me when you bring up Winston. What we felt for each other is dead and gone."

"Winston feels differently, Amy. I've seen him. He still loves you. In fact, he loves you so much he hasn't known a woman, er, in the biblical sense, since he gave up preaching and went to Manaus."

Her eyes flew open, and for one second her true feelings were exposed. Nile saw a yearning there that had always been so rigidly under control. Then it was gone.

"Whether you like it or not, Amy, you're the only woman for Winston, and I think he's the only man for you."

She straightened primly. "I have the mission. I need nothing else, especially a man."

Maddie was right: missionaries were a humorless, sanctimonious lot.

Nile decided he had tormented Amy enough. He rose from the railing. "I'm going to find Maddie. She's been in the river too long." He gave Amy a wink. "With any luck, an alligator's eaten her, and she'll be out of my hair once and for all."

That coaxed a smile out of her, and Nile knew she had forgiven him for being so hard on her.

"Let me show you where our bathing pool is," she called after him.

"No need," he called back. "I know where it is."

Let her think about that for a while.

Nile grinned and headed for the river.

The bathing pool was formed as the waters of a swiftly flowing stream fell over a waterfall on its way to feed the Amazon. The running water and shallow rocky bottom discouraged the dangerous river inhabitants that Nile had warned Maddie about, so it was safe for bathing.

He could hear the roar of rushing water before he came to the end of the jungle path and stood looking down into the pool. Maddie's clothes and a blanket that served as a towel were folded neatly and piled on a wide flat stone near the base of the waterfall, but there was no sign of her anywhere.

For a moment Nile could taste fear as his eyes scanned the jungle frantically for any sign of her. When he looked down at the water and saw a dark shadow darting just beneath the surface, he let out the breath he had been holding in a deep sigh of relief.

Then Maddie's golden head broke the surface like a pale bubble, and before Nile could think to turn away or make his presence known, she stood up.

She was naked.

Nile was not a man who enjoyed spying on women at unguarded, intimate moments, but he was unable to tear his eyes away from Maddie, for he felt like one of Brazil's earliest explorers coming upon a fabled Amazon woman.

As she stood knee-deep in water, wiping it out of her eyes, Maddie was a sight to behold, as primal and natural as Eve in the Garden of Eden. Her long golden hair clung to her head as slickly as a seal's skin, its wet ends curling like caressing fingers around her high, full breasts.

Nile found breathing almost impossible when Maddie gathered her wet hair and tossed it over her shoulders, causing her wet breasts to bounce provocatively. Her waist was long and perfectly indented, her belly as flat as his own. He was disappointed that her hips were more boyish than round, but her long, shapely legs more than compensated for it.

The moment Maddie started moving, those hips swaying ever so gently, Nile felt himself grow rock-hard.

Suddenly Maddie stopped and listened, a look of wariness on her face.

So, Nile thought as he watched her blue gaze search her surroundings, she is beginning to read the jungle and to sense when danger's near.

Then he felt her gaze on him.

Both froze, just staring at each other, eyes locked, for what seemed like hours. Nile knew he should just tear himself away, go back to the mission, and apologize to her later, but he couldn't.

Much to his surprise, Maddie didn't shriek in a fit of maidenly modesty or dive back into the pool to conceal herself from him as any other respectable gentlewoman would have done. Later he would wonder about that, but right now he was too busy watching her square her shoulders, calmly walk out of the water, and reach for her blanket. As she wrapped it around herself, her fingers were shaking and her cheeks were crimson with mortification. Nile could tell that beneath her brave, cool facade, she was furious and perhaps even a little frightened.

Even the steamy morning heat couldn't melt the ice in her voice as she said, "Have you looked your fill, Mr. Marcus? If so, kindly turn around so that I may have some privacy to dress."

He didn't. He wouldn't.

When he started down the path toward her, Maddie felt as though she were watching a jungle cat stalking its prey. She had learned to recognize danger in a man's eyes, the kind of calculating determination to take without asking that only flight could save her from. She saw it in Nile's hot golden gaze as he came toward her noiselessly and relentlessly, but Maddie didn't want to run this time.

She clutched the blanket to her chest. "Go away and leave me alone."

"Don't send me away," he said thickly as he came to stand before her. "Please."

Just one look at his tormented face told Maddie that Nile's emotions were warring within him. He wanted her, that was obvious, but something was holding him back. The fact that she was promised to another man, perhaps? Or, wonder of wonders, did the man have some semblance of scruples after all?

Nile's hand came up to cradle her cheek, his touch surprisingly gentle and reassuring for such a large, strong man. Maddie knew now was the time to pull away if she wanted to end it.

"Maddie."

When he said her name like that, she felt her iron resolve turn to water.

Something tells me I'm going to regret this, she thought, just before closing her eyes and standing on tiptoes to meet his kiss.

Nile's fingers tangled in her wet hair just before his warm, ardent lips sought hers. His mouth felt deliciously sweet and heavy, his kiss turning her insides all shivery and banishing all inhibitions.

Then her hands were sliding up his chest and snaking around his neck, only the blanket wedged between their bodies. As Maddie pressed herself against him shamelessly and parted her lips so Nile could deepen the kiss with his tongue, she felt his questing hands slide down her bare back, leaving a trail of fire in their wake.

When his fingers cupped her trim buttocks and began kneading the flesh in sensuous circles, Maddie broke free with a gasp of delight.

That's all the blanket needed to fall to the ground.

"You're so beautiful," Nile rasped, his eyes drinking in her loveliness like a starving man at a banquet.

Then he was raining kisses on her face and down her neck as he reached up to gently squeeze a bare breast.

Maddie felt her nipple tighten against his warm palm, and she shivered and leaned into it as a hard knot of desire slowly uncurled deep inside her and spread throughout her body, sapping her of her will to resist. Then when Nile lowered his head to tantalize the pink bud with his tongue and tug at it with his lips, Maddie lost all ability to think rationally. All she wanted to do was draw Nile down into her arms and give herself to him. She didn't care about consequences or tomorrows, she was on fire with the need to be possessed by this exciting and exasperating man.

"Nile? Maddie? Are you all right?"

The sound of Amy's shouting at the top of the path tore Maddie and Nile apart as if they were opposite poles of a magnet.

"Damnation and hellfire!" Nile swore under his breath before giving Maddie's naked form one last possessive look. Then he turned and strode away from her, calling, "We're all right, Amy. Maddie's just finishing dressing."

Taking his hint, Maddie grabbed her clothes, stepped behind a bush, and began dressing hurriedly with trembling fingers.

She didn't know whether to curse Amy for the interruption or to thank her.

11

After dressing, Maddie ran breathlessly up the path to where Amy and Nile stood waiting for her.

She flashed an apologetic smile at the other woman. "I'm sorry I worried you by tarrying, but it's just that I haven't had a real bath in so long, I couldn't resist the urge to indulge myself."

If Amy suspected what had really transpired at the pool, she didn't show it. She took Maddie's arm companionably as they started walking back to the house, and said, "I know exactly what you mean. Living on a launch with only a bucket of river water to wash with hardly constitutes a proper bath!"

Maddie risked a glance at Nile, but he stared resolutely ahead and would not look at her. His inscrutable expression hid whatever he was feeling about their moment of mutual desire.

When they arrived back at the house, Nile mumbled some excuse about having to check on Jayme and the launch and went lumbering off. Maddie dried her hair, braided it, and joined Amy on the veranda for breakfast. Amy seemed most interested in hearing about the England she had left so long ago, so Maddie regaled her with stories of London and the countryside. An hour later, Amy asked Maddie if she would like to join her on a trip to a nearby native village, but Maddie declined, saying she had to get some writing done.

No sooner did Maddie get a few sentences written than Nile returned.

As Maddie watched him cross the yard in his smooth, silent stride, she felt her heart begin to race. The vivid memory of his hard, aroused body pressed urgently against hers derailed her train of thought and caused her pen to stop. The impressions she was trying to express on paper were erased by vivid recollections of Nile's warm, callused hands traveling down the wet skin of her back.

Maddie's fingers started trembling so badly she had to set her pen down lest it betray her true feelings.

As Nile climbed the veranda steps, he looked at Maddie; then his gaze slid away in shame. Finally he broke the awkward silence by saying, "Where's Amy?"

"She went to one of the native villages."

He nodded, then seated himself on the railing and turned toward her. "I think it's best that you remain here with Amy while I go to Iquitos to find Thomas."

Maddie just sat there dumbfounded.

Taking her silence for assent, Nile said, "I'm glad you agree. It's settled, then."

She set her papers aside and rose. "No, it is not settled. Our agreement was for you to help me find Ben Thomas, and if he's in Iquitos, then that's where I shall go. I'll be damned if I'll stay here twiddling my thumbs and worrying about you as I wait for your return!"

Nile rose from the railing, his thick brows together in a scowl, his golden eyes glittering dangerously. "Damnation and hellfire! How many times do I have to tell you, it's not safe!"

Maddie raised her chin obstinately. "We've had this same discussion several times before, and I'm growing tired of it! I've come this far without mishap, haven't I? I'm sure I can make the rest of the journey unscathed as well."

He whipped off his hat and ran his hand through his hair, mussing it. "This leg of the river is much more dangerous. There are more rapids and whirlpools, not to mention unfriendly natives with blowguns and poison darts waiting to ambush us at every turn. I'd be better off alone. Besides," he added in a wheedling voice, "I'm worried about Amy. She's all alone now. She'd appreciate the company of another Englishwoman."

"That's a low blow, Marcus, trying to play on my sympathies for Amy's lot out here. Well, it won't work. Amy has taken care of herself this long, she can take care of herself awhile longer."

He made an exasperated sound. "Please, Maddie. At least listen to reason."

Maddie shook her head. "No. I won't agree to it. I'm going with you, as we agreed. End of discussion." To emphasize her point, she sat back down, picked up her pen and papers, and went back to her writing, effectively dismissing him.

Or so she thought.

With a growl of rage, Nile strode over to where she was sitting, grasped her shoulders, and hauled her bodily from the chair so that she stood facing him.

This time, only Maddie's papers clutched in her hands stood between her and Nile, but unlike their confrontation at the pool, this one generated sparks of a different kind.

Maddie stared at his livid face, his eyes narrowed menacingly, and she was surprised to see real fear there as well as anger.

"I don't take orders from anyone, Miss Maddie-pigheaded-Dare," Nile muttered between clenched teeth, his fingers digging painfully into her shoulders as he shook her once. "If I say you're staying here, that's where you're staying, damned agreement or no damned agreement, is that clear?"

Maddie said nothing, just stared back at Nile, but her thoughts were racing almost as fast as her pulse. When she thought she had divined his true feelings disguised by this outburst, she said, "You're more of a danger to me than the Amazon."

Nile released her as if her shoulders had turned white-hot, and he stepped back away from her.

She continued relentlessly, "That's really what you're afraid of, isn't it, that you can't trust yourself to be alone with me?"

"And I have every reason to be afraid!" His jaw clenched and a muscle jumped with the effort of controlling himself. "Need I remind you of what almost happened down at the pool?"

"No."

"I . . . I almost forced myself on you." His voice shook with disgust and self-condemnation. "I'm nothing more than a . . . a rutting stallion."

Maddie touched his arm. "You mustn't blame yourself. I could have screamed, run from you, or dived back into the water until you had a chance to change your mind. But I didn't. You weren't entirely to blame. As I recall"—Maddie smiled at the pleasant memory—"I was not unwilling."

Nile's eyes narrowed suspiciously. "That did surprise me, considering that you are promised to another."

Caught off balance by the sudden shift in conversation, Maddie racked her brain, searching for some plausible explanation that didn't make her seem dishonest and faithless to poor Ben. After all, Nile didn't know the truth.

She hung her head as a blush heated her cheeks. "I just want you to know that I am not in the habit of making such brazen advances to a man, and I do apologize to you for my shocking behavior. I . . . I don't know what came over me, Nile. All I can say in my own defense is that I felt drawn to you because of all we've shared these past weeks."

Her explanation seemed to satisfy him. "And I thought I was strong enough to resist being alone with a woman, but I was wrong." A roguish smile twisted Nile's mouth as he looked her up and down in quick appraisal. "You are a beautiful woman, Maddie."

She returned his smile. "And it's taken you only five weeks to notice!"

"Oh, I noticed long ago, right from the first moment we clashed in the Explorers Club."

Nile's confession momentarily flustered her, and Maddie had to turn away from the relentless longing in his eyes.

"So the real reason you want me to stay here with Amy is so that I don't become a victim of your . . . masculine appetites, is that it?" she asked softly.

Nile sighed as he reached up and traced the line of her jaw with one finger. "I'm only a man, Maddie, with a man's desires. There's only so much temptation I can take."

She felt a shiver of delight skitter along her arms and had to resist with all her strength. "Sam told me you were dangerous."

"Did he, now? You should have listened to him. He knew what he was talking about."

Maddie hesitated. "Be that as it may, I must go with you to Iquitos. You know that."

Nile took his defeat gracefully. "I know. I promise to be on my best behavior from now on." His smile was bitter. "Once we find Thomas, I won't have to worry, now, will I?"

Without waiting for an answer, he turned and strode off.

Maddie watched him go, her thoughts in turmoil. Sam had warned her about the dangers of being alone with Nile Marcus, and she had been too arrogant and confident to heed him. Maddie had crossed paths with all types of men in her work, from tough, uncouth dockworkers to smooth, polished aristocrats, and always she had managed to remain aloof and unmoved by their blandishments. Even Ben had never had this effect on her. But Nile Marcus was different. She had never met a man quite like him before.

"Maddie, Maddie . . ." she murmured aloud. "Did you really expect to share a cage with a jaguar and come out unscathed?"

She sighed and forced her thoughts to return to her writing.

Amy stopped by the graveyard on her way back from the village.

As she stood beside Freddie's grave, she waited for the feeling of comfort to envelop her as it always did, but today there was nothing. All she felt was that terrible weight pressing against her shoulders like a gathering of storm clouds.

She clutched her cross and closed her eyes, but only the words of the Twenty-second Psalm would come: "My God, my God, why hast thou forsaken me? Why art thou so far from helping me, and from the words of my roaring?"

Still the Lord did not answer her.

Amy thought of her life here, seven years of doing the Lord's work without complaint or thought of reward, and all she could recall was hardship and misery rather than satisfaction. She thought of the jungle and the diseases, the savages so resistant to salvation even as they were enslaved and sold by the rubber men, and she was filled with a desolation the likes of which she had never known.

Suddenly her mind was filled with soothing, peaceful thoughts of the idyllic life she had known and left in Devonshire, and Amy smiled at the tender memory. She saw the centuries-old field-stone farmhouse on the edge of sweeping moors blanketed in heather and dotted with woolly white sheep. Her mother stood in the doorway, a welcoming smile lighting her careworn face, and her lips moved. Amy strained to hear what her mother was trying to say to her, but she couldn't because the words were spoken without sound.

The scream of a jaguar deep in the jungle sliced through Amy's consciousness like a knife, and her mother vanished immediately, taking the feeling of comfort with her. Amy knew great resentment, and tried to call the pleasant vision back, but Mary was hurrying toward her with an anxious expression on her face.

Amy waited for her, all thoughts of her home forgotten in the face of the present's demands.

After spending three days at the mission, Maddie was more convinced than ever that there was something wrong with Amy, and she resolved to discuss it with Nile the first time they were alone.

That opportunity occurred after supper one night, when Nile excused himself, saying he wanted to go down to the river to check with Jayme about the launch's readiness to continue on its journey.

Maddie rose hurriedly to follow. "Do you mind if I join you?"

Nile hesitated, and by the look in his eyes Maddie could see he was questioning the wisdom of being alone with her. But he shrugged. "Suit yourself."

They walked down the path toward the dock together, and when they were out of earshot Maddie said, "Nile, I think something's wrong with Amy."

He stopped in his tracks and looked down at her. "What do you mean?"

"Well, you've known her longer than I have, but doesn't her behavior strike you as a little odd?"

"Odd in what way?"

"She seems ... well, brooding and preoccupied all the time. She stares into space, and you have to call her name several times to catch her attention. Don't tell me you haven't noticed."

Nile gave her an exasperated look. "Of course I've noticed, but that's to be expected. Her brother died a short while ago. One can't expect her to be lighthearted and carefree under the circumstances, now, can one?"

"Of course not, but ..." Maddie groped for the right words to convince him. "Oh, I don't know. You're going to think me crazy for saying this, but it's just a feeling I have. I think Amy is on the verge of some sort of mental collapse."

"Oh, and now I suppose you're going to add physician to your long list of accomplishments?"

"I'm no expert, but I am a newspaper reporter with the capability of reading people. I saw something similar when I was in Africa. There was a woman missionary who behaved much the same as Amy"— Maddie took a deep breath—"just before she killed herself."

Now she had infuriated him. "Amy kill herself? Never! Amaryllis Gates is one of the strongest, sanest women I've ever known, present company included. If she weren't, she wouldn't have lasted this long out here."

He started walking fast as if to escape, but Maddie increased her stride and followed him.

"Just because she's survived this long doesn't mean she'll survive in the future," Maddie pointed out. "And you must admit, the Amazon has taken its toll on her physically. She looks ten years older than she really is."

That caused Nile to stop and regard her thoughtfully.

She continued. "Before, Amy had her brother to rely on for strength and support, as well as other missionaries. But they've all died, one by one, and now she's alone. How long can she be expected to carry on here by herself?"

"But she's not alone," he pointed out with maddening reasonableness. "She believes her God is with her."

"Perhaps God is telling her it's time to pack her bags and go elsewhere."

Her dry tone coaxed a smile out of him, but only for a second. He was serious almost immediately. "What do you suggest I do?"

"Talk to her. I would, but I'm afraid she would view my interference as presumptuous, since I'm a virtual stranger. Let her know we have her best interests at heart, and that it may be time for her to admit defeat and leave this place."

Nile shook his head. "Amy admit defeat? Never."

"Then she must be made to see reason."

They said nothing more about Amy as they walked down to the river together. They heard Jayme's soft, sweet voice even before they saw the launch, and after consulting with the Brazilian about the craft's readiness, Nile and Maddie walked back to the house.

The light was already fading, darkening the jungle around them and bringing out mosquitoes. Maddie found herself slapping her arms and neck almost without thinking, the moment she felt one of the insects alight.

By the time they got back to the house, the candles were already lit. Amy was seated in her wicker chair, her worn Bible cradled in her lap. But she didn't appear to be reading it. Her vacant stare was directed to someplace only she was aware of, and she gently rocked herself back and forth.

Maddie placed her hand on Nile's arm and gave him a look filled with the significance of what she had said earlier.

Nile's jaw tightened. "Amy?"

She didn't reply.

"*Amy!*" he called, louder and more forcefully this time.

She started, her head jerking up as recognition flooded into her eyes.

"I'm sorry," she murmured with an apologetic smile. "I must have been woolgathering and didn't hear you coming up the path."

As they climbed the steps to the veranda, Maddie asked, "What passage were you reading?"

Amy didn't reply at once, but glanced down guiltily at her Bible. "Why, the Psalms. I read them every evening before retiring. I always find them so comforting."

But Maddie suspected Amy had been caught up in her own world and wasn't reading anything at all.

The following morning, Nile awoke in a foul mood and with a headache so painful he felt as though he had drunk five bottles of whiskey.

But as he washed and shaved, he realized the throbbing was not due to intoxication, but from the sheer weight and magnitude of the problems he faced. First and foremost in his mind was finding Ben Thomas, for he was the key to learning who had murdered Provvy. Then he had to fight his unexpected and growing attraction to Maddie and the prospect of being alone with her. Now there was Amy to contend with.

As he dressed, he considered Maddie's words carefully. If she was right, if the Amazon had finally taken its toll on Amy, Nile had to find some way of persuading her to leave the mission and return to Manaus with them for her own safety.

He sighed heavily. That task was going to be the equivalent of emptying the Amazon with a teaspoon. This mission was the cornerstone of Amy's life, the tangible result of her beliefs. Her brother was buried here. She would not give it up without a fight.

"But if Maddie's right," he muttered aloud, glancing at his distorted reflection in the cracked mirror, "Amy will leave this place whether she wants to or not."

When Nile found Amy alone on the veranda, with Maddie nowhere in sight, he realized she had absented herself on purpose to give him time to talk to Amy alone.

"Good morning," Amy said, greeting him with a smile.

She seemed more herself this morning, her eyes bright and alert, without the vacant, hollow look Nile had seen there last night.

"Good morning," Nile replied, seating himself while Mary hovered at his side, serving *cafèzinhos* and a thick cereal made from manioc flour.

"So," Amy said, "when will you and Maddie be leaving for Iquitos to find this young man of hers?"

Nile sipped his coffee and shrugged. "First we have to pay a visit to Mr. Fitch's *estrada*."

Amy's gray eyes turned silver with anger and she shuddered. "Why would you want to go there?"

"Maddie wants to visit a rubber plantation and write an article about it for the *Clarion*. When Senhor Aguirre gave her a letter of introduction to the estimable Mr. Fitch, Maddie jumped at the chance."

Amy shook her head. "Can't you dissuade her

somehow? You know what horrors go on there. She'll be so shocked."

"Oh, I don't think there's much in this world that shocks Maddie. Besides, when her mind is made up, even God can't change it."

"Hold your tongue, Nile Marcus! You may be a dear friend, but there are only so many of your blasphemies that even I will tolerate."

He grinned. "That's because I'm such an engaging fellow."

He hoped his light, teasing words would lull Amy into a false sense of security and keep her guard down, and judging by the amusement that lit her face, he was succeeding.

Nile sat back. "And how have you been keeping, Amy?"

"Why, just fine."

"Really?" He made his voice heavy with skepticism.

Now a watchfulness crept into her eyes. "Yes, really. Why do you ask?"

"I'm just concerned about you out here alone in the wilderness, that's all."

"You needn't be concerned. God will provide, as He always has."

Did He send a bushmaster to poison Freddie? Nile thought, but he never uttered the words, for he knew they would be futile and only wrap Amy tighter in the mantle of her deep religious convictions.

"But you're all alone out here, Amy," he pointed out, "with no man to protect you. All of the men have died. You're all that's left."

A shadow of pain crossed her face and she looked away. "That is true. But I've written to London, and hopefully, more will be joining me soon."

"How soon?"

"I really don't know." She sounded annoyed. "That is up to the mission to decide."

"And what are you going to do in the meantime?"

Amy laughed, a hollow sound. "Dear Nile, your concern is touching but unnecessary."

He fought to keep his temper in check. "No, it's not. Amy, you think of yourself as a missionary first and a woman second. Need I remind you that you're the only white woman around for miles? What if one of Fitch's men decides to . . . take advantage of your situation?"

Her cheeks turned a delicate pink. "Nile Marcus, such language! If that were to happen, then I shall accept God's will as part of His divine plan for me."

Nile groaned. "Amy!"

"You needn't fear for my safety. I enjoy Senhor Aguirre's protection, so I highly doubt that one of his partner's men would dare go against their *patrão*'s edicts."

"All it would take is one renegade, Amy. At least when Freddie and the other men were here, there was someone to look after you and protect you. But they're gone," he added gently.

Amy rose, visibly annoyed as she grasped her cross. "What is the matter with you, Nile? Why do you keep pressing this point? You know I'll never leave here."

He stood and went to stand behind her, his hands resting lightly on her shoulders in a gesture of comfort. "Did you ever stop to think that maybe it's time you did leave?"

She whirled around to face him. "How can you ever suggest such a thing? This mission is my life!"

"Even if it costs you your own life or your sanity?"

The force of his anger caused Amy to take a step back. "My . . . my sanity . . . What are you talking about? I'm not insane, Nile."

He mentally cursed himself for blundering. "I know that, Amy, but for how long? How long can you, a proper Englishwoman, live out here alone, among savages, among rubber men who are less than savages, and come out unscathed?"

"I am not going mad, Nile! I'm *not*! How can you, an old and trusted friend, even think that?"

"I'm not saying you're mad, Amy," he said softly. "But loneliness can do strange things to a person. And you are lonely without Fred, aren't you?"

Tears welled in her eyes, turning them into rain-filled pools. "Yes, I am. I miss him so much!"

Nile went to her, took her in his arms, and held her while sobs shook her shoulders. "I know, Amy, I know."

When she finally stopped crying, she sniffed, "I'm sorry for the outburst, Nile. I don't know what came over me."

"No need to apologize," he replied, releasing her. "I shouldn't have pushed you the way I did."

She smiled up at him. "No, you shouldn't have. But I forgive you. Friends again?"

"Friends." Nile turned to go, then hesitated. "Just think about what I said, won't you?"

"I promise I will."

"That's all I ask." Then he turned and walked away.

After Nile disappeared into the house, Amy sat alone on the veranda and smiled to herself.

How sweet and touching of Nile to be so worried about me, she thought, but there's no reason. With the strength of the Lord to aid me, I'll be fine.

Feeling suddenly drained, Amy closed her eyes and rubbed her temples. She was back in Devonshire again, standing on a hillside with the warm summer sun on her back and a cool breeze caressing her face. Contentment and joy surrounded her. She could see Fred standing at the foot of the hill, motioning for her to join him. He was trying to say something to her, but the wind kept snatching the words out of his mouth and garbling them. She wanted so desperately to hear what he was saying.

Amy felt an insistent hand on her shoulder, and the lovely vision vanished, leaving her with an aching disappointment inside.

"Is Mama all right?" Mary asked, her dark eyes filled with concern.

"Of course I'm all right!" The moment Mary's eyes widened and she stepped back in fear, Amy was filled with remorse. She rose and hugged the other woman. "Forgive me for snapping at you, Mary, but Mama still feels sad for losing Don Fred."

Mary nodded. "Don Fred a good man." Then she turned and walked away.

Maddie, who had been lurking in the house, pounced on Nile the moment he came inside.

"Were you able to convince her to leave?" she asked.

"No. She's just as stubborn as you are." He rolled his eyes heavenward as if seeking strength. "Lord save me from stubborn women!"

"Perhaps I should talk to her."

Nile's hand on her arm stayed her. "I wouldn't, if I were you. Amaryllis, temperate soul that she is, just may lose her temper if she thinks we're all against her."

"I'll avoid the topic, then."

The moment Maddie stepped out onto the veranda and Amy greeted her with, "I suppose you're going to try to convince me to leave as well," she knew she would have to proceed carefully.

"No," Maddie replied, sitting down. "I'm merely here to ask you about Mr. Aguirre's partner, Haddon Fitch."

"That bastard!"

The vehemence in Amy's tone caused Maddie to rear back in shocked surprise.

Amy was contrite at once. "Lord forgive me. I know I should be more charitable, but that man is so vile, so despicable, I just can't bring myself to feel anything for him other than loathing."

Sensing a story, Maddie leaned forward. "Why do you hate him so?"

Amy sighed. "Oh, I'm sure he's no worse than any of the other rubber barons, but his atrocities are still an affront to decent God-fearing human beings."

Maddie understood at once. "Nile has told me how they enslave the Indians to work for them."

"Slavery . . . One man actually owning another in this day and age! And the women . . . Do you know that a man may buy—*buy*—an Indian woman for fifty pounds? They prize the *mulheres frescas*, the young girls, most highly."

"How terrible. Why hasn't anyone tried to put a stop to such practices?"

"Who's to stop them? There's no law out here. The Winchester repeating rifle is the only law, and might makes right." Amy fingered her cross and regained some semblance of control.

"It must be very frustrating for you, to try to help these people against such overwhelming odds."

"Oh, yes," Amy said bitterly. "We've had to look the other way because we rely on his protection and Senhor Aguirre's good graces even to be here." She looked at Maddie long and hard. "Take my advice: stay away from Haddon Fitch. You and Nile just go back down the Juruá and up to Iquitos to find Ben Thomas."

"I can't. First and foremost, I'm a newspaper reporter, and I know my readers would be interested to read about a rubber plantation. Since Senhor Aguirre has given me a letter of introduction, I can't waste it."

Amy studied her again. "You are a most remarkable woman, Maddie."

"Oh, no, it's you who are remarkable." Maddie looked around at the forest all around, the wildness of the place. "You face danger each day just by living out here, and you manage to survive."

A strange look passed across Amy's face. "But just barely . . ." she murmured so softly that Maddie had to strain to hear her.

"Then why do you stay?"

Anger flashed in Amy's eyes for a second, to be replaced by a stoic calm. "Because I could no more stop being a missionary than you could stop being what you are."

Maddie just stared at her in surprise, then nodded in mute understanding.

The following morning, Nile and Maddie packed their few belongings, said good-bye to Amy, and joined Jayme in the launch for the ride upriver to Fitch's *estrada*.

12

Jayme's launch hadn't traveled half a mile down the Juruá River when it was accosted by a larger launch filled with a dozen vicious-looking men bearing rifles.

Maddie stepped closer to Nile. "Who are those men, and do they mean us harm?"

"They are part of Fitch's army," he replied, never taking his eyes off the rapidly approaching launch.

She was both surprised and curious. "The man needs an army? Whatever for?"

"To protect his investment. Aguirre doesn't own this river, he merely took it over by force and controls it through brute strength, but he needs armed guards to make sure his rubber is delivered without interruption. On land, more men patrol the *estradas* to make sure the *seringueiros*—the men who tap the rubber trees—do their work."

"And these are part of the six-hundred-man army you once told me about?"

"The very same."

Maddie glanced at him. "I am impressed."

"You're supposed to be."

As the other launch drew alongside Jayme's boat, one of Fitch's men called out something in Portuguese that sounded suspiciously like a warning. Nile merely waved, smiled, and said something in return that must have convinced the other man they meant no harm, for he nodded curtly and signaled them to proceed.

Maddie was conscious of a dozen dark eyes staring at her in blatant interest, but she kept her own gaze averted. She heard one man make a comment to his compatriots, followed by laughter that could not have been construed as anything but ribald.

When the boat full of leering men had passed them, Maddie said to Nile, "What did that man say about me?"

"Something very crude that I will not repeat."

"I suspected as much."

Nile looked at her, a flash of annoyance in his eyes. "What do you expect? You're a beautiful white woman out here in the middle of nowhere where the men outnumber the women by probably a thousand to one. You're a rarity, a commodity many of them would fight for."

"A commodity! Well, thank you very much!"

Her indignation amused him, for a smile tugged at the corners of his mouth, then vanished, to be replaced by a more somber expression.

"That's all you are out here," he said, "a commodity, like rubber or soap, to be acquired and used, with no value beyond what someone thinks you're worth. I'll have you know that men have fought and died over women out here."

Maddie frowned in distaste. "How barbaric."

"Yes, it is."

"And I suppose the women have no say in the matter."

"Those who are the strongest have the greatest say."

"Then why wasn't Provvy's woman ever harmed, or Amaryllis?"

Nile rested his forearms on the railing and leaned against it as he stared out into the jungle. "He did have to fight another man for her once."

That startled her. "Did he win?"

"They fought with knives and Provvy won by slitting his opponent's throat. But after that, the other men respected his right to Inge and left them both alone. As for Amaryllis, she enjoys Aguirre's protection, but I still fear for her safety."

"Perhaps when we return from Iquitos with Ben, we can persuade her to leave the mission and come with us."

Nile's jaw hardened. "We'll have to do something. I don't want her to disappear into Fitch's brothel."

"He has his own brothel?"

"Of course. But it's not like the brothels of Manaus. There the women are free to come and go as they choose. Fitch's brothel is filled with captive Indian women who are nothing more than slaves for his men."

Maddie reared back in indignation. "That's horrible! Can't anything be done to stop such a practice?"

"No," Nile replied wearily. "As I told you countless times before we started on this expedition, nothing can be done. And if I so much as catch you trying, I'll take you over my knee and make sure you don't sit down for a week."

"If you so much as touch me, Nile Marcus, I'll—"

"Maddie, this is not some child's game we're playing!" He whirled on her, grasped her shoulders in a desperate grip, and shook her for emphasis. "You mustn't interfere with anything you see, no matter how horrible. It could mean our very lives. You may not care about yours, but I hope to live to a ripe old age." His tawny eyes bored into hers. "Do you understand?"

She stared at him for what seemed like hours, her idealism and sense of justice warring with the reality of their situation and the truth of Nile's words.

Finally she said, "No matter how outraged I become, I'm not about to do anything that will jeopardize our lives. I wouldn't want your blood on my hands."

His hands fell away from her shoulders and he drew his forearm across his brow. "I know that. But I also know you're independent, strong-willed, and hate injustice."

"True. But I'm not a fool. This is Haddon Fitch's domain, and I can accept the fact that his word is law and nothing can be done to change that."

Nile scowled, then turned away from her.

"What's the matter now?" Maddie demanded. "I've just promised not to put us in any danger."

He shrugged. "I know that. It's just that I have a bad feeling about this. I think we should just forget all about Fitch, turn around, and head straight for Iquitos."

"But I have Aguirre's letter of introduction," Maddie pointed out. "Surely that guarantees us a welcome from Mr. Fitch, as well as his cooperation."

Nile rubbed his jaw. "I suppose I am being overly cautious. Fitch knows me, and as much as I despise him, I've never had any problems with him. He seems to respect me."

"See, there's nothing to worry about," Maddie said. "If I didn't need an article about a rubber plantation for the *Clarion*, I'd be the first one to say let's bypass it and go straight to Iquitos. But I do need such an article, so let's make the stop, then be on our way."

Nile agreed, and they fell into a companionable silence.

Maddie couldn't believe her eyes.

On the left-hand side of the river stretched a long pier, and tied to it were dozens of dugout canoes filled with what looked like huge black smoke-cured hams. Other canoes were coming down the river toward them, and as these boats pulled up to the pier, more workers began unloading them, all the while watched over by armed men.

Maddie observed the steady stream of canoes come and go, her interest heightened. "What's going on here?" she asked Nile.

"Today is Saturday, Fitch's delivery day," he replied. "Once a week, all of the tappers from the *estradas* upriver deliver their rubber consignment for the week."

"Those jiggling black balls are rubber?"

Nile nodded. "They're called *peles* and they weigh about two hundred pounds. The tappers collect the white sap from the trees, then bring it to their smokehouse to be cured over a fire of oily palm nuts. They dip the broad blade of a long wooden paddle into the latex, building up layer after layer of the stuff until it forms the hard ball you see there of the high quality called 'Pará Fine Hard' rubber."

"Fascinating. Then what happens?"

"The *peles* are delivered here, to Aguirre's *barracão*, the main trading post, where they await the steamships to take them to the warehouses in Manaus. From there, they're shipped to Liverpool or New York to make Aguirre and Fitch even richer than they already are."

Maddie wrinkled her nose as she sniffed the air. "Rubber, the perfume of the Amazon."

Nile nodded and smiled as he remembered the quote and where they had first heard it. "The scent of money."

Maddie peered beyond the busy wharf, her reporter's curiosity whetted even further. "And what's back there?"

"The trading post itself and Fitch's residence,

which is much grander than the mission's. Back farther still is a barracks for his men, the stables and . . . other buildings."

Maddie knew he was referring to the brothel, but she resolutely put such thoughts out of her mind. She was here to write an article, not to judge what went on here. She would not jeopardize their lives for something she could not hope to change.

Jayme docked the launch at the busy pier, and Nile disembarked, then assisted Maddie.

The moment Maddie stepped onto the pier, all work ceased simultaneously for several seconds, and once again she felt dozens of greedy dark eyes roaming over her, lighting up with expectation as they brazenly drank their fill.

For the first time in a long while, Maddie felt the stirrings of uneasiness. She had the unmistakable sensation of being surrounded by wolves just waiting for their leader's signal to attack and devour her.

Instinctively Maddie's hand tightened on Nile's arm and she moved closer to him, publicly acknowledging him as her protector. The men saw the gesture, backed off mentally, and returned to their work.

Nile spoke to one of the men, received his answer, and started leading Maddie away from the pier.

"What did you say to him?" she murmured, feeling those eyes boring into her back as she moved past.

"I asked him where his *patrão* was," Nile replied. "His patron, Mr. Fitch, is at his residence, so we shall make ourselves known to him and present him with your letter of introduction and hope he sends us on our way."

"Now, Nile . . ."

"I can't help it. This place makes me uneasy."

"I know what you mean." Maddie shuddered. "I could feel those men undressing me with their eyes."

Nile stopped and looked at her, appeal written on his face. "It's not too late for us to turn back."

"I would if I could, but I need my story. Sam specifically asked for an article about a rubber baron, and this is a perfect opportunity." Maddie smiled mischievously as she slipped her arm through his and continued walking. "Besides, with the King of the Orchid Hunters to protect me, I have nothing to fear from any man."

"Hmph. I hope you're right."

"Oh, I have every confidence in you."

As Nile had promised, Fitch's main house was much larger than Amy's at the mission, but was built in a similar style with a veranda running the length of the house and topped with a thatched roof. It was set in a large clearing, but bounded on three sides by the jungle.

When they approached the front of the house, Maddie noticed three young Indian women on the veranda. One was seated in a rocking chair, fanning herself lazily with a palm frond, while the second was having her hair combed by the third. The first two wore demure white dresses similar to the kind Mary wore at the mission, but the third was completely naked, save for a loincloth.

Maddie heard Nile make a strangled sound deep in his throat, and when she looked over at him, she saw that he was blushing and trying not to look at the woman.

"That is Fitch's personal harem," he whispered to Maddie. "Those are his concubines."

Her eyes widened. "He dallies with three women? Rather greedy of him, don't you think?"

"I daresay he doesn't dally with all three at once."

"I should hope not," Maddie murmured. "They are beautiful."

"They're all *mamelucas*—half white, half Indian, handpicked by Fitch himself for just that very reason. It's one of the reasons Amy despises him so much."

Maddie squared her shoulders and took a deep breath. "A veritable *ménage à quatre*. Well, this is certainly going to be an interesting visit, I must say."

"Fitch is a law unto himself, more like a dictator than a king. He can do anything he wants out here."

When they approached the veranda, the women stopped what they were doing and stared at Maddie and Nile out of curious black eyes, but said nothing. The half-naked one made no attempt to leave or cover herself, even in Nile's presence.

Nile greeted them in some strange tongue Maddie had never heard him use before, but assumed it was the women's native language, for two of them smiled shyly and made a brief reply.

"Well, well," came a booming but unmistakably English voice from the doorway. "What have we here? Guests?"

Maddie turned her head to see a tall, thin man dressed casually all in white emerge from the doorway. He had curly rust-red hair, a freckled face, and an impressive pointed mustache. Attached to his belt was a whip.

He smiled, revealing perfect white teeth save for a chipped front tooth. "If it isn't Nile Marcus."

"Fitch," Nile said, extending his hand.

Fitch grasped Nile's hand, but his pale blue eyes were on Maddie. "And who is this divine creature?"

"Maddie Dare," Nile replied, releasing the other man's hand. "This is Haddon Fitch. Fitch, this is Maddie Dare."

Suddenly Fitch noticed his women. His face reddening further in anger, he shouted something in their native tongue that caused the half-naked one to shrink away as if every word were a whip's lash and slink away back inside the house when he was done.

When his anger cooled, he turned back to Maddie with an apologetic smile. "You must forgive Tia. She is still something of a savage, I'm afraid, with no sense of modesty where company is concerned." Fitch took her hand and bowed over it. "The pleasure is all mine, Miss Dare."

Maddie inclined her head. "Mr. Fitch."

When he raised his head again, he studied her as he stroked his mustache, those light eyes roving over her with interest and approval.

"Tell me, Miss Dare," he said, "what is a lovely Englishwoman such as yourself doing in this god-forsaken wilderness?"

"I am a journalist for a London newspaper called the *Morning Clarion*," she replied, "and I'm here to find my lost fiancé."

His rusty brows rose. "A lost fiancé ... how intriguing."

Maddie reached into one of her skirt's deep pockets and pulled out her letter of introduction. "I also have this letter from Senhor Aguirre."

Fitch took the letter, scanned it, then handed it back to her. "If Antonio wants me to offer you our hospitality and assistance, I shall be only too happy to oblige. Why don't we get you settled and then find you something to eat. I'm sure you're famished after your journey. I, regrettably, must attend to some estate business, so if you'll excuse me ..."

After giving instructions to an older, dour-faced woman who must have been his housekeeper, Haddon Fitch left them.

"So, what do you think of our host?" Nile asked Maddie.

They were sitting alone on the veranda, having

just finished a pleasant, filling meal of fish and spicy rice.

"Why, he's perfectly charming," Maddie replied.

"You seem surprised."

"I must confess that I am. He's not at all what I expected."

"And what did you expect?"

Maddie grew quiet and pensive. "Someone uncouth and tough. Someone with horns and cloven hooves, I suppose. Someone cold and soulless, like Calistro."

"Don't underestimate him. He *is* like Calistro. Haddon Fitch may be a cultured English gentleman on the surface, but he's as ruthless and tough as they come. He couldn't survive out here otherwise."

"I'll remember that."

"See that you do, because our estimable host returns."

Maddie looked to see Fitch come striding through the clearing with an air of absolute authority about him.

He skipped up the veranda steps, then whipped off his hat and ran a muscular forearm across his sweaty brow. "Damned heat. It never ends. One would think one would grow used to it, but one never does." Then he looked at Maddie and smiled. "Are the accommodations and food to your liking?"

"Just perfect. At last I'll be able to sleep in a real bed rather than a hammock or bunk."

"We do the best we can," he said, seating himself.

"Your best is excellent, as always," Nile said.

Fitch inclined his head to acknowledge the compliment, then turned to Maddie. "Do tell me about this quest of yours, Miss Dare."

Maddie told him all about Ben's disappearance, how she had come to Brazil to find him, and where their quest had taken them.

Fitch scowled. "A photographer, you say? I do

remember him stopping here, but he didn't stay. He went back to Provvy Brown's." He shook his head. "Poor Provvy. You know, of course, that he's dead?"

Nile leaned forward in his seat. "Amy told us. Do you know who could have killed him, and why?"

Fitch spread his hands in an apologetic gesture. "I haven't a clue. Inge insisted the photographer fellow murdered him for some uncut diamonds, but I didn't put much stock in her story. I questioned all of my men, and they didn't know either." He paused, then added, "You know how it is out here, Marcus. There is no law, except for myself."

The moment he spoke those words with such confidence, Maddie felt a shiver run up her arms at the blatant reminder.

Nile rose and went to lean against the veranda's railing. "Maddie's fiancé was the last man to see Provvy alive, and once we find him, I'm sure he'll be able to give us some clue as to who murdered Provvy."

"If it's one of my men," Fitch said, his voice hard, "I can assure you that he'll pay for what he's done."

Nile nodded, obviously moved by the other man's offer.

Seeing the pain etched in Nile's face, Maddie said to Fitch, "And what is an Englishman such as yourself doing out here? Why aren't you enjoying the amenities of Manaus like Senhor Aguirre?"

He smiled. "It's quite simple, Miss Dare. I'm here so both Don Antonio and I will enjoy bigger profits from our endeavors. If I were to stay in Manaus, we would just have to hire someone else to oversee the *estradas*. Since I thrive on the adventurous life almost as much as Marcus does, I remain here while my partner remains in Manaus. Such an arrangement suits us both."

He shrugged. "It won't last forever. Someday I shall return to England a rich man, but right now, here is where I shall stay."

What man wouldn't find such an arrangement suitable? Maddie thought. Your own harem, all the authority of a tyrant, and a fortune accumulating in some bank besides.

She just smiled. "You're very fortunate."

He returned her smile. "I think so."

Later that night, after a yawning Maddie had excused herself and retired, Nile sat on the veranda with Fitch, smoking cigars and drinking *cachaça*, a potent rum made from sugarcane.

They spoke of the future of Amazonian rubber for a while, with Fitch telling Nile about his expansion of the rubber *estradas*; then Nile told him about Manaus.

Finally they got around to Maddie, as Nile had suspected they would.

"Your Miss Dare is quite a stunner," Fitch said. "My men have been talking of nothing else all day. And my women are consumed by jealousy at having such a beauty in their midst."

Nile sipped his drink slowly. "Maddie is uncommonly beautiful."

Fitch exhaled a puff of smoke. "Is she your mistress?"

Nile didn't take offense at the blunt question. "No. She is my employer and I am her employee, hired to guide her on this fool's errand, that's all."

Fitch's light eyes widened as he took a long drag on his cigar; then he shook his head and chuckled. "How have you been able to keep your hands off her all this time? I know I wouldn't."

Nile stared into the depths of his glass and thought of that morning at the pool. He almost hadn't been able to resist her then.

He tossed down the last of his drink. "It's been hell, but she's a lady," he said, as if that were explanation enough.

"Would you sell her to me?"

The request took Nile by surprise, but he gave Fitch a cold, calculating stare. "She's not mine to sell."

Fitch shrugged as he flicked the ash from his cigar. "No one would have to know. We could make our . . . arrangements and you could leave without her."

"Amaryllis Gates would know."

"She's insignificant. Besides, all of those missionaries are dead, so she'll be leaving soon herself. Antonio is growing tired of being charitable."

"And what about Antonio? He's given Maddie his protection."

"Don't worry about Antonio. I can handle him."

Nile leaned back in his chair and studied the other man for a moment. "Do you really want her, Fitch?"

He shrugged again. "She would be an interesting diversion. I haven't had a white woman in so long I've forgotten what it feels like."

"And when you grow tired of her?"

"I'm sure one of my *seringueiros* would take her off my hands."

Nile felt sick to his stomach, and tried to hide his revulsion. Here was Haddon Fitch discussing Maddie as if she were a brood mare to be bought and sold without any consideration for her desires.

"I can't let you do it, Fitch," he said, his voice low.

"What are you going to do to stop me?" he said, plainly amused.

Nile's body went rigid. "I know I can't stop you from taking her, if you really want to. But at least I can try. And I will try, make no mistake. You may kill me, but I won't go down without taking a few of your men with me. The woman is under my protection, and I take my duties seriously. It's a matter of honor with me. You understand that, don't you, Fitch?"

The other man stroked his mustache and studied him out of hard, expressionless eyes. Nile's mouth tasted sour with fear and the realization that he was a dead man if Fitch so desired it.

Then Fitch broke out in his wide smile. "I've always admired you, Marcus, and because I do admire you so much, I'm going to let you keep her, if she means that much to you."

As if Maddie were even his to give so magnanimously.

Nile said nothing, for he couldn't bring himself to thank Fitch, even for his life. He rose instead. "If you'll excuse me, I'm going to bed."

Fitch rose with him. "If you, ah, would like some company tonight, I can vouch for any one or all three of my women, especially Tia, who seems to have taken a fancy to you herself."

"You're too generous," Nile said, fighting to keep his face from showing the disgust he felt, "but I'm exhausted. I'm afraid I couldn't do the ladies justice tonight."

Fitch burst out laughing and clapped him on the shoulder. "I think it's thoughts of your Miss Dare that exhaust you, my friend."

Nile managed to force a smile in return. "You're probably right, Fitch, you're probably right."

"Sick, depraved bastard," Nile muttered under his breath.

He suspected Fitch had given him the room next to his for the express purpose of shocking or tormenting him. As Nile lay on the comfortable bed, his hands behind his head as he stared at the filmy mosquito netting, he could hear the unmistakable sounds of fornication through the thin walls.

Three female voices and one male moaning and giggling in the night . . .

Nile closed his mind to the distraction and forced himself to concentrate on other thoughts, notably Fitch's offer for Maddie.

"It would have served her right," he muttered to himself. "I warned her time and again the Amazon was no place for a lady, but she wouldn't listen."

But no, even Fitch was too high a price for being strong-willed and stubborn. Still, Nile wasn't above telling Maddie later of the fate that had almost befallen her.

As the sounds from next door grew more frenzied, Nile found himself losing control of his thoughts. He imagined Maddie lying beside him, her soft golden hair spread out on the pillow, her blue eyes dark with invitation. He longed to taste her breasts again, as he had at the pool, but this time he wouldn't stop. He would taste every inch of her, and then, when he had her writhing helplessly in his arms, he would possess her with infinite slowness until she was truly his.

Nile ground his teeth together as he felt his manhood throb and swell with a desire demanding to be slaked. Swearing under his breath, he swung his legs over the edge of the bed and buried his head in his hands, breathing deeply.

It didn't help. He was on fire for her. He had to have her. It didn't matter that she belonged to another. It mattered even less that she might not want him.

He rose, slipped on his trousers, and headed for the door, his steps resolute. When he came to the door, he paused, and that was when he noticed that the other room had become abruptly silent, as if its occupants were listening and waiting to see what he would do.

Nile stood there, white-hot anger replacing desire as comprehension dawned. He turned, crossed the room, and unbuckled his belt, letting it fall with his trousers so that the buckle made an audible clunk as it hit the floor. Then he went back to bed.

He would not be raping Maddie tonight for Fitch's perverted amusement.

He closed his eyes and breathed slowly through his open mouth. Gradually the fire died, leaving him cold with the agony of longing, but triumphant.

He heard laughter next door, then silence.

The next morning, as Maddie and Nile were having breakfast alone on the veranda, he surprised her by saying, "I think we should leave here as soon as possible."

She regarded him with a flash of annoyance. "But we only just arrived yesterday. And besides, I haven't gotten enough information about rubber to write my article."

His golden eyes darkened with anger. "Damnation and hellfire! Is that all you ever think about, your damned articles!"

Maddie sensed at once that Nile was furious about something other than her writing. "What's wrong?" she asked softly. "Why are you being such a beast this morning?"

Before Nile could answer, Tia—fully clothed this time—came out on the veranda and stood there at the other end, not acknowledging their presence.

"It's nothing," Nile muttered, and Maddie knew better than to press the issue.

The sound of hoofbeats distracted her, and she looked up to see Haddon Fitch come riding up to the house. He was mounted on a small black horse and leading another. His whip lay coiled against his thigh like a snake.

Fitch looked up at her and called, "I hope you can ride, Miss Dare."

"I can," Maddie replied.

"Good, because it's the only way you'll see rubber being collected. So, if you'd care to join me . . ."

Before Maddie could reply, Nile rose to his feet and said to Fitch, "Where are you taking her?"

Fitch smiled. "Just to one of the rubber *estradas*. You needn't worry. She'll be perfectly safe with me."

Nile didn't look at all pleased, and Maddie wondered why. Something must have happened between the two men after she had retired last night, for she sensed an undercurrent of tension between them. She would speak to Nile later.

Maddie left the veranda and mounted the horse Fitch held for her, then waved to Nile as they started off.

They rode in silence until the house was out of sight; then Fitch turned in the saddle and said, "How much do you know about rubber, Miss Dare?"

Maddie, who always did exhaustive research before beginning an article, replied, "I know that rubber wasn't truly usable until the vulcanization process was invented in 1839."

Fitch nodded in approval. "Before that, it tended to harden in cold weather and turn into a sticky mass in the heat, rendering it impractical."

"And I also know that you owe your prosperity to the invention of the inflatable tire some ten years ago."

"Don't forget those most wonderful inventions that use inflatable tires, the bicycle and the automobile," Fitch added with a laugh.

They fell silent again as their horses waded through a shallow creek, the jungle rising thickly all around them. Even though it was not yet mid-morning, Maddie felt as though she were breathing in a steam bath, the heat was so oppressive.

Soon they reached what looked like a wide path cut through the jungle. Fitch stopped his horse, reached for a tin canteen slung over his saddle, and handed it to Maddie.

After Maddie drank her fill of cool, refreshing water, she handed the tin back to Fitch, who drank and started riding again.

"This is one of hundreds of rubber *estradas* Aguirre and I own," he explained. "Each trail forms a loop, and every day our tappers follow their routes, collecting rubber from the *Hevea brasiliensis* trees."

In the distance, Maddie heard a dull thwack-thwack sound that grew louder with every step their horses took.

"What's that sound?" she asked.

"That's the sound of a machete cutting into the rubber tree's bark. When the cut is made, a tin cup is attached to the tree to collect the latex. Later on in the day, the tappers return to empty the full cups into larger containers. Each man has a quota to fill."

And if he doesn't fill that quota? Maddie asked herself.

As they rounded a bend in the trail, Maddie saw a tapper hard at work. He was dressed all in white, with a wide-brimmed palm-frond hat on his head and a collection of tin cups attached to his waist. When he heard the sound of approaching hoofbeats, he glanced up once, then returned to his work, swinging the machete slowly and cutting a deep gash in the silvery bark of a rubber tree. As the sap oozed from the cut like white blood from a wound, the tapper quickly attached a cup to catch the precious liquid. That done, he walked on to the next tree, his tin cups clinking together with his every step.

Maddie noticed that the rubber trees didn't grow together, but were spaced far apart, and she mentioned this to Fitch.

Her observation amused him, for he grinned. "This is the jungle, Miss Dare, not some nursery with trees in neat, orderly rows."

"So your tappers might have to walk a great distance before they come to another rubber tree."

"Oh, yes."

Maddie shook her head. "What a way to earn one's daily bread."

Fitch just shrugged. He ruled here. His tappers' welfare was obviously of no concern, as long as they produced and filled his pockets.

"Do you know that most of the tappers collect the rubber without ever even knowing what it's for? They've never seen an inflatable tire, let alone a bicycle or an automobile."

Maddie made no comment, for even as indignation swelled in her breast at the man's callous indifference, she remembered Nile's countless warnings never to interfere, so she kept still.

"Seen enough?" Fitch asked.

I'd like to see your brothel, Maddie said to herself, and all the unfortunate Indian women you've enslaved there.

But she managed to smile and nod.

"Let's get back to the depot, then."

They turned their horses and rode off.

When they arrived back at the house, Nile was waiting on the veranda. Maddie had never seen him look so relieved.

"Did you get enough information for your article?" he asked.

"Yes," she replied, dismounting. Then she looked

up at Fitch. "It was all very fascinating. I'm sure my readers will be interested as well."

"Glad to be of service," Fitch said, his pale eyes twinkling. "Now, if you'll excuse me, I have work to do today."

Once Fitch was out of earshot and Maddie joined Nile on the veranda, he turned to her and said, "Let's walk down to the launch. I've got to talk to you. In private."

Before Maddie could say another word, Nile had grasped her elbow and was guiding her off the veranda and down the path leading to the pier.

"What's wrong?" Maddie kept her voice low as several armed men walked by. "You've been skittish ever since last night."

"We've got to leave as fast as we can. We're in danger here."

"In danger? Mr. Fitch seems most hospitable, for all his depravity."

"You weren't with us on the veranda last night." He squeezed her elbow, making her wince. "He wanted to buy you, Maddie."

She stared at him. "Buy me? You can't be serious."

"I am deadly serious. And so was Fitch, the bastard."

"What did you tell him?"

"That you weren't mine to sell, and ..." He hesitated, then made a dismissing motion with his hand. "Let's just say I convinced him otherwise."

Maddie slipped her arm through Nile's, for she felt in dire need of his strength as the enormity of her situation hit her. If Fitch really wanted her, there was nothing Nile could do, for he was outnumbered. Though Nile hadn't said as much, Maddie suspected that he would fight to protect her, even to the death.

"When should we leave?" she asked.

"Tomorrow," Nile replied. "Just tell Fitch your

fiancé awaits you in Iquitos and you're eager to find him. You'll thank him for his hospitality, but insist that we be on our way. I'll have Jayme get the launch ready and we'll leave tomorrow morning."

"I think that would be most prudent."

"Damn right," Nile replied.

That afternoon, Maddie told their host they would be leaving tomorrow morning because she was eager to travel on to Iquitos and her fiancé. Fitch charmingly pressed her to remain for a few more days, since he enjoyed his countrymen's company so much and had so little opportunity to indulge it, but Maddie remained firm.

When evening came, she retired early to her room to start work on her latest article, but merely describing a rubber plantation sounded so dull. She needed something to pique her readers' interest, perhaps even shock them out of their complacency. She'd have given anything to see Fitch's brothel with her own eyes.

The next morning at daybreak, Maddie awoke to the sound of screaming.

She sat up in bed, her heart racing. She listened. There it was again, a scream too human and too much in agony to be made by any howler monkey. Then it stopped.

Maddie waited. When nothing broke the silence, not even the sound of Fitch or his women stirring in the house, she rose, hurriedly dressed, and left to investigate.

The sky was barely pink, and patches of mist still rose from the ground as Maddie hurried toward the only other path leading away from the house. She looked and listened for any sign of Fitch's armed guards, but it must have been too early for them to be up and about yet.

Maddie followed the path into the jungle, taking

care not to trip over vines that sometimes curled over the path. Within minutes she came upon the source of the screams she had heard.

In a small clearing stood a whipping post, and bound to the crossbeam was an Indian woman, her bowed head and buckled knees indicating she was either unconscious or dead from the brutal beating she had received.

Maddie clapped her hand over her mouth to physically stifle the scream of horror and revulsion that rose to her throat. The woman's bare back was cross-hatched almost to the bone with deep, bloody cuts inflicted by a whip with a strong arm behind it.

For an agonizing moment that seemed like a hundred years, Maddie just stood there paralyzed with shock and indecision. Should she see if the woman was still alive? Cut her down? Tell someone and bring aid?

Then Maddie recalled Nile's admonition to never interfere, so she stifled her outrage, whirled on her heel, and started back to the house.

She couldn't let her pity for the hapless woman override her own instincts for survival. She couldn't.

When Maddie reached the house, she managed to slip back unseen to her room. There she mentally prepared herself, forcing herself to forget what she had just seen until she and Nile were away from this horrible place and its depraved master.

Maddie stood on the launch's deck with Nile, watching Fitch's trading post disappear behind a bend in the river.

She didn't know how she had managed it, but she had saved them.

All morning she had kept her emotions under tight rein, acting as though she were nothing more than a woman in love eager to be on her way to be reunited with her fiancé. She had smiled when she felt like screaming, moved with confidence when she felt like shuddering. She must have been very convincing, because even Nile hadn't suspected the agony that was eating at her insides like acid.

But he would soon know.

Without warning, Maddie began shaking so hard she didn't think she'd ever stop. She crossed her arms and almost doubled over.

"Maddie, what's wrong?" Nile barked, at her side in an instant, one hard, strong arm around her.

She opened her mouth to speak, but only strangled sobs emerged from her throat, dry and swollen from her efforts to keep her emotions locked in.

Nile enfolded her in his arms and she clung to him so tightly it was as though she would melt into him. But he offered her the strength and comfort she so desperately craved.

He just held her tightly, her head pressed against his shoulder, and when her shuddering subsided somewhat, he murmured, "Maddie?"

She stepped back but couldn't bear to release him, looking deeply into his puzzled eyes. "Oh, Nile, it was horrible, just horrible!"

He still held her. "What was so horrible? Tell me."

And she did, in a trembling, stammering voice, watching his face turn ashen with each revelation.

When she finished, Nile's reaction startled her. He grasped her shoulders, his fingers digging into them painfully as he shook her.

"You fool!" he rasped. "Didn't I tell you not to go snooping? You could have gotten us both killed!" Then he flung her away and went to lean against the rail to cool his anger.

Maddie didn't defend herself, because Nile was right. She just stood there hugging herself in her misery and feeling so stupid.

"Why was the woman beaten?" she asked.

"The Indians are regularly beaten," Nile replied wearily. "There's a saying here: 'They're not people, they're animals.' So if the men don't work, they're beaten. If the women don't . . . please their masters, they're beaten. What you saw was common practice among the rubber men. The Indians are nothing but animals to them, so they're beaten like animals."

Maddie shivered again. "I wish I could have helped her in some way."

"There's nothing you could have done. Just be thankful one of Fitch's men didn't see you and we were able to get out of there alive."

Maddie nodded and wiped her eyes with the back of her hand, then headed for her cabin down below. Just as she was about to descend the stairs, Nile said, "Congratulations."

She turned and looked at him in puzzlement. "For what?"

"For keeping your head this morning around Fitch. To see what you saw and to act as though nothing happened . . ." Nile shrugged. "That took a great deal of courage."

His compliment pleased her, for they weren't freely given. "Thank you. If you'll excuse me, I think I'll lie down for a while."

Lying in her bunk, Maddie tried to put the horrors of Fitch's heartless world out of her mind. Instead, she thought of Ben waiting for her in Iquitos, but that didn't comfort her. This entire venture seemed so pointless now. All she wanted to do was accomplish what she had set out to do and return to England.

But once they left the Amazon, that meant leaving Nile behind as well.

13

"Ben isn't here."

Maddie knotted her fingers together in helpless frustration and rising panic as she strode around Mr. Hessel's parlor. Her nerves were shattered, and she felt as though she were drowning in a cold, dark sea.

In the four days since she and Nile had arrived in the Peruvian city of Iquitos, a dismal, squalid place standing high on a bluff above the Amazon at the end of a bay, they had tramped through every raucous, dirty lodging house in the city searching for any sign of Ben. Maddie, with a watchful, armed Nile standing guard, had shown Ben's photograph to so many people, it was now worn and grimy from being handled and passed around so often. Each showing had been accompanied by a shake of the head. No one had ever seen this man. Ben was nowhere to be found.

Iquitos itself was taking its toll on Maddie, turning her short-tempered and cross. She had been expecting a city like Manaus, prosperous from the rubber boom, with some rudiments of civilization, not a hopeless backwater of open drains and pigs in the street gorging themselves on piles of stinking refuse left around even the most respectable-looking houses. Having to shoo away pecking chickens and dirty ducks waddling in dirtier puddles did nothing to improve Maddie's sour disposition, but when she and Nile just missed being splashed and soaked by the contents of a chamber pot thrown from an upstairs window, her normally iron resolve broke. After screaming at Nile that she was not going to spend a moment longer in this miserable city, even though they had comfortable lodgings with a German businessman, Maddie turned on her heel and returned there.

Now she stopped long enough to rub her aching forehead in vexation. "Ben's not here. We've looked everywhere in this stinking city, and no one has seen him." Maddie flung her hands into the air. "Where in the devil is he?"

Nile went to the window and gazed down at the river, its waters low at this time of year. He looked just as tired, with dark shadows underscoring his eyes, and shoulders slumped in fatigue. "You're asking me? I'm as much in the dark as you are."

"I don't understand it!" Maddie resumed her pacing. "Amy said Ben told her he was traveling upriver to Iquitos, so why isn't he here?"

Nile rubbed his hand across his face. "I don't know. As much as I hate to say this, maybe something happened to him along the way. Maybe he didn't reach Iquitos at all."

Maddie stopped, feeling the color drain from her face. "If he met with an accident or foul play, surely we would have heard something—anything— along the way."

It had taken them four days to reach Iquitos from the mission, and at none of the stops they made for fuel and food had anyone mentioned an accident on the river.

"Not necessarily," Nile said gently. "It's true that such news usually travels fast, but if something happened and no one witnessed it ..." He shrugged. "It could be weeks before anyone knew of it."

"But he was traveling by steamer, not a launch," Maddie pointed out, her voice rising in desperation. "There were many other passengers with him. Surely if all were lost—"

"Steamers have been known to go down without leaving a single survivor."

"You're very reassuring, you know that?" Maddie snapped, fighting back the tide of despair threatening to engulf her.

Nile was at her side in three strides. He took Maddie's icy hands in his and held them tightly. "I'm merely being realistic," he said. "I know this has been hard on you, especially after what you witnessed at Fitch's depot, but you have to face the fact that Ben Thomas may not be in Iquitos because he's become another casualty of the Amazon." Nile took a deep breath. "Either that, or he changed his mind after he left the mission and went somewhere else."

"But where else could he possibly go?"

"Back downriver, to Manaus."

Maddie pulled her hands free of his strong, warm clasp and shook her head in denial, the words pouring out of her heedlessly. "No, that's impossible. He's got to be here somewhere. That's the way we planned it."

The moment Maddie realized her mistake, she hurried to cover up. "Er, he's supposed to be here because Amy said he was going to Iquitos."

Nile grew very still, and his heavy brows came down in a scowl. "What did you say?"

Maddie widened her eyes innocently. "I said, Ben is supposed to be here because—"

"Before that. I distinctly heard you say, 'That's the way we planned it.'" His voice grew soft and menacing. "Planned what, Maddie?"

She smiled and tried to make light of a situation

that was growing more tense by the second. "Why, nothing. Nothing at all."

But Nile would not be dissuaded that easily.

He stood with his feet slightly apart, crossed his arms over his chest, and studied Maddie with his disconcerting, probing stare. She could read his very thoughts just from the subtle changes in his expression. First he narrowed his eyes in speculation as he considered and discarded possible implications of her imprudent words. Then his eyes widened in stunned disbelief, and finally his whole face went rigid with raw fury as he guessed the truth at last.

"Ben Thomas was never really lost at all, was he?"

Maddie knew there was no point in trying to evade the truth any longer. She was just too exhausted and overwrought to go on lying. She and Nile had shared much together these last few months, and he deserved better.

"No," she said. "I've known all along where he would be. I just pretended to follow his trail."

Nile just stood there looking as though he had been struck by lightning.

Maddie turned away, unable to bear the horrible accusation in his eyes a moment longer. "I guess I owe you some sort of explanation."

She felt herself grabbed by the shoulders in a painful punishing grip and whirled around to face a man who looked as if he could cheerfully feed her to piranhas.

"You *guess* you owe me some sort of explanation?" Nile roared. "Damnation and hellfire! You hire me under false pretenses, you risk both our lives, all for a . . . a *hoax*?"

Maddie would have shrunk back from his righteous wrath, but he held her so tightly she could barely move. "If you'll kindly release me, I'll explain."

He shook her once, then flung her away as if he couldn't bear to touch her. "Talk. And it had better be good."

Maddie took a deep breath to compose herself, but her heart kept racing out of control and her voice trembled. "You're right. My search for Ben Thomas is nothing but a hoax dreamed up by Sam Vincent and me to sell newspapers. We thought it had all the makings of a tearing good story. You remember . . . 'LADY REPORTER SEARCHES JUNGLE FOR LOST LOVE'? Only Ben Thomas isn't my fiancé."

Nile's jaw actually dropped. "He isn't your . . . ? Damnation and hellfire, so you lied about that too?"

The scorn dripping from every word made Maddie avert her eyes to the plush carpet at her feet. "Yes. It made for a better story, you see. Gave me a personal stake in the outcome, as it were. And since Ben was willing to go along with it, we didn't see the harm in stretching the truth just a bit."

Maddie added quickly, "Actually, at the time, I wanted Ben to be my fiancé. I've always loved him—or thought I did—from the first moment we worked together at the *Clarion*, but he always treated me rather like a little sister. I thought that if I followed him to the Amazon and pretended to rescue him, we would have the entire voyage home to be alone together. He would see me in a new light and perhaps fall in love with me."

Nile's sharp bark of laughter caused her to flinch. "What a bunch of idiotic drivel! And you pride yourself on being the equal of any man? . . ." He shook his head. "I'll tell you one thing. No man I know would ever be that stupid."

Maddie felt her cheeks grow pink, but she ignored his gibes. "So the three of us worked everything out down to the last detail. Ben would leave for Brazil ostensibly to take photographs for the *Clarion*. After a certain amount of time, his letters were to cease. I would become worried and hire a guide to help me track him down. After following Ben's trail, I was to discover him in Iquitos, well and unaware that his letters had never reached me in England. It wasn't as dramatic as finding him wandering around the jungle, being held hostile by ruthless savages or a victim of amnesia, but it was more realistic. We would return in triumph to the adulation of thousands of readers and an appreciable increase in the *Clarion's* circulation."

Nile raised his hands and clapped them together slowly, mocking her. "Bravo, Miss Dare, bravo. I applaud you for the liar and fraud that you are, and for concocting such a diabolical, deceitful plan. But the end justifies the means, doesn't it, as long as you get your precious story?"

"No, that's not—"

"You must be so proud of yourself. It's a pity you had to spoil it all by telling me."

She took a step forward, then hesitated. "I was going to tell you the truth, Nile, I swear it."

"When? When we found Thomas?"

"Yes."

"Why didn't you tell me the truth when you hired me?"

"Because Sam and I were afraid you wouldn't agree to be my guide."

"Well, both of you were right!" Nile strode over to her and grasped her face in one large hand, holding her steady while he gazed into her eyes. "If I had known what you were planning, I would have told you in no uncertain terms what you could do with your thousand pounds. I don't claim to be a saint, but I consider myself to be a man of some scruples and integrity. I would no more be party to such a hoax than I would beat a weak, defenseless woman, but damnation and hellfire, you sorely tempt me, Maddie Dare."

When he released her, Maddie said, "I don't blame you for being angry with me."

"Angry? Ha! That's an understatement if ever I heard one."

"And . . . and I wouldn't blame you if you washed your hands of me and left me here to rot."

He glared at her. "Don't even tempt me."

Maddie felt the panic rising again. "But it's gone all awry. Something has happened to Ben, and you've got to help me find him."

"I don't have to do a damn thing. You've made your bed, and now you can lie in it. I resent being tricked, lied to, and made to feel like the world's biggest fool."

"I'm sorry," Maddie murmured, forcing back tears. "I know I've hurt you, and I don't expect you to forgive me."

"Good, because I won't." He turned away from her, trembling with the force of his anger. Then he spun around. "Dammit, Maddie!" he cried. "I trusted you. How could you do this to me?"

Tears spilled onto her cheeks. "I'm sorry. I didn't mean to hurt you."

"Well, you did."

They fell silent, Nile bristling with indignation and Maddie contemplating the enormity of what she had done.

Finally she broke the silence. "But Ben doesn't deserve to suffer for my mistakes. He doesn't deserve to be abandoned."

Nile sighed heavily. "I agree. Despite what I think of you, I'll help you to find him."

Maddie felt faint with relief. "Thank you, Nile."

He didn't soften toward her. "But understand this: if I didn't need Thomas to help me find

Provvy's murderer, I would be leaving the both of you here to rot."

Maddie bowed her head contritely. She sensed rather than heard Nile approach, and raised her head to find him standing just inches away from her, his golden eyes still smoldering with some strong emotion she couldn't identify.

He reached up and slowly drew the backs of his fingers down her cheek in a sweet, soothing caress.

"You know," he murmured, his voice soft and seductive, "I was beginning to think I was wrong about you. I was even beginning to admire your spirit and courage and tenacity. There were times when I even desired you as a woman." Then a chill glazed his voice like a killing frost on a blade of grass. "But now I see that I was right about you all along."

His hand fell away and he stared at her with loathing written on his face. "You're nothing but a liar, a cheat, and a fraud. Christ, I've bedded whores with more morals than you! At least they were more honest."

Maddie flinched as if he had struck her, but said nothing in her own defense. What was there to say?

Nile whirled on his heel and left her standing there.

When Nile's footsteps faded away, Maddie sank onto the sofa, rested her elbows on her knees, and cradled her whirling head in her hands, cursing herself for her slip of the tongue.

She didn't know what was wrong with her. She had weathered adversities greater than this and her courage had never failed her before. Maddie Dare had always prided herself on her ability to make the best of a situation and bounce right back with more determination.

The Amazon had finally overwhelmed her, sap-

ping her strength. The heat, the insects, the barbaric Haddon Fitch ... And to top it off, Ben was
not where he was supposed to be.

Maddie straightened and leaned back. Where in
the hell was Ben? Once he had made what should
have been an uneventful trip up the Amazon to
Iquitos, leaving a trail so obvious even a blind man
could follow it, he was supposed to have found
rooms in a lodging house and wait for Maddie to
arrive and "rescue" him. But he hadn't.

The plan had gone awry somehow.

If something has happened to him, it's all my
fault, Maddie thought. I was the one who urged
him to agree to this, and I'm the one who'll never
forgive myself if he's come to any harm.

Yet as she sat there, she realized her concern for
Ben was not based on love, but guilt. That guilt had
caused her to lose her composure and blurt out the
truth to Nile.

If only he hadn't been so quick to pick up on her
slip of the tongue ...

Maddie rose and went to the window, but she
drew back when she saw Nile on the veranda, leaning on the railing and staring down at the river.
She could see only his profile, but she could tell he
was still infuriated.

Her own feelings astonished her. She had not
expected that revealing the truth to him would cut
her this deeply, making her feel as though she had
committed some unpardonable crime. Maddie was
a newspaper reporter, and the story always came
first, even at the cost of personal feelings. Yet that
thought didn't comfort her this time. She had lied
to Nile and betrayed him. He had every right to
think her contemptible.

"I promise you, Nile," she said aloud, "that I'll
make it up to you somehow."

Satisfied with that, Maddie turned and went back to her room.

Back on the river two days later, Nile still hadn't spoken to Maddie beyond a chilly, "It's time to eat," or "I'm going to bed."

He was still so furious with her he couldn't bear to look at her without feeling the anger well up anew like bile. So he busied himself with cleaning the guns, tending the steam engine under Jayme's alternately puzzled and amused direction, and watching the river for any sign of sandbars or submerged trees.

Maddie wisely stayed out of his way, keeping to the aft end of the launch, where she continued to scribble down more lies. Every once in a while, Nile would catch her staring at him hopefully, but he pointedly ignored her. Finally she gave up and returned to her writing.

Nile knew, however, that she wouldn't avoid him forever.

As he sat there cleaning one of the Winchesters for what seemed like the thirtieth time, he saw Maddie set down her papers and rise. Then he turned his attention back to the gun in his lap, though he could see her out of the corner of his eye, marching toward him in her determined stride.

"Well, Nile Marcus," she said, "do you intend to ignore me all the way to Manaus?"

He rubbed an imaginary spot on the barrel. "Yes."

She made an exasperated sound. "I never thought you were the sort of man who held a grudge."

He looked up at her. "And I never thought you were the sort of woman who would lie and cheat. I'm disappointed in you, Maddie."

Two spots of pink appeared on her cheeks. "How many times do I have to say I'm sorry for lying to you? I'll admit I should have told you the truth the moment Sam hired you."

"Ah, but you're not sorry for instigating this hoax in the first place, are you?"

She balled her hands into fists at her sides and whirled around. "You just don't understand."

Nile set down the gun and rose. "What is there to understand? You're deliberately duping people. You're making thousands of readers believe that you came to the wild, dangerous Amazon searching for your lost fiancé, when the real truth is that he wasn't lost, and he wasn't even your fiancé to begin with!"

"But it makes for a more exciting story," Maddie wailed.

"That's a lame excuse, and you know it. There's nothing you can say to justify your actions. It's fiction, not the truth. If your readers wanted some tall tale, they would read books, not a newspaper."

She shook her head again.

Nile continued with, "You're betraying your readers, people who look up to you and respect you. I saw them all come to see you off in Southampton. I heard them call out their good wishes for your safety and success. And you feel no remorse about lying to them. That's what infuriates me the most."

Maddie turned and faced him again, her chin raised an angry notch. "Well, what do you expect me to do, write an article exposing the hoax?"

Nile nodded benignly. "That would be only right."

"Even if I were to write such an article, Sam would never agree to publish it."

"So you think that lets you off the hook, do you? Well, I'm sure there are other newspapers in London that would be only too eager to publish such an exposé about a competitor."

"Are you daft?" Maddie scoffed. "That would mean the end of my career, and I won't do it."

Nile raised one brow. "Your work is worth compromising your integrity?"

"My work means everything to me. It's what I do, and what I am."

"If that's all you have in your life, I feel sorry for you."

She colored again and took a step toward him until they were almost nose-to-nose. "You can keep your pity, Nile Marcus, because I don't want it!"

"Evidently you don't want my respect either." His eyes roved over her face, seeking to melt her resistance. "There was a time back at the mission—at the bathing pool, to be precise—when I felt that my respect mattered a great deal to you, Maddie."

She took a deep breath, and he could tell that she was wavering. "It does matter to me, more than you think."

"Then prove it. Do what's right."

"It's not that simple, Nile."

"Why not?"

Maddie looked away and folded her arms, effectively creating a physical barrier between them. "Honest Nile Marcus. It must be wonderful to always know you're right about everything. Life is so clear-cut for you, isn't it? Always simple. Always black and white, with never any shades of gray."

"Not always," he replied, taken aback by her bitter, mocking tone, "but in this case, it seems pretty clear-cut."

"Well, it's not." She turned away from him. "There are several gray areas to this matter."

He came up behind her and let his hands hover over her shoulders as if he were about to touch her. But he didn't.

"Tell me what they are, Maddie," he murmured. "I like to think I'm a reasonable man. I want to understand why you did this, and why you feel you can't make it right."

"I . . . I can't."

Her refusal to trust him cut him sharply, and he backed away. He could feel her erect a wall between them, and he wanted to shake her.

"I'm listening, Maddie."

"There is no good reason," she replied flatly. "I agreed to do it to raise the *Clarion*'s circulation, that's all. I'm just as false and base as you think I am."

Even as she said it, she looked so unhappy that Nile sensed she was holding something back. "Suit yourself," he said.

Then Maddie said, "When we get back to London, are you going to expose me?"

Nile shook his head. "Don't look so scared, Maddie. I won't ruin your little scheme, because I don't intend returning to England with you. I'll stay with you until we find Ben Thomas to see if he knows anything at all about Provvy's death, but after that, we'll be free of each other. You can make up all the stories you want once you're back in England; I won't stop you. All I ask is that your boss sends me my fee, plus a little extra for duping me."

"Fine," Maddie said, surprising Nile by sounding more defeated than relieved.

Then she returned to her end of the launch and left him alone after that, keeping up that wall of coldness between them.

That evening, just as the sun was going down, Nile couldn't resist watching her standing there at the rail, for she always drew him like some sea siren and he seemed incapable of resisting her.

As she stood there, the red setting sun turning her ivory face into a mask of molten gold, Maddie looked both pensive and troubled, as if she were wrestling with private demons. Her smooth brow was furrowed, and her lips were tightly compressed into a thin, uncompromising line.

Despite his anger at her, Nile wanted to go to her, to hold her and cajole her into telling him what was wrong. He sensed there was more to this hoax than Maddie was telling him, something that was disturbing her, and he wanted to find out what it was. But whatever she had locked away inside of her, she wasn't about to share with him, and he wasn't going to push her. Her lack of trust both annoyed and saddened him.

Then, in a blinding flash of clarity, he realized why he was so angry with her. Part of it was because of the ease with which she seemed capable of deception. But what really bothered him was her confession that Ben Thomas never had been her fiancé. For in admitting that, Maddie had taken away one of Nile's chief reasons for keeping his distance. Now there was nothing to stop him from taking advantage of her except his own scruples.

As the sun set, Maddie raised her hand to brush back a stray tendril of hair that had escaped to brush her cheek. It was an unself-conscious gesture, yet so sensual in its grace that Nile had to swallow hard and look away.

He turned on his heel and went below before he did something he would surely regret.

Another day passed before they reached the mouth of the Juruá River.

Maddie, who had kept to herself with a kind of resolute wistfulness all that time, said to Nile, "Are we going to stop back at the mission before proceeding to Manaus?"

He nodded. "I'm going to make one last attempt to persuade Amaryllis to leave the mission and come with us."

"Do you think she will?"

"She's got to. It's too dangerous for her to remain out here alone."

Maddie looked out at the thin line of jungle. "Are you going to tell her what I did?"

Nile was silent for a moment, then said, "Your tawdry little secret is safe with me."

Maddie glanced at him gratefully. "Thank you."

"Why should you care what Amaryllis thinks of you?"

Maddie shrugged. "I like her. I just wouldn't want her to think ill of me, that's all."

Nile gave her an odd look, but said nothing.

As Jayme maneuvered the launch out of the Amazon's swift current and into the mouth of the Juruá, Maddie left Nile and returned to her chair, where she sat with her back toward him. She prayed that Nile would be able to convince Amy to join them. The building tension would surely have to ease if the missionary were on board for the rest of the journey.

Jayme's launch was barely into the mouth of the Juruá when Maddie saw one of Fitch's own patrol launches appear almost out of nowhere and come steaming toward them at a good clip.

A vision of the Indian woman, her back flayed open and running with rivulets of blood, flashed before Maddie's eyes, filling her with fear.

"Nile!" she cried, jumping to her feet.

He was at her side more quickly than she would have expected, concern registered on his face. "What is it?"

Maddie pointed to the other launch. "Fitch's men. What if they know I saw the Indian woman? What if they've come for us?"

"Don't worry," he said soothingly. "It's only a routine patrol to see who's invading Fitch's territory. Once they see who we are, they'll let us pass on to the mission."

"I hope so."

"Really, there's nothing to worry about." Then he went forward to greet Fitch's launch.

Maddie stayed where she was, for she thought it was best to keep in the background and let Nile deal with them. Just the memory of the rapacious way those swarthy men had eyed her the last time they had landed at Fitch's trading post was enough to set her teeth on edge.

Then the unexpected happened.

When the other launch was about fifty feet away and closing rapidly, Maddie saw Nile call out a greeting and raise his arm to wave. Without warning or provocation, two of Fitch's men raised their Winchesters to their shoulders, aimed, and fired.

Two shots rang out, shattering the stillness like breaking glass.

Maddie watched in horror as Nile's body jerked from the impact of bullets hitting him; then he pitched over the railing and plummeted headfirst into the river before she could think another thought.

"*Nile!*" she screamed as she watched him sink into the turbulent waters of the Juruá.

Maddie ran to the spot where he had been standing, clutched the railing, and leaned over, her eyes frantically searching the river for any sign of him.

"Nile!"

There was nothing, not even bubbles breaking the surface. He was gone.

"Jayme!" Maddie screamed.

Just as she turned to the Brazilian captain for aid, the sharp bark of more gunfire filled the air. Maddie watched in horror while bullets whizzed by her like angry wasps and tore into Jayme's defenseless body. He jerked violently several times from the impact, then slowly drifted to the deck of his beloved launch like a falling leaf, a look of surprise and denial passing across his features before they relaxed in the dark eternal sleep of death. Jayme would sing no more.

Shock eclipsed all rational thought from Maddie's mind, leaving only a red haze of murderous rage in its wake. She saw one of Nile's Winchesters lying there, picked it up, and aimed it at the men in the other launch, which was drawing ever closer.

One of Fitch's men shouted out what sounded like a warning to drop the gun, but Maddie was beyond caring what happened to her.

"Damn you!" she screamed, intending to kill several of them before she went down.

The men all dived for cover or flattened themselves on the deck as Maddie's finger convulsed on the Winchester's trigger, but instead of roaring, all it did was utter a feeble click-click-click.

Then she remembered. Nile had been cleaning the gun just before he died and hadn't bothered to reload it.

She swore, her eyes searching frantically for the bullets even as her tormentors rose and came out of hiding, brave and swaggering now that the mere woman was unarmed and no longer a threat. Before she could find the ammunition, the other launch had come alongside hers and some of Fitch's men were already climbing inside and securing it. She swore again between clenched teeth and flung away the useless weapon.

Maddie just stood there, her back straight and her arms rigid at her sides, her head raised proudly as they kept a wary distance.

I can't fight them all, she thought, so I will not debase myself by even trying. I will not cry and I will not scream. I will not give them the satisfaction of groveling for my life. If I'm to die, let it be with dignity and courage, as Nile did.

Out of the corner of her eye she saw two of the men lift Jayme's lifeless body and heave it overboard as if it were as unimportant as a sack of garbage. While her heart screamed in protest, she said nothing, but the resounding splash echoed like an explosion in her mind.

The men just laughed.

Now the man who appeared to be their leader walked toward her slowly, his cruel black eyes raking her up and down. But since he was several inches shorter than Maddie, she was able to look down her nose at him, and this simple physical advantage gave her courage.

He shouted some order at her in Portuguese.

"I speak only English," she replied haughtily, resisting the impulse to claw out his eyes or spit in his face.

The man may not have understood her words, but he did not mistake the utter contempt in her tone, for his swarthy face darkened and she saw murder in his eyes.

She held his gaze, refusing to look away, no matter how dire the consequences.

Victory was hers when he muttered something, walked over to her chair, and pointed at it, obviously meaning for Maddie to sit down. Holding her head as high as a princess, she strolled over to the chair and sat down, not letting her spine touch its back as she folded her hands in her lap.

One of the men took the wheel, ignoring the fact that he was standing in Jayme's blood. Fitch's launch turned around and started back upriver, followed meekly by its prize.

Maddie refused to think of Nile.

As she sat in her chair, staring straight ahead and ignoring the men around her as if they were invisible, she forced all thoughts of Nile and the violent way he had died out of her mind. There would be time to mourn him later, time to give in to the mindless grief lurking at the edge of her consciousness, waiting to take control and plunge her into blackest despair. But right now she couldn't afford the luxury. She needed her wits about her, for she had a feeling a greater ordeal for her was soon to begin.

Maddie began thinking logically like the reporter she was.

It was clear that Haddon Fitch wanted her alive. These were his men, and they wouldn't have killed Nile and Jayme without Fitch's orders, the same orders prohibiting them from harming or killing her, even when she had tried to kill them and insulted their leader.

Why did Fitch want her?

Maddie could think of only two reasons: either he had discovered she had seen the Indian woman he had ordered flogged to death, or he wanted her for one of his concubines.

That thought made Maddie's hands tremble in her lap, but she stopped it with the sheer force of her will before panic and fear reduced her to a blithering idiot.

Whatever Fitch's reasons for wanting her, he was responsible for the deaths of two men, and somehow she was going to see that he paid.

Only then did Maddie let shock wrap her in its soothing embrace until she felt and saw nothing, not even the mission's dock as they steamed by.

Maddie felt a rough hand shaking her shoulder and babbling something incomprehensible at her.

She came out of her trance to discover they had arrived at the trading post and Haddon Fitch himself was standing on the pier, his feet apart and hands on hips like some pirate king gloating over his captive.

Maddie took one deep, steadying breath, gather-

ing her composure and pushing back the wild, shrieking rage lurking at the back of her mind like a
caged beast waiting to be freed. Then she rose,
smoothed her skirt as if she were going to tea at
Buckingham Palace, then disembarked from the
launch, deliberately ignoring Fitch's outstretched
hand and jumping nimbly onto the pier.

As she faced him, she once again resisted the
impulse to strike and claw. She looked him squarely
in the eye and said only one word: "Why?"

His eyes widened and he shook his head in disbelief, something like respect in his voice as he said,
"You are a cool one. I'll say that for you."

Maddie waited. All the other men on the pier
stopped what they were doing and waited in silence as well, as if to see how their boss would
handle this woman.

"You saw something you weren't supposed to see,
my dear," Fitch said regretfully. "If it were anyone
else, I would merely overlook it and let you go on
your way, for Indians are flogged every day in the
Amazon. But you are a reporter for a British
newspaper, and our countrymen have invested a
great deal of money in our profitable undertaking
here. I can't take the chance that you might prick
their consciences and incite an investigation."

He shrugged and smiled. "Merely self-preservation
on my part."

Maddie smiled dryly at the irony of her situation. If she were an ordinary woman and not a
newspaper reporter, she would be free and Nile
and Jayme would still be alive.

"Did you have to kill Nile and Jayme?"

"You need to ask? I'm surprised at you. How
could I possibly get you away from Marcus while
there was still a breath in his body? No, I'm afraid
he had to die, and it saddened me as much as it
saddens you. I quite admired the fellow. And with

the launch's captain as a witness . . ." Fitch shrugged again. "I'm afraid he had to die too."

"Why didn't you have your men kill me as well, and be done with it?"

Fitch looked offended. "My dear Miss Dare, you mortally wound me. Why, I would no more dream of killing an Englishwoman than I would allow my Indians to escape the lash for laziness. I am an English gentleman, after all."

Maddie tried to repress a shudder at the man's callousness, but failed. "What do you intend to do with me, then?"

Fitch put a finger to his lips in an attitude of contemplation. "I haven't decided yet. Perhaps I shall keep you for myself. Perhaps I shall give you to my men."

He spoke casually, as if Maddie were some brightly wrapped Christmas parcel he couldn't quite decide whom to give to.

He is as mad as a March hare, she thought to herself, but as long as I can stay alive, the better my chances of escaping.

Maddie squared her shoulders. "Since it appears that I am to be your guest for an indefinite period of time, Mr. Fitch, I would appreciate being shown to my quarters. It has been a fatiguing morning, and I would like to rest."

"Brava, Miss Dare!" he exclaimed, his eyes lighting up in unexpected delight at her insolence. "I do so admire a woman with spirit, and I think we're going to get along famously together."

When Fitch crooked his arm and offered it to her as if he were escorting her to dinner in his manor house, Maddie ignored it and took a step forward, intending to precede him across the pier and up the path to his house. Suddenly she felt her braid grasped and yanked, sending flames of pain shooting across her scalp and causing her eyes to water.

With a gasp, she came to a standstill as her head was forced back against Fitch's shoulder.

"Don't push me, Miss Dare," came her captor's low, dangerous growl, his breath hot against her ear, the sharp scent of him filling her nostrils. "I will tolerate high spirits in a woman only so far. When I graciously offer you assistance of any kind, you will accept it. Is that clear?"

"Y-yes."

He released her at once and the pain stopped. "Fine. Let's try that again."

This time, when he offered his arm to Maddie, she took it without looking at him and just managed to keep from shuddering in revulsion.

As they walked back to the house, Fitch's good mood returned, and he chatted amiably to Maddie about all the comforts and limited privileges she would enjoy as his honored guest. But he quickly assured her that one of those privileges did not include her ever seeing or communicating with Amaryllis Gates, for obvious reasons. He also warned her against trying to escape, because not only was escape impossible in these impenetrable jungles patrolled by his own army, but also it would displease him, and then he would have her killed in a slow, unpleasant manner. He would regret taking such drastic measures, of course, but she had to understand he could not allow her to flout his will.

Perversely, Maddie found this threat reassuring rather than intimidating. She knew there were some fates worse than death, and at least Fitch was unwittingly giving her a way out if her captivity became intolerable.

When they reached the house, Maddie endured the sharp, gloating stares of Fitch's three concubines before being shown to the room that was to be her prison.

"I'll leave you alone now," Fitch said. "Despite

your brave facade, I know you'll want to break down and have a good cry. Any woman would, after seeing her lover murdered before her very eyes."

"Nile wasn't my lover," Maddie replied dully, feeling exhausted, yet needing to get in the last word.

"Oh, but he wanted to be. He told me so himself."

She turned to ask him what he meant, but Fitch was already gone and the door closed behind him before Maddie could utter another word.

When his footsteps died away, Maddie just stood in the center of the room and tried to resist the hysteria welling up inside her, fighting for dominance. She didn't want to break down and lose control, because once she allowed the shrieking to start, she knew she wouldn't be able to stop it, and she didn't want to give Fitch the satisfaction.

But then she thought of Nile.

He was dead, his life snuffed out like a candle flame pinched between two fingers. And it was all her fault. If he hadn't been with her, he would still be alive. He had given his life for a hoax.

Maddie opened her mind to the pain, welcoming it and letting it twist her insides and squeeze her heart dry. She hugged herself to keep from flying apart as her knees buckled and she sank to the floor. Then she screamed and kept on screaming until she ran out of tears and her throat closed up.

The last thing she remembered before sinking into blessed darkness was the faint sound of laughter.

14

Nile clung to the half-submerged tree with his good arm, his head out of water as he watched the launches turn and steam back upriver. When he was sure no one could see him, he swam for the bank a short distance away.

The moment his feet touched the muddy river bottom, he reached for one of the many vines overgrowing the steep bank and started hauling himself out. Each time he grasped a vine and put half of his weight on his left arm, it burned and hurt worse then an aching tooth where the bullet had grazed it, causing Nile to gasp in pain. Since his lungs were ready to burst after his long swim underwater to escape his attackers, he could barely afford the extra exertion.

In his weakened state, the riverbank loomed like a veritable mountain, but he was determined to conquer it. His will to survive was greater than his beaten body's desire to rest.

Nile concentrated his thoughts on Maddie, and the pain shrank to manageable proportions. He continued climbing, even though the bank was slick with mud beneath the rushes and lianas seeking to hinder his every step. Soon he was halfway up the slope. Minutes later, he reached the top.

Gasping and exhausted, Nile allowed himself the luxury of collapsing where he stood, but only until his pounding heart slowed. Then he got to work.

First he examined his wound and was relieved to see that while it was painful, it wasn't deep and nothing vital to his survival had been damaged. Still, it had to be attended to, so he removed his knife from the sheath strapped to his calf, pulled out his sodden shirttails, and proceeded to cut a strip of cloth to use as a bandage. Once he stanched the blood, he rose to his feet and looked around.

Luckily for him, Amaryllis' mission was on this side of the river. If he followed the riverbank, taking into account the thick jungle he would have to traverse, he would probably reach it in two hours if he didn't collapse from exhaustion first.

Fleetingly he wondered why Fitch's men had attacked them and tried to kill him, but he put the thought from his mind. There would be plenty of time to think about that later. Right now, his own survival was uppermost in his mind.

Gritting his teeth in determination Nile grasped his knife in his good right hand and eased himself into the jungle.

A face floated above him. It wasn't the face he longed to see, but an Indian woman's, familiar somehow. She was saying something, but seemed to be speaking from a great distance and he couldn't understand the garbled words.

"Nile!" Another voice, more distinct this time and even more familiar. "Nile, it's Amy. Can you hear me?"

His eyelids felt as heavy as stones, but he managed to open them. Amy's face, sick with worry, wavered, then slowly came into focus. "Amy?"

She smiled. "Yes, Nile, I'm here. We've found you and we're going to bring you back to the mission. Don't worry. Everything is going to be all right now."

He felt himself being lifted by several pairs of strong hands, and then he felt no more.

When Nile next opened his eyes, he was lying naked in a hammock with only a thin blanket covering the lower half of his body to preserve his modesty. A fresh, clean bandage was wrapped around his upper arm, and the pain had subsided somewhat. He recognized the room as being one in the mission house and he breathed a sigh of relief. Safe at last—at least for the moment.

He heard footsteps, and then Amy was standing there looking down at him.

"Ah, you're awake," she said with a smile. "How do you feel?"

"I'm parched and my arm hurts like hell, but other than that . . ." He shrugged.

Amy went over to a table, poured a tin cup of water, and brought it back to him. He drank it greedily and asked for more.

While Nile was drinking the second cup, Amy said, "Are you strong enough to tell me why Mary's tribesmen found you wandering around the jungle with a bullet wound in your arm? And why Maddie isn't with you?"

When Nile finished the water, he handed the cup back to her and cleared his throat. "Fitch's men attacked us."

Amy froze, and her gray eyes widened in disbelief. "Fitch's men? Are you sure?"

"Oh, yes. We were on our way back from Iquitos and had turned up the Juruá to come here to see you, when one of Fitch's launches started coming toward us. The next thing I knew, they were firing at me."

Amy gripped her silver cross, her face as white as the moon. "Dear Lord! What did you do?

Nile took a deep breath as he relived the event he had managed to suppress until now. "The second I felt one of the bullets graze my arm, I knew I'd be a dead man if I stayed on the launch, so I decided to take my chances in the river.

"I went over the rail. The minute I hit the water, I swam for my life as fast as I could."

Amy put her hand to her face, closed her eyes, and trembled. "Dear God, Nile. The blood could have drawn piranhas or caimans."

"My options weren't any better back at the launch, Amy, not with Fitch's men out to murder me. Luckily for me, any piranhas were feeding elsewhere. I managed to surface for air once or twice without being noticed. Then I swam for shore, and here I am."

"But what about Maddie and your launch's captain? Did they kill them too?"

A muscle twitched in Nile's jaw. "I don't think so, but I don't know for certain. I did hear several other shots after Fitch's men boarded the launch." When Amy turned even paler, Nile said sharply, "Amy, are you all right?"

She brushed away his concern with a wave of her hand. "I'll be all right. I'm just . . . stunned, that's all. Why would Haddon Fitch even do such a thing? I know he's barbaric to the Indians, but he's never threatened any whites before. We've coexisted rather peacefully with him, and even enjoyed his protection."

Nile sighed heavily and closed his eyes. "I think it may be because Maddie saw something she shouldn't have when we were there."

"What did she see?"

"The morning we left for Iquitos, the little fool decided to go for a morning walk. She came across one of Fitch's whipping posts. The Indian woman who had been flogged to death was still tied to it."

"Oh, dear God!" Amy swayed and just managed to sink into a nearby chair before she collapsed.

"She prudently kept what she had seen to herself

until we were well away from the trading post—I will say that for her. But somehow Fitch must have found out about it. Perhaps one of his men saw her on the path that morning and reported it to Fitch. He knew we'd come back this way to see you, so he had his men lying in wait for us, and they ambushed us."

Amy scowled. "But why would he kidnap Maddie? It's common knowledge that the rubber patrons flog the Indians, and it's accepted. Even if she were to report him to the authorities, no one would take any action against him."

"That's what's so puzzling. Maddie is no threat to Fitch." But Nile had another fear, one he could not bring himself to verbalize.

Amy did it for him. "She is a beautiful woman, and those are few and far between out here. Perhaps Fitch wants her for one of his concubines."

"That's what I'm afraid of." Nile averted his eyes and focused his attention on the clear blue sky just visible through the window and tried not to let his anger overwhelm him. "When we were there the first time, he offered to buy her from me. I refused, of course, telling him she was not mine to sell, so I guess he just decided to take what he wanted after all."

Amy said, "What are you going to do?"

He turned to her. "I'm going to get her back."

"How? Fitch's depot is an armed camp. You'll be outnumbered a hundred to one."

"But I have one tactical advantage: Fitch thinks I'm dead."

"Even so, Nile . . ."

"Amy, don't be such a pessimist. I've got to try. I can't just leave Maddie at Fitch's mercy. You know what a sadistic bastard he is. When I took this job, I agreed to protect her, and I will, or die trying."

He decided not to tell Amy about the hoax and

how he and Maddie had been at odds for the last several days. That seemed so insignificant now.

"Well, the good Lord must have saved you from the river for a purpose. Perhaps that purpose is to rescue Maddie."

"I fully intend to."

"But you're still weak, and even though I've dressed your wound, that arm is just about useless."

He grinned at her. "After a hot meal and a good night's sleep, I'll be as good as new." He glanced down at the blanket. "And by the way, where are my clothes?"

"Mary's washing them. And you needn't worry, Nile Marcus. Mary's tribesmen undressed you and put you in that hammock, not I."

"I was beginning to wonder."

The teasing light faded from Amy's eyes, and she grew pensive once again as she rose. "If you succeed in rescuing Maddie—"

"*When* I rescue Maddie."

"When you rescue her, what will you do to Fitch?"

"As much as I'd like to tear out his heart with my bare hands, I realize I'm not likely to get the opportunity if I want to get us out of there alive. So I'll content myself with getting Maddie away from him."

"And I will have to abandon the mission, won't I?"

Nile reached out and took her hand. "I won't lie to you, Amy. Yes, you'll have to come with us, with only the clothes on your back—otherwise Fitch will take his anger out on you, and I can't have that. I won't save Maddie at the price of your life."

"But what will become of Mary and the others who have converted? I can't just leave them behind, Nile."

He squeezed her hand, hard. "You have to. We can't bring them with us. Don't worry about them,

Amy. They'll survive as they always have. I'm sure of it."

She closed her eyes and shook her head. "All of our work here will be for naught. I don't want to do this."

"You must. There have been too many martyrs already." He grinned. "Besides, Winston would have my head if I let anything happen to you."

She didn't return his smile or make any comment about Winston Belgrave. All she did was sigh, her expression bleak. "Deep down inside, I always knew it would come to this one day. I just pray that the Lord grants me the peace to accept it."

Without another word, Amy turned and walked out.

When Nile was alone, he allowed himself to think of Maddie, and, once she was acknowledged, the thoughts roiled in his mind like a bubbling caldron.

He knew she was alive. He would have sensed it if she weren't, a sort of mental severing followed by a feeling of grief and loss. Besides, he knew Fitch all too well. The Englishman would never let a beautiful woman like Maddie go to waste.

"Oh, no," he murmured, "she's alive, all right."

What was she thinking and feeling? he wondered. She had seen him shot, seen him fall into the river. When he closed his eyes, he could still hear her screaming his name. She probably thought he was dead. Did she feel sorrow? Grief? Despair?

Suddenly Nile was overcome by remorse. The way he'd been treating her lately, he was lucky if she spared him a second thought.

Remorse was quickly replaced by self-righteousness when he thought of the hoax she had so willingly taken part in. Damnation and hellfire! The woman was a liar and a cheat.

Yet, except for lying about Ben Thomas, Maddie

had never played him false or disappointed him. He remembered the way she had cared for him so selflessly when he had had his bout of malaria, the way she had always taken his orders without question for the good of their party.

No, he wasn't about to let her down.

He stared up at the ceiling and began to plan.

Haddon Fitch was insane.

As Maddie sat at the table with the madman and the Indian women she had dubbed the Witches of Endor, she kept her eyes on her plate so she wouldn't have to watch Fitch knead Tia's bare breast.

He said something in their native tongue and the women looked at Maddie and giggled. She kept eating her beans and rice, for she had to keep up her strength if she were to survive.

"I told them you were blushing," Fitch said. "Tell me, Miss Dare, does my behavior offend you?"

Maddie raised her eyes to his and kept them there. "I am not accustomed to seeing behavior more appropriate to a brothel being indulged in at table, so, yes, you could say I'm offended."

Fitch chuckled as he feigned a shudder. "Such cold disapproval in your tone ... I fear I may freeze to death, which would be something of an accomplishment in this climate."

Maddie said nothing, just lowered her eyes to her plate and resumed eating.

"Are you thinking about Nile Marcus? We all heard you sobbing your heart out a few hours ago, so he must be on your mind."

At the mention of Nile's name, Maddie felt the beginnings of treacherous tears sting the backs of her eyes, but she fought them back with superhuman effort. She would not give this monster the satisfaction of seeing her break down.

"Look at me when I speak to you!" Fitch roared, slamming his open palm down on the tabletop.

Maddie started, and did as she was commanded.

Fitch's eyes were glittering with inhuman savagery. "I asked you if you were thinking of Nile Marcus, Miss Dare, and I expect an answer."

Maddie willed her voice not to quaver as she replied, "No, I am not. I was thinking of myself and what is to become of me."

He put his elbows on the table, steepled his fingers, and rested his chin on them while he studied her. "I haven't decided. Oh, don't look relieved just yet, Miss Dare. Many tantalizing possibilities have offered themselves, but I just haven't made up my mind."

When Maddie remained silent and refused to provide him with an entertaining retort, Fitch looked annoyed. "Wouldn't you like to hear what they are?"

"Not particularly."

He leaned back in his chair. "You are a singularly contrary woman, my dear. First you tell me you are thinking of what is to become of you, and then when I offer to tell you, you say you're not interested." Fitch smiled. "Well, I think I shall tell you anyway, whether or not you wish to hear it.

"First of all, I had thought to give you to my women as their own personal slave."

Maddie felt the blood draining from her face at that prospect.

Fitch pounced at once. "Ah, I can see that upsets you, but surely a woman of your formidable intelligence can see the irony of the situation. It would be such a novelty to see an Indian enslave an Englishman for a change, wouldn't it?"

"I fail to appreciate the irony, Mr. Fitch."

He laughed, while his women looked puzzled, not understanding their master's amusement. "My, my, you are so droll! Now, for my second idea, one I think will be more to your liking." He paused to heighten the suspense then said, "I thought of giving you to the man who killed Nile Marcus."

Maddie couldn't restrain herself this time. "No!"

Her tormentor raised his rust-colored brows. "No? Oh, yes, my dear. If that is what I wish to do to you, you will be given to him, make no mistake about it."

She sat there rigidly, fighting to retain control of herself, for she could see that Fitch took sadistic delight in provoking such responses from her.

"I wonder what it would be like for a woman to lie in the arms of the man who killed her lover?" he mused, his eyes never leaving her face. "Would she eventually come to love him as well?"

"I rather doubt it," Maddie replied coldly. "No woman could love a murderer. She would kill him, or herself, at the first opportunity."

He knew she was referring to him as well, and his eyes twinkled with delight. "Oh, you are a brave one. I do so admire courage in a woman, because it is so rare."

I don't feel particularly brave, Maddie said to herself. I feel like screaming until I can't scream anymore but I have to hold on. I can't give him the satisfaction of breaking me, I just can't!

Fitch began writing invisible words on the table with his fingertip. "And then there is my third idea. Would you care to hear it, Miss Dare?"

"Of course, since it involves me."

His features turned sly. "I had thought to make you the mother of my heir."

What Fitch obviously thought of as the most horrible of fates was nothing to Maddie. She knew it was physically impossible for her to be the mother of anyone's heir, but he had no way of knowing that.

Now was the time for her to appear to give Fitch what he wanted.

"You monster!" Maddie cried, bolting to her feet, letting her indignation come spewing out. She started for him with upraised fists, but before she could reach him, the three Indian women swooped down on her, grasping her arms and pinioning them at her sides, their black eyes glittering with anticipation.

Fitch regarded her with contempt. "You disappoint me, Miss Dare." He made a dismissive wave of his hand and said something to his women. As they started leading Maddie away, he said, "I told them to take you back to your room and keep you there until I decide what to do with you."

Now that she had spoiled his sport, he no longer found her amusing, but Maddie couldn't have been more pleased.

Once she was alone, she sat on the edge of the bed and hugged herself tightly, trying to keep herself from flying into a thousand little pieces. Then she screwed her eyes shut and jammed the knuckles of one hand into her mouth to stifle her sobs.

She still couldn't believe Nile was dead. One moment he had been standing so vital and alive beside her, and two seconds later he was gone, swallowed by the waters of the Juruá. She would give anything to relive that moment, to have a second chance. But nothing could bring him back now.

Regret tore at her like the talons of an eagle. She was sorry she had lied to him about Ben, and she was even sorrier Nile had died when there was such anger and bitterness between them. Now she would never have the opportunity to make amends.

She took a deep breath and wiped her eyes. "Courage, Maddie," she said, letting the sound of her own voice bolster her. "You can't give up, no mat-

ter what Fitch does to you. Nile would have wanted
you to go down fighting."

She found herself wondering if Fitch was going
to come to her tonight and make good his threats.
Since he delighted in stretching out his torments,
Maddie rather doubted it.

She would be ready for him.

Amaryllis stood before her brother's grave to say
a final good-bye.

There was so much she wanted to say to him
about the mission and how she regretted leaving
her life's work after all these years of struggle in
God's name, but her thoughts were so jumbled and
scattered, she just couldn't make sense of them or
bring them together to form a coherent thought. It
was as though her life in the Amazon had all been a
dream.

When she thought of her life in Devon, however,
the images were vivid and comforting.

The moment Amy closed her eyes, she saw her
family as they used to be in happier, more carefree
times. Papa, his staff in one hand, was walking
behind their herd of sheep and waving to her. Fred,
happy and forever young, smiled down at her from
his upstairs bedroom window. And there was her
mother, standing in the doorway, beckoning to her
and speaking words that Amy could never hear.

"Speak up, Mama," she said. "I can't hear you."

Amy wanted to run up to the door and go inside,
but something kept holding her back. She tried to
run, but her feet felt rooted to the ground and
wouldn't obey her.

"Amy?"

The weight of a hand on her shoulder startled
her. Amy shook her head to clear it, and found
herself standing in the mission cemetery with the
frightening dark jungle and its unknown terrors

lurking just out of sight. Her childhood home was gone. When she tried to bring it back, she couldn't.

She turned irritably, to see a man standing behind her, a puzzled expression on his face.

"Are you all right?" he asked. "You looked a million miles away just then."

Who was this man, and why was he bothering her? She remembered just in time.

"More to the point, how are you? It's too soon for you to be out of bed, Nile."

He shrugged. "I feel better now, truly. My arm's still sore, but I'll survive." He was silent for a moment as he studied her. Then he said, "I've figured out a plan to rescue Maddie, but I'm going to need your help."

What rescue? And who was this Maddie he was talking about? Of course! Now she remembered. Maddie had been kidnapped by Haddon Fitch and Nile was going to rescue her.

"I'll do anything I can," she said.

"Good. Now, here's what I'm going to do . . ."

As they walked back to the house together, Amy didn't really want to hear Nile's plan. She wanted to return to Devon and hear what her mother was trying so hard to tell her. She wanted to walk through the door and be safe again. But she forced herself to listen.

Then they went into the house to prepare for tomorrow.

Nile felt as though he were being baked alive as he lay curled beneath a blanket at one end of Amy's dugout canoe. Sweat trickled down his face, but he didn't dare reach up to wipe it off. He was supposed to be a rather large pile of manioc or bananas, so he couldn't move.

He was comforted by the fact that Fred's loaded Winchester was within reach. That, plus a can of kerosene and matches, was all he needed to put his plan of rescue into action.

"How far do we have to go?" he murmured to Amy, who was sitting up front, paddling the canoe with slow, deft strokes.

Fortunately for them both, Amy and her dugout loaded with foodstuffs and merchandise to trade were a familiar sight on the Juruá. None of Fitch's men would question her harmless presence.

"Not far," she replied. "One of Fitch's launches just passed us heading upriver."

Nile breathed a sigh of relief. If they hadn't been suspicious of the missionary's cargo, then Nile's ruse was working.

Now, if only he could depend on Amy.

She had scared him half to death yesterday when he came upon her in the cemetery. When she turned to him without any recognition in her expressionless eyes, she was like a stranger. Then she recovered herself quickly and from that moment on had been completely lucid, listening to Nile's plan objectively and even adding some suggestions of her own for its success.

Nile prayed she had only been daydreaming, but he recalled Maddie's insistent assessment that Amy was on the verge of a mental collapse. If that were true, he would have to worry not only about getting Maddie away from Fitch, but also about Amy's safety.

"Damnation and hellfire," he muttered under his breath.

He needed to be able to count on her, otherwise all would be lost. Nile wasn't sure he believed in Amy's God, but he uttered a short prayer nonetheless.

"Can you see the pier yet?" Nile asked.

"Yes," Amy replied. "And we're in luck. No one is delivering rubber this morning. In fact, there seems to be only one man armed with a machete guarding it, and he doesn't look as though he's expecting trouble."

"Good. Do you see Jayme's launch there?"

"I can't tell. There are several of them."

Nile grinned. "Kind of Fitch to leave them for us, don't you think?"

When Amy made no comment, Nile got worried. "Amy? Are you sure you can go through with this?"

"Of course," she replied with a touch of asperity. "I agreed to it, didn't I?"

Nile felt his confidence return. His plan was going to work. It just had to.

"And what about your sore arm?"

"It'll be all right. It hurts a little when I use it, but it's nothing I can't tolerate."

Moments later, when Amy said, "Get ready," Nile knew she had paddled the canoe over to an area not far from the pier where the dugouts were usually moored. He took several deep breaths to calm himself, and waited.

"Now!"

At Amy's signal, Nile peered over the edge of the blanket in time to see the guard turn and stroll down the other end of the pier. Nile flung back the blanket, jumped from the dugout, and grabbed the kerosene and rifle. Before the guard could turn around and stroll back, Nile was already up the path and into the jungle.

He ran silently down the *estrada*, his senses alert for any sign of danger, but all he heard were a few rustles of animals fleeing unseen and the outraged squawks of parrots overhead. As he passed rubber trees with their cups already attached, he smiled to himself. He had timed it just right. The *seringueiros* had already made their first pass of the day and wouldn't be coming back to collect the latex until much later. So Nile would have no witnesses, and no one to question his presence here.

He had chosen this particular *estrada* well, he thought as he loped down the path. It was far enough away to draw Fitch and his men away from the house, giving Nile enough time to rescue Maddie and escape before Fitch realized what had happened.

Nile stopped and looked around. This was as good a place as any. Here the rubber trees grew a little closer together than usual, so Fitch would feel their loss more acutely.

He took his can of kerosene and began dousing the underbrush and rubber trees. As luck would have it, this was the dry season and the vegetation was likely to burn well.

When Nile struck his first match and ignited the kerosene-soaked underbrush and watched it burst into flame, he decided there must be a God after all.

Then he turned and started down the *estrada* and toward the pier, the crackle and hiss of the greedy flames sounding like music to his ears.

Maddie was sitting on the veranda, having breakfast with Fitch and his silent, watchful women.

"I'm sorry I disappointed you," he said in an intimate, lazy drawl.

She raised her brows. "I beg your pardon?"

He leaned forward in his chair. "By not coming to you last night."

"On the contrary, you did not disappoint me."

In fact, she had spent half the night wide-awake and in mortal fear that he would force his advances on her as he had threatened. But as the night wore on, with each second after agonizing second seeming like an hour, and he never came, Maddie realized he had no intention of ravishing her—at least not right away. Sadistic monster that he was, Fitch preferred letting her suffer in shuddering anticipation of the horrors to come. Finally, she had just fallen asleep.

"Oh, but I have, my dear. Those dark smudges beneath your reproving blue eyes tell me you didn't get a wink of sleep, and it's all my fault. There you were, in eager anticipation of my embraces, and I never came. I'm such a cad."

He grinned that taunting smile Maddie loathed. "I shall have to remedy that situation tonight. I mustn't keep a lady waiting."

He would tell her now, thus leaving her the entire day to dwell on what was to happen to her tonight.

How long could she endure such mental torture before going insane?

"Oh, dear, I seem to have upset you. Let me—"

Fitch was interrupted by the shouts of several of his men running toward the house. He was on his feet in an instant, Maddie forgotten in the face of new danger. He conferred with the men for a moment, then turned back to Maddie, his pale eyes filled with an emotion she had thought him incapable of—fear.

"One of the *estradas* is on fire," he explained. Then he sketched a mocking bow. "As much as I enjoy conversing with you, Maddie, my love, I must put duty first. Just so you won't feel my absence too acutely, my women will accompany you back to your room, where you will remain until I return."

He said something to the women, who rose and started dragging Maddie up out of her seat. One of the men brought Fitch's horse around, so he mounted quickly and went riding off, giving Maddie a grin and an insolent salute.

As Maddie was escorted down the veranda, she could see huge clouds of black smoke billowing into the air and soiling the hazy blue sky.

"I hope this place burns down with everyone in it," she muttered.

Then she would finally be free of Haddon Fitch.

Panic reigned supreme. Men were everywhere, shouting and cursing.

Dozens of *seringueiros* went racing past Nile, all of them so intent on reaching the fire and putting it out that they didn't notice him traveling in the opposite direction. With his straw hat pulled low to hide his face, his own mother wouldn't have recognized him.

Suddenly he felt the ground shake beneath his feet, and he knew there was a horse approaching. Nile risked a glance and saw Fitch himself come galloping down the path.

For one second Nile contemplated raising his Winchester and shooting the man who had ordered his death, but he fought down the impulse. If he did that, Fitch's men would be swarming all over him like fire ants, and he wouldn't have a chance of rescuing Maddie.

He lowered his head and kept on walking. Fitch galloped by without a glance, dismissing Nile as just another one of his many faceless, nameless *seringueiros*.

"Someday," Nile muttered under his breath.

When he reached the pier, he found it deserted except for Amaryllis wringing her hands and pacing back and forth.

"Nile!" she cried in relief when she saw him. "You're safe."

"For the moment." He scanned the launches moored there.

When he saw Jayme's, he strode down the pier, followed by a hovering Amaryllis. He checked the steam boiler to make sure it had enough water, then shoveled in some coal and began starting the engine while Amy stood guard. He wanted the launch ready to go when he returned with Maddie.

Nile forced himself to curb his impatience as he kept checking the gauges every two seconds. "Rise, damn you! I haven't got all day."

The engine cooperated, and when the launch's engine was finally humming, Nile stepped onto the pier.

"Watch the launch," he ordered Amy over his shoulder, "but stay out of sight."

"What if Maddie isn't in the house?" she asked. "What if—?"

"Stop worrying. I told you I know Fitch. He wouldn't put her in his brothel right away."

Without another word, he was gone, striding down the pier.

With everyone diverted by the fire, Nile reached the house without seeing another soul, but he knew better than to become complacent. Fitch could return at any time. And there was no telling who had been left back at the house to guard Maddie. Nile was willing to bet on Fitch's three women, but even then he couldn't be sure.

Holding his rifle at waist level, with his finger on the trigger, he climbed the veranda's steps slowly and as silently as he could. When he reached the veranda, he saw only a table strewn with half-empty cups of *cafèzinho*. He counted them. There were five.

Maddie was here.

Nile resisted the impulse to relieve his building tension by calling out to her. That would only warn his enemy of his approach, when he wanted to surprise them.

He entered the house, moving silently from room to room, his ears attuned to the slightest sound, the creak of a floorboard, a soft footstep.

All of them were empty.

Nile licked his dry lips. Beads of sweat that had nothing to do with the heat rose on his brow. His wounded arm began to throb. What if they had taken her somewhere? What if she wasn't here after all?

And then he heard a familiar voice as clear as a bell: "If you witches don't take your hands off me this instant, I'll claw your eyes out."

He had found Maddie.

Inside her room, Maddie shook Tia off and took a step back. She had had quite enough of these women always grabbing her arms and leading her somewhere. If they wanted a fight, she was determined to give them one.

Tia's black eyes narrowed in hostility, and her supple body gathered itself for an assault. But just as she was about to spring, there came the resounding crash of the door being flung open and hitting the wall.

The noise startled Maddie, but no more than the sight that greeted her disbelieving eyes.

"Nile!"

If he were a ghost, he was a magnificent one, his tall, imposing body filling the doorway. But the moment he stepped into the room, his golden eyes glittering in triumph, like a stalking jaguar closing in for the kill, Maddie knew he was flesh and blood.

And he had come to save her.

"Step back," he commanded, his eyes never leaving the women. "And whatever you do, don't get in my line of fire."

"What are we going to do with them?" she asked.

Before Nile could answer, Tia screamed and lunged for him with the speed of a striking bushmaster, but he was faster. Before Maddie could blink, Nile had swung his Winchester around and let the charging woman run right into the rifle butt. Her head connected with a sickening thud and she slumped unconscious to the floor.

But Maddie had no time to waste her sympathies on Tia. One of the other women screamed and charged at her. Almost without thinking, Maddie drew back her arm and aimed her fist at her adversary's midsection. When the punch connected, the woman went down with a loud "woof" and lay curled on the floor, fighting for breath.

Maddie just stood there staring down at her and uttering an appalled, "Oh, my. I haven't killed her, have I?"

"Don't worry, she'll be fine."

Seeing her fallen sisters was enough to give the third woman pause, and she hung back.

Nile handed Maddie the rifle. "You hold this while I tie them up." He reached for the rope looped to his belt like Fitch's whip. "Shoot them if you have to."

Thankfully, Maddie didn't have to. Nile moved so swiftly that he bound and gagged Fitch's women in what seemed like a minute. Then he turned to Maddie and took the rifle out of her shaking hands.

"Let's get out of here."

Maddie hesitated. There was so much she had to say to him. So much—

"Now is not the time, Maddie," he growled, reading her mind. "We've got to get out of here before Fitch gets back. Come on!"

Then he was running, and all she could do was follow or be left behind.

Just when they reached the end of the corridor, Nile stopped abruptly, muttered something under his breath, and grabbed Maddie around the waist with his free arm, whirling her around and back against him. Before she could even squeal in surprise, Nile's mouth came down on hers for a hard, quick kiss that was over before it had even begun.

Dazed, every sense aroused and blazing to life at Nile's exquisite touch, Maddie just stood there staring into those passion-darkened eyes.

"I thought you said we didn't have time for this," she murmured breathlessly, running her tongue over her lower lip to taste the remnants of his kiss.

Those eyes roved over her face possessively. "We don't, but I couldn't wait to do that any longer. Now, let's get out of here."

As they ran from the house, Nile moved fast, forcing Maddie to hurry to keep up with him, but she did so gladly. Even though Nile was too busy scanning the area for Fitch's men to even spare her a glance or a reassuring smile, she couldn't take her eyes off him, even when she tripped over an upraised root and almost went sprawling in the dust.

"Don't dawdle!" he snapped as she recovered herself and rushed to keep up.

Maddie couldn't help herself. She had thought he was dead, and now here he was, right by her side, so very much alive. And he had risked his own life to rescue her.

"Did Fitch hurt you?" he asked.

Feeling giddy with elation, Maddie replied breezily, "He pulled my hair once."

"That's not what I meant."

"I know, but it still hurt like hell."

"Maddie . . ." His tone held a warning.

"No, he didn't touch me." She shuddered in spite of the heat. "Not physically, anyway."

Nile did glance at her then, a knowing look filled with a mixture of sympathy and murderous outrage, and Maddie feared what he would do to Fitch if the man were so unlucky as to cross their path.

Suddenly Nile stopped and flung out his arm to restrain her.

"Amy should be waiting for us at the pier," he whispered. "I hope nothing's happened to her."

Maddie hoped so too.

Amy had gone down below to hide as Nile had instructed.

As the endless minutes ticked by with agonizing slowness, she stopped worrying and tried to pray, but as always these days, the words wouldn't come and she gave up.

Where was he?

Something had gone wrong. Maddie wasn't in the main house after all. Fitch had put her in his brothel, and now Nile was trying to get her out.

Amy's head began throbbing, and she put her hand to her forehead to try to soothe it, but it was no use. Nile's daring, dangerous plan had failed. They were all doomed.

"It would appear that I shall meet my maker sooner than I had anticipated," Amy muttered to herself.

Then she heard it. Footsteps.

"Nile!" She ran up the stairs. "Did you find Mad—?"

The guard was back, a machete in his hand.

Amy froze.

"What are you doing here, *senhorita?*" he demanded. "Why has this boat been made ready? The patron has not ordered it."

Amy thought fast. "The patron has given it to me as a gift to take back to the mission."

The guard eyed her suspiciously. "He said nothing to me of this gift."

"I tell you he gave me this *lancha.* Surely you would not go against your patron's wishes."

The man was unconvinced. "Come, *senhorita.* We will find the patron."

"No!" she cried, panicking.

Amy jumped off the launch and started running down the pier. She could hear the thumping of heavy footsteps following her, growing closer and closer. Then an arm encircled her waist, and she was lifted off her feet and flung down onto the pier. As she looked up, all she could see was the gleaming blade of the machete looming over her head. . . .

Then it was gone and she was back in Devon again. Her mother was standing in the doorway, smiling and beckoning. This time, when Amy tried to run to her, her feet glided over the earth as though her heels wore wings. And this time, when her mother spoke, Amy heard her ever so clearly.

"Welcome home," her mother said.

Amy went inside, home at last.

"Amy!" Maddie shook her shoulders, trying to ignore the dead guard that Nile had just shot.

Nile knelt by her side. "Is she . . . ?"

"No. The machete didn't touch her. I think she just fainted. Help me get her into the launch."

Nile handed her the rifle and managed to lift Amy's unconscious form into his arms in spite of his wound. Then he took her below deck to his cabin while Maddie nervously stood guard.

When Nile emerged, he said, "The engines are ready. Just let me set the rest of the launches on fire, so Fitch can't follow us, and we'll be on our way."

Maddie stood there, her nerves screaming with impatience as she watched the path. At any moment, she fully expected to see a wild-eyed Haddon Fitch with an army of men come charging after them. But before that could happen, Nile was releasing the launch from its moorings and steering it away from the pier.

Minutes later, the other three launches were burning like bonfires, the orange flames licking at the sky.

15

Maddie went to the other end of the launch, clutched at the rail so hard she thought her knuckles would break through the skin, and watched until there was nothing of Haddon Fitch's compound to see except rising gray smoke smudging the tropical sky.

Her ordeal was over.

She sighed, shivered, then crossed the deck to where Nile stood at the wheel. The moment Maddie slipped her arms around his waist and clung to him, her face pressed against his broad back, she felt as though a dam had burst inside, sweeping away all her fears. She started crying, great hiccuping sobs that barely let her draw another breath.

Nile unclenched her hands from around his waist and turned so he could draw her toward him and enfold her in his embrace. She went willingly, her body starved for the sheer comforting presence he offered.

His muscular arms formed an iron cocoon, sheltering and protecting her as they tightened. "Hush, Maddie, don't cry. It's all over. Fitch can't harm you. Please don't cry."

"Oh, Nile," she sobbed, her face hard against his, "I thought you were dead."

She felt him smile. "It takes more than a few bullets to kill me—don't you know that by now?"

Maddie had to chuckle in spite of herself.

"That's better," he said.

She closed her eyes and just let him hold her for a few moments while she gathered her scattered wits. Once she felt her runaway emotions slow down, she became impatient, realizing at last that she was hoping Nile would tilt her head back and kiss her as he had that day at the bathing pool.

When Maddie looked up at him, she was astounded and dismayed to see only a neutral expression in his eyes rather than the blazing desire she had hoped for.

So, he was still holding the hoax against her.

She stepped away and smiled brightly to hide her disappointment. "How did you save yourself? I saw you fall into the river." She didn't tell him she had felt like jumping in after him.

Nile's face tightened in pain and Maddie noticed for the first time that his left shirt sleeve had a rip in it and there was what looked like a bandage beneath the material.

"What happened to your arm?" she asked.

"That's where the bullet grazed me," he replied. "I knew that if I stayed where I was, they would kill me, so I decided to take my chances in the river and come for you later."

While Maddie listened, he told a harrowing tale of swimming to shore before any piranhas could make a meal of him, and struggling his way through the jungle to get to the mission.

When Nile finished, Maddie said raggedly, "They killed Jayme, you know. They shot him to death right in front of my eyes, then threw his body overboard."

Nile swore softly and blinked hard several times. "Poor Jayme. He never stood a chance." He looked at her. "I take it Fitch wanted to make you one of his ... concubines."

She shook her head, then told him the primary reason Haddon Fitch had kidnapped her.

Nile looked stunned. "So he was afraid you'd expose him once you returned to England."

"That's what he said, but I wonder. I know the press has great power to sway public opinion, but this is Brazil, a country thousands of miles away. Even if I did write an article about Fitch's abominable mistreatment of the Indians, what could anyone in England possibly do?"

"Quite a lot, actually," Nile surprised her by saying. "First of all, Fitch is a British subject. And if British banks have invested money in Aguirre's company, they have a stake in what goes on here. They wouldn't want to be thought of as sanctioning such barbarism."

He rubbed his jaw thoughtfully. "I would say you have a real opportunity to bring Fitch and Aguirre down, Maddie."

She smiled a slow, satisfied smile. "After what that bastard did to me, it will be my pleasure."

"I thought you said he didn't touch you."

"Oh, not physically, but mentally . . ." His gaze weighed too heavily on her and she had to turn away from it. "He delighted in telling me, in exacting detail, everything he was going to do to me. And he gave me plenty of time afterward to dwell on it. Anticipating something can sometimes be worse than experiencing it."

Maddie clenched her hands into fists, the nails biting into her palms. "First he said I was going to become his concubines' slave. Then he considered giving me to the man who killed you, and last but not least, he thought he might make me the mother of his heir." She laughed bitterly. "And I can just imagine what that honor would entail."

For a moment Nile did nothing, and Maddie assumed she had stunned him speechless. Then he came up behind her and placed his hands on her shoulders, but it was a curiously impersonal touch, something he might have done to comfort anyone. What Maddie wanted and needed so desperately was for him to take her in his arms and reach out to her with a passion that told her he truly shared her pain, not merely sympathized with it.

All he said was, "That must have been hell for you."

Then his hands fell away and he returned to the wheel.

Maddie pushed aside soft feminine feelings and began thinking like a journalist again. "Do you think Fitch may have burned to death back there?"

"Not a chance. I only set part of an *estrada* on fire as a distraction to get them all away from the house. I'm sure they put it out before it could do any real damage."

"What a shame." Maddie's gaze scanned the river behind them. "What if Fitch wants me stopped? What if he follows us?"

That thought mustn't have occurred to Nile, for he turned pale beneath his bronze skin. "That's possible. He's a determined bastard, especially when he's crossed."

"As well as being a madman. Don't forget that charming aspect of his character."

Nile's expression hardened. "Then we shall have to sail this river as though we're running for our lives."

"We may very well be. And if he catches us, he won't let any of us live this time."

"Including Amaryllis."

"Amaryllis! I had forgotten all about her. I'd better go below and see how she's faring."

Maddie needed the excuse to get away from Nile, so she turned and left him.

* * *

Nile watched her disappear below, his heart aching for her and the anguish she had suffered at Fitch's hands.

He knew that when she had come to him, she wanted more than the simple comfort another human being could provide. He could see the longing in her tear-filled eyes, feel the desperation in her touch, hear the pleading in her voice for him to respond to her. But he couldn't.

Not that he didn't want to. He freely admitted to himself that he desired Maddie as a woman. Once he had even thought he loved her. Yet he couldn't admire her as a person. She had lied to him. No matter how hard he tried, he couldn't overlook such an important aspect of her character. If Maddie could lie so glibly about something so important, she could lie again and again. How could he ever trust her to be faithful to him?

Nile turned the wheel, keeping the launch on course in the middle of the river, then glanced back over his shoulder for any sign of Fitch. When he saw nothing, he turned his attention back to where he was going.

Still, even though there was this unbreachable chasm between himself and Maddie, he would do everything in his power to see that Fitch didn't harm her.

He owed her at least that much.

In Nile's cabin, Maddie shook Amaryllis'-shoulder. "You can wake up now. We're safe."

Amy's eyes flew open and she stared at Maddie. "Who . . . who are you?"

"It's Maddie."

Amy sat up and swung her legs over the bunk. "I'm sorry, but I don't know anyone named Maddie."

Oh, dear God, Maddie thought, aghast.

She tried again. "Yes, you do. I'm Nile's friend, remember?"

The gray eyes held no hint of recognition. "I'm sorry, but I do not know you." Then her face brightened and sent Maddie's hopes soaring. "I have it! You are very pretty, so you must be Lady Trevellyn."

"Lady Trevellyn?" she echoed. "Who is she?"

"Why, you are! You live in the castle high on the hill near our farm. I've seen you riding by on your big white horse."

Maddie tried to fight down the rising waves of panic, but she had to warn Nile. She said to Amy, "Will you wait here for a moment, until I get back?"

Dismay furrowed Amy's brow. "Where are you going?"

"To tell a friend that I have found you."

"Oh, I'd like that! I don't have many friends."

But you do, Amy, Maddie said to herself. More than you know.

After admonishing Amy not to move, Maddie left her and went above deck to find Nile still at the wheel.

"Where's Amy?" he asked. "She's all right, isn't she?"

Maddie placed her hand on his arm. "Nile, I don't know how to tell you this, but I think Amy's finally lost her mind."

His face registered disbelief, then anger. "That's absurd. Amaryllis Gates is the sanest person I know."

"Nile, listen to me, please. When I went down there just now, she didn't recognize me at all. She told me I must be some Lady Trevellyn, who lives in a castle near her farm, wherever that may be."

"Amy's parents owned a farm in Devon," he said thickly.

"She . . . she seems so simple and childlike. It's as though her mind has retreated back to England and her childhood."

Nile shook his head in denial. "There's got to be some reason for such behavior. Maybe she hit her head when that *seringueiro* threw her down on the pier."

"Or perhaps her backbreaking life out here and her brother's death finally unhinged her. We both saw how strangely she was behaving at the mission the first time we were there."

"Damnation and hellfire, not Amy!"

Maddie said softly, "Why don't I bring her up so you can see for yourself?"

Nile nodded, his eyes bright as he fought to compose himself.

Maddie went below again and found a docile Amy still sitting exactly where she had left her.

Maddie extended her hand. "Come with me."

Amy clasped it as if she were a trusting child. "Where are we going?"

"I told you, to see a friend."

"What's her name?"

"His name is Nile."

"Nile . . . What a funny name. Is he a very good friend?"

"Yes, Amy, a very good friend."

She smiled then, the sweet, innocent smile of a child about to be given a special treat, and Maddie thought her heart would break.

When they emerged, Maddie brought Amy forward and said softly, "Amy, this is your friend Nile."

The other woman looked at Nile with blatant curiosity, then lowered her head shyly. "He's not my friend. I don't even know who he is."

Nile swore.

"Don't!" Maddie snapped as Amy cried out and cowered against her. "You'll frighten her."

He ran his hand through his hair, fighting for

control. When he was calmer, he said, "But I know you, and your brother too."

Amy's face brightened at once. "Freddie? You know my brother, Freddie?"

"I knew . . . know him very well."

"Then you must be my friend. Papa says Freddie is very smart, and if we weren't so poor, he'd go to Oxford or Cambridge."

"Yes, Freddie is very smart."

Maddie had to speak with Nile alone. So she indicated a chair at the other end of the launch and said to Amy, "Why don't you go sit over there and watch the river go by?"

Amy said, "The Exe is such a lovely river, isn't it?" and did as she was told.

Maddie turned to Nile. "In her mind, she's a child still living in England. She doesn't even know where she is."

Nile looked at her sitting in the chair so docilely, and his face softened in pity. "Poor Amy."

"Don't forget poor Winston Belgrave," she added, keeping her voice low. "He'll be devastated when we bring her to him like this."

Nile inhaled and let out his breath slowly. "I hadn't thought of that. You're right. He loves her more than life itself, and to see her this way . . ."

He added, "No woman belongs out here. Winston wanted to give her a life of ease and beauty. Now that he's about to get that chance, the Amazon snatches it away."

Maddie sighed. "I'm beginning to agree with you. No woman does belong out here. Oh, don't look so shocked, Nile Marcus. I'm the first one to admit it when I'm wrong."

He snorted. "Fine time for you to realize I was right all along."

He winced in pain and began rubbing his arm.

"Is your arm hurting you?" Maddie asked. "Shall I change the dressing?"

He dismissed her dithering with a wave of his hand. "I'll live." Then he surprised her by turning somber and placing a hand on her shoulder. "Listen, Maddie, with Amy the way she is, you and I are going to have to work three times as hard if were going to come out of this alive."

She glanced at the other woman. "I know. We've lost our captain and we're trying to navigate a dangerous river by ourselves. I don't know how much you know about running a steam launch, but my expertise in nonexistent. I also suspect any money we had is at the bottom of the Amazon, and that we have very little food. And with Amy being so unpredictable, she may be an additional liability."

When Nile said nothing, merely stared at her owlishly, Maddie gave him a wry smile. "What's the matter, Mr. Marcus? Surprised that a mere woman can comprehend the seriousness of our situation?"

"That's unfair. I never doubted your intelligence."

Only my morals, she thought dismally.

She raised her chin, hiding behind a brave and sassy facade. "I fully intend to come out of this alive, Nile. I'll do whatever it takes for the three of us to survive. All you have to do is tell me the truth of our situation and what I have to do to help."

Her boast coaxed a tiny smile out of him. "Sit next to me while I steer this magnificent vessel and I'll tell you."

Maddie sat right down on the deck, curled her legs beneath her, and listened while Nile began speaking.

Later, he concluded with, "And even if we do make it to Manaus, that doesn't mean we'll we safe."

Maddie groaned. "Dare I ask why not?"

"Fitch is no fool. He'll get word to Antonio Aguirre to tell him to be on the lookout for us."

For the first time, she noticed a dark stain on the deck that could only have been Jayme's blood, and she felt her own sense of outrage rallying her courage and strength.

She looked up at Nile. "I'm not going to let him beat us. I won't let him get his hands on me again."

Before he could comment, Amy jumped to her feet and went running to the rail. "Look at the pretty bird! It's all blue and yellow and red. I've never seen one like that before."

Maddie pursed her lips. Even more than her own safety, she feared for Amy's if Fitch ever got his hands on her, and one glance at Nile told her he felt the same.

They would just have to make it. They just had to.

By the time darkness fell on the river, Maddie was ready to drop from sheer exhaustion.

After they had reached the mouth of the Juruá and set sail down the Amazon, Maddie had almost relaxed, until Nile reminded her that they would soon be coming to the rapids they had conquered on the way upriver. This time, however, they were sailing downriver with the current, so Nile managed to navigate the dangerous rapids with a finesse that would have made Jayme proud.

That evening, thanks to Nile's skills as a fisherman, they were able to dine heartily on fish and turtle eggs, and after the launch was securely moored for the night, Maddie said good night to Nile, who would be sleeping in a hammock on deck, put Amy to bed in his cabin, and retired for the night in her own.

Even though her body was exhausted, her mind refused to rest.

As she listened to the mosquitoes humming around the netting swathing her bunk, she wondered if Haddon Fitch was somewhere out there, moored on the river just as they were, waiting for dawn to continue the chase. Even if they escaped him and were able to reach Manaus safely, they still didn't know what had happened to Ben.

Ben . . . Maddie had almost forgotten about him.

She closed her eyes. She was beginning to regret ever becoming involved in this scheme. All she wanted to do was return to London and resume her life as the *Clarion*'s best reporter. But what about Nile?

Maddie's eyes flew open and she stared out into the darkness. Doubtless, once they eluded Fitch and found Ben, Nile would remain behind to bring Provvy's murderer to justice, then return to England. Once Maddie's story hit the streets, Nile would be able to take his pick of orchid-hunting expeditions. Her life would go on as it always had.

But there would be something missing now.

"Face it, Maddie," she muttered, "once this is over, you'll never see Nile Marcus again."

Only when she forced that reality from her mind was she finally able to fall asleep.

Maddie awoke to the sounds of Nile starting the steam engine rather than the usual roar of the howler monkey, so she knew it wasn't even dawn yet.

Stifling a yawn and wishing for a bucket of water to wash in, Maddie wondered how she was ever going to survive the four-day voyage downriver without bathing or changing her clothes. She decided the sacrifice would be worth it if it helped them elude Fitch. Then she rose and joined Nile in the launch's tiny boiler room.

"Good morning," she mumbled.

Nile smiled. "It's barely that, but I wanted to get

the engine ready so we'd be able to leave the minute I'm able to see where we're going."

"You can bet Fitch is doing the same." When Nile made no comment, she said, "Do you mind if I watch?"

"If you like."

So she watched Nile add water to the boiler and check gauges as the engine hissed like a startled cat, then started purring like a contented one. Finally, when he was satisfied, they went above deck and Nile got the launch under way.

Once they were in the current again, he said, "We should be coming to a settlement soon. At least we'll have a place to dock so I can go into the jungle and hunt for some food."

Hope flooded through Maddie. "Perhaps the people there can help us against Fitch."

"No, Maddie, this is our fight and no one else's. I'd hate to think what Fitch would do to anyone he suspected of helping us. He'll have armed men with him, remember?"

Her spirits plummeted. "I hadn't thought of that. I certainly don't want anyone's blood on my hands."

Then she looked back over her shoulder, but the river was blessedly empty.

"We'll be doing a lot of that during the next few days."

"Doing what?"

"Looking over our shoulders."

The sound of footsteps on the stairs claimed their attention as Amaryllis appeared, yawning and stretching as she emerged from below deck.

Maddie felt Nile stiffen beside her, and she knew he was also wondering if they were going to see Amaryllis the woman or Amaryllis the child.

To Maddie's sorrow, the look in the gray eyes remained ingenuous.

She looked at Nile briefly and shook her head

before saying, "Good morning, Amy. Did you sleep well?"

"Oh, yes. Now I'm ready for my cocoa and porridge."

"I'm afraid we don't have any right now," Maddie said gently, "so you'll have to wait."

Amy scowled. "But I'm hungry now!" And she burst into tears like a petulant child.

Nile swore in exasperation, but stopped when Maddie shot him a reproachful glance. Then she put her arm around Amy and mollified her by promising her a special treat later, if only she would be good for just a little while longer.

Several hours later, when the sun was a hot white ball inching higher in the sky, they arrived at the settlement Nile had mentioned. Leaving Maddie alone with Amy, he took the Winchester and went into the jungle. Several shots rang out, and when he returned a half-hour later he had freshly killed game, which they cooked over a clay stove.

Maddie and Nile stuffed themselves and urged Amy to do the same, until she finally rebelled and refused to eat another bite. She had no way of knowing this might be her last meal for the rest of the day, and Maddie wasn't looking forward to the child-woman's next demands for food.

When they were finished, they resumed their flight.

They hadn't been traveling for more than two hours when Maddie noticed something was wrong with Nile.

As he stood at the wheel, his head kept nodding as though he were falling asleep on his feet. Then he would catch himself, his head would jerk up, and he would stare at the river ahead in grim determination. Every so often he would draw his arm across his forehead.

"Nile, are you all right?"

His face was mud-colored and his whole body was quaking with the chills. "No, I . . ."

While Maddie watched in horror, Nile sank to his knees, sending the launch veering to the right as he clutched at the wheel to break his fall.

"Nile!"

Maddie wanted to go to him, but with the launch bow suddenly pointing toward shore, her first concern was getting it back on course into the current, where the waters ran deep, before they ran aground in the shallows. Pulling Nile's hands away, she turned the wheel slowly. The launch responded like a docile puppy, obediently changing direction.

Her heart in her mouth, Maddie held the wheel steady until she had the launch right where she wanted it, then knelt down to see to Nile. Even before his body started jerking, she knew he was having another malaria attack.

"Fine time for you to pass out on me, Marcus," she muttered.

She felt pulled in two directions. There was Nile, lying at her feet and shuddering in the throes of fever, and the Amazon, waiting to lead their launch to destruction.

"Amy, come here!" Maddie called. "Now!"

In one second, Amy was by her side. "Yes?"

Maddie licked her dry lips. "Amy, we're going to play a little game. Would you like that?"

"Oh, yes! Freddie and I always play lots of games."

"Good." She drew Amy over to the wheel. "I want you to see how long you can hold this wheel without moving it. Can you do that for me?"

"That's easy." She held on to the spokes of the wheel with sheer determination.

Maddie waited, and when it appeared the launch was going to stay on course, at least for a little while, she went to tend Nile.

"Nile, can you hear me?" she asked as she knelt beside him.

He stirred, and his eyes flew open. For an instant they stared at Maddie blankly; then gradually recognition registered in their golden depths.

"Maddie?"

"You're having another attack of malaria," she said urgently. "I've got to get you to bed, but I'm going to need your help."

With Maddie's assistance, Nile struggled to his feet, where he swayed precariously. He seemed dazed as he looked around, but with Maddie's shoulder to lean on, he managed to stumble below deck and collapse onto his bunk.

"Don't worry, Nile," she murmured. "When we get some quinine in you, you'll be better in no time."

But when she went to her own cabin to search for her medicine case, she couldn't find it.

As panic overwhelmed reason, her search became more frantic. Damn! The bastards must have taken it when they docked the launch at Fitch's compound.

Without quinine, Nile's fever would just have to run its course, and there was no telling how long that would take. Hours? Days?

Maddie swallowed hard. With Nile incapacitated, she was the only one left. She would have to pilot the boat by herself, and find them food.

She was their only hope of ever coming out of this alive.

Maddie's nerves were stretched as tautly as piano wires. Her palms were sweaty and tended to slip off the wheel unless she held the spokes in a relentless grip. The only time she released it was to draw her forearm across her brow before the stinging sweat fell into her eyes and blinded her.

She had managed to navigate the river for the

rest of the afternoon without mishap, and she was beginning to wonder if the ghost of Jayme was standing at her elbow, whispering in her ear and guiding her. She tried to remain calm and recall what he had told her about reading the river.

The main thing she remembered was that the fast water was the deep water.

So she watched for dead leaves and floating logs moving swiftly, and she followed them, for Jayme had said they were in just as much of a hurry to reach the sea as the Amazon. This advice served her well when she passed the mouths of small tributaries that joined the main river. If Maddie hadn't been watching the moving debris, she might have become confused, sailed up one of these little rivers, and become lost for sure. By the same token, when she saw debris collecting in any one spot, she steered clear, and always sighed in relief when the launch kept moving.

As far as the engine was concerned, Jayme's ghost always seemed to warn Maddie when it needed tending. At those times, she would have Amy play their little "game" with the wheel while she ran below deck to add more coal or water to the boiler.

Each time, Maddie spared only a few seconds to check on Nile. She was always dismayed to find him lying there unconscious, muttering something unintelligible, his clothes fever-soaked. She gave him water, wiped his brow, and returned to the wheel.

Maddie lost all concept of time. All she saw was the river ahead of her, and she was ever conscious of the possibility that Fitch was creeping up behind her. That alone made her stay at the wheel, when all she wanted to do was collapse and sleep for a hundred years.

Finally, when twilight fell and Maddie couldn't read the river anymore, she headed for shore, seeking a deep place out of the current where she could moor the launch for the night.

Remembering what Jayme had said about the deepest water being near steep banks, she searched for one and almost cried for joy when she found such a spot. Afraid that she would go crashing into the bank, she shut off the engine. But it turned out to be too soon, causing the launch to come to a halt too far away for her to moor it.

Cursing roundly, Maddie got out Jayme's long pole, stuck it in the water, and pushed with all her strength. Inch by inch, the launch drew closer to shore. Then she reached over and tied its line to a stout tree jutting out into the water.

Maddie collapsed where she stood, incredulous that she had survived her first day.

"Nile?" Maddie called his name softly.

He didn't hear her. He lay shivering, his skin hot to the touch, just like the first time Maddie had witnessed the progress of his malarial fever. Only, unlike last time, she would not be getting into bed with him to keep him warm. She thought it best to sleep on deck tonight, in the hammock.

Pulling back the mosquito netting, she leaned over and kissed him on his rough, unshaven cheek, but even the tender touch of her lips didn't rouse him.

As Maddie left Nile's cabin, the sound of muffled sobbing met her ears, but she hardened her heart against it. Earlier that evening, a ravenous Amy had demanded food, and since she was incapable of understanding why there was none to be had, she threw a tantrum. Frustrated when her efforts to appease Amy failed, Maddie responded in the only way she knew how—she sent Amy to bed without her supper.

A rumbling deep within her own stomach told

Maddie that she was going to have to find them something to eat tomorrow, though for the life of her, she didn't know how she was going to accomplish that feat without money. With Nile incapacitated, he couldn't go hunting at the next settlement.

Feeling the sting of a mosquito on her neck, she hurried across the deck, got into the hammock, and pulled the netting over her like a shroud and closed her eyes.

That night, Maddie slept fitfully. Every time she heard the launch creak or moan, she thought it was Fitch coming aboard, and she awoke wide-eyed and trembling, her fingers reaching for the rifle on the deck. When she did manage to doze, she dreamed of rapids and spinning whirlpools sucking her down, down, down, until she awakened with a scream in her throat, her body bathed in cold sweat.

Just when she fell into the deep sleep of exhaustion, the roaring of monkeys jarred her awake.

Morning had come too quickly and it was time to begin the grueling ordeal all over again.

"I'm hungry. I want my cocoa and porridge!"

Maddie glared at Amy and fought down the impulse to push the other woman overboard and be done with her whining demands. Immediately she was filled with remorse. Amy was not responsible for her actions.

But Maddie wasn't having an easy time of it either. The moment she had awoken, she rushed to Nile's cabin, expecting to find him up and about, his fever broken. Her high hopes were dashed when she found him still in malaria's unrelenting grip. She could not count on him.

Still, she managed to get the launch into the current without any mishap and start the engine.

When Amy came on deck, her demands for food

only reminded Maddie of her own gnawing hunger with its accompanying light-headedness.

"We'll eat soon, I promise," Maddie said.

"I'm hungry now. My stomach hurts."

Maddie just gritted her teeth and ignored her, praying that there was a settlement up ahead.

It was midmorning when Maddie first noticed the other launch.

She had just come on deck from having checked on Nile's condition when she saw it steaming down the river toward them. It was still too far away for her to make out its occupants, but she knew who it was.

"Fitch!"

Nausea clutched at her midsection, and the deck teetered crazily beneath her feet. Maddie sucked in great gulps of air, refusing to faint, and gradually the deck righted itself.

Somehow, in some way, Fitch had closed the gap between them.

Maddie turned this way and that, trying to decide what to do. If she wanted to outrun them, she would have to add more coal, but she didn't know how much was too much. She could cause the boiler to explode.

She looked back over her shoulder. The other launch was slowly gaining on her. She could now see figures on its deck.

Turning her attention back to the river, Maddie noticed a small settlement not far ahead. Perhaps someone there would be willing to help them. She kept telling herself that as she steered the launch for the pier.

She glanced down at the rifle at her feet. If she had to, she could kill Haddon Fitch before she let him harm Nile or Amy.

Maddie didn't look back as she headed for the

pier and the cluster of buildings on the riverbank. The launch commanded all her attention, for she knew if she didn't shut off the engine at just the right time, they would go plowing into the pier. It was only after she had cut the engine that she turned around again, fearing what she would see.

The other launch was only thirty feet away.

Fitch had won.

Then, as Maddie took a closer look, she noticed something about the other launch's occupants: Fitch wasn't among them, and the small group of men on the deck didn't appear to be armed. In fact, they looked like Brazilian farmers.

The other boat hadn't been pursuing them after all.

Relief made Maddie dizzy, and she had to clap her hand over her mouth to contain her rising hysteria. They were still safe.

Maddie managed to dock the launch, with the assistance of several others, and tried to explain that she needed food. But what did she have to trade? She was seriously considering trading the Winchester, but then she noticed Amy's silver cross.

"Amy," she said, smiling sweetly, "if you want anything to eat, you'll have to give me your pretty necklace."

Amy handed it over without a word.

They would dine well tonight thanks to a cross made from "tears of the moon."

16

Maddie had her routine memorized and could perform it with the efficiency of a trained dog.

Most of her time was spent behind the launch's wheel, navigating the river. Every so often she would have Amy play their "game" while she ran below to add coal and water to the steam boiler or to check on Nile, who was now sleeping the oblivious sleep of exhaustion, the malarial fever having finally released its vicious grip. Once Maddie was back behind the wheel, she looked over her shoulder constantly for any sign of Fitch.

The ordeal was taking its toll physically. Maddie had been staring at the river for hours, her vision beginning to blur, and she had to blink several times and rub her eyes before the landscape stopped dancing. Her shoulders and legs ached from standing at the wheel so long, and her fingers were cramped from clutching at the spokes. She was past noticing the appalling heat that roasted her, and she had come to welcome the sudden afternoon downpours, finding the rainwater refreshing as she let it soak through her clothes and drench her skin.

At least she wasn't hungry. Amy's silver cross had been traded for a good supply of jerked meat and fresh water. Maddie had carefully rationed it between herself and a greedy Amy, leaving the lion's share for Nile when he was better.

But the constant combined threats of nature and

Haddon Fitch were taking a far greater toll, gnawing away at her iron resolve like rats feasting on cheese. Not being able to let down her guard for a second had stretched her nerves to the snapping point.

Then she would hear that little voice inside her head, the one that always appeared when she was at the lowest ebb in her life.

"Not ready to quit already, are you?" it drawled. "Come, come now. You're brave Maddie Dare, the equal of any man, remember? You can't quit. Because if you do and Fitch catches you, Nile will die."

Nile will die.

That blunt reminder was all Maddie needed. She ruthlessly pushed all doubts out of her mind and gathered the courage to do what had to be done.

But she hadn't counted on the sand flies.

Maddie was beginning to feel as though she were traveling down the mythological river Styx when she first became conscious of the droning, humming sound. She ignored it until she felt a bite more painful than any mosquito on her cheek, followed by another and another.

When Amy started whimpering and flailing the air, Maddie sent her to her cabin to escape the insects, but there was no escape for her. Without her hat and netting to protect her anymore, she had to endure the onslaught as best she could. Even though she constantly brushed them away, the army of flies was persistent and she still felt their stinging bites.

She tolerated them because if she let down her guard for one second, Nile would die.

Nile's eyes flew open, and for a moment he didn't know where in the hell he was. Then his mind cleared of cobwebs and he recognized his cabin. He lay there for a moment, his body feeling as stiff and sore as if it had been tortured on the rack.

Finally he was able to sit up and swing his legs over the side of his bunk. His head swam, and for a moment he thought of lying back down again and sleeping for twenty years like that Rip Van Winkle character Provvy had once told him about.

Then he remembered why he was here, and all thoughts of sleep vanished.

Maddie.

As Nile rose, the weakness took a crushing hold of him, but he leaned against one wall and fought it off. When his legs felt more solid and able to bear his weight, he staggered across his cabin and up the stairs.

The moment he emerged from below deck, the brilliant light hurt his eyes, and he had to squint.

"Welcome to the land of the living," a familiar voice said.

Nile opened his eyes. The sight that greeted him both gladdened his heart and ripped it right from his chest, because what he had predicted in the Explorers Club that damp, gray March day had finally come true. Three months ago, he would have gloated; now he could only regret he had been right.

Maddie stood at the wheel, but it was a Maddie he didn't recognize. Her shirt was sweat-stained and her split skirt torn. The silken blond hair that had once begged to be sifted through a man's fingers had escaped from its neat braid and now hung in limp, snarled locks around her shoulders.

And her face . . . Her porcelain skin was a furious pink from sunburn and her cheeks and neck intermittently dotted with black blisters where sand flies had feasted.

Yet what disturbed Nile the most were her eyes, no longer sparkling with defiance but lackluster and remote, like those of a whipped dog trying desperately to endure one last beating before giving up.

Nile took a deep breath and staved off tears by lashing himself with anger and remorse. He never should have agreed to this in the first place. Never.

Her voice cracking, Maddie said, "How are you feeling?"

Like a first-rate bastard, he said to himself. To Maddie he said, "Much better."

"Good. There's some jerked meat over there, and I'd recommend eating it before Amy does. She's had hers already, but"—Maddie smiled, but the mirth never reached her eyes—"you know how she is."

Nile looked around. "Where are we?"

"I don't know," Maddie replied, staring straight ahead. "We've been on the river for three days, so I would assume we're nearing Manaus."

"You've been sailing this launch for three *days*?" His voice rose incredulously.

The confident Maddie returned. "I'll have you know I managed to sail this river all by myself, without blowing up the launch or running it aground."

She didn't need to mention that she had done it all while contending with a madwoman and a sick man; all Nile had to do was look at her to know it hadn't been easy. Well, she wasn't alone anymore.

"Maddie . . ." He held out his arms to her.

At first she stared straight ahead at the river, appearing not to notice him. Then her lower lip began trembling, and her face crumpled.

"Oh, Nile . . ." she cried, flinging herself into his arms and clinging to him as if she'd never let him go. "Hold me. Please hold me."

He held her as tightly as he was able, his arms wrapped around her, his cheek pressed against hers. "Hush, Maddie, it's all right now. You did fine, but you don't have to be brave anymore."

Great sobs shook her frame as she let go, allowing herself to share the burden she had been carrying alone for so long. Nile just held her until the crying stopped and she went still.

She looked up at him. "I had to keep going, otherwise you would have died. I couldn't let that happen because I . . . I love you, Nile."

He felt an involuntary surge of pleasure. "What did you say?"

"I said that I love you. I never realized how much until Fitch took me prisoner and I thought you were dead."

As Maddie waited for his response, Nile's emotions were in a turmoil. He knew he felt something for her, but was it love? And even if it were, a part of him couldn't overlook the fact that they wouldn't be in this predicament in the first place if she hadn't lied to him about Ben Thomas.

She sensed him mentally drawing away from her, for she stepped back out of his arms, her eyes wide with disbelief and denial. "Why are you treating me this way, Nile? Why are you suddenly so . . . so cold?"

"Maddie, I . . ." He shrugged, at a loss for words.

"It's the hoax, isn't it? You won't forgive me. You're still holding that against me, aren't you?"

He couldn't meet her fierce, wild gaze. "I can't help it, Maddie. If you hadn't lied about Ben Thomas, we wouldn't be in this situation now."

"You self-righteous bastard!" Her lower lip was quivering from the exertion of suppressing tears. "You've got to throw that into my face at every opportunity, don't you? Yes, I lied, lied, *lied*! But I also saved your life. And Amy's. But that doesn't count, does it?" she added bitterly. "In your eyes, I'm still a liar and a cheat and nothing I can do will make up for it."

Nile felt the first stirrings of shame. Maddie was

right. No one was perfect, least of all himself. What right had he to condemn her? It was time to put it all behind him.

He was about to open his arms to her again, when Maddie laughed hysterically and muttered, "Well, I might as well be hung for a sheep as a lamb." When she looked at him, her eyes glinted defiantly. "I've got a confession to make, Nile. My real name isn't Maddie Dare, it's plain old Janie Japes. You'll be pleased to know my whole life has been one lie right after another."

Before she could elaborate, Maddie fell to the deck in a dead faint.

When she came to, she found herself lying in the hammock, a cool wet cloth across her forehead. Nile was standing at the wheel, steering the launch, while Amy sat on the deck beside him.

Maddie couldn't bear to move. It felt so good to just lie there without a care in the world and let someone else worry about eluding Haddon Fitch. But the blissful feeling didn't last. After her last outburst, she realized she owed Nile an explanation.

"Nile?" she called, surprised at how feeble her voice sounded.

But he turned as if he had been listening and waiting for her to speak. He left the wheel and stood over her, his expression unreadable. "Yes?"

"We've got to talk. I've got something very important to tell you."

"Let me moor the launch for the night."

Once that was accomplished, he returned to her side and leaned against the railing. "How are you feeling now?"

"Exhausted," she answered truthfully. She didn't tell him that her skin felt as if it were on fire from all the insect bites she had endured.

"Then I'd better let you rest."

"No. I'll be all right, truly. There's something I've got to tell you before I lose my nerve."

A ghost of a smile lit up his handsome, careworn face. "Maddie Dare lose her nerve? Never."

She looked down at her hands and focused her attention on one black blister at the base of her index finger. "But that's just my point: there is no Maddie Dare. She doesn't exist. I made her up."

"She looks pretty real to me," Nile said gently.

"Well, she's a lie. And she is not the daughter of a country parson from Somerset. She's nothing more than the daughter of poor factory workers and she grew up in a series of London tenements."

"Janie Japes," Nile said. "Why don't you tell me about her?"

Maddie hesitated. She had never told anyone about Janie, not even Sam Vincent, a man she trusted and looked up to. She had always been so ashamed of her past. In fact, she didn't know why she was telling Nile now, except that she felt he had a right to know.

"I lived in various two-room tenements with my parents, three brothers, and three sisters," she began. "When I was ten years old, my mother was killed when she fell into her machine at the factory where she worked."

Nile stirred, and she could sense his outpouring of sympathy even before he said, "I'm sorry, Maddie. That must have been difficult for you."

"It was. My mother and I were very close, and when she died, I felt as though I had lost my best friend. You see, your mother may have left you to go traveling the world, but at least you had a mother. Even though two of my brothers were older and stronger than I, I had to do everything—take care of the four younger children, cook, clean, and mend their clothes—otherwise my father would give me a whipping, especially when he was drunk, which he usually was.

"But that wasn't the worst of it." Maddie forced herself to look at Nile and prayed for courage. "I don't know how to tell you this, but I want to warn you that what I'm about to say will offend your sensibilities."

Nile stepped away from the rail to tower above her. "What is it, Maddie? You know you can confide in me."

She took a deep breath and let the words come pouring out in a rush: "When I was twelve, my older brother Dickie started ... started ..." She hesitated. "Nile, we became lovers."

Nile's eyes became as round as saucers; then his lip curled in disgust. "Your own brother?"

Desperation made Maddie's words come faster. "I was only a child, Nile. He said it would be all right, that what we were doing wasn't wrong. I swear I didn't know any better, and ... and ..."

"Hush, Maddie, it's all right," he crooned, reaching out to stroke her tearstained cheek. "I know it wasn't your fault. Please don't think I'm blaming you."

Maddie's frantic breathing slowed down when she saw Nile regarding her with more compassion in his eyes than she had ever hoped to see there.

"Your brother should have been shot for what he did to you, the little bastard."

"We were ignorant and poor, Nile. Dickie didn't know any better either."

"Still, I'd like to get my hands on him for just a few minutes."

Then Maddie said, "There's more, Nile, and I'm afraid it's not pleasant." She sighed and closed her eyes, forcing the words out: "I became pregnant at thirteen."

Those damning words echoed through the tropical stillness, seeming to grow in magnitude like a rising wind until Maddie thought she would go deaf.

"Oh, Maddie ..." Then she felt Nile grasp her hand and hold it tightly. "How terrible for you." He hesitated for a moment, then said softly, "What happened to your baby?"

Without his comforting touch to give her strength, Maddie knew she would never have had the courage to go on. "I lost it," she said heavily, "and the ability to have any more children of my own."

Without uttering a sound, Nile sank to his knees beside the hammock and drew her into his arms. She felt him tremble, and then his tears were dropping onto her cheek. "My poor, poor Maddie."

"Don't cry for me, Nile," she murmured, reaching up to stroke his hair. "It happened so long ago, and I've come to accept it."

Finally he rose and returned to the rail, where he stared out into the jungle.

"About that time I met the woman who was to be my salvation," Maddie continued. "She was a wealthy widow by the name of Stephania Raleigh, and we first met when I was thirteen and went to work for her as a maid. She saw something in me that no one else had, least of all myself. She paid my father a princely sum to adopt me legally, and then she went about molding and educating me into the daughter she had never had. I never saw my family again, though my brother tried to see me once or twice."

"You were very fortunate this Mrs. Raleigh took a fancy to you," Nile said.

"Very fortunate. Once I learned to read and write, I devoured every book in her extensive library and practiced making up stories of my own. I made remarkable progress, if I do say so myself, and Mrs. Raleigh was delighted to have her faith in me affirmed. When I was older, she introduced me into her august social circle and even took me traveling abroad as if I were her own daughter. It was she who convinced me to become a newspaper reporter."

"So she's the one I have to blame."

Maddie smiled at his gentle teasing. "She's the one."

She tried to rise, but fell back with a gasp, bringing Nile to her side at once, his eyes dark with concern. "You've strained yourself. Why don't you rest and we'll talk tomorrow?"

"No. I've got to finish what I've started before I lose my nerve. I've got to make you understand." She looked up at him. "I needed a new name to go with the new life I had forged for myself, for the new person I had become, thanks to Mrs. Raleigh. Poor, ignorant Janie Japes didn't exist anymore. So I became Maddie Dare to reflect the daring, confident woman I had become."

Maddie took a deep breath. "Now we come to the difficult part. I am only Maddie Dare because of my writing, Nile. It sets me apart, makes me special, and gives my life purpose. Without my writing, I feel worthless."

"You're not worthless, Maddie. Don't ever say that."

His words gave her courage. "That's why I could no more give up writing than I could stop breathing. And it's why I helped Sam to concoct the hoax, even though I knew it was wrong."

She raised her eyes to his, searching their golden depths for any clue to his feelings, but his gaze was veiled and she couldn't tell.

"I've never told another soul about Janie Japes," Maddie said quietly.

"I'm honored and flattered that you told me."

His words filled her heart with hope. "I thought if you knew what private demons drive me, you'd understand and be able to forgive me for deceiving you."

Nile reached over to touch her cheek. "Why don't you try to get some sleep? I have a lot of thinking to do."

Maddie watched him walk away, but instead of sleeping, she stared at the launch's roof.

She realized she had taken the gamble of her life by telling Nile of her bleak, deprived childhood. She knew she had shocked him to the core. Any good, respectable middle-class Englishman would be when confronted with such an incredible story, since it was out of the realm of such people's experience. But Maddie couldn't help being born poor, just as she couldn't help being the victim of her father's drinking and her brother's unnatural desires. She prayed Nile understood that and didn't condemn her.

He's got to understand, she said to herself. He's just got to.

Then she closed her eyes and finally dozed.

When Maddie next opened her eyes, she felt much stronger, as if a heavy burden had been lifted from her shoulders. It was almost twilight, and Nile was hovering above her.

"I'm sorry," he said.

Maddie's hopes rose. "For what?"

"For being such an ass." He dropped down on one knee so his face was level with her own. "Will you forgive me?"

"There's nothing to forgive, Nile."

He took her hand in his. "Oh, but there is. I've been stupid and blind. You were right when you said I see everything in terms of black and white. But now I can see and understand that your reasons for going along with this hoax aren't so cut-

and-dried. Your being a newspaper reporter is your life."

"Yes, it is." Maddie gripped his hand firmly, her voice edged with steel as she said, "I'll never go back to the way I was, Nile. Never. It was a terrible life of deprivation and hopelessness."

"You won't have to."

A strange expression crossed his face, and he swallowed firmly, as if gathering his courage to say something to her. When he murmured something unintelligible, Maddie said, "What did you say?"

"I said, I love you, Maddie."

She searched his face, daring beyond hope that she had heard him correctly. But it was written there for anyone to see. Maddie reached out to cradle his cheek in her palm, her eyes damp. "Oh, Nile . . ."

He closed his eyes with a sigh and turned his head so he could kiss her palm, his lips warm and insistent against her flesh. Then he looked over at her, his eyes shining with the same hunger they had had that day at the bathing pool, a look Maddie had thought she would never see again.

"I love you," he said again. "I never suspected how much until Fitch abducted you. I remember thinking how furious I was that he dared take something that belonged to me, and I was ready to fight him to the death, if need be, to get you back."

Then Nile fell silent as though waiting for Maddie to make some comment. When she didn't, he grinned. "Aren't you going to voice your objections to being considered a man's possession, Miss Dare?"

"No, Mr. Marcus," she replied lazily. "Any woman would adore being fought over." She let her gaze fall to his lips. "Especially by such a handsome, virile specimen as yourself."

Maddie heard the hiss of his sharply drawn breath, and then Nile's mouth was on hers, his hard lips warm and demanding, expertly coaxing hers to respond to him. Maddie closed her eyes, luxuriating in the voluptuous feelings his touch aroused in her. When she parted her lips and sought to possess his mouth with her tongue, Nile drew away.

"Do that and I'll be taking you on the deck," he growled.

Maddie chuckled. "You're forgetting about Amy."

"Maybe I could lock her in her cabin." He looked so determined, Maddie laughed again.

Then Nile became serious. "I knew I had to get you away from Fitch, but at the time, I didn't know why. I thought it was just because I felt honorbound to protect you. But now I realize it was because I had fallen in love with you and had to get you back."

Her heart singing, Maddie said, "What is it about me that you love best? My strong will? My cutting wit? Come, come, a woman likes to know."

"All that and more." Nile sat back on his heels and hung his arms over his knees. "After I rescued you, you didn't have an attack of the vapors as any other woman would. And as we made our escape, we worked together. It was as if we were of the same mind. You didn't ask for special treatment, you just did what had to be done without complaint. I don't know any other woman who would have done that."

"Haven't I always told you I'm extraordinary?" Maddie said, giving him a teasing smile.

"You proved that these last few days, sailing this launch by yourself."

"Don't tell my readers, but I was terrified."

"But do you know what really humbled me?"

"No, what?"

"When I came above deck, your first thought was for my welfare, not your own. There you were, looking so frightful I almost didn't recognize you, and—"

"Frightful?" Maddie patted her hair, alarmed to feel it all snarled and tangled. Then she blushed and averted her eyes. "I must look a sight."

"You do," Nile agreed, chuckling at the reappearance of her vanity. "But you're the most beautiful sight I've ever seen."

He knelt again and lowered his face to hers. Maddie reached up and entwined her arms around his neck, drawing him closer. She closed her eyes as he slipped his left arm beneath her shoulders to support her, and then he was kissing her again, harder this time and with raw, unrestrained possessiveness. The world around them ceased to exist. There were only Maddie and Nile and their burning newfound love for each other.

Abruptly Nile stopped and pulled away. When Maddie regarded him with a questioning look, he said, "After what your brother did to you, are you sure you want me to . . . to . . ." Words failed him and he looked away.

"It's all right," she said softly, to erase all doubts. "What Dickie did didn't make me fear a man's advances, Nile, or make me unfeeling. Please don't stop now. I want you so much."

With a sigh of relief, Nile moved his lips against hers, and she abandoned herself to his touch, both arousing and soothing. She felt the first jolt of pleasure rock her to the core, then slowly spread throughout her body like a slow flame as Nile claimed her.

With one quick thrust, his tongue slid into her mouth, causing Maddie to groan as she welcomed the sensuous invasion. At the same time, she felt his fingers move down the front of her shirt, deftly undoing one button after another. Maddie held her breath, waiting, praying for him not to stop. Nile didn't disappoint her. He parted the material and slid his hand beneath both the shirt and the lawn camisole.

The moment Nile's warm, rough hand closed around Maddie's bare breast, she felt him retreat from the kiss. She groaned in wordless protest and sought to pull his head back down so she could continue devouring him.

"Love-greedy woman," he whispered, amusement in his voice. "I just want to be able to see your face while I do this . . ."

His fingers closed gently on her nipple, and Maddie's eyes flew open as white-hot desire uncurled deep in her belly. She stared up at Nile, his face inches from her own, his golden gaze pleased with his masculine ability to awaken her in just this particular way. She could see her own face reflected in his irises, the double images' languid wantonness of her half-closed eyelids and slightly parted lips exciting her almost as much as Nile's relentless caressing of her breast. He deepened his hold on her captive nipple, causing Maddie to groan mindlessly as she surrendered more and more of herself to him.

"Poor Maddie," he said, his tone mocking.

She could feel Nile's hot breath blaze a trail down her neck and chest as he lowered his head to her breast. With a whimper of urgency she arched her back, offering herself up to him. Nile chuckled as his tongue flicked over the straining peak, teasing it until Maddie thought she'd go mad.

"Nile, please!"

His mouth closed over the rosy nipple and he suckled first one breast, then the other, with agonizing slowness, causing Maddie to writhe beneath his mouth.

"Sweet, lovely Maddie . . . let me make love to you," Nile murmured raggedly.

"Oh, yes, Nile! Please!"

Suddenly a voice called out, "What are you doing? Praying?"

Maddie and Nile jumped away from each other.

"Damnation and hellfire! I had forgotten about her," Nile muttered under his breath as he started swinging to his feet.

Maddie's fingers flew down her shirt, closing buttons before Amy could see her in such wanton disarray. "Yes, dear," she replied sweetly, even as her body screamed in protest at its denial. "Nile and I were just saying our prayers."

Nile's look of resentment and frustration was comical to behold as he watched Amy saunter across the deck, oblivious of what she had just interrupted.

"I always said my prayers at bedtime," Amy said. "My mama would listen to them."

Maddie rose from the hammock, surprised that she was able to stand after Nile had turned her body into clay ready for molding. She said, "Why don't you lie in the hammock for a while and watch the beautiful sunset? The mosquitoes will be here soon anyway, and we'll have to go to our cabins."

Amy smiled and did as she was told.

"And I think I'll go chop wood," Nile muttered.

Maddie suppressed a smile. "We have no ax."

"Then perhaps a swim in the river will cool me off."

She drew him aside, out of earshot of Amy lying blissfully in the hammock. "We can't do anything with Amy around. We can't risk her interrupting us again."

Nile ran his hand through his hair, his whole body visibly shaking with the need to touch her, a need Maddie shared. All she wanted to do was fling herself into Nile's arms and have him make love to her.

"Why don't we take a little walk into the jungle?" Nile suggested, his eyes glittering with anticipation.

"There are snakes in there and who knows what else!"

"Blood-sucking vampire bats and leeches, not to mention swarms of mosquitoes."

"Wonderful! No matter how much I want you, Nile Marcus, I have no intention of letting swarms of mosquitoes feast on my exposed body."

His eyes twinkled as his gaze fell to her breasts. "And a lovely body it is."

Maddie blushed to the roots of her hair as she tried to ignore his relentless teasing. "Besides, we can't leave Amy alone. There's no telling what she would do."

"Point well taken."

"What about your cabin, after Amy's fallen asleep?"

"Bad idea. I'm a noisy lover. She wouldn't be asleep for long."

They both fell into frustrated silence.

Finally Nile let his hot gaze rake her over. "When I make love to you, I want a bed big enough for four people. I want to take my time undressing every lovely inch of you." He lowered his voice to a seductive growl. "Then I'm going to make you burn for me, Maddie Dare, until you beg me to take you."

Nile's words were as potent and arousing as his touch, and Maddie felt the embers of desire start to smolder again. She swallowed hard. "If you keep this up, I'll never reach Manaus, Amy or no Amy."

"By the time I'm through with you, you'll know you belong to me and no one else."

"I do like the sound of that."

He grinned, a wolfish baring of teeth. "You won't be sorry."

"And will Luizhina vouch for you?" she said archly.

He took an involuntary step toward her. "You

little minx. Just for that, I'm going to keep you in bed until you're too exhausted to move."

The delicious implications almost drove Maddie over the edge. "Nile, will you stop it?"

He raised his brows and his expression changed to one of angelic innocence. "I know you're longing to tear off my clothes, but you'll just have to restrain yourself."

Maddie was spared from responding when they heard a sharp wail of protest from Amy as she came bounding out of the hammock, waving her hand in front of her face to ward off the mosquitoes.

"Bedtime," Maddie said, casting a sidelong glance at Nile.

"I wish."

Maddie was instantly roused out of a deep sleep when she was thrown out of her bunk and landed on the floor in a tangle of mosquito netting. Panic and a sense of danger overwhelmed her as she fought her way clear and rose to her feet. As she staggered forward and fumbled for the door in the dark cabin, she realized the floor was teetering crazily to the side.

When she noticed her feet were wet, she screamed Nile's name as she flung open the door.

"Maddie, are you all right?" his voice called from above, and she could see his large form silhouetted against gray sky.

"Yes. What's happening to us? There's water down here."

"We slipped our mooring, floated downriver during the night, and crashed into a log. Get Amy and let's get out of here before the launch sinks. Hurry!"

Don't panic, Maddie told herself. The worst thing you can do is panic.

"Amy?" she called.

A shrill cry of confusion and fear greeted her

ears as she opened the door to the other cabin. In the dimness, Maddie could discern Amy sitting on her bunk, her legs tucked beneath her.

Maddie extended her hand. "Amy, come with me. Quickly!"

"But the floor's wet."

Maddie lost all patience. Grabbing Amy's hand, she pulled her off the bunk and started dragging her out of the cabin. "That's why we have to leave."

When Maddie emerged from below, she found the deck was not so steeply sloped that she would lose her balance and go sliding off. She looked around in the thin gray light of predawn, fully expecting to be trapped in the middle of the river, with the shore miles away on both sides. She was relieved to see that at least the launch had gone aground very close to shore.

"Why is the boat stopped?" Amy whimpered behind her.

"Hush," Maddie said, putting a comforting hand on the other woman's shoulder. "You must be very quiet, Amy, and very brave. You've got to do whatever I tell you. Promise me."

"I . . . I promise. But I'm afraid!"

"There's nothing to be afraid of. You know Nile and I won't let anything happen to you."

Nile materialized before her, his sheer physical presence solid and reassuring. "It could be worse," he said. "We should be able to wade to shore. I just hope I don't get the Winchester wet."

Maddie noticed he was tying a length of rope to the railing. "What's that for?"

"I'm going to stretch this rope across the water and tie it to that other log onshore. That way, you and Amy will have something to hang on to."

She smiled. "Always so considerate."

Nile looked at her. "I don't want to lose you. Not now. Not like this."

His words and the deep affection in his rough voice warmed her, almost making Maddie forget the question uppermost in her mind: how were they ever going to escape Haddon Fitch with the launch disabled? But she couldn't bear to voice it, not yet.

Nile went to the rail. "I'll go first. You and Amy should be safe here for a while yet."

"Be careful," Maddie called after him as he lowered himself over the side.

When she heard the splash, she fought her way down the deck, holding on to one of the poles supporting the roof. She bit her lower lip as she watched Nile sink below the surface of the water for a moment, wetting the rifle in the process. His head bobbed to the surface almost at once, and after he discarded the useless weapon, he began swimming with sure, steady strokes.

Suddenly he stopped.

Maddie envisioned him being attacked by a stingray or an eel, and her heart flew to her throat. She let out a sigh of relief when she saw that Nile was wading now, the water up to his armpits.

"Sandbar," he called back.

There came another patch of deep water that forced him to swim, but it was for only a short distance. Then he was wading again, this time through waist-deep water. Finally he was standing on a long stretch of flat shore and tying the rope around the log.

When he was done he waved to her to signal they should come ahead.

Maddie looked at Amy and thought this would be the perfect time for the missionary to regain her lost wits. But she knew that life seldom worked for her convenience, so she took a deep breath and prayed Amy would do as she was told.

When Maddie explained to Amy what she had to

do, the other woman's eyes widened in terror. "I can't!" she cried. "I'm afraid!"

"You've got to be brave, Amy. Freddie would want you to be brave."

Her brother's name opened all doors to Amy. She went to the rail and eased herself into the water, grasping the rope. For one terrifying moment she went under, but emerged gasping and sputtering. Then she did as Maddie instructed, letting the rope guide her as she moved through the deepest parts of the water, and wading through the shallows.

"Good girl," Maddie murmured.

Then it was her turn.

Maddie banished all thoughts of dangerous river denizens from her mind as she climbed over the rail and held on to the rope. The waters below looked murky and bottomless, but she took a deep breath and resolutely eased herself into the Amazon.

Surprised that the water could be so chilly, Maddie almost panicked when she went under, but then her head broke the surface and she was floating. At first she thought she could swim without the aid of the rope, but she found her skirt was weighing her down and she was forced to move hand over hand, occasionally fighting to keep her head above water. Once she almost screamed when she felt something brush against her leg, but she fought down the panic and kept on going.

To Maddie, the distance between the launch and the shore seemed like miles, but before she knew it, she was wading through the shallows toward Nile, who had come in the water after her.

His arms went around her, offering her shelter, and she clung to him, their wet bodies pressed together as they stood thigh-deep in water. His hard, brief kiss spoke volumes; then they headed for shore, to where Amy was sitting on the log.

Once Maddie made sure Amy was all right, the

three of them just sat there in silence for a few moments.

Then Maddie said to Nile, "What do we do now? We're stranded here. And as much as I hate to mention it, our present situation does not bode well for us in our struggles to outrun Mr. Fitch."

Nile said, "We're close to Manaus now. A boat should be coming along soon."

Maddie just prayed it wasn't Fitch's boat.

"We've been very lucky," Nile went on. "The launch could have drifted into the current. Also, if this were the rainy season, all this land and a good part of the jungle beyond would be underwater right now."

"If Fitch catches us, we're going to wish we were underwater," she muttered.

Nile's arm was around her shoulders in an instant, his rugged face close to hers. "I promise you we'll make it somehow, Maddie. We can go through the jungle if we have to."

She looked into his eyes and saw the raw determination there. "You haven't let me down yet."

"I never will."

Maddie smiled and rested her head against his cheek, but her idyll was short-lived.

Amy whined, "I'm all wet."

"You'll dry off soon," Nile said. Then he whispered into Maddie's ear, "Do you know, you look nearly naked in that wet shirt?"

His words were so unexpected, they caught Maddie offguard, and her face turned scarlet. "Nile Marcus!" But he was right. The wet cloth of her shirt and camisole clung to her breasts provocatively.

She lowered her gaze to his trousers. "The same could be said of you."

He sighed. "Perhaps both of us should concentrate on getting us out of this predicament rather than out of our clothes."

"An excellent idea."

But she wondered if they ever would get out of this alive.

Maddie watched the morning sun rise above the treetops, and she felt her spirits plummet. They had been sitting here all morning, and not one boat had steamed by.

As she watched Nile traverse their sandy patch of shore, she could tell that he was beginning to worry too, and trying valiantly not to show it. But the facts of their situation were grave. Even though Nile had found a freshwater stream to slake their thirst and some manioc root to ease their gnawing hunger, they had no weapons save Nile's knife to defend themselves against larger predators, and nothing to protect them from tiny stinging ones that could be just as deadly.

Suddenly the sound of a jaguar screaming close by in the jungle made Maddie jump and Amy cry out with fear. However, something else had claimed Nile's attention.

"Maddie, come here!"

She rushed to his side. "What is it?"

"Look," he said, pointing upriver.

There, coming toward them, was a dugout canoe paddled by two Indians.

As the canoe drew closer, Maddie murmured to Nile, "Are they friendly? Do you think they'll help us?"

Nile just shrugged.

"Even if they agree to it, that canoe is not big enough to carry five people."

"Then I'll just have to stay behind."

Maddie stared at him in alarm. "No!"

"Maddie, don't argue with me. Just watch the canoe."

Unlike the launch, the canoe easily negotiated

the shallows and sandbars, and within minutes its two occupants were pulling it onto the shore. Maddie felt a fluttering of fear when she noticed the bows and blowguns in the bottom of the boat, but she was relieved when the Indians remained unarmed.

For a moment the two Indians just stood there eyeing Nile and Maddie warily, their black eyes both suspicious and curious.

"Smile, Maddie," Nile said.

She did so, and the Indians began talking excitedly between themselves.

"Do you understand what they're saying?" Maddie asked through her smile.

"Not one word," Nile replied.

One of the men boldly strode toward Maddie, and she had to fight the impulse to back away. Much to her surprise, the Indian reached out and began stroking her hair. When he stopped, he said something to his companion, who also came over and touched her hair gingerly, as though it were something truly wondrous.

"They seem quite taken with your hair," Nile said. "Perhaps they think it's 'sweat of the sun.'"

Suddenly Maddie had an idea.

She reached back and grabbed a long hank of her hair. First she pointed to it; then she pointed to the two men, indicating that she wanted to give it to them. Their broad faces registered astonishment, then blatant interest. Walking over to their canoe, Maddie pointed at it, hoping they would understand that she wanted to trade.

Nile looked incredulous. "You're going to trade your hair for their canoe?"

"Why not? I've got something they want—even though they could easily kill me for it—and they have something I want. Do you think they understand?"

"We'll soon find out." Nile reached down and slipped his knife out of its sheath on his calf.

"Why don't you get Amy into the canoe?" Maddie suggested. "That should make our intentions clear."

Nile did so, and when the Indians didn't object, Maddie assumed they understood what she wanted.

"Just think what a story this will make for the *Clarion*," she said as Nile started cutting her hair. " 'MADDIE DARE TRADES GOLDEN LOCKS FOR CANOE.' "

When Nile was finished, Maddie turned away, unable to look. Out of the corner of her eye she saw him divide it in two and hand one hank to each Indian. To her relief, they babbled excitedly and grinned, obviously delighted with the trade.

Nile said to Maddie, "Now, let's leave before they realize they've gotten swindled."

Her heart pounding wildly, Maddie walked toward the canoe, where Amy was sitting docilely watching the Indians with less fear than childlike curiosity.

"Help me push off," Nile said, and Maddie did so, wading into the water.

Within seconds they were seated inside, paddling away for Manaus.

When Maddie looked over her shoulder, the two Indians were disappearing into the jungle at a lope, never realizing they had saved the white men's lives.

17

Winston Belgrave stood before the mirror tying his tie. Then he ran a comb through his hair, and when he was satisfied with the way he looked, he strode over to his bedroom window and watched as the setting sun turned the sky over Manaus a brilliant orange.

Usually sunsets never failed to move him. They signaled the end of another profitable day. But for the last few weeks he had felt a palpable dissatisfaction with his life. It wasn't that he was tired of making money or the comforts wealth bought. It was ... The real reason eluded him, dancing just out of reach.

Winston brushed his forelock out of the way impatiently. No, that wasn't true. He was just deluding himself. The reason for his dissatisfaction was, as always, Amaryllis Gates.

He loved her. He needed her to become a complete man again, to supply something that was woefully lacking.

"It's all Nile's fault," he said aloud to the empty room.

Seeing Nile together with Maddie had reminded Winston of all that was missing in his life. Even though Maddie was promised to another, there was no denying the bond between her and Nile. Even when the two of them were at odds with each other, there was something there. It was a shame that, once they found her fiancé, she and Nile would go their separate ways. And that, thought Winston, would be a tragic mistake, because he had never met two people more suited to each other than Nile and Maddie, whether either of them realized it or not.

As the vivid orange sky began to fade to bright pink, Winston wondered what was happening to them. A day hadn't gone by that he didn't think of them without a tremor of fear for their safety. But always there was that conviction that Nile would keep them from harm.

Finally he sighed and turned away. He wasn't really looking forward to the opera tonight, but it would fill his evening and console him for losing Amaryllis, at least for a few hours.

There came a knock on his door, followed by the appearance of Bento.

"Senhor Marcus to see you, *senhor*," he said.

Winston just stared at his servant in disbelief. "What did you say?"

When Bento repeated himself, Winston's initial shock was replaced by excitement. "And Senhorita Dare as well?"

Bento inclined his head in assent. Winston brushed past his servant and hurried down the upstairs corridor, all the while wondering what kind of state he would find Nile in.

He found his answer when he came trotting down the stairs to see his friend standing in the foyer, one outstretched arm propping him against the wall, his back facing Winston.

"Welcome back, O King of—" He stopped in mid-sentence and halted halfway down the stairs when Nile turned around.

The man looked half-dead. He swayed on his feet, keeping himself upright only through the sheer force of his will. Nile's eyes were tired and bloodshot, lines of strain and exhaustion etched on his grubby, unshaven face. His clothes were filthy and torn, the left sleeve of his shirt sharply slashed, as from a bullet or a machete.

"My dear Marcus," Winston said softly, appalled. "You look as though you've been through hell."

"I can't spare the time for our usual pleasantries, Win," Nile said, "so just listen to me, and listen carefully "

Winston's mind roiled with questions but he knew he had to do just as Nile asked. "Go on," he said, descending the rest of the stairs.

"Maddie and I have Amaryllis with us."

Winston's heart surged with hope. "She's here? She came back with you? That must mean—"

"Will you keep quiet and just listen to me!" Nile roared.

Winston fell silent as his friend grabbed his arm in a grip surprisingly strong for his condition.

"She's not well," Nile said bluntly, his eyes soft with compassion. "There's no easy way to tell you this: she's lost her mind, Win. Amaryllis has gone mad."

He shook off Nile's arm and took a disbelieving step backward. "No! That can't be! Amy's the sanest woman I know."

Nile passed a weary hand over his eyes. "Win, I . . ." He shrugged and groped for words. "It kills me to have to tell you this, but it's true. In her mind, she's become a child again, always talking of her home in Devonshire and of Fred. I just wanted you to know so that when you see her, you won't be shocked if she doesn't recognize you."

Winston grappled with the terrible devastation threatening to paralyze him, and fought it back. He would deal with it later. Right now, Amy needed him.

"Where is she?" he said.

"In the drawing room, with Maddie."

Without a backward glance at Nile, Winston strode over to the closed double doors, stood before them in silence while he collected himself, then opened them.

The two women seated on the sofa rose and turned to him as he came walking into the room.

"Winston," Maddie said with a wan smile. "It's good to see you again."

He forced himself to look at her rather than Amaryllis, to prepare himself. When he saw what the Amazon had done to the poor woman, he knew she was lucky to have gotten out alive.

"What happened to your hair?" he asked.

Maddie reached up and fingered the jagged ends that reached only to her chin. "Sacrificed in the line of duty," she said with a weak laugh.

Then she put her arm around Amaryllis, and Winston knew he could avoid the inevitable no longer. His gaze slid over to the other woman and froze there.

It was not Amy's tangled hair or dirty face that broke his heart, but the lack of spirit in her pewter gray eyes. They were as transparent as glass, with no life behind them, no internal energy of any kind. They were the windows on a dead soul.

He forced himself to smile, when all he wanted to do was scream. "Hello, Amy. Do you remember me?"

With each passing second that she stared at him, Winston's hopes soared higher and higher. But then her gaze fell and she said, "No."

"Mr. Belgrave is a friend of Freddie's," Maddie said gently.

Amy's head shot up and her face became animated. "You know my brother?"

"Yes, Amy, I do."

"Mama said Freddie is very smart, and if we weren't so poor, he would go to Oxford or Cambridge."

Winston whirled around so she wouldn't see his savage anger and mistakenly assume it was directed at her. When he noticed that Nile had followed him into the room and was leaning against the door-jamb, he said, "You all must be starving and exhausted. I'll have Bento bring you something, then serve dinner, and then you can tell me what happened."

Nile stepped away from the door. "Winston, you don't—"

"If you'll all excuse me," he said, trying to keep his voice from breaking, "I have to be alone."

Nile stepped aside and Winston fled with his anguish.

After telling Bento to serve his guests a light collation, then summon him for dinner, Winston retreated to his study. He closed the door behind him and sagged against it heavily, his mind whirling.

Amy ... his beautiful, spirited Amy, had become nothing more than a stranger, a shell, a child in a woman's body.

Winston pressed his head back as hard as he could against the door, letting the wood dig into his scalp until tears of blessed pain welled in his eyes.

It was all his fault. God was using Amy as divine retribution for Winston's many, many sins. Clever God. Why punish Winston Belgrave himself when he will suffer so much more exquisitely if someone he loves is punished instead?

He stepped away from the door, his hands clenched into fists. He glowered up at the ceiling as if God were there looking down upon him.

"Why?" he cried, his voice ringing in the small room as he shook his threatening fist at the Almighty. "Why must you make her suffer for something I did? She's innocent. Innocent, damn you!"

He sank to the floor, great sobs racking his body. "Please make her well again. I'll do anything you ask. Anything."

He lay there whimpering until he heard Bento's cautious knock on the door. Then he rose, humbled at last, for he knew what he had to do to redeem himself.

". . .so instead of docking at the wharves, where one of Aguirre's men could see us," Nile concluded, "we moored the canoe on the outskirts of the city and walked."

Nile, Maddie, and Winston were seated around the dinner table after ravenously eating their fill of the sumptuous meal Win had provided. Maddie had already tucked the exhausted Amy into bed, and though Nile had urged her to go to bed as well, she had refused, preferring to sit up with the men while Nile told Winston the story of Provvy's death, their encounter with Haddon Fitch, and the subsequent harrowing escape down the Amazon.

Win leaned back in his chair and toyed with the stem of his wineglass. "So you really think Fitch was chasing you?"

Nile shrugged. "I do. Look, he tried to kill me, and kidnapped Maddie because he believed she could bring his little empire down. If I were in Fitch's shoes, I wouldn't let her get away. I'd try to stop her. I'd also telegraph my partner to stop her just in case I failed."

"I haven't heard anything about it," Win said.

Maddie smiled. "I think you'd be the last person Aguirre would say anything to, considering that you and Nile are such good friends."

"True," Win agreed.

"That's why we came here instead of going to a hotel," Nile said. "I don't want anyone knowing we're in Manaus. Not that we're going to stay here for very long."

Win looked at him sharply. "Don't be foolish. Of course you're going to stay here for as long as you like."

Nile shook his head. "I won't put you in danger too, old friend."

"Where will you go?" Win demanded in exasperation.

He put his elbows on the table and laced his fingers together. "I have a place in mind, but now's not the time to discuss it. Maddie's going to nod off into her dessert any minute now, so I think it's time she went to bed."

She stifled a yawn. "But before I do that, I would like to take a long hot bath."

Nile wrinkled his nose as if he smelled rotten eggs. "Now, that is a wonderful idea."

Maddie straightened in her chair and gave him a supercilious stare. "I'll have you know I'm not the only one who needs a rendezvous with hot water and a bar of soap, Mr. Marcus."

He grinned as he held up his hands in surrender. "Touché, Miss Dare."

As Maddie rose, Win said, "I'll have Bento draw your bath and leave you some salve for those insect bites. If you'll leave your clothes outside your door, they'll be laundered and mended by tomorrow morning."

Maddie gave him her heartfelt thanks, then added, "Don't worry, Win. I know Amy is going to be all right. It may take a little time, but I know she's going to be herself one day."

Then she bade the men good night and left.

Nile's eyes followed her out of the room. When Maddie's footsteps died away, he turned to Win and said, "Now we can really talk."

Win shook his head. "You're damned lucky you got out of this alive, O King of the Orchid Hunters."

"None of us would be alive today if it hadn't been for Maddie," Nile said.

"Do my ears deceive me, or am I talking to the same man who was reluctant to be burdened with a woman on this expedition?"

"The very same," Nile admitted. "You should have been there, Win. She was remarkable. Not only did she keep a cool head during our escape, when any other woman would have had hysterics, she navigated the river herself when I was out with another attack of malaria."

Win's eyes widened. "You're joking."

"If that's your reaction, imagine how I felt when I came staggering up the stairs to see Maddie at the wheel and our launch halfway down the Amazon."

Win raised his fine pale brows. "Do I detect a note of admiration in your voice?"

Nile sipped his wine, feeling bone-tired but unwilling to succumb until he had said everything he was going to say. "Admiration, respect, and—God help me, Win—I think I even love that exasperating virago."

For once, his friend didn't make a humorous retort. "It's quite wonderful, isn't it, when the right woman comes along?" he muttered wistfully.

Nile propped his elbows on the table and rested his head in his hands. "You know me Belgrave. I've never felt the need for a permanent relationship with a woman. Temporary ones have always suited me just fine. But it's different with Maddie. The thought of not having her in my life . . ." Words failed him and he just shrugged.

"But what about Ben Thomas?" Win said, his pale eyes filled with pain for his friend. "Once you do find him, you'll have to give her up."

"Ben Thomas isn't her fiancé," Nile said. "Right

from the start, this entire expedition to find him has been a hoax."

While Win just sat there dumbfounded, Nile told him all about the hoax Maddie and her newspaper had perpetrated, and how he had discovered it when they didn't find Thomas in Iquitos, where he was supposed to be.

"She's got brass, I'll say that for her," Win muttered. Then he added, "I can just imagine your reaction when she confessed all this to you."

"I wanted to wring her neck," Nile said. "I called her a liar, a cheat, and every other insulting name I could think of."

"Obviously you have changed your opinion of her base character."

Nile nodded solemnly as he recalled Maddie's outburst on the launch. "She reminded me that none of us is perfect. She also gave me several valid reasons why she had done what she did."

When Nile thought of Maddie's childhood and why she needed to be a journalist so badly, he felt himself draw even closer to her.

Win brushed his forelock out of his eyes. "I'm delighted for you, my friend."

"Your support means a great deal to me," Nile said. He studied his friend for a moment. "What about you and Amy?"

An expression of bleak despair shadowed Win's face. "I'm going to take her back to England. I'm sure there are medical specialists there that will be able to help her. And if they can't . . ." He looked at Nile. "I'll never leave her now, even if she remains a child for the rest of her life."

The fervor in Win's eyes was so intense that Nile knew better than to voice the objections that sprang to mind. Whether Win's motives were based on love or guilt or restitution, this decision was his and his alone to make.

"Before you go, will you do me a great favor?" Nile asked.

"What is it?"

"See if you can find out if Ben Thomas returned to Manaus. He's my only link with Provvy's killer."

Win nodded. "So, you have restitution of your own to make."

Nile nodded as the fatigue he had been staving off for hours finally wouldn't be denied. "I've got to get to bed before I drop."

Win pushed back his chair and rose. "You go ahead. I have some thinking to do."

Nile rose and slowly made his way out of the dining room. He would look in on Maddie before going to bed. He grinned to himself when he thought of Maddie and bed in the same breath.

He grabbed the banister and started climbing the stairs.

Maddie reclined in the tub, the back of her head resting on the rim, the steaming soapy water up to her neck.

When she first stepped into the bath, she scrubbed herself clean with a vengeance and washed her hair. Once basic cleanliness was accomplished, she anointed her burned, bitten face with the salve Bento had left, then turned her attention to the sybaritic pleasures of bathing. For the past half-hour she had been lying here like Cleopatra with her eyes closed, letting the hot water soothe her tired, aching muscles and draw the tension from her shoulders and back.

She couldn't believe she—they—had survived their impossible trek down the Amazon. It had challenged her mental and physical powers to the fullest, even more so than Africa, and Maddie had survived.

She was safe now. Safe.

Maddie opened her eyes and stared at the golden

arabesque on one of the bathroom tiles. She mustn't let the water lull her into a false sense of security. Antonio Aguirre and Haddon Fitch could be looking for them right this very minute. And even if they weren't in danger from that quarter, there was always the mystery of Ben Thomas to contend with.

Where is he? she wondered. Is he connected with Provvy's death somehow? God help him if he is, because Nile will have his head.

The unexpected sound of the bathroom doorknob turning jerked Maddie out of her daydream. She sat up abruptly, causing a bit of the water to slosh over the tub's rim and onto the floor.

"Excuse me," she called out, "but this room is occupied."

"I know," a familiar voice replied as the door swung open and Nile stepped inside. "That's why I'm here."

"Nile Marcus, how dare you interrupt a lady while she's bathing!"

He shut the door and grinned. "You've been in here so long I thought you might have drowned or at the very least turned into a wrinkled prune."

Maddie drew her arm across her breasts as she glared up at him. "Well, I haven't, so you can turn around and leave."

But Nile was making no move to do so. He just stared at her hungrily out of weary eyes, and Maddie felt herself blush.

"At least be a gentleman and avert your eyes," she said.

"You're far too enticing to do that. Besides," he added softly, "I've seen it all before."

"If you won't think of my modesty, then think of Winston. We are guests in his house, and if he hears you up here with me, he'll be shocked out of his mind."

"True," Nile agreed. He took her towel and held

it for her. "So I think it's time you got out of that tub and went to bed."

Maddie knew Nile wasn't going to look away, so she rose and was immediately enfolded in the towel he held. Then he grasped her hand to steady her as she climbed out, but the moment both her feet touched the floor, he pulled her into his arms.

Maddie held her breath as she gazed at him. Gaunt as Nile's face was, and hard with strain and fatigue, Maddie thought she would never get tired of looking at him for the rest of her life.

Nile closed his eyes and wordlessly rested his forehead against hers, his body radiating contentment as his arms held her.

"We made it," Maddie murmured, her lips grazing his. "We beat the Amazon."

His eyes flew open and he drew his head back so he could look at her. "No one ever beats the Amazon, Maddie. We survived because the Amazon let us."

His words shook her because she knew them to be true.

As her eyes roved over his face, she whispered, "Will you stay with me tonight?"

Nile looked as though he had been given a great gift, and he responded by cupping her cheek with his palm. "I want that more than anything in the world, but there are Winston's feelings to consider. We are guests in his house, and I wouldn't want to offend his sensibilities. The man is a dear friend, but he is as straitlaced as an old tabby."

"I understand. We're probably too tired anyway."

A teasing gleam appeared in Nile's eyes. "I'm never too tired for that, Miss Dare."

"Soon, then?"

"Maddie, Maddie, what you do to my self-control. Yes, soon. I promise."

She kissed him again, slowly. "Until tomorrow, then."

"Until tomorrow."

"Maddie, wake up."

Maddie tried to ignore the insistent voice by turning over and burrowing deeply into the pillow, but it was no use. When an insistent hand kept shaking her shoulder, disturbing her sleep, she opened her eyes gradually to see Nile already dressed and sitting on the edge of her bed.

"Don't you know that a gentleman should never be alone with a lady in her bedchamber?" she grumbled.

"As you so often remind me, you are not a lady, but a journalist," he retorted, his voice filled with laughter, "so I may be alone with you in your bedchamber all I like. As long as Belgrave doesn't catch me, of course."

"Leave it to you to throw my words back at me." She squinted against the bright light flooding the room. "What time is it?"

"Past noon," he replied.

Maddie rolled over on her back and looked up at Nile. "I must have really needed my sleep."

He looked well-rested himself, his eyes sparkling and alert. "Wasn't it wonderful to sleep without mosquitoes buzzing all around?"

"And in a real bed instead of a hammock." She yawned and stretched like a contented cat. "I am also looking forward to real food for breakfast instead of jerked meat."

Nile's expression suddenly turned grim. "We can't afford to become too complacent. We still have to try to find Thomas as well as evade Aguirre and possibly Fitch."

That sobering reality was like a splash of cold water in Maddie's face. She sat up, taking care to make sure the dressing gown she had slept in was wrapped tightly around her so as not to distract Nile.

"Do you think we have a chance of finding Ben?" she asked.

"If he's in Manaus, we'll find him. We assume he came back downriver, and if so he at least had to pass through here." Nile rose and went to the window. "I hope he's still here, because if he isn't, he could be anywhere—Pará, Rio de Janeiro, or even Paris for that matter."

Maddie was silent for a moment. "You think Ben murdered Provvy for the diamonds, don't you?"

Nile turned and looked at her, his countenance bleak. "I'll be honest with you, Maddie. Yes, I do. He was the last one to see Provvy alive, according to Inge. And what made him go back downriver when he was supposed to meet you in Iquitos? Sounds to me like he suddenly came into money and decided he didn't need to be a photographer for the *Clarion* any longer."

Maddie ran her hand through her cropped hair in frustration. "What you're saying makes sense, Nile, but"—she shrugged helplessly—"I know Ben Thomas. He was never the kind of man who would murder someone."

"A fortune in uncut diamonds can tempt even the strongest man."

"I hope you're wrong."

"So do I, for your sake." Then Nile turned away from the window and headed for the door. "You'd better get dressed. We have plans to make and Belgrave should be back any minute with your disguise."

She perked up at that. "My disguise? And what might that be?"

"You'll see," Nile said with an enigmatic grin. Then he left her to dress.

Maddie found her clothes laundered and mended just as Winston had promised. As she dressed quickly, she couldn't help but think about Nile's theory concerning Ben.

She had been so attracted to Ben at one time that she tended to overlook his faults, seeing only what she wanted to see—the handsome, charming rogue. But now that she was no longer under his spell, she could view him with a reporter's objectivity. As she thought about it in greater depth, she recalled Ben's oft-spoken dissatisfaction with his position at the *Clarion*, his conviction that someday his luck would change. Maddie hadn't paid attention to it at the time because everyone at the *Clarion* grumbled about the long hours and low wages.

"But would he kill someone for personal gain?" she said aloud to herself.

Then Maddie put Ben out of her mind as she stood before the mirror and critically examined her reflection. Her sunburned skin was no longer red but as bronze as Nile's, making her blue eyes an even more startling color in contrast. The salve had worked wonders, taking the sting out of the insect bites and easing the tightness of her skin. But she frowned in dismay at her poor cropped hair that would take years to grow out to its former luxuriant length.

Resigned, Maddie muttered, "Oh, well, it was sacrificed in a good cause," before tucking it behind her ears. Then she grinned. "My, don't you look just like a strapping lad."

Little did she realize how her altered appearance would benefit her as she went downstairs to join Nile.

Maddie stared at the white linen trousers and jacket Nile had just given her.

"This is my disguise?" she squeaked.

"Ingenious, isn't it?" Winston said. "The fit may not be quite right, but it was the best I could do on such short notice."

Nile's eyes gleamed wickedly. "You've always boasted that you're the equal of any of my sex, Maddie, so let's see how good you are at impersonating a man."

She flung the suit at his amused face. "Beast!"

He caught it expertly. "Now, now, Miss Dare . . ."

Maddie folded her arms. "Why do I need to wear a disguise at all?"

"Because we're going into hiding until we know for certain that Aguirre isn't after you," Nile replied.

"I thought we were in hiding right here," she said.

"Win will be better able to spy for us if Aguirre doesn't think he's seen us."

Winston frowned. "You make sense, Nile, but I'd rather you stayed here and let me take my chances."

Nile shook his head. "We can't risk it. Too much is at stake."

"And what about Amy? Are we taking her with us?" Maddie asked.

Winston looked pained. "She'll stay with Bento and his wife. She'll be safe there."

Nile looked out the window at the vibrant sunset, then handed the suit back to Maddie. "You'd better put this on. We'll be leaving as soon as it gets dark."

Three hours later, Maddie was walking beside Nile through the streets of Manaus.

"Stride, don't mince!" Nile hissed. "You want to walk like a man, not a woman in a suit."

Maddie automatically lengthened her stride. "You're enjoying every minute of this, aren't you?"

"Every minute." He glanced down at her, his golden eyes dancing with mirth. "It's a good thing you bound your, er, chest, otherwise no one would believe you're a man. And try to keep your hips from swaying."

"Nile Marcus, when this is over, so help me God, I'm going to—"

"Don't say another word. Your voice is too high for a man's, so you'll be better off if you don't say anything at all."

"So you can torment me and I can't retaliate, is that it?"

"How astute of you. Now, not another word out of you."

Maddie clamped her jaw shut and forced herself to concentrate on her performance in an attempt to keep her temper from boiling. Soon she was duplicating Nile's stride and enjoying the freedom of trousers, though the jacket and tie were making her swelter. But when several *senhoritas* passing in a carriage gave her flirtatious looks from behind their black lace fans, Maddie's success was complete.

As she walked silently beside Nile, Maddie noticed that the streets were changing, becoming narrower, darker, rougher. She found herself becoming more alert, wishing she had eyes in the back of her head, and more than once she had to fight down the impulse to cling to Nile's arm.

"Just where is this hiding place of yours?" Maddie murmured.

"You'll see."

The moment they rounded a corner and started down yet another dark narrow alleyway, Maddie sensed danger ahead. No sooner did she lay a warning hand on Nile's arm than they heard sounds of a scuffle followed by a thin, sharp scream. She stopped, giving her eyes time to adjust to the darkness. Then she saw the three figures, two standing and the other lying on the ground not twenty feet away.

"Stop!" Maddie cried without thinking.

She felt Nile's hand digging into her arm, restraining her. "Don't be a fool!"

But it was too late. The two assailants froze and stared at them. Nile swore under his breath and tensed for a fight. Without warning, the two assailants turned and fled, running down the alley toward the other end, where a solitary streetlight glowed in the moist tropical night.

"Let's see if we can help that poor bastard," Nile said, walking toward the fallen man.

He was so intent on the crime's victim that he paid no mind to the fleeing assailants, but Maddie did. The weak arc of light revealed something astonishing.

"Nile!" she said, grasping his arm. "Those two are women!"

He stopped and stared, but they had already rounded the corner of a building, making good their escape even as the echo of their footsteps rapidly faded away.

Maddie glanced at the man lying on his back, his arms close to his body. "Shouldn't we try to catch them?" she asked Nile, who was kneeling beside the supine form.

When Nile swore, Maddie asked, "Is he . . . ?"

"Dead? Oh, yes. They stabbed him in the gut." He looked up at her, a queer expression on his face. "It's Calistro."

Maddie's eyes widened as her hand flew to her mouth. "Calistro?" she gasped.

"See for yourself."

Maddie took a deep breath to gather her courage, and peered over Nile's shoulder. Even in the semidarkness of the alley, she recognized the man responsible for Zosia's death. Those black eyes, so cold in life, appeared just as cold and lifeless as onyx in death.

She shuddered and turned away. "Good riddance."
As Nile swung to his feet, Maddie said, "What are
we going to do about him?"

"Leave him to the dogs, before we're accused of
his murder."

He started walking down the alley and Maddie
followed.

"Those two women ... Do you think the twins
killed him?" she asked.

"We'll never know for certain," Nile replied, "but
I'd like to think so."

"So would I," Maddie uttered with such vehe-
ment satisfaction that Nile looked at her sharply.

They resumed their walk to Nile's hiding place.

From the foyer, Maddie surveyed the plush noisy
parlor that smelled of smoke, perfume, and licen-
tiousness.

She glared up at Nile in outrage. "Your idea of a
suitable hiding place is a brothel?" she hissed into
his ear.

His eyes twinkled with mischief. "Chloe's is the
perfect place. No one would think of looking for us
here."

"I beg to differ," she retorted hotly. "It's the first
place anyone would think of looking for *you*!"

Nile shook his head. "Maddie, Maddie, you do
disappoint me. You're not being very daring at all."

"I'll have you know I've been in brothels before,"
she said. When Nile's eyes widened in shock, she
added, "Only as a reporter, of course."

"Of course."

"It's not the place, it's the way the women are
looking at you." She clenched her teeth. "As if
you're an old and valued customer."

Of the twenty or so women seated around the
room in various states of undress, ten of them were
blatantly giving Nile inviting glances. Every one of

them was stunning, and there was something for every taste. Whether a man's preference ran to the boyish or the voluptuous, dark- or fair-haired, simple pleasures or more decadent offerings, there was a woman for him at Chloe's. As Maddie scanned offerings of every nationality, she found herself wondering which had been's Nile's favorites.

"You're jealous!" he crowed in delight.

"If you don't lower your voice," Maddie said, "they're going to question your masculinity. I'm supposed to be a man, remember?"

Flustered, Nile cleared his throat and stepped away from Maddie just as a woman with Oriental features came up to them, gave Maddie a sharp, appraising look, and said something to Nile in Portuguese.

"What did she say?" Maddie asked.

"Chloe wanted to know what I was doing with a woman dressed as a man."

Maddie turned away and coughed into her hand to hide the very feminine blush that rose to her cheeks.

Nile conversed with Chloe for another minute, then turned to Maddie and said, "She's agreed to hide us. Follow me upstairs, and try to be inconspicuous."

Maddie did as she was told, and Nile led her to a room at the end of the hall. After locking the door behind him, Nile swooped Maddie into his arms, holding her tightly against him as his mouth found hers.

He kissed her relentlessly, until Maddie was breathless and weak-kneed, and when they finally parted, he stared down at her with a look of blazing triumph.

"I finally have you where I want you, Maddie Dare."

"I know. You intend to sell me into white slavery."

Nile shook his head. "Do you know why I chose Chloe's as our hiding place?"

"No. Tell me."

"What did I promise you that night on the launch, when you so brazenly offered yourself to me and I had to refuse reluctantly?"

Maddie smiled slowly at the memory. "You said you wanted to make love to me in a bed big enough to hold four people."

Nile nodded toward the other end of the room. "Will that do?"

Her face lit up when she saw the huge ornately carved four-poster bed standing against the wall. "I think it would do very nicely."

He tilted her head back and ran his lips down her neck. "What else did I promise you that night?"

She shuddered deliciously at his expert touch. "That you wouldn't let me out of bed for at least four days."

"Make it five."

Maddie entwined her arms around his neck. "No Amy, no Winston, no interruptions."

"Exactly."

"Clever Nile Marcus."

Suddenly the teasing light faded from his eyes, and he looked at Maddie strangely.

"Nile, what is it?" she asked in alarm.

"Maddie, do you really want to make love to me?" He drew the backs of his fingers down across her cheek.

"Of course I do! I wouldn't be here with you if I didn't."

Nile took a deep breath. "After what your brother did to you, I . . . I wasn't sure how you would feel."

"That was a long time ago, Nile," she said softly. "I've never been with a man since, but that's because I never met another man I wanted to go to bed with. I'm not afraid to try with you."

He looked relieved. "I had to be sure. I don't want to hurt you, Maddie."

"You never could."

He closed his eyes and rested his forehead against hers for a moment. Then he said, "Let's get you out of that suit."

As Nile reached for Maddie's jacket, she placed her palms against his chest to restrain him. "You know, Nile, you've seen me undressed three times—"

"Two and a half. You were only half-undressed on the launch."

Maddie suppressed a smile. "I stand corrected. But in any case, I've never seen you undressed. So why don't I get you out of that suit first?"

"You're thoroughly brazen and shameless," he whispered, but the sparkle in his eyes belied the words.

Maddie divested him of his white linen jacket quickly, but she took her time with his shirt, unbuttoning it with such maddening slowness that Nile finally yanked out the shirttails himself and finished the job.

"Now my trousers." His voice was rough and thick with passion.

"Not yet." Before Nile could protest, Maddie slid her hands across his broad chest, reveling in the wiry hairs sprinkled across it and the tense muscles underneath. Then her caressing fingers glided over his shoulders and down arms as hard as steel. She felt him tremble with the effort of holding himself back, and she felt her own excitement begin to blossom.

As she reached for his trouser waistband, her fingers began to tremble ever so slightly, and she hesitated, feeling suddenly shy.

"Maddie, what is it?"

She shrugged apologetically and focused her attention on Nile's chest. "I've seen a man before, but with you I feel as though it's my first time."

He raised her chin, forcing her to look at him. "If you want to stop right now, just say so."

In reply, she began unbuttoning his trousers. She could tell he was already almost fully aroused. When she tugged and the trousers fell to the floor in a soft rustle, she finally saw Nile in all his naked splendor. And he was magnificent.

Maddie sucked in her breath but couldn't take her eyes off him. When her curious fingers touched the long, thick shaft, it jumped and throbbed as though alive.

Nile groaned between clenched teeth. "Any more of that and I'll be useless. Why don't we go to bed?"

When Maddie smiled and her hand fell away, Nile began undressing her, but he was not as slow as she had been with him. In seconds Maddie's suit was scattered on the floor and Nile was undoing the strip of cloth binding her breasts.

"I feel like one of those Egyptian mummies in the British Museum," Maddie mumbled, her arms raised in the air to facilitate the process.

He grinned wickedly. "I feel as though it's Christmas morning and I'm opening a particularly longed-for gift."

Maddie chuckled at that, but her laughter died when she was finally rid of the binding and she noticed the way Nile was looking at her, like the predatory jungle cat she had always thought he resembled.

Suddenly she stepped back and looked down at his feet.

"What are you doing?" he asked.

"Looking to see if your feet are on backward," she replied with an impish grin.

Nile threw back his head and roared with laughter. "So you think I am a *boto*, do you?"

"A river spirit assuming human form to seduce this poor maiden."

"I'll show you just how much of an animal I am."

Then he swept her into his arms as though she weighed nothing and carried her over to the bed. He set her down gently, then followed her down.

Maddie watched as Nile propped himself on one elbow and stared down at her while he smoothed her hair with his free hand. Then his lips were all over her face, kissing her forehead, her cheeks, and finally her mouth. As he plundered that with his tongue, his hand was gliding down her body, lingering on her breast only long enough to tease the rosy nipple to life, before continuing on its leisurely exploration of her flat abdomen and boyish hip.

Maddie stiffened only briefly, as dark, searing memories of her brother's illicit caresses came flooding back, but she reminded herself that she had nothing to be ashamed of, and this time it was right and good.

She felt herself blossom beneath Nile's coaxing mouth and hands, as though a cold knot in her center was finally thawing. When Nile's burning lips began trailing down her neck, Maddie began returning his caresses, glorying in the sensuous texture of rock-hard muscle beneath silky skin.

She held her breath as his head moved down, for she knew what was going to come next and her body quivered in sweet anticipation. The touch of Nile's hot breath against the tip of her right breast made her groan even before his tongue began flicking over it, teasing the nub into aching fullness. Then he switched to the other breast, giving it just as much loving attention and sending Maddie rising on a widening spiral of pleasure.

He kept suckling her with slow deliberation, first

one breast, then the other, until Maddie's groans of abandon deepened and she was panting and writhing helplessly beneath him. She was lost. Nile was her master. All she could do was obey.

He loved her slowly and thoroughly, and just when she thought she would go mad with pleasure, Nile raised his head, kissed her gently, then parted her thighs with one knee. He poised himself over her, then entered her slowly, gently.

Maddie's eyes widened and she gasped as he took complete possession of her. When he began moving, she joined him in the ageless rhythm, her desire rising higher and higher with every thrust, all reason finally dissolving in a blazing burst of ecstasy that tore Nile's name from her parted lips.

Her uninhibited response plunged him over the brink, for he threw back his head and bellowed her name before shuddering and collapsing against her.

Later, as they lay entwined in each other's arms, replete and exhausted, they fell asleep murmuring words of endearment.

18

Maddie awoke slowly, one sense at a time.

She first became aware of light pressing against her eyelids and nudging her into a state of languorous semiconsciousness. Through half-open eyes she saw she was lying on her side in a bed in a strange semidark room with windows shuttered so tightly that only the faintest threads of morning light were visible between the slats.

Next she became aware of her own body and was faintly puzzled. It was bare, and it felt both tired and exhilarated at the same time, awakened, renewed somehow. Her flesh tingled, as though it had been stroked and kneaded to new glowing life and awareness, and the insides of her thighs ached pleasantly from some half-remembered exertion.

As the rest of her brain began functioning, Maddie suddenly remembered just what those exertions had consisted of, and she smiled at the memory of last night. Nile had made love to her. Not only had he mastered every inch of her body with his hands and mouth until he knew her intimately, he had made their thoughts one as well, and sent them soaring.

Maddie rolled over carefully, half-fearing he would be gone. But there he was, as real as Maddie herself, lying on his back and still sleeping on the other side of the bed.

She stared at him, her eyes drinking their fill of

his tousled hair, lined face relaxed in sleep, and jaw now shadowed with rough stubble. She watched his broad chest rising and falling, and remembered what it had felt like to be held in those arms now lying still at his sides, to feel his hips moving against her, relentlessly yet with such perfect control. Never had she expected to find such joy in a man's arms. And she wanted to experience it again and again.

When Maddie recalled her own passionate response to him, her wild wanton cries and mindless beseechings, she blushed to the roots of her hair. How could she possibly face Nile after reacting in such an uninhibited manner?

But once her nervousness faded, she felt her body stir with desire. Reaching out, she began to arouse him, stroking him while her gaze never left his face.

Nile's eyes flew open and he awoke like a wild animal, fully alert and cognizant of his surroundings. He stared at Maddie, his tawny eyes sharp and piercing.

She released him as she dropped her eyes to his chest and felt her cheeks grow pink with embarrassment. It was one thing to share such intimacies with a man at night, and quite a different matter entirely to face him across rumpled sheets the next morning.

Then she felt her chin raised so that she had to look at him. All she saw reflected in his eyes was sympathy and understanding.

"The morning after is always a bit awkward at first," he said kindly. "But there is a way to ease it."

"And what is that?"

He nuzzled her ear while whispering, "By loving me all over again."

Then Nile took her hand and put it against him, and Maddie felt his flesh quiver and harden at her touch. Emboldened, she clutched and caressed it in the way that brought him the most pleasure.

Nile gasped, then rolled onto his back, where he lay shuddering, a slave to his body's demands. "God, Maddie . . ."

The awkwardness disappeared. Maddie leaned over and kissed his flat nipples, then ran her tongue down the ridges of his ribs and along his smooth belly, circling the navel before plunging her tongue inside. A spasm of delight jerked Nile's body, nearly raising him off the bed.

"Enough!" he growled, reaching for her at last.

Much later, when they both lay sated and panting, Maddie discovered no traces of awkwardness remaining. She felt as though she and Nile had been lovers for years. When he propped himself up on one elbow and let his eyes rove over her, not even a hint of a blush stained her cheeks this time.

"You are magnificent," he murmured, smoothing back her damp hair with one large hand. "And definitely worth waiting for."

Maddie gave him a coquettish smile. "Am I better than your Luizhina?"

"You will be . . . with practice."

Maddie reached out and shoved at his chest, pushing him over. "Beast!"

Nile just laughed, a deep, contented sound. When Maddie sat up and turned away from him, apparently still furious, he just encircled her waist with one arm and pulled her back against him.

"Do you know how happy you make me?" he asked, his lips against her hair.

"No. Do I really make you happy?" she murmured uncertainly.

"Yes, you do. Why would you doubt it?"

She swallowed hard. "Because I'm so different from the kind of woman you seem to want."

"And what kind of woman do you think I want?"

"Oh, one who stays at home, darning your socks, not one who goes traipsing around the world writing newspaper articles. A conventional woman, not"— she closed her eyes—"a woman like your mother."

With an audible sigh, Nile released her and turned her to face him. "I may have wanted a woman like that once, Maddie, but no longer. I admit that my resentment of my mother once prejudiced how I felt about you, but when we were escaping Fitch together and you saved our lives, I finally realized how much I need the kind of woman you are, the kind who's going to be a partner."

Her smile was tremulous. "You don't know how much it means to me to hear you say that, Nile. You're finally accepting me for what I am."

He kissed the tip of her nose. "About time, don't you think?"

Maddie nodded happily as she nestled her head against his shoulder, feeling warm and secure. She wanted to talk about what would happen when their Amazon adventure was over and they returned to England and their everyday lives, but she didn't want to spoil the perfection of this moment. Perhaps Nile wasn't thinking beyond the present. Even though he had said he loved her, that didn't mean he meant marriage or a future with her. After all, she could never bear his child. No, she would just have to settle for whatever time they did have together and worry about tomorrow later.

That is, if they had a tomorrow.

She stirred against him. "Nile, do you think we will ever get out of Manaus alive?"

He rubbed her arm absently, his voice grave. "I won't lie to you, Maddie. I don't know. It depends on whether Belgrave can find Thomas before Fitch and Aguirre find us. Aguirre may be powerful in this city, but I'll promise you this: he's not going to take us without a fight." His arm tightened around her. "I'll die before I let him harm you."

She hugged him with all her might as she felt her eyes fill with tears. No man had ever loved her enough to lay down his life for her, and she was moved beyond words.

"Let's hope it doesn't come to that," she murmured.

"But I've got to find Ben Thomas," Nile said, "even if it means risking capture by Aguirre. I owe that much to Provvy."

Maddie said nothing. Part of her wanted to forget all about finding Ben and just get them all out of Manaus with their skins intact, but another part of her realized that this was something Nile had to do. It was a part of his personal code of honor as a man to avenge the death of a man who had been like a father to him, and he would do it or die trying.

She thought of Nile dead and shuddered.

"What's the matter? Are you cold? You trembled just then."

Maddie smiled to herself. "How could I be cold with your arms around me? No, I was thinking of Calistro," she lied.

"Oh."

"Do you think someone found his body?"

"Probably, by this time, if the vultures didn't pick it clean first."

"Do you think the authorities will connect his death to the twins?"

"I doubt it. We were the only witnesses and we're obviously not coming forward with that information." Nile gave her a little shake. "Besides, I didn't see who did it, did you?"

"No. The alley was so dark that I didn't get a good look at them." Maddie snuggled closer. "As terrible as this sounds, I'm glad Calistro is dead. Now he won't be able to lure innocent women into a life of degradation. And Zosia's death has been avenged. I also think it's ironic that the twins were the instruments of that vengeance. I shudder to think what's been done to those poor girls to turn them into murderers."

Maddie was interrupted by a soft knock at the door, and while she pulled the sheet up to her chin, Nile slipped out of bed and put on the silk dressing gown that had been left for him. He went to the door, opened it, and came back bearing a tray laden with a veritable feast.

Maddie grinned when Nile set it on a nearby table and she saw rolls with imported preserves, thick slices of imported ham, and steaming *cafèzinhos*.

"Chloe must think quite highly of you to provide such a feast," she said with a teasing chuckle.

Nile shrugged. "I used to be a good customer."

Maddie picked up a pillow and tossed it at him, but Nile ducked quickly and it missed him. "Monster!"

"But you love me anyway."

"I do, Nile, with all my heart."

His golden gaze softened as he reached out to stroke her cheek. Then he said, "Enough of this sentimental blather, Dare. We have to keep up our strength, so let's eat."

"Why do we need to keep up our strength?"

"As soon as we finish eating, I'll show you."

And he did.

By the third day, Maddie was ready to climb the walls. She and Nile had spent all that time confined to their room, and while she had to admit that a great deal of that time was spent in the pleasurable pursuit of getting to know each other, the forced confinement was beginning to place quite a strain on her. She could spend only so much time in bed or in the adjacent bath.

Maddie crossed her arms and began pacing the floor. "Can't we at least go downstairs? I feel as though I've been locked in a prison cell, with my meals served to me through the door!"

"As I've told you for the hundredth time, we can't go downstairs because one of the customers might see us. No one is supposed to know we're here."

"Surely Chloe's girls must suspect," she pointed out.

"Those that do have been warned to tell no one on pain of losing their lucrative livelihoods," Nile replied.

"Well, if they know about us, can't I at least go talk to some of them? I'm sure it would make a fascinating article for the *Clarion*."

He smiled indulgently. "It is only ten o'clock in the morning, my dear. The poor girls were working until four A.M., so take pity on them and let them get some sleep."

Maddie went to one of the windows and peered through the slats at the sunny day outside. "I wish we'd hear something—anything—from Winston."

"I'm sure we will, sooner or later."

Just then, there came a knock on the door and Nile went to answer it. Maddie heard him speaking in Portuguese to someone, his voice growing more animated.

Finally he turned to her and said, "Get dressed. Winston is waiting downstairs."

Fifteen minutes later, Maddie and Nile were being ushered into a small antechamber on the first floor.

Winston appeared ill-at-ease in such surroundings, for his fingers kept flicking nervously and his boyish face was grim.

The moment Maddie saw him, she said, "Winston, how's Amy?"

"The same," he replied bleakly. "But Bento and his wife are taking good care of her."

Nile said, "Why have you come? Do you have news for us?"

Winston nodded. "Much news. Sit down and I'll tell you."

Once Maddie and Nile were seated on the edge of a plush velvet sofa, Winston took a deep breath and said, "Haddon Fitch is dead."

"What!" Maddie and Nile cried out in unison, then exchanged astonished looks.

Winston nodded. "An accident on the river. His launch got caught in a whirlpool and he and a boatload of his men drowned. Don Antonio himself told me the sad news at the opera last night."

"Don Antonio?" Nile looked puzzled. "You spoke to Aguirre at the opera last night? Why? He's our enemy."

"You surmised wrong, old friend," Winston said with a grin. "From what I was able to determine last night, Fitch never got word to Aguirre about what Maddie had seen and why he was chasing you. Evidently his confidence was so overwhelming that he thought he could stop you without his partner's help."

"So Fitch never sent Aguirre a telegram about intercepting us," Nile said.

"Apparently not."

Maddie added, "So we don't need to stay in hiding."

Winston raised one hand to brush his forelock out of the way. "When I spoke to Aguirre, he seemed genuinely puzzled that Fitch was even sailing to Manaus in the first place. He also didn't know that you, Nile, and Maddie were in Manaus, because he asked if you had found your fiancé yet."

"Perhaps he was only acting," Nile suggested, "to make you relax your guard and betray us."

"I don't think so. He seemed sincere. In any case, I didn't tell him you were in the city."

Maddie reached over and squeezed Nile's hand. "Better safe than sorry. I'm glad we were cautious."

Nile leaned back and shook his head. "So Fitch is dead. Now all we have to do is find Ben Thomas and learn what he can tell us about Provvy's murder."

Winston stuffed his hands into his pockets and regarded them solemnly. "I know where Thomas is."

Maddie's jaw dropped and she jumped to her feet. "Ben is here? In Manaus?"

Nile was not far behind. "Where did you see him?" he demanded.

Winston held up both his hands for silence. "Now, I can't be sure because I saw his photograph only once, but the man I saw looked remarkably similar."

"Where did you see him?" Maddie asked.

"Also at the opera," Winston replied, "sitting in the private box of one of Manaus' wealthiest bankers."

Maddie felt her blood run cold as she exchanged looks with Nile. "How can a mere photographer afford to keep company with a wealthy banker?"

"Unless he's come into a great deal of money himself," Nile added.

"Provvy's uncut diamonds," Winston said.

"We don't know that!" Maddie cried. She still couldn't bear to think that Ben might be capable of murder.

Nile placed a hand on her shoulder. "What else could it be, Maddie?" he asked gently. "Where else would Thomas get that kind of money? And why wasn't he waiting for you in Iquitos as you had planned?"

"Perhaps he was consulting with a banker for a loan, to open his own photography studio here in Manaus."

Nile said, "You're just making excuses for him, Maddie."

She bowed her head and rubbed her forehead in defeat. "I know."

"You may be convinced that Thomas is guilty," Winston said, "but proving it is a different matter."

That observation did not please Nile. "What do you mean?"

"Who saw him kill Provvy?" Winston pointed out with maddening logic. "No one. Only Inge insists that it was Thomas, and she's disappeared altogether. And where are these uncut diamonds Thomas is supposed to have stolen? You can't have a man arrested just because he didn't meet you where he was supposed to."

Nile's expression was a mixture of impatience and frustration for a moment; then he brightened. "What if we go around to all of the diamond merchants in Manaus, show them Ben's photograph, and ask if the man sold them any uncut gems? Wouldn't that prove he stole Provvy's diamonds?"

Winston rubbed his jaw reflectively, causing his emerald ring to sparkle with every movement of his hand. "We could do that, I suppose. Of course, there's no guarantee they'll tell you anything."

"It's the only way we'll get enough proof to go to the authorities," Nile said.

"Not that they'll do anything anyway," Winston reminded him.

"Then I'll just have to take care of matters myself, won't I?"

Maddie looked at Nile sharply, for she had never heard such coldness in his voice before, or seen such deadly determination in his eyes.

"Aside from seeing Ben at the opera," Maddie pointed out, "you don't know where he's staying."

"But I do," Winston said. "In the lobby during intermission, I overheard Thomas talking about the small house he had rented." He reached into his breast pocket, took out a slip of paper and read, "Ten Dolorosa Street."

"That's all we need," Nile said. "Let's start visiting diamond merchants."

Maddie went back to Winston's house while the men went to question the diamond merchants. Nile had seemed surprised that Maddie didn't want to go with him, since she usually had to be in the center of the action, like a good newspaper reporter, but he said nothing.

Yet Maddie needed to be alone to think about Ben.

As she slowly paced around Winston's drawing room, her hands clasped behind her, she tried to reconcile the Ben Thomas she knew with the man he had evidently become, a ruthless man willing to kill for personal gain.

She remembered the first time she had ever met him. She had already been working at the *Clarion* for four years when he was hired as a photographer. Maddie had been sitting at her desk writing when she noticed this man staring at her with an intensity that unnerved her. She had tried to ignore him, but to no avail. Finally she got up, walked over to him, and demanded to know why he was staring at her. He apologized profusely and explained he was the new photographer. Then he told Maddie she provided such a contrast to all the male reporters, he wanted to take a photograph of her hard at work, surrounded by men.

She must have fallen a little in love with him right then and there, for he didn't want to photograph her for her beauty, he wanted to photograph her for what she did, what she was. How could she not love a man like that?

Ben took that photograph and many others. When

Maddie went out on assignment in London, he often accompanied her to take photographs that would later be converted into illustrations for the *Clarion*. He would always take the time to explain his work to Maddie, never resenting her questions or tiring of answering them.

He had always impressed her as a kind, thoughtful man as well, insisting they stop for hot tea on a cold rainy day, and even protecting Maddie on those occasions when people resented the intrusion of a newspaper reporter in their lives.

But what attracted Maddie the most to Ben Thomas was the fact that his background was what hers could have been like if her mother hadn't died and her father had been more ambitious. Ben also came from a large poor family, but his parents had been good decent folk determined to keep their family together. Maddie always listened raptly when Ben spoke so warmly and lovingly of his family.

As time passed, Maddie and Ben became close friends, yet they never achieved that closeness that turned friends into lovers. Though Maddie was too proud to reveal her true feelings to him, she secretly hoped he would one day realize he loved her and begin calling. But he never did. That was why Maddie had been so surprised when he agreed to her wild idea of posing as her fiancé for the hoax.

Now Maddie stopped her pacing long enough to look out the window. Ben had always been so industrious and obviously enjoyed his work. It was impossible for her to reconcile the man she knew with the man who could have killed another.

She turned away from the window and pressed the heel of her hand to her forehead. Yet the damning evidence was there, piling up against him.

Suddenly the sound of the front door opening pulled Maddie out of her deep reflections. She turned to see Nile come striding into the drawing room. One look at his triumphant face told her that he had met with success.

Maddie took a hesitant step forward. "You've found something." It was a statement rather than a question.

Nile nodded. "One of the diamond merchants I went to remembered Thomas right away. 'How could I forget the man who sold me one of the largest uncut gems I have ever seen?' he said."

Maddie sighed in despair. "Then Ben did kill Provvy."

"I'm sorry, Maddie, but it certainly looks that way."

"What are you going to do now? Inform the police?"

He regarded her calmly. "I still don't think I have enough proof. Thomas could have gotten that stone anywhere. I can't prove it belonged to Provvy."

"So what are you going to do?"

"I'm going to search his house. Perhaps there is something there that I can connect to Provvy. If I can prove the connection . . ." He shrugged.

Maddie already knew what Nile planned to do if he couldn't prove anything.

She looked around Nile. "Where's Winston?"

"I don't know. We thought it would save time if we went our separate ways."

"Shouldn't you wait for him?"

"The fewer people, the better."

Maddie looked at him. "You're not going alone. I'm going with you."

Nile shook his head emphatically. "It's too dangerous."

"Just as my navigating the launch down the Amazon was too dangerous?" she shot back.

"Maddie, this is different."

"No, it's not. If you didn't want me to come with you, you shouldn't have come back here. You should have gone to Ben's house directly from the diamond merchant's. Now that you're here, I'm going."

Nile's eyes hardened. "Maddie . . ."

She walked up to him and placed her hand on his arm. "I'm going! I have a stake in this too, remember? Ben Thomas was my friend. I even thought I loved him once, God help me. I want to be there when he explains himself. Besides, I have a plan."

"Dammit, Maddie! I don't want anything to happen to you!"

"Nothing will. You'll be there to protect me." She took a step toward the door, turned, and faced him. "Now, are you going to listen to what I have to say?"

Nile surrendered and followed her.

Maddie felt as though her stomach were filled with thousands of fluttering butterflies as she stared at the little house on Doloroso Street.

"I don't like it," Nile muttered, "not one bit."

"It's our only chance," Maddie said. "I'll confront Ben while you enter the house through the back. With any luck, he'll tell us all we need to know and you'll overhear him."

"And if he doesn't?"

"Then you can take whatever action you feel appropriate."

"Fair enough. But I still don't like the idea of using you as bait, Maddie."

She smiled up at his beloved face and placed her palm against his cheek. "Don't worry, Nile. Nothing will happen to me."

Nile scowled at the house. "What if he has servants?"

"We'll just have to chance it."

"We're leaving a great deal to chance."

"I know, but it's the only way."

"We could wait until tonight. Thomas will probably leave for the evening. The house would be empty then and we could search it without being disturbed."

"We don't know for certain that he is going out for the evening." She placed a hand on his arm. "Besides, I have to confront Ben myself for my own satisfaction. I have to know why he betrayed the *Clarion* and, most of all, himself."

Nile looked at her long and hard for a moment, then nodded wordlessly.

Maddie gave him one last smile and started across the street while Nile headed for the back of the house.

When she reached the front door, she waited for several minutes to give Nile some time to get into position. Then she took a deep breath to settle her insides and rang the bell.

Several seconds later, the door opened.

"Hello, Ben," she said.

Just seeing the expression on his handsome face, a mixture of wide-eyed astonishment and guilt that would have been comical to behold under any other circumstances, was worth the potential danger to Maddie.

She raised her brows. "You seem surprised to see me. I wonder why."

He recovered himself beautifully; she had to say that for him. That heartbreaking lopsided grin lit his face, and she could almost see his mind racing as it grasped for excuses. "Why, Maddie . . ."

"Aren't you going to invite me in?" she asked. Surely Nile had gotten into the house by this time. "Or do you intend to keep me standing on your doorstep?"

"Of course not."

"Good, because there is much we have to discuss, and somehow, I doubt that you will want your neighbors to hear what I have to say."

Something like fear flickered through his pale

blue eyes, but was gone in a second. He stood back so she could enter. "Come in."

As she slowly entered the foyer, she looked around. "What a charming little house you've got here, Ben."

"I'm only renting it." His voice shook just a little as he closed the door behind them.

She turned back to look at him and noticed his upper lip had become shiny with nervous sweat. "I wasn't aware that one could rent such a house on what the *Clarion* pays us."

He shrugged. "Rents are so much cheaper here."

Maddie knew that to be a bald-faced lie, but she said nothing.

He grinned, seeking to disarm her. "Well, it's so good to see you, Maddie." But when he reached for her as if to embrace her, she stepped back out of range.

"Why weren't you in Iquitos where you were supposed to be, Ben?" she asked, keeping her voice level. "You had been leaving an obvious trail for me to follow up until then. My guide and I scoured the city for days, but you were nowhere to be found. It soon became obvious that you were never there at all." She listened for any small sound that might tell her Nile was nearby, but to her dismay, she heard nothing.

"Come into my study," he said. "I'll explain everything."

"I hope so. Sam isn't going to be pleased with the way this expedition has turned out."

As Maddie followed Ben down a short hallway, she glanced left and right, hoping to see Nile hiding somewhere, but again, there was no sign of him. Then Ben was standing aside and indicating a doorway to what Maddie presumed was his study, so she stopped looking for Nile and walked past Ben.

"Please sit down," he said.

Maddie took a seat across from his desk and waited.

Ben's smile was charming and confident as he sat down himself and said, "I apologize for not being where I was supposed to be and for making you go all that way for nothing, Maddie. But the truth of the matter is, I've gone into partnership with an entrepreneur here in Manaus and I'm quitting the *Clarion* for good."

Maddie's look was frankly skeptical. "For a partnership to succeed, both of the partners usually have to make some monetary investment. I know for a fact that you're not a rich man, so why should someone take you on as a partner? Because of your good looks and charm?"

Anger tightened Ben's features. "You know, Maddie, a sarcastic tongue is a very unattractive trait in a woman. No wonder no man ever wanted you."

Maddie thought of all the times Nile had loved and wanted her and she just laughed. "If you think you can hurt me, you're wasting your time." She regarded him in silence, watching him. "So tell me, Ben, where did you get the money for all this?"

"I've told you all I'm going to," he said, his voice cold. "I don't have to justify myself to you."

"You don't have to because I already know where you got the money for this partnership," she said. "You murdered a trader named Providence Brown and stole a fortune in uncut diamonds from him."

For one second Ben looked as guilty as if Maddie had caught him holding the murder weapon; then his expression changed, becoming bland and unreadable. "That's ridiculous!" he cried with a sharp bark of laughter. "I've never even heard of this . . .what's-his-name."

"Brown, Providence Brown. And don't play the innocent with me because I have several witnesses willing to swear to the fact that you were his guest on the Juruá River."

"They're lying."

Maddie shook her head. "I know about Brown because he and my guide were once very close. My guide and I stopped at Brown's settlement and learned what had happened from a missionary woman living farther upriver. Did you think I would somehow bypass the Juruá on my way to Iquitos and never learn of what you had done?"

"Murdered traders, uncut diamonds ..." Ben chuckled. "Maddie, your imagination is running away with you. You've been working for the *Clarion* too long."

"Don't patronize me!" she snapped, leaning forward in her chair.

Then Maddie heard it, a faint squeak outside the study door, as if someone had stepped on a loose floorboard. She held her breath and watched Ben's face closely for any sign that he had heard it too, but he appeared too preoccupied with extricating himself.

Suddenly he went on the offensive. "All right, so I did stop at Brown's settlement. That doesn't prove I killed him or stole his diamonds."

"But I can prove it, Ben," Maddie said, feeling sorry for him in spite of what he had done. "You sold one of the diamonds to a merchant here in the city who is willing to identify you."

Ben went very still. Then, right before Maddie's eyes, he changed. His pale blue eyes froze into a cold, compassionless stare devoid of any humanity, and his handsome face became ugly with desperation and rage. Maddie wondered fleetingly if this was how Ben had looked when he plunged that knife into Provvy's back.

He sighed as he opened the top drawer of his desk. "Maddie, I'm truly sorry you became involved in this," he said, his voice heavy and regretful, "because now I'm going to have to kill you as well."

When his hand came out of the drawer, it held a pistol. And it was aimed straight at Maddie's heart.

The shock gave her an unpleasant jolt and her mouth felt dry as the butterflies took possession of her stomach again, but she forced herself to remain calm and drag her gaze away from that tiny black hole of death and back up to Ben's face.

"Even if you kill me, someone will find you. There are others who know where I am and what has happened. You can't escape, Ben."

He rose and shrugged carelessly. "Manaus isn't the only city in the world. There's Rio de Janeiro, even Paris. I'll be out of here before anyone realizes you're missing."

Maddie rose as well, hoping her knees wouldn't knock together to betray her fear. "Why? Why did you do it?"

"Why should I make any last-minute confession to you?"

"Why not? You're going to kill me anyway. What could be the harm in it?"

His lip curled in contempt. "Why do you think I did it? For the money, Maddie, more money than I could ever hope to make in a lifetime of slaving at the *Clarion*. One night I heard that old fool and his hag of a wife talking about their treasure, so I waited. When he went to his cache, I followed him. At first all I was going to do was steal it and leave, but he caught me. He would have killed me if I hadn't killed him first."

Maddie looked at him pityingly. "Whatever happened to the Ben Thomas I used to know?"

"He got tired of watching everyone else get rich."

When Maddie made no response, he said, "Well, I guess this is good-bye, Maddie."

"Thomas!"

In the second it took for Maddie to turn and see Nile looming in the doorway, the knife had already left his hand and was flying toward its target like a falcon seeking its prey. Before Ben could take aim, the weapon buried itself in his abdomen. His eyes widened in surprise, his face the picture of disbelief as his left hand encircled the knife's hilt in a pathetic futile attempt to soften the blow and keep himself from dying. His aim spoiled, the gun went off with a boom that echoed throughout the room, but the bullet hit the opposite wall rather than its intended target.

Ben dropped the gun, then looked down at the blood seeping between his fingers. His last word was, "Maddie ..." before he closed his eyes forever and toppled forward.

Nile strode into the room and looked down at him. "That was for Provvy."

Maddie's knees suddenly buckled with relief and she had to grab the back of her chair for support. "I was beginning to wonder if you were ever going to get here."

Nile strode over to her, grasped her shoulders, and shook her. "You little idiot. You pushed him too far. You could have gotten yourself killed."

She smiled over at him. "But I knew you would rescue me, just as you rescued me from Haddon Fitch."

He drew her to him for a fierce, possessive hug. "I think I'll have to spend the rest of my life rescuing you, because you are more precious to me than sweat of the sun, tears of the moon, or diamonds."

Maddie hugged him back, her heart singing with joy. When they parted, she glanced down at Ben. "What do we do now?"

"First I'm going to search the house for the diamonds, then I'm going to summon the police."

"And when you find the gems, what are you going to do with them?"

Nile looked thoughtful as he held on to her arms. "I'm going to give them to Inge, if she can be found. They were Provvy's and they rightfully belong to her, now that he's gone."

Maddie nodded. "You're a generous man, Nile Marcus. Those diamonds are probably worth a fortune. You'd be set for life if you kept them for yourself."

"I don't want them. I have you, and that's all I need."

Then he drew her into his arms for another long, leisurely kiss, and when they parted, they went in search of the diamonds.

An hour later, they found the diamonds hidden beneath a loose floorboard in Ben's bedchamber.

Nile opened the leather pouch and shook the contents into his hand.

Maddie tried to hide her dismay. "They don't look like much."

"These are literally diamonds in the rough. They may not look like much, but I suspect they will be, once they're cut," Nile replied, turning about a dozen small hard lumps over in his hands. "Two people have already died for these stones. I wonder how many other lives have been lost?"

Maddie shuddered. "As long as they're not ours."

Nile nodded solemnly, then put the stones back in their pouch and he and Maddie went to summon the police.

19

Maddie sat back in her chair and smiled in satisfaction at the papers she held.

Finally she had the entire story of her incredible Amazon adventure down on paper, and as she re-read it for the third time, she was filled with pride of accomplishment. It was definitely the best article she had ever written in her entire career as a journalist. Sam was sure to be pleased with it. Her readers would devour every word. The *Morning Clarion*'s circulation would soar. She would return to England in triumph, to acclaim that would be the envy of all of Fleet Street.

Her smile grew even wider when she set aside the article and thought of Nile. Even six months ago, she never would have admitted that anything except writing could make her feel so happy or so complete. But now she could admit to herself that her relationship with Nile Marcus was just as fulfilling. She had never dreamed a man could make such a difference in her life.

"Maddie Dare, you've fallen in love," she said aloud, "and fallen hard."

When she thought of Nile, she became as excited as a schoolgirl in the throes of first love. She would catch herself humming little ditties under her breath, and she never walked anymore, she floated as if she wore wings. Whenever Nile was close by, she always sensed his presence somehow even before she heard his footsteps. And when he was in the room, she never could tear her gaze away. Just one look from those hungry golden eyes was enough to turn her insides all shivery.

What was most gratifying was the fact that Nile was just as besotted with her. Since he was not sharing Maddie's bedroom out of respect for Winston's feelings, his desire for her had intensified. Whenever they were alone, he never could resist pulling her into his arms for a passionate embrace. Seated at the dinner table, he virtually ignored Winston and Amy to hang on Maddie's every word.

Now Maddie rose and began pacing around Winston's study, for in spite of her great joy, she was troubled. Even though she didn't doubt Nile's love for her, she often wondered about the future. What would happen once they returned to England? Would they marry, or merely live together out of wedlock? And if they married, would Nile continue to hunt orchids for collectors? Maddie fully intended to remain with the *Clarion.*

Maddie frowned. She and Nile had much to discuss before they left for England with Winston and Amy in three days' time.

Her thoughts were interrupted by a knock on the door, and when she responded, "Come in," and the door swung open, she was delighted to see none other than Nile himself standing there.

Maddie said nothing at first, just content to look at him. She wondered if she would ever get tired of looking at the man she loved.

Nile stood for a moment framed by the doorjamb, his predatory gaze locked on her. Then he grinned, closed the door behind him, and entered the room with the feline grace that was so much a part of him.

His eyes left her only long enough to glance about the room. "Are we truly alone? Belgrave isn't hiding in a corner somewhere, is he, waiting to wag a disapproving finger at us?"

Maddie laughed as she extended her arms to him. "We are truly alone, O King of the Orchid Hunters. I heard the estimable Mr. Belgrave tell Bento that he was taking Amy to a dressmaker today to have her outfitted for the return to England."

Nile enfolded her in his crushing embrace, nearly sweeping Maddie off her feet. Then he set her down and kissed her until she was breathless and dizzy.

"How long do you think they'll be gone?" he whispered, nuzzling her ear.

"Oh, for hours and hours, I would expect."

Nile's face twisted with longing. "Then why don't we take advantage of it? My bedroom is just upstairs."

Maddie felt a hard knot of desire uncurl within her, filling her with sweet anticipation, but she managed to resist. "As much as I would love to, I think we had better talk, Nile."

His face fell. "Talk? About what?"

Feeling suddenly unsure of herself, Maddie stepped back out of his arms and turned away. "About . . . about what happens to the two of us when we return to England."

He was silent for a moment as he rubbed his jaw. "Well, I had thought that I would try to find another expedition, perhaps to Burma this time, and you would go right on working for the *Clarion*."

Maddie took a deep breath to fight down her rising panic. "But what about us, Nile?"

"I don't understand."

So, he was going to feign ignorance again and force her to be the one to bare her soul.

She turned around and regarded him in exasperation, pleading for his understanding and compassion, but Nile's face was a blank mask. She would get no help from him. If she wanted him, she would just have to tell him. This was no time to let foolish pride stand in her way.

Maddie placed her hands on his arms while she looked deep into his eyes. "I love you, Nile, and I don't want to lose you. You are my lover and my friend, and I can't imagine a life without you."

He shrugged. "But you have your work at the *Clarion*, and it's very important to you. You even told me so yourself."

So that's what he wanted from her, an admission that the *Clarion* wasn't her whole life, that there was room in her heart for him too.

"But I need you as well, Nile," she said softly. "I don't want this happiness to end once we return to England. I want it to go on forever ... I want you by my side forever."

It was humiliating to sound so needy, so desperate, but Maddie couldn't help herself. She wanted and needed Nile more than she needed her foolish pride.

His eyes narrowed. "Maddie Dare, are you proposing to me, bold, brazen wench that you are?"

When she caught the laughter behind the sternness in his voice, she retorted, "Why, yes, Nile, I think I am." She dropped down on one knee like a lovestruck suitor, clasped her hands together beseechingly, and gazed up at him. "Nile Marcus, I'm asking for your hand in marriage. Will you do me the great honor of becoming my husband?"

He fought to control himself. "Since my own father is no longer alive, perhaps you should ask my Uncle Winston for his consent."

Then his shoulders started shaking and he began laughing so hard, tears formed in his eyes. "You were aptly named, because you are truly both mad and daring, Maddie Dare." Then he pulled her to

her feet, grasped her waist, and spun her around.
"Of course I'll marry you!"

As Maddie held on for dear life, she laughed
with joy, her heart almost bursting with happiness.
"Oh, Nile . . ."

But when he stopped and set her on her feet
again, Maddie's jubilant mood faded. "Are you
sure?" she said softly.

"Of course I'm sure. I just accepted your proposal,
didn't I? And I am a man of my word."

"Even though you know I'll never give you children, a son to carry on the Marcus name?"

He took her in his arms again and held her fiercely.
"I'm marrying you for yourself, Maddie, not what
you can give me. All I want is you, sweetheart."

She smiled at him through her tears. "I think I
love you even more for saying that."

"Why shouldn't I say it? It's the truth."

Maddie stepped back. "If we're going to Burma,
I'll have to quit the *Clarion*, of course."

"Unless Sam Vincent wants another installment
of 'The Adventures of Maddie Dare.' "

"Maddie Marcus," she corrected him.

"Maddie Marcus. Now, that does have a nice
ring to it."

She slipped her arms around his waist and said
hopefully, "If I do have to quit the *Clarion*, I thought
I might write a travel book similar to the kind your
mother used to write."

Nile looked pensive for a moment, then smiled
and nodded. "I think my mother would have liked
that, just as she would have adored you."

She sighed with contentment. "You don't know
how happy it makes me, to hear you say that."

Then she turned, went to the desk, and picked
up the article she had been writing. She handed it
to Nile. "This may very well be the last story I ever

write for the *Clarion*, so I would like you to read it and tell me what you think."

His eyes sparkled as he took it. "I'll read it right now."

"And I'll go wait for Winston and Amy so I won't distract you."

When Maddie left the study for the drawing room, Nile was seated at Winston's desk reading her article.

Five minutes later, Maddie heard the front door open, and when she went out into the foyer, an excited Amy came rushing forward.

"You should see all the beautiful dresses Winston bought for me!" she cried, clasping her hands together in childlike delight. "Wait until Mama and Papa and Freddie see me in them."

"I'm sure you'll look lovely," Maddie said kindly, trying to ignore Winston's hopeless expression.

Amaryllis' mental state had not improved since her return to Manaus. In her mind, she was still a little girl living on her family farm in Devonshire. But at least she had come to accept Winston as a friend, and Maddie thought that was a good sign.

To ease the lines of worry from Winston's face, Maddie said, "Come into the drawing room. I have something to tell you."

Winston smiled. "Judging from that sparkle in your eyes, it's something wonderful."

"It is."

"I'm hungry," Amy said, and started for the kitchen.

"Let her go," Winston said wistfully. "She wouldn't understand anyway."

Maddie suddenly felt guilty for having so much happiness when Winston and Amy had so little. "Don't worry, Winston. Once you get her back to England and the fine doctors there, I'm sure Amy will get better."

He sighed. "I hope so, Maddie, I certainly hope

so." Then he grinned. "But enough about my problems. You have something to tell me?"

As soon as they entered the drawing room, she said, "Actually, I should wait for Nile as well, because my good news concerns him as well."

Winston's green eyes widened. "He's asked you to marry him."

"Actually, you have it backwards. I asked him to marry me, and he accepted!"

"Oh, Maddie, I'm so happy for you!" Winston grasped her hands tightly in his and leaned forward to kiss her on the cheek.

She blushed. "Thank you, Winston. I know you are."

"Well, this calls for a celebration." He strode over to the sideboard and drew out a bottle of Cordon Rouge champagne. "Where is the King of the Orchid Hunters?"

"In your study, reading my account of our Amazon adventure," Maddie said as Winston popped the cork and began pouring. "He should be here any minute."

Footsteps sounded outside the drawing-room entrance just as Winston finished pouring the champagne, and Maddie looked up to see Nile, her article in hand, standing in the doorway.

One look at his face told her something was dreadfully wrong.

Winston, with his back still toward Nile, noticed nothing. "Congratulations, O King of the Orchid Hunters!" he said heartily, taking a glass in each hand. As he turned around, he said, "Maddie just told me your wonderful news, and I—"

"Nile, what's wrong?" Maddie said, taking a hesitant step toward him. She stopped when she saw the mixture of disappointment and anger in his eyes and felt a palpable coldness radiating from him.

Winston stopped in his tracks and scowled at his friend. "Yes, what is it?"

Nile came into the room, his footsteps heavy. The contemptuous way he was looking at Maddie made her feel as though she were a murderer caught in the act of committing some horrendous crime.

"Leave us, Belgrave," he snapped. "This is between Maddie and me."

Hearing the seriousness in his friend's tone, Winston quietly set down the champagne glasses and left the room, closing the door behind him.

When Nile and Maddie were alone, he came to stand before her and glanced down at the papers he held.

"I read your article, and I see that you still intend to claim that Thomas was your fiancé."

So that was the cause of Nile's displeasure.

"Oh, Nile, what can be the harm?" She smiled up at him, her voice cajoling as she tried to make him understand. "It makes for a more exciting story that way."

His eyes were dull and oh, so cold. "Did it ever occur to you to tell the truth, that what started out as a hoax turned into a search for a murderer and thief? That sounds like an exciting story to me."

Maddie's gaze slid away. "But that would tell the *Clarion*'s readers that we had been duping them all along. I couldn't do that to Sam."

"What about for your personal integrity?"

She wanted to touch him, to place her hands on his arms, but she knew they would be stiff and unyielding, so she didn't. "Nile, try to understand. If I expose the hoax, I'll be telling my readers that I'm dishonest, that I can't be trusted. My reputation will be blackened and I'll lose readers."

"You should have thought of that before you agreed to this . . . this fraud."

Maddie released him and turned away. "Yes, I

should have. But what's done is done. I've got to make the best of the situation." She turned back to him. "I promise I'll never do it again. From now on, all of my articles will be the truth, I swear it. But that article has to run just as I've written it."

Nile flung down the papers, letting them scatter on the floor. He glared at Maddie. "Didn't anything I said to you in Iquitos touch you? Do all the promises you made to me about honor and integrity mean nothing?"

"You . . . you don't understand." Maddie had to make him understand. She just had to!

"I understand perfectly," he said, sounding tired and drained. "You told me how sorry you were for carrying out the hoax, and your reasons for doing it. But I thought you had learned your lesson. I thought you had changed. And now I read this article and discover you haven't really changed at all. You're bound and determined to carry it through to the end, no matter what the cost."

"It will only be this once, Nile, I promise."

He sighed. "Don't you care about what I think? Don't you have any consideration for my feelings?"

"Of course I do."

"Then prove it. Rewrite this article and tell the truth."

Maddie stood before him, her hands clasped before her. "And if I don't?"

Nile regarded her in silence, his handsome face inscrutable. A sad smile played about his mouth for an instant, then disappeared. "I can't love a woman who is dishonest, Maddie. I need a woman I can trust." He sighed heavily. "I thought you were that woman, but evidently I was wrong."

She stared at him in shock and disbelief. "What are you saying?"

"I'm saying it's over between us. Once I walk out that door, we'll never see each other again."

Maddie reeled from his hurtful words as if they were physical blows. "You could leave me, after all we've shared, after all we've meant to each other?"

"It won't be easy," he admitted. "I loved you more than any woman I've ever known."

Her heart filled with hope and elation until she heard his next words: "But being alone is preferable to living with a woman without scruples. I'm sorry, Maddie, but that's the way I feel."

As Maddie stared at him, she sensed the distance growing between them like a yawning chasm. Any love Nile had once felt for her had been replaced by contempt, and her despair suddenly turned to self-righteous anger.

"And what about me? What about my feelings?" she cried. "I must always see your point of view, but you never consider mine or make any attempt to understand me."

Nile just shook his head pityingly. "You just don't understand, do you?"

She turned away from him, her back stiff and unyielding. As much as she longed to fling herself into his arms and promise to do whatever he said, another part held her back. She needed Nile, but she also needed the *Clarion*.

"I can't do it, Nile," she said, trying to stop her voice from shaking. "I can't do what you're asking."

"Then I guess there is nothing else to say, except good-bye."

Maddie stood there, her eyes brimming with tears as she waited for Nile to gently turn her around so he could kiss her one last time. But all she heard were quick, sure footsteps crossing the room, followed by the sound of the door closing.

Go after him! a little voice shrieked inside her brain. She ignored it.

Moments later, when she heard the door opening again, she whirled around expectantly, but her hopes were dashed when she saw it was only Winston, his boyish face somber and his green eyes filled with sorrow.

"Just me," he said, his fingers flicking open and shut nervously. "I don't mean to pry, Maddie, but even a dolt such as I can see that something is amiss between you and Nile."

She brushed at her eyes with the back of her hand. "It's more than amiss, Winston. We've decided to go our separate ways, that's all."

He sighed deeply and looked genuinely troubled. "I'm sorry to hear that. I thought you and the orchid hunter were eminently suited."

Maddie managed a tremulous smile. "Evidently not suited enough. It appears we cannot reconcile our differences."

"Knowing Nile, I'm sure he's the one who refuses to do the reconciling."

"Oh, I wouldn't say that. I'm partially to blame."

Winston was silent for a moment, then said, "I know this isn't the right moment to ask this question, Maddie, but what are you going to do now?"

She took a deep breath and gathered her courage. "I'll return to England and my position at the *Clarion*. If you don't mind, I'd like to accompany you and Amy. I'm sure I'll find your company very comforting."

"Of course you're welcome to join us."

Maddie tried to thank him, but her lower lip was trembling so hard that she couldn't get the words out. Then the awful realization that she would never see Nile again exploded in her brain, and she dissolved into tears.

Winston was at her side in an instant and gathered her in his arms. He didn't offer any useless words of comfort because he knew there were none to be had. He just held her, letting her sob her heart out, and Maddie clung to him, absorbing his strength because she knew she would need it in the lonely weeks and months and years to come.

That night, Maddie was awakened out of a fitful sleep by the sound of footsteps outside her bedroom door. Then the door opened and he was standing there.

"Nile?" she called out sleepily, raising herself on one elbow.

But when Maddie became fully awake, she realized the bedroom door was still closed and she had wanted Nile to return so badly that she had imagined hearing his footsteps.

She was alone. And likely to remain that way.

Maddie lay back on the right side of the bed as if Nile would soon return to occupy the other half. She missed him so much it was like an acute physical pain that left her body both aching and numb. Even when she slept, her mind was filled with so many images of him that her body responded to the mental stimuli. When she closed her eyes, she could feel his strong, hard body next to hers, his hands and mouth fondling her into ecstasy.

Knowing that would soon lead to madness, she angrily fought off the sensations and moved to the center of the bed.

Get used to it, Maddie, she admonished herself. Nile's not coming back. You're going to be all alone again.

She sat up in bed and drew her knees up to her chest. Being alone wasn't so terrible. She had been alone for most of her life and had come to treasure her independence, the fact that she alone was responsible for herself and had no one to answer to.

However, when Maddie thought of Nile and how he had protected and cared for her on the expedition, she had to admit that it was wonderful to depend on someone else for a change, to have a strong shoulder to lean on when one's own strength had gone.

Feeling restless, she rose and went to the shuttered windows and asked herself for the thousandth time why she hadn't agreed to Nile's demand that she change her article. Yet she already knew the answer. Being a newspaper reporter was so ingrained in her, so much a part of who she was, that she couldn't risk damaging a reputation she had fought so hard to build.

Even if that reputation was partially built on a lie? her inner voice asked.

The thought made her so uncomfortable that she tried to put it out of her mind, but it kept coming back to haunt her for the rest of the night, poking and prodding at her conscience until she couldn't think clearly anymore.

Finally Maddie began sobbing again, letting the pain wring all emotion out of her. When she couldn't cry any longer, she finally fell into the deep sleep of exhaustion.

The following morning, a somber-faced Winston handed her a note that Nile had left under the front door. In it, he said good-bye and wished her the best of luck in her journalistic endeavors.

Dry-eyed and emotionless, Maddie folded the note carefully and stuffed it in the pocket of her skirt, then, with her heart breaking, discussed the return trip to England with Winston.

The violent October wind drove the rain before it in slanting sheets, turning Dover Street slick and shiny.

Inside the hansom cab, Maddie shivered. She remembered that time in the steam heat of Brazil how she had yearned for a cold English rain; now she would have given anything to be back on the Amazon again, with Nile.

Don't think about him, Maddie girl, she admonished herself, or you'll just start crying again.

Taking a deep breath, she closed her eyes, but it was no use. A tantalizing image of Nile danced through her thoughts. How she longed for the sheer physical presence of him, to see his golden eyes dancing with laughter and humor again, to bask in his love.

Almost four months had passed since Maddie had returned to England with Winston and Amy, and she still missed Nile. She suspected she always would.

The hansom stopped before her terrace house and Maddie stepped down and paid the driver, who tipped his hat and rattled off in search of another fare.

She shivered again as she turned up her collar and bowed her head into the driving rain before racing up the slick steps to her front door. Fumbling for her keys, she found them and proceeded to unlock the door.

But the door was already unlocked.

Maddie stood there frozen to the spot while the rain pelted her mercilessly and ran down her neck. Someone had broken into her house. She swallowed hard, her heart beating faster. Every instinct screamed at her to get away as quickly as possible and to summon a policeman, but another part of her was outraged that someone had dared break into her house and violate her sanctuary.

Her rage was so great that she wanted to march right in there and confront the person, even though she realized such an action was foolhardy and might even result in her being injured or killed.

Steady, Maddie, she thought, don't panic. Whoever was there is probably long gone by now.

Then she noticed that there was a light coming from her parlor window. Peering through the thick curtains as best she could, she noticed there was someone in her parlor, sitting as cozy as could be in a chair near the fireplace.

She hesitated a moment, trying to decide what to do. Whoever had brazenly broken into her house had certainly made himself at home, and didn't seem in the least bit threatening.

Maddie took a deep breath to bolster her courage, opened the door, and went inside. She didn't bother to remove her sodden redingote, she just walked through the tiny foyer and stood in the parlor doorway.

A man rose from the chair. "Hello, Maddie."

She stared at the intruder in disbelief, blinking several times to clear her vision, but he didn't vanish like some wraith. "Nile."

He had changed since that day in Manaus, when he had walked out on her. He was thinner, causing the dark wool suit he wore to hang on his large frame as though it had been fitted for someone else. Nile's face was haggard and drawn and he looked very discontented. That should have pleased Maddie, but it only tore at her heart.

She looked into his eyes, usually blazing with wild, animalistic energy, and found them to be as dull and lifeless as scratched glass.

"I didn't know you had numbered housebreaking among your talents," she said.

A wisp of a smile touched his mouth but never reached his eyes. Then he started toward her. "Let me take your coat," he said. "You're soaking wet and you'll catch a chill."

His words reminded her that she was wet and cold, and so shocked to see him, that she began shaking all over. Maddie just stood there, not caring if she ruined her Turkish carpet by dripping water on it, while Nile approached her as silently as a panther. She hadn't the strength to unbutton her redingote, so he did it for her, saying nothing as his blunt fingers started to undo the buttons as gently and carefully as one would with a child.

In spite of Nile's disconcerting nearness, Maddie refused to let herself feel anything for him, and kept her unblinking gaze on his tie. He had torn her self-respect to shreds that day in Manaus, and she wasn't going to let him open those painful wounds again.

When the buttons were all undone, he stood behind her and took her coat, being careful not to touch her, then hung it on the rack in the foyer. Maddie continued to stand there shivering in silence, wondering what he was going to do next.

"Come sit by the fire and get warm," he said, placing a tentative hand on her elbow. Did Maddie imagine it, or were his fingers trembling just a little?

"You've certainly made yourself at home," she said wryly as she entered the parlor.

Much as she hated to admit it, Nile looked as though he belonged here as much as she did. The few guests that she had invited into her home always looked so out-of-place, like elephants in Trafalgar Square, but not Nile. The home that she guarded so zealously, without even a cat or bird to invade her privacy, welcomed this man who had so devastated her heart.

"I was wet myself from the rain," he said, "so I didn't think you'd mind if I built a fire and put the teakettle on."

She didn't, not when she went to stand before the fire and gratefully let its heat leach the chill out of her bones. But she still felt so cold inside.

Finally Maddie seated herself, but Nile chose to remain standing, one arm braced against the mantel while he stared broodingly into the fire, his brow furrowed in contemplation.

Maddie twisted her fingers together and blurted out, "Why have you come here, Nile? The last time we were together, you made it perfectly clear that you thought me beneath contempt and never wanted to see me again. So I must confess that I'm quite surprised to see you."

He kept gazing into the fire as if he could find the answers he sought in the burning coals. "That's exactly how I felt about you after I finished reading your article," he said heavily. "I booked passage on the first ship I could find leaving for England. I had to get away from you. But in doing that, I discovered I was only trying to run away from myself."

"What do you mean?"

He dropped his arm and stood to face her. "I missed you so much, Maddie. I felt as though someone had cut out my heart."

She felt a great surge of happiness, but she didn't trust the permanence of it, so she forced the emotion back. If Nile wanted her, he was going to have to convince her on his own. She had been hurt too badly to give herself so willingly to him this time. She would not help him.

She rose, but did not go to him. She turned away as she said, "You said some horrible, unfair things to me that day, Nile."

"I know, and I've regretted them ever since."

Maddie waited for him to make his usual counter-accusation that her unwillingness to expose the hoax made her morally deficient somehow, but he didn't this time.

"What?" she said, turning to face him, her brows raised in astonishment. "Do you mean to say that you no longer consider me to be a liar and a cheat?"

He sighed heavily. "I had plenty of time to think about it on the trip back, and even more time to think when I arrived."

"And what did you decide?"

"I came to the conclusion that I was seeing the situation in black and white again, in my usual thickheaded fashion. I put myself in your place and saw the situation from your point of view. And I decided I didn't care what kind of story you told to the *Clarion*. That didn't change the person I knew, or how I felt about you."

He took a step toward her, his handsome face vulnerable and pleading with her to understand. "I still want you, Maddie, just as you are, but I won't blame you if you tell me to go to hell and be damned. I hurt you badly, and I know I have no right to expect you to forgive me."

Maddie just stared at him, unable to believe that this proud, stubborn man had just humbled himself.

Nile must have interpreted her silence as rejection for a wild, desperate fire flared up in his eyes and he was at her side in three strides, his hands imprisoning her wrists to keep her from fleeing.

"Maddie, you can't turn me away, you—"

"Nile, let go of me."

"*No!* Never again!"

She grinned at his beloved face. "Now, that's more like the Nile Marcus I know, so fierce, so possessive."

Before she could take another breath, he dropped her wrists and took her into his arms, crushing her to him in a hug.

"Maddie, my life . . ." he murmured into her hair. "I never want to lose you again."

He stepped back and just looked at her, his eyes wandering over each feature in wonder, as if he couldn't believe she was standing before him. His contemplation lingered on her lips before his eyelids drooped and his own mouth sought hers.

The breath was squeezed out of Maddie's body as Nile drew her even closer to him, settling her down the length of him while he took possession of her mouth. Maddie slid her arms around his neck, determined to give as good as she got and to truly show Nile that she had forgiven him and wanted him just as much as he wanted her.

As his warm, hard lips teased and tasted hers with such consummate skill, Maddie felt the languorous warmth she had only dreamed about ever since Nile had left. Now he was here, in the flesh, and she was going to savor every moment.

She reached up to run her fingers through his hair, relishing its thick, silken texture as she pressed her body to his. Maddie frowned in dismay, for the steel ribs of her corset formed a rigid barrier between them.

Nile stopped kissing her and looked over at her in chagrin. "You're wearing a corset."

"I'm back in England, remember?" Maddie smiled seductively. "My clothes wouldn't fit if I didn't. But we can soon remedy that."

His eyes darkened with passion. "Are you sure?"

"Quite sure."

"Maddie, love . . ." His voice was rough-edged and husky.

Maddie stepped back. "Nile, before we . . . retire to my bedchamber, there's something I've got to tell you."

His expression was both wary and fearful. "What is it?"

She took his hands in hers. "I quit my job at the *Clarion*."

Nile just stared at her as if he had turned to stone. "You *what*?"

"I quit my job at the *Clarion*."

"But . . . but why, Maddie? That job meant everything to you!"

She smiled ruefully as she dropped his hands and walked over to the fireplace. "It did mean everything to me—once. But after you left, I also had plenty of time to do some thinking." She turned to look at him. "I thought about what you said and I took a long, hard look at myself, Nile. And I didn't like what I saw. No matter how hard I tried to rationalize it, the hoax was still dishonest. So when I returned to London, I told Sam Vincent what had happened to Ben, and I also told him I wasn't writing the final article about Maddie Dare's Amazon adventure."

Nile's face glowed with delight. "I'm proud of you, Maddie. I know how much being a newspaper reporter means to you, so it couldn't have been easy."

"It wasn't, but it made me feel good, as if I had redeemed myself somehow."

"What did Sam say when you told him?"

"He was furious, of course, at the prospect of the *Clarion* losing all that money, especially since he had just paid your fee. I think he also felt that I had betrayed him personally. He told me to write the article or find a new place of employment."

"And did you?"

She shook her head. "No. Sam has seen to it that no other newspaper will hire me. And that's unfortunate, because I wanted to write an article exposing Antonio Aguirre's enslavement of the Indians."

Nile just shook his head.

Maddie smiled bravely. "There's no need to worry about me. I have my savings to rely on, and I'm writing a book. I intend for it to outsell any of your mother's, I'll have you know."

Nile grinned. "I bet it will."

Maddie's hand swept the air, as if the book's title were emblazoned across the sky. "*My Amazon Adventure*, by Maddie Dare."

He came toward her, arms extended. "I think 'Maddie Marcus' has a better ring to it, don't you?"

As she went to him and slipped her arms about his waist, Maddie felt her heartbeat begin to race out of control. "Why, Nile Marcus, is that a marriage proposal?"

"A proper marriage proposal this time—that is, if you don't mind spending your honeymoon in Burma."

"Burma!"

"That's where one of my former clients is sending me, to find more blue vanda orchids for his collection."

Maddie stepped back in surprise. "Someone is financing an expedition for you?"

He nodded. "It seems the hunter he sent there came back empty-handed, so now he wants me to try Burma for him."

"Oh, Nile, that's wonderful!" Maddie cried, hugging him.

"We'll have to celebrate."

"Oh, yes," she said breathlessly as she gazed into his eyes. "And I know just the place."

"Where?"

"Upstairs." She took him by the hand and showed him the way.

Afterward, as Maddie lay curled against Nile and listened to the sound of the rain drumming on the roof, she sighed in blissful contentment.

He brushed his lips against her hair. "What are you thinking?"

"I was just thinking what a happy life we're going to have together, and just wishing that Winston and Amy could be as happy as we are."

Nile drew her close. "So do I. But the least we can do is love each other to the fullest. That would honor the memory of what they once had and lost."

"I never want to lose you, Nile. Never."

"And you never will, Maddie, as long as I have breath in my body."

"I love you, Nile."

"And I love you, Maddie."

She smiled up at him seductively. "Show me again."

And he did.

Epilogue

Maddie stared at the pile of trunks stacked in her foyer and smiled over at her husband.

"It feels so good to be home, don't you think?"

Ten months had passed since they had last set foot in the terrace house, and Maddie was glad to be back among familiar surroundings.

Nile grinned as he grasped her around the waist and drew her into his arms. "It feels good just to be wherever you are, my love."

After he was through kissing her, Maddie smiled. "Well, you've certainly made your client one happy man. I thought he was going to expire of ecstasy when he saw all the blue vandas and the other orchids you brought from Burma."

Nile nodded with satisfaction. "You brought me luck, Maddie. Only a few of the plants died on the return trip, and he thinks I can all but walk on water."

Maddie chuckled at that as she removed her straw boater and set it on the table, then proceeded to pull off the white sheets covering the furniture. "As much as I enjoyed Burma, I can't wait to get settled in here again and begin work on my new travel book. I hope it's—"

The sound of the doorbell ringing interrupted her. She frowned. "Now, who could that be?"

"I'll get it," Nile said. "It's probably Sam Vincent here to offer you your old job back."

But when Nile shouted, "Belgrave!" Maddie knew it wasn't her former employer, so she went rushing into the foyer to greet their old friend.

"Winston!" she cried, extending her arms to him as he crossed the threshold.

Winston Belgrave hadn't changed a bit since the day he had been Nile's groomsman at the wedding. But now his boyish face was wreathed in smiles and there was a rare sparkle in his green eyes.

The next words out of his mouth were, "Nile and Maddie, I've brought someone to see you."

Then he stepped aside to reveal Amaryllis standing on the doorstep.

"Hello, Maddie," she said, beaming. "Hello, Nile."

Maddie stood there in shocked silence for a moment, then let out a whoop of delight. "Amaryllis, you recognized us. You're all better!"

"Yes!" Amy replied, both laughing and crying as she hugged Maddie, then Nile.

Winston said, "The doctors at the Viennese clinic made a breakthrough about three months ago. Amy finally stopped living in the past and came back to us."

"Came back to you, Winston," she said, her gray eyes softening as she took his hand.

"Well, let's not all stand here like statues," Maddie said. "Come into the parlor and sit down. I can see we have much to talk about."

While Maddie and Nile listened, Winston told them all about the private clinic in Austria he had taken Amy to, and how the doctors there had helped her.

Amy reached out and clasped Win's hand again. "Not only did they help me to reconcile myself with Fred's death, they helped me to finally realize that I loved Win, even though we had taken divergent paths in life."

Winston dragged his adoring gaze away from his

Amy long enough to say, "We've been waiting for you two to return so you'll come to our wedding."

"You're getting married?" Maddie cried. "I'm so thrilled for you!"

Amy nodded happily. "It's about time I came to my senses, don't you think?"

Nile took Maddie's hand and stared lovingly into her eyes. "I think we all came to our senses just in time."

"Our good fortune calls for a toast, O King of the Orchid Hunters," Winston said. "Do you have any Cordon Rouge for old times' sake?"

"I'm afraid sherry will have to do," Nile said, and went in search of a bottle and four glasses.

Minutes later, when everyone had a glass, Nile raised his. "To the Amazon, where we all found our destinies."

"To the Amazon."

Their toast drunk, Maddie smiled at her husband over the rim of her glass, for she had found her destiny—and her happiness—at last.

About the Author

Leslie O'Grady was born and raised in Connecticut, where she lives with her husband, Michael. A graduate of Central Connecticut State University, she has worked as a public relations writer for a television station and a hospital. When not writing, Ms. O'Grady enjoys movies, museums, and collecting books about nineteenth-century England. She is the author of several romance novels, including *So Wild a Dream*, which is available in a Signet edition.